BOOK TWO OF THE SONS OF STEEL SAGA

Sons of Steel

Cyberwars

G. L. Keady

ALSO BY

G. L. Keady

DREAMRAIDERS

Sons of Steel Saga

FUTURES END

First published in Australia in 2023

by Big Island Productions

Big Island Productions
PO Box 3027, Tuross Head, 2537, NSW, Australia
www.bigislandprod.net

ISBN:
Ebook: 978-1-923038-07-3
Print: 978-1-923938-06-6

Edited by: Joan Grady
Cover design: Brandon Evans-Keady
Illustrations: Pierre Jackson. Colourist: Nestor Redulla Jr.

Is life an illusion? If I make the syllogism: "I am not myself" is that
not an oxymoron? Referring to myself is claiming singularity but am
I not composed of individual atoms?

Black Alice

TABLE OF CONTENTS

CHAPTER 1
VANISHING POINT

ALICE wiped a dribble of blood from his battle-scarred brow. He glanced at the ferry captain, out cold on the floor beside him, and at the dazed face of Hope, who still clutched the remains of the bottle she had used to knock him out in her hand. His best friend and fellow peace activist, Mal Function, was now conscious, leaning against the cabin wall, gasping for breath. He was battered and bleeding, cut in a dozen places from the window that had shattered during their brawl.

Alice shot him a derisive grin, and with his usual swagger proclaimed: "Glad that's over!"

He grasped Mal's hand and helped him up.

"Sorry for doubting you, Al," said Mal, wiping blood from the corner of his mouth. "Now I get what you were trying to do."

Alice stepped towards him. "Function, you turd ... Argh!" He froze in agony, grabbing at his back. "I've done me back in," he groaned. "Help me onto the floor, mate," he gasped through gritted teeth.

He sprawled out on the deck.

Mal was holding Alice's arm when its solidity began to fade and recover, in and out of phase, right before their eyes.

"Jesus!" Mal exclaimed, dropping Alice's arm like it was a hot potato. He looked down at his friend, bewildered. "What the stuff's happening, Hope?"

"Mal, I feel weird!" Alice spluttered, holding his forehead. "Like I'm about to cash my chips or something. What's the story, Hope?" He groaned, confused. The bridge was shimmering; the walls were bulging. "Not again, not again," he groaned, losing it.

Hope knelt beside him, looking concerned. "I think you're beginning to de-molecularize again," she said. "It seems to happen when you're excited or under stress. The increased neural activity activates the rogue strand of DNA Secta implanted in your genome."

The mention of Secta fired him up.

"Him again!" he yelled. Then his face contorted and he screamed, struck by a pain in his arm, which again began to pulse slowly into transparency and back again.

"Calm down!" Hope warned. "You have to calm down!" Despite her scientific perspective, she was a compassionate woman, and found herself fighting back tears. She had gone out on a limb against her brother, Secta, and her employer, the Oceana State Government, risking charges of treason to support Alice in his quest. Now, even though they had succeeded, things were becoming even more insane. Aware that she couldn't let emotion get the better of her, she took a deep breath.

"The more fired up you get, Al, the more you'll slip out of phase," she said, gently.

"What is this phase crap, Hope? The only phase I know about is three-phase lighting at gigs."

"Yeah, mate, me too," Mal managed a grin, despite his anxiety. But Hope wasn't amused. "This is serious, Al. If the process can't be stopped, you'll slip out of phase completely, probably into another dimension. That's what Secta and I have been perfecting: digital matter transfer."

"Easy for you to say, Hope..." Alice growled. "But I'm no Doctor Who — I'm just a frigging rock singer."

Her eyes fixed on him as she sought a strategy. Her gaze sharpened. "I need to get you back to the lab," she said.

"Stuff that!" he replied, struggling to get up. But the movement only made matters worse. His entire body began to slip in and out of visibility. He flopped back to the deck, defeated.

Mal knelt down beside him, and looked up forlornly at Hope.

"Can't we do something for him, doc?"

"Nothing," she replied, coldly scientific and resigned, all trace of the emotional girl gone. "He'll disappear in a few minutes. I can only give him some educated guesses.

"Al," she went on, "My hunch is that your being is about to slip into a parallel dimension. Could be the future, could be the past, I can't tell which. But you'll have to find your own way. You managed it before, and you'll do it again. Maybe then we'll be able to stabilize you. Alice? Do you hear me, Alice?"

"Yeah, yeah, yeah," he mumbled. "Stabilize me, find my way back..." His entire body was phasing in and out of visibility, pulsing rapidly.

Hope moved closer, touching his cheek. "Listen, Alice, it's important. If you appear in another dimension, it could be in a different body. Try to keep a grip on your own identity."

"Eh?" said Mal, confused. "How's that?"

The weather over Sydney was worsening. Hope had to raise her voice to be heard.

"He might phase-shift into another person in another time dimension," she said. "If that happens, some of his neurons will carry the memory of his own identity. They'll just need to be triggered so he can recall."

Gently placing her hand under the back of Alice's head, she lifted it slightly, and spoke calmly and deliberately, even while tears shone in her eyes. "Alice." she said "Alice. Remember. You. Are. Black. Alice."

Flicking on and off like a blinking fluorescent light, Alice mumbled: "I... I'm Black... Black... Black... I'm..."

Then he was gone.

In a strange dimly lit otherworldly void — a netherworld — Alice was sitting on the floor staring intently at a glowing orb the size of a basketball, that was suspended supernaturally in the air. The greenish light emanating from it pulsated each time the entity from within it, known as En-Ki, spoke.

"And so, you managed to change destiny, Alice. You altered the timeline."

"And brought about the futures end. I wiped out my friends … Zule, Kinks, Ex and Djard…" he lamented. "All the time travel should've ended there but it didn't, did it?"

"No," said the alien, "it was not my fault the experimental formula Doctor Secta had used to alter your molecular structure had serious side-effects."

"That my friend is the understatement of a lifetime. Continue…"

A dazzling lightning bolt flashed Alice's mind's eye.

Senior Inspector Honor was seated in a swivel chair behind a gunmetal grey, government-issue desk in a small windowless basement office at Oceana State Security Directorate HQ. A call came through on her mastoid implant.

"Yes, zis is she," she barked in reply, her Eastern European accent being particularly suited to barking. "Oh, good morning, Miss Vallins. He does? In fifteen minutes? Off course, no problem. Zank you."

She stood up, flustered, wringing her hands. Being summoned before the President was never a good thing. And following the Black Alice fiasco, after he had somehow managed to escape imprisonment, flee the SSD and get to the peace demonstration they'd tried so hard to keep him from, it was even worse. Senior Inspector Honor was, in fact, feeling extremely worried.

She nervously checked her image in a small mirror on her desk. The black eye she had sustained from intimate contact with Alice's fist had faded to yellow. She opened a compact and carefully dabbed at the bruise. Then she touched up her scarlet lipstick and hauled her long black hair into a neat bun. "Zere," she said, glaring at herself in the mirror. "I am presentable."

She gathered the things she might need at the meeting; a folder and a flash-drive containing relevant case files. Then, nervously brushing some non-existent lint from the front of her knee-length black skirt, she straightened her red-piped black jacket and took a deep breath. She was as ready as she would ever be. Honor strode decisively out of her office to take the elevator to the President's penthouse suite.

On seeing Honor exit the elevator, the President's receptionist gestured imperiously for her to sit in the waiting area. Honor, however, elected to stand, gazing thoughtfully out at the panoramic view of Sydney Harbour available through the automatic anti-glare four-metre windows that extended from ceiling to floor. She wasn't going to be told what to do, she thought inwardly. So she stood, and studied the distant view of the massive American nuclear submarine docked at Garden Island. The morning sun was glistening off the conning tower, on which she could clearly, even at a distance, see the registration number: 666.

"Zere you are," she thought. "Ze vun zat has caused me so much trouble…"

The receptionist interrupted her reverie, voice as cold as ice. "Senior Inspector Honor," she snapped. "You may enter now."

"Zank you, Miss Vallins," Honor smiled falsely on the way by.

Walking towards the oak doors to the President's office, she stopped at a mark on the crimson carpet as protocol demanded. A red laser scanned her from head to foot, before issuing a beep to signify that she was unarmed. With a loud click, the doors unlatched. She stepped inside.

The President's impressively plush office added to her already nervous state. For some reason, tough as she was, senior authority had always affected her that way. The President was seated behind an ostentatiously large old oak desk. A rotund Asian man with a clean-shaven head, he was dressed in a well-decorated black military uniform. Firing Honor a welcoming sneer, he motioned for her to sit on a sofa facing a window even larger than the one she'd just left. She sat, waiting for the President to lever his large frame from behind his desk and join her.

His presence, despite his bulk, was overwhelming. Whenever Honor met him, she wondered how a man who had lost all his hair could have such remarkably bushy black eyebrows. The impression they made was so forceful that they seemed to add yet more lines to his brow when he turned his stare on any given object. They formed two great black wings on either side of his nose, and made eyes black as tar seeming like fathomless, inky depths in which many a soul might have been lost. Speaking into his implant, he ordered his secretary to bring in coffee for two. And some biscuits.

The man crammed himself into a lounge chair reserved for his use alone. Ignoring its groans and protestations, he made himself comfortable and fixed his eyes on Honor. She remained quiet, aware of her place.

"There seems to have been a surprising number of injuries from what I had assumed would be a simple operation, Senior Inspector Honor," he began, politely. "You are aware that the eyes of the world are upon us, thanks to the visit of the American nuclear submarine? Of course you are. So you know that all we needed was to avoid diplomatic embarrassment from Black Alice and his tree-hugging Octagon comrades. Yet still, somehow, the Octagon ferry managed to stage its protest with, I understand, Alice at the forefront. Which brings me to my question." Honor shifted uncomfortably. The President's tone of polite enquiry wasn't fooling her.

"Why, Senior Inspector," the man went on, "Why was I told that Dr Secta's experiment had been successful when our dissident friend was clearly and visibly on board that ferry?"

Honor had been thinking fast. She had to redeem some credit for herself and her assistant Karzoff. She had to give the President some kind of believable but carefully inexact explanation, while brownnosing as much as possible. It seemed the safest way. When in doubt, one couldn't beat the classics.

"Vell, sir," she proclaimed. "Your brilliant stratagem of using Secta's experiment to eradicate Black Alice vas based on experimental new technology — vich, in fact, successfully completed ze mission. Alice vas eliminated, exactly as you anticipated and planned. Even you could not have predicted zat he vould return. How zat happened ve do not know, but ve are taking strenuous steps to find out. And ven ve find ze person or persons who assisted him, ve vill make very sure zey are made a very public example of!"

The President appeared to be listening intently, but was distracted by Miss Vallins entering the room with a tray carrying two mugs of steaming coffee and a plate of biscuits. He eyed her hungrily as she placed the tray on the coffee table in front of him, making sure he got a good view down her blouse as she passed him a mug. Honor looked her over. Mid-thirties, great figure, well-shaped legs. Pale complexion, blue black hair. Irritatingly perky breasts. She looked away from the overt display of sexual energy between these two ill-matched people, apparently studying a large painting on the wall. Suddenly she gasped as the painting changed and the wall behind it went from wood panelling to a warm blue.

The President grinned. "The latest thing," he said. "Programmable holographic wallpaper and art. Sensors detect the general mood in the room and change the décor accordingly. Splendid, don't you think?"

"Yes. It could revolutionize interior design," Honor agreed.

"Another of Dr Secta's remarkable inventions!" the President crowed. "He really is a genius. Which is why he, at least, will not be punished for this Black Alice debacle."

Honor looked at the floor, where Miss Vallins' feet were still present as she placed a plate of biscuits near the President's chair. Crimson toenails tipped long, elegant toes peeping from Louboutin black, high-heeled sandals.

"Speaking of punishment," the President went on, "What news of Dr Hope?"

Honor blinked. The man flashed a lizard smile. "I understand it was Dr Hope who helped Black Alice escape the building?" he said.

"Zat … zat is correct, sir," stammered his Senior Inspector. "She has, off course, been stood down, and I vill interrogate her personally ven she is brought into custody. But for now, our primary focus must be on finding and recapturing Black Alice."

"Very well, Honor," rumbled the president, flashing an eagle glare at her from under those brows. "Get things in hand and report back to me. I warn you, I will tolerate no more incompetence. From you, or from that partner of yours. Where is he, by the way? I expected you both here."

"Karzoff, sir? He is in zi hospital."

"Oh? Why so?"

"He was electrocuted as he tried to prevent Black Alice from escaping, and shot, sir."

"Ah, I see. That reminds me, what happened to my 2-4-D prototype cyborg? I was quite fond of it, you know. Another fine example of Dr Secta's genius."

Honor flushed, wincing at the recollection of her encounter with the malfunctioning cyborg unit. "Ze dissident destroyed ze robot, sir," she said, as sulkily as she dared. "I vas badly … burned as a result." Honor indicated her bandaged thigh.

"Well I hope Secta is building a new model," said the President, with utter unconcern. "The concept of organic binary science he is perfecting is simply brilliant. Now. Run along, please. Sort out Dr

Hope, but remember that she is Dr Secta's sister, and his assistant. Secta is vital to the future of Oceana, and I do not want his work unduly affected. So, focus on finishing what you should have finished already — get rid of Black Alice and his damned Octagon!"

"Copy that, sir," said Honor, poker faced. She stood, nodded and strode toward the door, brimming with indignation.

CHAPTER 2
ROAD KILL

THE FUTURE. Not the future Alice has experienced before: an alternate. 2087, and the world has been ravaged by a devastating seven-year conflict: Cyberwars. Civilization has reverted to a state almost parodying the ancient movies about the Wild West. Millions have died from fallout poisoning following nuclear strikes on the world's major cities. In Australia, Sydney has been levelled, as have Canberra, Melbourne and other strategic centres around the country. The same story is played out around the world — cities bombed and left gutted, ruined, void of human habitation. The rule of law has broken down. The jails have emptied. Everyone carries arms, order is of the past.

The chasm between rich and poor is now greater than ever. There is no middle class, only common folk protecting themselves against the tribal gangs that roam the countryside, preying on the vulnerable. They're forced to pay exorbitant fees to gang overlords for the privilege of shelter in their heavily fortified compounds. There's little work, and the overlords are often more cruel than the brutal feudal lords of medieval history. The Dark Ages have returned.

There had been no victor from the Cyberwars. After the global databanks had been hacked, then erased, and while chaos reigned, all critical infrastructures had failed — all satellite telecommunications were gone, electricity grids and water supply quickly followed. Every conceivable apparatus reliant on computers had gone down worldwide, and they'd taken society with them. Oil refineries and all forms of commercial transportation were non-existent, and gasoline had become a currency. Food could no longer be farmed and was a scarce commodity even in the 'richest' remaining zones. No meat, no fish, no eggs, no dairy. The only animals to be found were deadly groups of non-native predators that had escaped from zoos and bred in this new landscape, together with wild dogs and feral cats, hunting in packs and competing with humans for survival. There was a thriving black market for the ever-dwindling supplies of canned food. Some generators had survived or been repaired, supplying minimal power, but they needed gasoline and that was costly. Roads were littered with cars left derelict after running out. Stripped, burnt-out, rusted carapaces, were all that remained, relics of a bygone epoch of human civilization.

But the wars had not only scarred the cities and the land. Soldiers who had somehow survived the horrors were returning home, wounded to their very core...

South Coast, New South Wales, Australia, 2087

The asphalt highway stretched like a long black conveyor belt, cutting thick eucalypt forest as though the largest scythe in the world had swung through, just once. For a man standing by the roadside, the searing heat caused the entire world to shimmer in a mad, hypnotic dance. Along the road, what was left of telegraph poles stood like broken teeth. Once the proud conveyors of vital electricity and communications to towns along the coast, they were no more than ghostly reminders of an era gone past; miraculously-remaining vestiges of humanity, along with trashed cars dotted along the road and the lone figure of a man. Dressed in black, with a kitbag slung over his broad shoulders, he stood in the blazing sun at the edge of the road, looking and feeling like the last man on earth. Six foot six, rugged, muscular, with a face wearing a menacing stare and showing all the signs of a youth ill spent in the pool halls of life.

This proud first nations man of the Yuin mob, was the product of intensive military training — a walking lethal weapon — returning home from the wars and a stint in military prison. He was heading to what was left of home, hoping for a chance to reinvent himself. He knew adapting to what now passed for civilian life would be a challenge, but he hoped returning home would calm the beast war had released in him.

On the side of the road, he noticed a big buck kangaroo, dead, hit by one of the few vehicles still running. It had blown up big time. On its back with its feet in the air, it looked like the world's weirdest balloon. If you stuck it with a pin, it would probably explode. He moved clear but couldn't avoid the stench. With his hand covering his mouth and nose, shook his head sadly as he passed. "Poor bugger," he muttered. "Used to be king of country, now you're nothing but a bag of worms…"

A rustle came from the trees nearby. Senses on high alert, he looked sharply in the direction of the noise. Another rustling, this time from across the road. Sensing a threat, with cool deliberation, he lowered his kitbag, dug inside and came up with a pistol. He checked the clip. Six bullets — they would have to do. He knew instinctively he was up against animals, not humans. They were too low to the ground and moving too fast through the scrub.

His instincts proved correct — a huge German shepherd leapt from the bush nearest him and propped. Bugger. Wild dogs. There would be more of them than his limited ammo could hold off. The shepherd snarled, yellow teeth bared. The man knew the dogs wanted the roo, and saw him as competition. He started backing away. He'd have to take out the leader if it charged. If they attacked as a pack he wouldn't stand a chance.

Two more dogs appeared on the opposite side of the road, mongrels, but no less ferocious. Then two more from behind one of the burnt-out cars. They were ready to attack. No time to back away, he needed to scare them off. The leader had to be the shepherd. Even as he had that thought, the biggest pit-bull the man had ever seen appeared behind it. Seriously battle-scarred, it looked like it could kill a wild boar by itself and eat it for breakfast.

He crouched onto one knee, took aim, and as the shepherd and pit-bull thundered towards him, he fired. The first shot exploded the shepherd's skull, but the second missed the pit-bull. The remaining dogs had joined the charge. His next desperate shot hit the pit-bull in the hindquarters, but even a shattered leg didn't stop it. The man swung around and aimed at the others — three bullets left, four dogs, and the pit-bull was still coming, dragging its back leg.

Whump! He took out the lead of the other four dogs, and the rest took fright and fled. But the pit-bull had arrived, and even though it was bleeding like a stuck pig, it launched itself into the air. Whump! Whump! The man emptied the chamber into the dog while it was still in the air. Another canine head exploded with the first shot. The second almost cut it in half. It landed at his feet, a mess of blood and steaming guts. The man looked down at it. "Mongrel thing," he growled. "Wasted three good bullets on you!"

He tucked his gun away and, slinging his kitbag back over his shoulder, started walking, hoping the surviving dogs would be content to eat their friends and leave him alone. Suddenly, the rumble of an oncoming vehicle attracted his attention. Brushing the ever-present flies from his face, he dipped his head and looked back under the broad brim of his hat to see an SUV heading his way. He stuck out a thumb.

The SUV was really travelling. When the driver hit the skids, the tyres squealed and bellowed smoke. A blacked-out driver's side window opened a few centimetres and a gruff voice snarled from inside.

"Hey, you! Over here."

The hitchhiker strolled over. Cautious, but in need of a ride after dealing with the dogs, he stopped at a safe distance and said, in as friendly a voice as possible: "G'day! How about a —" Before he could finish his sentence, he was staring down the barrel of a 44-magnum.

"What's in yer kitbag, buddy?" the driver asked.

"A gun, personal stuff, mostly clothes — no money, if that's what you're after," the hitcher replied.

"Money? Hah! Money means nothing these days," said the voice. "Tip it all out on the ground. Now!"

The hitcher tried: "Ah, come on, feller, give a bloke a break..."

"Do it now or you'll be joining all the road kill there!"

The driver wasn't messing around. The hitcher couldn't have read the tone clearer if he'd said it himself. Hard experience had taught him the only sane response was compliance, so he sighed and emptied his kitbag into the dust.

"Now, take off yer left boot."

With a deep sigh, he reluctantly obliged. Standing on one leg, unwilling to place his bare foot on the molten asphalt, he felt like an idiot.

"Right," the driver said smugly. "Now put the bare foot on the pistol."

Once again, he complied.

"Keep it there," the voice demanded. "Now reach down slowly and remove the clip."

Again, he did as he was told. As he began to straighten, the voice barked again. "Wait! Keep your foot where it is. Now pull the trigger."

"Where would you like me to aim it: your front tyre?"

"Don't be smart. You know what to do."

The hitchhiker rolled his eyes, a stream of sweat dribbling from under his hat and sizzling onto the road. He pulled the trigger. A click — the chamber was empty.

"Good," said the voice. "Now lean over — slowly — and drop the clip through the window. Got it? On my order!"

The magnum cocked, ready to fire.

"Right. Do it!"

The hitchhiker straightened up, very slowly and deliberately, and slipped the magazine through the gap in the window.

"Good. Now kick the clothes on the deck around with your bare foot."

"What the stuff for!" he spat, now furious.

"To make sure there's no knife."

As he kicked his clothes around he muttered, "Are you bloody paranoid or something?"

"Absolutely," was the uncompromising reply.

"Look, it's a thousand degrees out here. I've been walking for a damned day and a half, I'm not gonna attack you. I just want a…"

The driver cut him off mid-sentence. "Alright. Grab your stuff and get in."

He opened the door to the SUV, and suddenly it all became clear. He was hit by a waft of perfume and the sight of the hottest looking female he had laid eyes on in seven long years.

She pointed a finger at the pistol balanced on her lap and, looking over her sunglasses with big blue eyes, said: "One false move and you're dead meat. Got it?"

"No problem," he said, unable to keep the smirk from his stubbly face.

"Now close the door. You're letting all the good air out."

He slammed the door and instantly felt the air-con begin to dry the sweat on his body. She handed him a bottle of water, and he took a revitalizing swig.

Her bare foot slammed down on the accelerator, and in a New York second, they were doing a hundred and fifty clicks.

"Name's Rita," she said, glaring at the road. "What's yours?"

"Turk," he said, contorting a leg to pull on a sock, his foot near the air-conditioning duct.

"Jesus, mate!" said Rita. "You have been walking a while, haven't you? Your feet are seriously on the bugle!"

He smiled in spite of himself, and as the two of them laughed, the mood lightened. He glanced at her, taking in rich red lips, English-rose complexion, long sandy hair, a delicate nose. She must be in her mid-twenties. A pretty girl like this out here all alone? Must be able to handle herself. His gaze travelled to her bare feet and red painted toenails. She caught him staring.

"Scrounged some cosmetics off a bloke," she said. "You got a foot fetish or something?"

"Don't know," said Turk. "I could maybe get one — you've got nice feet. Not like mine." He grinned again.

"What's with the name?" She didn't beat about this bush, this girl.

"Had it since I was a kid," he said. "Sure beats Bruce."

"That your real name?"

"What, Bruce?"

She ignored his feeble attempt at wit. "Alright," she said. "Where you headed, Bruce?"

"Snake Ridge," he said. No point arguing with her, he had a decided feeling he'd lose. "Then on to Blanket Bay."

"Fine. Snake's near the coast. I'm going through there."

"Good-o," he said, relieved. "If it's all right with you, I'll grab some shuteye. It's been a long hike."

"No sweat," she smiled properly for the first time, showing perfect, pearly-white teeth.

"Not any more," he mumbled, already dozing off. "Air-con..."

Shaking her head gently, she smiled as he dropped into sleep, then triggered some relaxing music on the sampler. The blazing day slid gradually, almost imperceptibly into night.

A little while later, with the headlights of the SUV slicing a path through the pitch-black darkness, high beam headlights in the rearview mirror temporarily blinded her.

Turk casually lifted his hat and sat up, squinting against the bright light.

"There's a damn bus tailgating my butt," Rita complained. "I don't like it."

"I guess it finds your butt attractive," wisecracked Turk. Rita opened her mouth to fire a shot back, when the bus suddenly swerved onto the other side of the road and overtook them, almost forcing Rita onto the shoulder.

Fighting to stop the SUV from skidding, she cursed out loud: "Bloody goose! I hate these renegade drivers. Eventually they run out of fuel and just dump the bus and its passengers anywhere. It's a hell of a risk to drive or catch one. Idiots," she finished, still grumbling, as a wall of red dust engulfed them and filled the headlights.

"Where are we?" asked Turk.

"About forty minutes out of Snake, I'd say," she said. "Man, did you sleep or what? And what the hell were you dreaming about? The war?"

"Probably," he said. "Crap comes back to dump on you once you've spread enough of it around."

"Ha! Too true. So, you did the war then?"

"Yeah, I did my bit. I'm still wondering why."

She let that comment go — too complicated, too personal. Too much like talking politics with a total stranger.

"You from 'round here?" she asked, instead.

"Yeah, Blanket Bay," said Turk. "'S a fishing village a few clicks outta Snake."

"Don't know it. Got family there?"

"Just my young sister. Folks are dead."

"When did you see her last? That is, if you don't mind me asking."

"I don't mind. I guess about seven years ago. She was eight or nine when I left."

"She's a teenager now, huh? Bet she's buzzing about big bro coming home…"

"Nup. She doesn't know. It's … sort of a surprise." Turk sighed. "She hasn't heard from me in a while."

"How come?"

He paused for a second, his eyes far away. "Let's just say it was tough getting word out from where I was," he replied.

Okay, conversation over, she thought. Turk's body language indicated a truckload of pent-up emotional baggage. She questioned him no further.

Out of the dark ahead, red taillights glowed like the eyes of a crazed animal. The tailgating bus had stopped to let off a passenger. As Rita drove past, she hit the horn and held a bow-finger out the window. "Arsehole!" she yelled, savagely. Predictably, before long, the high-beam lights were once again blinding her.

"What's with this idiot?" she scowled, and then slowed to move over, leaving room for the bus to pass. But it didn't. It just sat there, right on her hammer. "I'll fix this bloody fool!" she hissed, as her foot stabbed the brakes, thinking it would force him to back off. Instead a loud bang shook the SUV as the bus rear-ended it. Rita slammed her foot back on the accelerator. But no matter how fast they went, the bus kept right on her tail.

Turk peered over his shoulder. "This ratbag needs to be taught a lesson," he growled.

Suddenly, the bus slowed. A passenger wanted off. Rita's SUV was finally able to pull away, the driver chuckling as he watched her tail lights dwindle into the dark. No matter, he'd catch her up again, cheeky little bitch. He pulled out and continued into the night. A little way down the road he saw someone in the light of his headlights, signalling to be picked up. Pulling the bus over, he opened the doors.

The man stepped on board. But instead of taking a seat, Turk flew at the driver and grabbed him by the throat.

"Listen, shit-for-brains," he snarled, eyes ablaze. "I'm the dude from the truck you've been messing with. You've been risking the lives of me and my friend, not to mention your passengers. So, we're gonna have a chat."

The driver writhed free and dived for the gun under the dashboard, but Turk grabbed his wrist, quick as a snake strike, and twisted the weapon out of his grasp. The driver gasped, which Turk took as an invitation to shove the barrel of the pistol into his open mouth, smashing his front teeth in the process.

Turk cocked the pistol. "Message got through to you now?" he hissed. "Anything I need to add?"

Mouth bleeding, the wide-eyed driver shook his head frantically.

Turk nodded, pocketed the weapon and calmly stepped off the bus, accompanied by rousing applause from the twenty or so appreciative passengers.

He climbed back into the SUV, parked off-road with the lights off, and handed Rita the pistol. "Not exactly the perfect start to my homecoming," he said. "But at least it ended well."

"No-one dead, you mean?" she was laughing. "Mate, I could hear the applause from here. Well done."

Turk shrugged. It was normal for him to take the law into his own hands. More often than not, to his own peril.

CHAPTER 3
CLOUD CHAMBER

ONLY A FEW hours after Black Alice had vanished from the bridge of the ferry, Dr Secta was busy in his SSD underground lab. An incoming implant call interrupted him. Irritably, he flicked his shoulder-length white hair out of his eyes and gazed up at the ceiling. He detested interruptions.

"Yes?" he barked. "Declare yourself!"

"Senior Inspector Honor."

"Oh." That cheered him up. He was always happy to partake in some verbal jousting with his favourite antagonist. "How's your nose?" he asked. "Still sore where Alice thumped you? And what on earth have you done to my robot? He'll never be the same after what you did to him… virtual sexual harassment, I'd call it!"

Honor tried to ignore him, but the memory of Alice throwing her onto the lap of a short-circuiting robot, and the awful burns she'd sustained as a result, made it difficult not to rise. The fact that he had recently crushed her ego by refusing her advances had only made matters worse. She had committed herself to a policy of overtly displaying her distaste for him whenever the opportunity arose, and she summoned it now.

"Secta," she said, as smoothly as she could. "I haff detained your sister, Hope. She vill shortly be undergoing interrogation. You have zi right to be present, off course."

Secta allowed her statement to sink in. "U-huh," he said, non-committal. "Detained on what charge, Honor?"

"Treason!" she barked, bluntly.

"Treason?" Secta didn't even try to hide his amusement. "Didn't that go out with the Spanish Inquisition? What treason, for goodness sake?"

"Ze same as yours, Secta," hissed Honor. "Aiding and abetting an enemy of ze state — in ozzer vords, Black Alice."

"Ugh," sighed Secta. "What a pile of hyperbole. Like most people who speak too much, Honor, you actually know very little. I did what was asked of me. I sent Alice to oblivion. Isn't that enough for you?"

"Hope helped him to escape our headquvarters, as you very vell know," snapped Honor, her patience wearing thin. "And you allowed him to materialize back out of ze hologram. He told us himself that you had helped him in ze future. How do you explain that?" Her tone was triumphant.

"How can I make sense of something that happened in the future, Honor?" he asked. "That simply doesn't make any sense…"

"I do not care if it makes sense or not, Secta! Ze fact remains zat it happened!"

"I'll need to speak with Hope," he said. "We might be able to work it out together. Send her to me," he demanded.

"I do not zink zat vould be a vise idea," she said, her voice menacing now.

"Oh, but vhy not, Honor?" he mocked. "I'm full of vise ideas. That's vhy the government pays me bucket-loads of money. So send Hope to me, or I'll simply call ze President."

There was a slight pause on the other end of the call. Then "No," said Honor. "I vill allow you to be present at zi interrogation, but zat is as far as I will bend for you."

"I don't want you to bend for me at all," he snapped back. "I thought I'd already made that clcar."

"Take it or leave it, Secta," she snapped. He knew when to stop pushing a point. "All right, Honor," he sighed. "Don't get your knickers in a knot. Just let me know when you're ready and I'll be there."

With the call terminated, he chuckled to himself. "God, I'm clever!"

Honor was pacing the interrogation room like an agitated cat. Secta and Hope were seated calmly at a large table. The panoramic view of Sydney Harbour, twinkling in the morning sunlight, had Secta captivated. Honor spoke, snapping him out of his daydream.

"Zis interview conducted by Senior Inspector Fanny Honor, vith Professors Secta and Hope of ze Oceana Science Division, is now being recorded and auto time-stamped," she declared. "Dr Secta, I shall first give you ze opportunity to explain yourself."

Secta leaned back in his chair. "Well, basically I'm human," he purred, caustically. "Though at times I have questioned that fact. I think there could be a hint of god in my DNA. Divine genius at least."

Hope grinned. Her brother had many faults, but he could turn almost any situation into a theatre of the absurd. But today Honor wasn't going to stand for it. "Cut ze asinine imbecilic answers, Secta!" she roared.

"No, no, no, Honor," said Secta, a patient teacher explaining to a particularly dim pupil. "Asinine and imbecilic? Tautological! That should be totally completely clear, even to you. Now, what exactly would you like me to cut? You did ask me to explain myself..."

Honor had had enough. "Guard!" she shouted.

The door opened and an armed, uniformed trooper stepped in.

"Ma'am?" he asked diffidently.

She made an exhibition of turning the recorder off.

"Shoot doctor Secta in ze left knee," she commanded. Secta made a campy display of covering his left knee with his hand, but Hope jumped up.

"No, Honor!" she shouted. "Tell him to put it away. I'll tell you what you want to know."

A smile of satisfaction broke on Honor's face. Clearly, she was making headway. She motioned for the guard to leave, resumed the recording and seated herself, cross-legged, on the edge of the table to hear Hope's confession.

For her part, Hope knew her brother had gone too far, and she needed to do something to ease the tension. Even though she had promised the Octagon not to tell what had happened on the ferry, and she would honour her promise to try to save him, she knew she'd have to give something away. It was the only way to control his interrogation.

"Alice has gone, Honor," she said. "While he was still on the ferry his condition deteriorated beyond our control. We lost him."

Honor resumed pacing. This was more like what she wanted to hear, but she needed to be convinced that Alice was gone for good — dead, disintegrated, whatever — anything but hidden away somewhere by the Octagon.

"Go on!" she snapped. "Convince me!"

"It was a side-effect of the hologram process," Hope went on. "It isn't stable." She glanced at Secta. He nodded his approval.

"It's too early to say why, Honor," she said. "We need to do a lot more research. But about Black Alice you can rest assured. He's gone."

"Vun quvestion remains, however," purred Honor. "Can he return?"

"I don't think so," Secta chimed in. "I told you. I gave you what you wanted. Alice is gone — post hoctor proc — est mortuus — kaput! Can't prove it, all I can tell you is that he is no longer."

Honor turned to face them, a satisfied smirk on her gaunt face.

"Ze process vorks zen?"

"Of course it works, Honor," said Secta, blithely. "But it is not, alas, flawless."

Suddenly, Honor surprised them, announcing: "Interview concluded." She turned to Hope. "Rest assured, Doctor, zis is not over for you," she sneered. "Zere vill be repercussions viz regard to you helping zi dissident to escape. Dr Secta, I require a full report on ze outcome of ze experiment on my terminal vizin twenty-four hours. Now, get out. Not you, Hope. You go novhere wizout ... supervision."

Later, escorted by her two trooper babysitters, Hope stopped outside Secta's underground lab. She inserted her index finger into the fingerprint identification passkey beside the door, but it responded with a red light and an indignant "Oh, no!" Angrily removing her finger, Hope stepped back and defiantly folded her arms. The troopers stared at her. She sighed noisily.

"Obviously I've been barred," she barked.

Nodding, the larger guard pushed her aside and shoved his finger into the device. "Oh, yes!" it purred, and a servo whined as the door slid open.

Secta looked up from his computer. "I hardly think an escort is necessary in here, gentlemen," he growled, irritably, to the troopers. "I only need to speak to Hope, not to you. Go on, shoo!"

Hope waited patiently for the door to close behind the troopers, then turned to her brother. "So, brother dear," she said. "What's with the sudden change of heart?"

He continued typing. "I have no idea what you're talking about," he said, shrugging.

"You had the chance to give me up for siding with Alice and the Octagon," said Hope. "But you didn't. I want to know why not."

He turned in his seat. "Not likely, little sister!" he chortled. "I know how you like to take the moral high ground. Who am I to deprive you of the opportunity?"

"You're such a drag, Secta," said Hope, smiling in spite of herself. "Unlike you, I have a social conscience."

"Sure thing, whatever," said Secta, shrugging again. "You want the truth? Your help is too valuable to lose. You're the only other person who understands my work."

"Gosh. Thanks," said Hope, facetiously. "I was worried for a minute there. Thought you might actually care what happens to me."

"As if," Secta snorted. "All the same, sister of mine, be careful. Honor is paranoid about failure, and obsessed with ridding the world of Black Alice and the Octagon. If she finds any hard evidence that proves you helped them—" He let the sentence tail off.

"Tell me," said Hope, her mind already elsewhere. "What happened to Alice — did you know it was a possibility?"

"That depends," said Secta. "What exactly did happen?"

Hope flopped into the chair Secta had used to de-molecularize Alice and lock him in his holographic prison. "Well," she said, "Alice freed me from the lab that you, in your loving brotherly fashion, locked me into..."

"Get to the point Hope, don't bleat."

"...And, long story short, we made it to the ferry, managed to avert a collision between it and the nuclear sub. Afterwards, we were on the bridge of the ferry and his cellular structure simply collapsed. He vanished."

Secta, grasping his chin, lapsed into deep thought. "Hmm," he said. "We might have expected that, actually. Yes. Yes, out of phase ... Dimensional instability ... Molecular transfer ... Interesting..."

"Speak clearly,' Hope chided.

Secta turned back to his keyboard. "He's in another timeline, Hope."

"Well, duh," she said. "I'd already worked that much out. The question is why? And how do we get him back?"

Secta opened his desk drawer and gently pulled out a black and white rat. Placing the animal on his shoulder, he stood and began pacing the room, deep in thought. "I'll be honest with you, Hope," he said. "Until now I wasn't convinced that dimension matter transfer was possible. But since we now know that Alice managed to materialize from the holographic state into a future timeline, and that I — or at least, my future self — helped him to return to this one, I've looked at the physics again." He stopped pacing and looked at his sister. "There's no doubt," he said. "The process works. At least in theory."

Hope stared at him. "So what you're saying is that it's definite? Our formula can digitize organic materials and re-materialize them in another place? That we can carry out matter transfer?"

"Not sure about the *our formula* part, Hope, and you're not quite right," said her brother. "We seem to have achieved transference without digitization. A similar process, but sub-atomic. Alice, in theory, is proof that it works, if he is in fact alive and in another time. If I could determine that, then yes, it would be dimensional matter transfer. But there's always the possibility that he might have gone nowhere. He might simply have ceased to exist."

"Yes. Or he might be inhabiting another form," said Hope. "His awareness might never kick back in. Right?"

Secta nodded. "Another possibility, yes."

"I thought so!" cried Hope. "That's what I told him on the ferry, right before he disappeared. I was partly guessing," she added, "But it seemed right to try to get him to understand … just in case I was right. Dammit! I promised I'd try to find him. How do we even start looking?"

Sporting a devilish grin, Secta said: "You know I planted a sub-atomic radioactive marker in his DNA?"

Hope sat up abruptly.

"So if he has travelled to another dimension, we might be able to track him!" she said.

Secta waggled a hand. "Perhaps," he said. "But if I was to hazard an opinion that only a true potential Nobel laureate could, I'd say it's unlikely."

"Why not?" Hope protested, flopping back into the chair.

"Because there are an infinite number of dimensions," said Secta, patiently. "There's the past, the present and the future. Look, think of the pages of a book. Each page is a separate dimension. But the routes between them aren't linear." He picked up a textbook from his bench. "Alice could have travelled forwards," he said, riffling through the pages. "Or backwards," he went on, flipping the pages in reverse. "He might have jumped from page one to page fifty. He might be upside down, or reading from right to left. There's no real way to tell."

"But there's the marker signal," said Hope. "If it's strong enough, it might still be possible to determine his location."

"In theory, you're right," said Secta. He stopped pacing. "There's just one snag," he went on, holding his chin, thoughtfully. "I haven't invented a device to read the signal yet." Hope's jaw dropped. Her shoulders sank dejectedly. "Well, anyway, it's not as if it matters, Hope," her brother concluded. "We've done the job we said we'd do, and that's that…"

"Wrong, dear brother," said Hope. "You'd better get started on building that device, because as soon as we can determine where he is, you're going to join him."

"Hah!" laughed Secta. "No thanks, little sister. I've got plans of my own, far more beneficial to my health than that one."

"Listen Secta, you're the only one that can do this," said Hope. "We get you into the future, and you'll be able to create the means to bring you both back. Remember, you did it before."

"But that wasn't me, Hope," said Secta, beginning to look panicked. "That was … well yes, it was me, but it was another me. You can't hold that against me! Besides, why should I? He means zero to me!"

"Yes," said Hope, drily. "Zeros and ones."

"Very funny, Hope."

"Look," she said, firmly. "You caused his condition, Secta. This is on you. And don't forget, he saved you. You owe him, Secta. That's all there is to it."

"Saved me? Owe him? Unlikely!"

"Oh, but he did," said Hope. He saved future you from an eternity in your personal underground prison. Remember?"

"Well yes, alright, granted, but that will never happen now," Secta whined. "He's already altered the future, if quantum physics has it right. Anyhow," he said, assuming a primly angelic expression. "We must remember the prime directive — we never interfere."

Hope sighed. "That's Star Trek, Secta, not science. I do know the difference," she said. "Look, Alice prevented the collision between the ferry and the sub, yes? That changed the timeline. Potentially. But you still took the longevity serum didn't you, dear brother? So, who knows what else you might be facing in future? And who knows whether Alice has a role to play in saving you again?"

"All right — all right, Hope, fine!" Secta snapped. "God, I hate it when you bleat. But know this: I owe him nothing. I am, however, finding myself somewhat attracted to the challenge of locating him. If we can locate his marker — and I stress if —I'll consider it. But we have to find it first."

"Deal!" cried Hope. "What do you need me to do?"

"The gamma nuclide I attached to Alice's DNA will have left a residue, no matter which dimension he's in," said Secta, his mind already whirring with the challenge. "We'll need to create a cloud chamber to detect it."

"A cloud chamber?" asked Hope, eyebrows abnormally high.

"Yes, Hope. It's perfectly simple," said Secta, lapsing back into his usual condescending state. "A device filled with helium, like a small dirigible, which allows us to perceive the path of charged subatomic particles through the formation of droplets … that is, chains of ions generated by their passage."

Hope's eyebrows sank back down. "Boy, sometimes you make me feel like I'm back at school," she said. "Why Helium?"

"Because it doesn't freeze and it's a monoatomic carrier gas with a high nuclear binding energy," said Secta, as if it was perfectly plain. "The charge density of helium forms its own neutron cloud. It is mathematical underpinning, Hope, the manipulation of instantaneous signals. Anti-Einstein I know, but cosmic unity nevertheless. In the same way are fish unaware of the water in which they swim."

"That's seriously obtuse, Secta."

"Not at all," he responded, smugly. "It's simply sub-atomic holographic reality."

"Okay," said Hope. "A helium cloud chamber. But how will we detect Alice's signature?"

"We'll begin from his vanishing point, of course!" answered Secta, grinning at his own brilliance. He patted the rat on his shoulder. "You realise we're risking everything by undertaking this, Hope? If Honor finds out…"

"Oh, stuff Honor!" snapped Hope. "This is more important than her. Or than us, come to that." Secta looked doubtful, but Hope pressed on: "We'll have to take the cloud chamber to the ferry. Presumably we'll find radioactive residue from his dimension switch. Then we'll be able to measure the decay, and that should show us where he is in time." She looked up with smile, proud of her deduction.

"Oh, bravo, Hope!" Secta cheered. "You're almost as clever as I! Please note, I stress the almost."

CHAPTER 4
SNAKE RIDGE

T AROUND 9PM Rita's SUV rolled into Snake Ridge. There were few signs of life in the small town. The view out of the window was bleak.

"Has this place gone to seed or what? It used to be called Bodalla, you know?" said Turk, frowning. "It's Friday night — the town should be hopping!"

"Jeez, Turk" Rita chuckled, "Those days are long gone, buddy. This is how it is now, most places."

Snake Ridge had always been a one-horse town, but now it looked like the horse had bolted, leaving only ghosts. Still, with its old iron roofs, big old blue gums on both sides of the highway and sleepy fields beyond, and compared to the places Turk had occupied most recently, it was a picture of bucolic charm.

As they came over a ridge onto the main drag, memory hit him like a ton of bricks. In his mind's eye, he went walking along the side of the road, a youngster again, laughing in the rain with his best mates, Jonno and Reno. He remembered the three of them, late teens, stripping off and diving butt naked into the Tuross River. Good times. Times of innocence, when they knew nothing about life and the workings of the world outside.

The SUV hit a pothole and snapped Turk back to reality. The golden days had been replaced by hard experience. War had stolen the zest from his life. He'd give anything to get back to his mates and his youth.

The tiny town, bisected by the highway, had once had a population that floated around five hundred, but would periodically explode. "You should have seen this place during school holidays," said Turk. "Tourists used to flock here. I guess those days have passed."

"Mate," said Rita from the corner of her mouth, repositioning the gun on her lap and steering with one hand, "There's no such thing as school holidays anymore. Because there's no such thing as school. And that's because there's no such thing as kids. Keep your eye out for trouble, alright? My sixth sense is registering."

The dozen or so single-level shanty buildings that constituted the town were vacant, but still wore the signs that had advertised their former glory: antique shops, rustic restaurants, funky boutiques and art galleries. A local pub lay dilapidated and abandoned, but still had its slogan stencilled on the rusted roof: "McConkey's Pub — the Killarney of the south." Age and neglect had rendered the message almost unreadable to the untrained eye, but it was still discernible to Turk, because he knew it was there.

He sat forward in his seat and pointed to a block of shops. "There," he said. "That bar up ahead, with the neon. Reno's — see it? There's a yellow F-200 outside. Can you drop me there? I think it belongs to a buddy of mine."

Rita pulled up outside.

"I won't come in Turk," she said. "Bars aren't really my thing." She grinned, holding out her hand. "Got to keep moving," she added, taking Turk's big paw.

"I haven't asked where you're headed," he said, feeling the warm silkiness of a woman's hand in his for the first time in many, many years.

"Angel City," she said. "It's as far as this tank'll get me. She's not hybrid or nuke pelleted, and gas is hard to come by."

Their eyes locked for a few seconds. She was arousing something in him that had lain dormant for far too long. He smiled, and just for a moment something quivered between them, delivered through eyes and touch. Turk took a deep breath and broke the spell.

"Good meeting you, Rita," he said, gruffly. "Till next time?"

He dropped her hand, stepped out of the SUV, and reached inside to grab his kitbag. Rita flicked him a warm smile. "You're a good bloke, Turk," she said. "I'd like there to be a next time." She handed over his pistol. "Here. You might be needing this. It'd be more deadly if it was loaded, mind you."

"Ta," he grinned, taking it with a smile. He slung his kitbag back over his shoulder and shut the door. Rita didn't mess about, taking off in a cloud of dust with nothing more than a blast on the horn. He took a moment to watch the car thunder up the highway, thinking briefly about all the people in his life he'd left — or had to leave — behind.

"Chaa!" he mouthed after her. Hell of a woman, he thought, looking up at a crackling, half-busted neon sign swinging precariously overhead. It was hot and muggy. Remembering Rita's advice to look out for trouble, he slipped his pistol into the back of his pants, hefted his kitbag once more and ambled into Reno's Bar.

The bar was barren of customers. Half a dozen young girls lazed about in dim pools of light, listening to loud music. They were bored and it showed. At the sight of Turk, they all but clambered over one another to get at him.

"Hey, hey!" he protested loudly, shouting over the loud music. "Back off, ladies! I'm just looking for Reno."

"Who's after him, then?" A harsh female voice came suspiciously from the darkest part of the room, causing all the girls to freeze.

"It's Turk," came his laconic reply.

He tensed as a woman came rushing out of the darkness, screaming like a banshee, and threw her arms around his neck,

"Turk!" she squealed. "Turk! Is it really you?"

He recognised Reno's wife Elsa, and relaxed into a big bear hug.

"Elsa, it's good to see you, mate!"

She held him at arm's length and studied his craggy features. "Let me get a gander at that good-looking dial of yours, love," she said, fondly. "A few more lines, eh? And not the laughing kind. A new scar or two, but yep, that's you under all those years. Geez, it's great to see ya. Welcome home, love ... How did you get here, got wheels?"

"Na, military flew me into Merimbula and dumped me there to find my own way home," he said. "I walked to the highway, fought off a pack of dogs, hitchhiked a ride."

"Lucky you," said Elsa.

"What, getting a ride?"

"Nah, surviving a feral dog attack and then getting a ride that didn't kill ya," she replied. "No-one can be trusted any more mate, everyone packs a gun. Some'd kill ya just for your boots. Things have changed since you left."

"I've noticed," said Turk. "Looks like all the towns along the coast are deserted ... from what I could see from the plane in the dark, there's spot-fires burning everywhere."

"Yeah," said Elsa. "The dogs pretty much took over the towns, but they can't breed. They'll die out soon enough, just like the rest of us. The spot-fires are mostly the fracking mines, you know how there were lots of them. Somehow, they were all set on fire after the cities got nuked. Made 'em no-go zones. Radiation makes what's left of 'em glow in the dark. Eerie stuff. Anyhow," she finished, shaking her head and hugging him again. "That's enough doom and gloom, right?"

She put an arm around his waist and walked him over to a dark cubicle. He towered over her five-five frame. A pctite brunette in her mid-thirties, Elsa was all exuberant grace, despite a voice hardened by years of yelling over loud music in bars. They sat down under a tennis light that sensed their presence and automatically illuminated.

Squinting, Turk cased the place.

"So, when did you get this joint?" he asked. "Wasn't this the old post office?"

"Sure was," she said. "Reno and I bought it the year after you left."

He studied her cute round face, hazel eyes framed by a bob hairstyle with a fringe.

"And where is the old bastard?"

"In Angel City, love, he'll be back in a couple of days. Hey!" she added, suddenly. "Guess who I saw last month?"

"Who?"

"Jonno!"

Turk removed his hat, put it on the table, and flopped back into his seat.

"Bloody hell," he laughed. "I thought if anyone'd be dead by now, it'd be Jonno."

"Nar, love, still alive and kickin', still the same bloke," said Elsa. "And guess what?" She paused for effect. "He's married! Yeah! I know," she went on, laughing at Turk's astonished expression, "Last person you'd expect to be hitched, right? But hey, she's a nice bird. Her name's Trixy, they've got a bar in Angel City."

"Married!" gasped Turk. "I'll be stuffed! But what is it with all you guys and bars? When I left you and Reno were teaching kickboxing and Jonno was selling fish, for goodness sake!"

"Yeah, well, things changed, love," she said despondently.

The music suddenly cranked up another fifty decibels and the girls started dancing together: they liked the song. Elsa took exception and bawled over. "Girls! Turn it down! Can't you see I'm having a conversation here? Manners, girls, manners!" Her voice softened slightly as she addressed one of the girls. "Jenny, bring us some beers please darl!"

She smiled at Turk and went back to her friendly tone. "One voice for them, one for you, love." She reached out and took his hand, smiled warmly. "So tell me. How are you, darl?"

Before he could answer the beers arrived, delivered by Jenny: mini-skirt, long shapely legs — dark skin — no older than seventeen, about the same age as his sister. As she leaned over the table to put the tray down, Turk couldn't stop himself staring.

Elsa caught him. "Been a while has it, love?" she asked, wryly.

They took a beer each. Turk shot her a broad smile. "Yeah, it's bin a while all right," he said, ruefully. "Sorry for pegging her."

"Hey, can't blame you for being a bloke," said Elsa. "Besides, you're right. She's lovely. But tell me about your life!"

"I'd rather talk about her," he said, but registered her expression. This wasn't a stranger, Elsa was a friend. "Alright," he said. "I did my thing at the front, killing the enemy, whoever they were supposed to be. So that was five years out of my life. Then, 'coz of a momentary lapse of reason at a kickboxing match, I killed my opponent."

"What, hit him wrong?"

"No. He called me a bloody abo and I took exception. Saw red, landed a hard chin jab and crushed his larynx. Actually, to be more accurate, I pulverized his cricoid cartilage. Can't breathe once that's shattered. Anyhow, I got two years in the military big house."

"Holy heck," said Elsa. "Well, at least you won the fight. That's more than we can say for the damn war."

"You're not wrong there, Elsa," he agreed. "What a waste of time and lives."

They toasted in silent agreement and took a swig at their beers.

"Anyway," Turk went on. "I've had plenty of time to think. Now I'm out and I'm gonna steer clear of trouble and start again."

"Well, you've come to the right place for that," Elsa said, mournfully. "You'll find no trouble here. No customers left to cause any damn trouble! Half the time I wish there were, just to break the monotony. At least we might be turning a buck."

"How do customers pay? I've got money."

"Currency isn't much value."

"So everything I earned in the forces—"

"Ain't worth nothing love, sorry to say."

The realisation that his net worth was worthless made him flop back in his seat.

"Damn," he said. "All for nothing."

"Don't worry, love," said Elsa. "We all had to start over again. You'll be all right. And I bet Nora can't wait to see you."

"Haven't told her I'm coming," he admitted. "Kept it a surprise."

Elsa knew how much Nora loved her big brother. He was, after all, her only living relative.

"Ah, she'll flip out when she sees you!" she said. "And you'll flip out when you see her — what a honey she's grown into!"

Suddenly, the thunderous roar of motorbike engines drowned their conversation. The bar girls raced for the windows to check the bikes or, more likely, their riders.

Six Fatboy Harley choppers with extended forks had angle parked in a line outside Club Voodoo, just opposite Reno's. In the purple glow of the Voodoo neon, six heavily armed, leather-clad, tattooed, longhaired dusty bikers dismounted and cruised menacingly inside.

Jenny turned from the window and called back to Elsa: "Six Rebels, Mum. Gone into Voodoo."

"Voodoo was the Dairy Café, wasn't it?" asked Turk.

"Yeah, run by outsiders," said Elsa. "Started up same time as us, ran the old place right into the ground. Nothing more than a flophouse now."

Turk grinned at her. "Maybe your theory about trouble'll get tested tonight."

"Hey, we live in hope," she said. "But no, they'll probably stay at Voodoo. Get what they want over there, you know the drill. It's a grovel pit."

Turk downed his beer.

"Well," he said, "I'd better hit the frog and toad. It's a bit of a hike to Blanket—"

"No fricking way, feller!" Elsa cried. "Don't move a muscle! One for the road, then I'll drive you out there — and I won't take no for an answer. Jenny! Shots!"

Jenny jumped into action.

Turk loved the way Elsa took control. It reminded him of when they were kids.

"Do you remember us going skinny-dipping when we were teenagers?" he grinned.

"Yeah!" she answered, laughing.

Shapely Jenny arrived with a bottle of Tequila and two shot glasses. As Elsa poured, Turk caught an amorous little twinkle in Jenny's big brown eyes. Time seemed to slow down. In slow motion, Jenny flicked her head like a thoroughbred filly, then moved a strand of long auburn hair from her line of vision. Turk blinked, trying to restore real time, but even the music had slurred and he felt heady. He watched Elsa pouring the shots. Her mouth was moving but he heard only the sound of rushing water and tinnitus. Something was wrong with him — he could feel it — his mind was clouded.

Elsa dismissed her. "Thanks, Jenny," she said. "That'll be all, darl."

Turk snapped out of his fog and watched the girl float gracefully away, perfectly balanced on her high-heeled sandals, glancing back over her shoulder at Turk. "She's a bit of a worry, that one," said Elsa. "Fancies you, looks like."

Just as he and Elsa were downing their shots, two bikers with Rebels insignias on the back of their scruffy leather jackets entered the bar, looking like trouble going somewhere to happen. Sighting the pool table, they made a beeline for it.

Turk followed them with keen eyes — this was bad news, he could sense it.

Three girls moved in to hang with the bikers, while Jenny switched on the overhead light to fluoresce the table. Then she collected the set triangle, leaned over the table and racked the pool balls.

Turk groaned inwardly. He downed his second tequila and was about to get to his feet when a commotion broke out. One of the bikers had Jenny pinned against the pool table.

Turk instinctively went to intervene, but Elsa pulled him back down. He immediately realised she was more experienced and would probably handle the situation better. She got up and casually approached the biker molesting Jenny.

"Okay, fella," she said. "That'll do, this isn't Voodoo. Let her go, please."

The big biker offered her a grin full of rotten teeth. "Hey, get lost lady," he leered.

Turk noted Elsa change her stance and nodded to himself. She was setting herself up for a lethal kick. She was, after all, a kickboxing champion with a black sash.

The Rebel groping Jenny froze, recognising a threat. His hand reached slowly for his hip-holstered pistol. Elsa caught the move and forced herself to relax.

"You're supposed to surrender your weapons at the door, fella," she said.

The biker suddenly whipped out a blade and held it to Jenny's cheek.

Turk flinched, but stayed put, feeling that Elsa was still in control.

"Put that away!" she demanded. Then the other Rebel made a sharp move for his weapon. Elsa caught it and let go a side kick so fast it knocked the pistol out of his hand. "Alright," she said, her voice cold steel. "Let go of my girl and both of you get out. Right now, boys, before someone gets hurt."

The two bikers chuckled. Suddenly, the one Elsa had kicked flew at her, grabbed her from behind and bent her over the pool table.

Turk stood. "Quit it!" he growled. "Let 'em both go, right now!"

The biker holding Elsa whipped her around to face Turk.

"What's your problem fella?" he crowed.

"Stay out of it, Turk!" Elsa cried. But her plea ended in a gurgle as the biker holding her ripped his blade across her throat in one swift movement. He let her slide to the floor while her life gushed through her fingers. She shot Turk a dying look that would stay with him forever. He turned his head, he didn't want to watch her die. He'd seen too many blokes bleed out on the battlefield. He didn't want to watch it happen to his old friend.

Defiant, Elsa's murderer licked her blood from his blade, trying to provoke Turk. He succeeded. Turk went for his pistol, but unbeknown to him another gang member had entered the bar behind him. Before he could draw it, the newcomer had grabbed him and pinned his arms.

The girls huddled together in a frenzy of fear.

A trickle of blood ran down Jenny's cheek from the blade still held hard against her face.

Two more gang members stormed into the bar and Turk exploded into action. Shoulder-dropping the biker behind him, he let fly with a barrage of punches, pistol whips, and kicks that sent two of the biggest bikers to the deck, faces a bloody mess. But before he could take out any of the others, the fight became a Mexican standoff. The leader of the Rebels had heard the racket, and burst into Reno's brandishing a sawn-off shotgun. He shucked it and aimed it at Turk.

An imposing hulk of a man with a face that said take no prisoners, he snarled at Turk. "One more move, fella, and I'll kill everyone in town tonight, just for the hell of it," he leered.

Turk knew his gun wasn't loaded.

The other gang members chuckled. The Rebels that Turk had decked clambered to their feet. Turk kept his eyes trained on them.

The guy who had killed Elsa sheathed his knife and faced Turk. "I'd do what Duke sez,," he sneered. "He means stuff!"

"I don't care what Duke says," Turk rasped back. "Have a go. I'll take at least four of you with me. That'll leave just two of you against the rest of the town."

Duke grinned past the stogie cigar hanging limply from his battle-scarred, stubbly face.

"Hey, I like this dude," he said. "He's got guts!"

Turk knew his kind. They generally meant business. They had lived so long with the hourly expectation of savage death that there was no longer anything but wary animalism in their eyes. He'd seen the look before. The only thing that made them different to front-line soldiers at war was that these warriors had no principles, no honour, no just cause to fight for.

Duke took a step forward, studied Turk a moment then growled, "So, soldier boy, what do they call you?"

In a flash, before Turk could answer, Duke snatched the gun from his hand and pistol-whipped him hard across the face.

"There!" the man scoffed. "Didn't teach you that move in the army, did they?"

Turk stood his ground, nose dripping blood.

Duke turned his attention to the girls and pointed at Jenny. "You!"

The biker who'd been groping Jenny pushed her towards Duke.

Duke handed off Turk's pistol and stood, hands on his hips, staring at Jenny. Tears streaming down her cheeks, she froze, trembling.

Still restrained by a big Rebel, to distract Duke from Jenny, Turk spat at the big man. The bloody gob found its mark, and the Rebel's leader didn't like that at all. An evil grin cracked his face and he fired a sharp nod to his men. Without delay they attacked the trapped man. With his arms held from behind they punched him to a pulp. When it was over, the Rebel holding him let his limp, battered body drop to the floor, beaten nearly senseless. Turk expected his suffering would soon be over, as he slipped into unconsciousness toward death.

CHAPTER 5
CAFE EPIPHANY

HONOR WAS PACING the floor beside Inspector Karzoff's hospital bed. His outlandish bright-red hair was singed and his arm was in a sling. He had sworn to himself it would be the last time he'd try to be a hero. He'd been rewarded trying to prevent Alice and Hope escaping with a thorough toasting and being shot. Karzoff's watery eyes were trained on Honor pacing the floor. She stopped abruptly.

"I don't trust him, Karzoff," she said. "You know vhat zese academic types are like."

Karzoff stammered, "I wouldn't know … I … I think—"

"Don't think, dear toad," she cut him off. "You're hardly in any condition for such exertion." She despised the man, but still, he was one of her squad. A show of unity should be made.

"You haff everyzing you need here?" she demanded. "Is zere anyzing you vant?"

"No, I … I…"

Honor didn't wait for an answer, she simply strode to the door, turned and glared back at him. He was only valuable as someone she could bounce ideas off, someone to pick up the grunt work.

"I think I vill haff Secta followed," she mused. "Catch you later, toad."

She turned on her high heel and left.

Karzoff called after her feebly. "I could do with..." It was no use, she'd gone. He knew she hadn't really visited him to check on his condition.

As Honor was striding across the dimly lit hospital car park she made a call on her implant.

"Honor, Senior Inspector, two-four-D–Delta," she barked impatiently at the operator. "I vant surveillance on Dr Secta. Yes, zat is correct. Yes, he is from level seven. I know he is GPS chipped. I vant eyes and ears on him too. Twenty-four seven, reporting to me personally every zree hours. Put your best person on it." She disconnected. "Done!" she said smugly to herself.

Secta plunged his fork into the butterscotch toffee slice on the plate in front of him. The civvies he was wearing had transformed him: the cravat and tweed jacket made him look like the more louche kind of thespian. The café was his regular haunt, a place to sit, relax and contemplate. Preferably over a butterscotch toffee slice.

Hope had asked him why he spent so much time there. Seated in his favourite booth by the window, he simply answered: "I like contemplating my navel."

He never sat anywhere else. If he came to the café and his booth was taken, he'd return to the lab. It could only be that particular seat. Today he'd been lucky. With the pleasant aroma of freshly brewed coffee floating over his senses, he gazed into the night-darkened city and its chaos, his mind performing mental gymnastics on the value — or otherwise — of rescuing Black Alice.

It wasn't difficult for him to understand his sister's infatuation with the man, but he was beyond that. He needed other motivation — perhaps a Nobel Prize, he thought — Fame. Fortune ... A place above all others ... He smiled. That would be most fulfilling.

As he sat absorbed in his thoughts, he gradually noticed that the traffic outside had eased, but the plethora of pedestrians traversing the sidewalk hadn't. As he watched, the ambience of his surroundings blurred, and he imagined the pedestrians outside speeding up until they were moving in super-fast motion. Then he pictured Alice, moving at normal speed in the opposite direction. He was suddenly overcome by realisation. "I have to slow time!" he shouted, to the alarm of his fellow patrons. "No! Wait!" He spoke even louder and more fervidly. "Not time ... I have to slow the bridge, the route between dimensions! I need to spin time..."

He leapt to his feet, only then noticing the attention of his fellow customers. "I need to reverse the polarity of the neutron flow!" he proclaimed, an orator addressing his audience. "That should slow it enough to detect the marker! Brilliant!" He spread his arms to bestow a benediction on the astonished onlookers. "My goodness," he said. "I am brilliant." Bowing courteously, he was rewarded by a light round of applause from a bewildered but thoroughly entertained audience.

Turk woke with a start, wondering where the hell he was. Then the pain came, and he remembered – oh God, was there anyone left alive? He sat up and was immediately overcome by a fit of coughing, during which he spat out a wad of congealed blood and a couple of teeth. Sitting in a dried-up pool of his own blood, he wiped his mouth then squinted though blackened, swollen eyes to determine if he was alone. He was. "They must have thought they'd done me in," he mumbled. "Hah. Take more than that to kill me."

Elsa's body had been removed and her blood cleaned from the wooden floor. It was as though it hadn't happened. He wondered who had cleaned the mess, and why. Whoever it was, they'd chosen to leave him there. He concluded it was probably the bargirls. Without dwelling on it any further, he reached up, gripped the bar rail for support, and dragged his aching body to its feet. He wavered, but managed to steady himself, overriding a rush of pain, dizziness and nausea. Squeezing his eyes shut so he didn't pass out, when he opened them he was staring at a wall mirror. Just for a second, he didn't recognise his own reflection. For a fleeting moment, he thought he was looking at someone else. A few flying stars dotted his vision but once they cleared his legs accepted the message that they had to move. He staggered into the kitchen out back, found a sink and washed his face, the cool water providing some relief. He watched the crimson water swirl down the plughole, then spat a clot of blood that hung in a string from his lips. A couple of gulps of water from the tap and he was feeling marginally better. Checking his missing teeth in the mirror, he was more concerned by his swollen battered face. Nora will never recognise me, he thought. Hell, I hardly recognise me! Then he noticed something else in the mirror. There was a body on the pool table, covered in a bloody sheet. The bloodstain at the neck meant it was Elsa. He didn't bother to check, he'd return later to sort out a burial. Holding his aching brow, he grabbed his hat, staggered back through the bar and out onto the front porch.

It was only just past nine in the morning and already well over thirty degrees — stinking hot. He was sweating up a soup and it trickled down his cheek and dripped from his chin onto his bloodstained shirt. The glaring sun made his bruised eyes water. He checked his pockets, found his sunglasses miraculously unbroken and slipped them on, waiting for his blurred vision to clear. There were three Rebel choppers still parked outside Club Voodoo. He scowled at them, then turned towards a movement in the corner of his vision. Someone was opening a shop three doors down — a grocery and hardware store. He grinned, slowly, as an idea dawned. Limping over, he went inside.

He emerged after a few minutes, carrying a small paper bag. His appearance on the street had drawn the attention of a couple of inquisitive teenagers, who were now studying him with interest. He ambled past them, up to the closest chopper. Fighting off pain, he leaned down, drew half a dozen disposable cigarette lighters from the paper bag and flicked them one at a time into the exhaust muffler of the bike. Then he concealed a can of lighter fluid under the seat and flipped the spout. Job done.

As he moved away, one of the boys raced inside Club Voodoo to blow the whistle on him, while the other boy strolled over, hand out.

"How about sumthin' to keep me mouth shut?" he said, scornfully.

"Learn some dignity, kid!" snarled Turk, then limped across the road back inside Reno's.

Seconds later a big, grubby Rebel biker staggered out of Voodoo with a beer in hand, half stung, looking for whoever had been reported messing with his bike.

Turk stepped out of Reno's, kitbag over his shoulder, jangling Elsa's car keys. When he spotted the biker outside Voodoo, he stopped and eyeballed him. His memory was clear — it was the scumbag who'd cut Jenny. Turk climbed into Elsa's canary-yellow, customized Ford F-200 pick-up and cranked it up. It purred like a big cat. Then he pulled out and drove slowly past Voodoo and the biker. The big ugly Rebel watched him like a cat, and Turk returned serve aiming an index finger pointed like a pistol, and mimicking the recoil of a shot being fired.

The Rebel flicked back a bow-finger before hopping onto his bike to give chase. Two more staggered out of Voodoo and joined him. As he flopped onto the seat of his chopper and kick-started, the lighter fluid under the seat hosed his leg and the gas tank. He revved the engine and pulled out onto the road, the other two Rebels following suit.

Driving slowly, Turk adjusted his mirror for a better view. The doctored chopper made it only a short distance up the road. Whump! The cigarette lighters exploded and an almighty blast from the exploding fuel tank blew the rider clean off his bike and ignited the spilled lighter fluid. He landed on the road, ablaze, beside his burning bike.

A grim smile broke across Turk's battered, unshaven face.

The remaining two Rebels moved quickly to help their fallen comrade, splashing him with beer to douse the flames. The burnt Rebel tried to stand, but collapsed back to the ground. Confused, he looked down and realised what had happened — his severed leg was lying on the road not far away. Grasping the ragged stump that was jetting a stream of blood onto the hot bitumen, he screamed wildly at Turk. "I'll get you! ... I'll kill you!" Then he collapsed, a screaming heap gradually getting smaller in the rear vision mirror.

Only a little revenge, but it had been sweet. He planted his foot and the big, powerful, supercharged F-200 roared up the highway, bound for Blanket Bay.

CHAPTER 6
THE REBEL YELL

TURK WALKED SOLEMNLY towards the rusted front gate of the neglected Blanket Bay house, standing all alone in a relatively healthy thicket of native bush. He stopped at the gate, taking in the familiar surroundings. Memories flooded back: a ghostly bark from his dog, Tika, a crazy but loyal Kelpie-Rottweiler cross, who would run at the gate at a hundred miles an hour, barking his head off to greet Turk whenever he came home. He almost laughed — he'd loved that dog. Another memory surfaced as the familiar scent of jasmine wafted by. His mum had planted it at the gate when he was just a tike. She loved to treat visitors to her favourite fragrance.

The house was on a low hill, facing the lake. He looked over the expanse of water, recalling fondly the number of fish he'd taken from it over the years. Sadly, that wouldn't be the case anymore — a warning stench told him it was stagnant, rotting, polluted. Lifeless. It was far from the picture of beauty he'd remembered while fighting in the war, but even so it still held a special place in his heart.

He looked back at the old house, a ramshackle affair, built on stilts over fifty years ago using local timber. His father had built it, and had done a particularly good job. The iron roof had rusted and was in need of a good paint, and the chimney, still with a peculiar lean to it, was just as he always remembered.

The front door was ajar, and faded blue curtains shaded two large front windows. The veranda porch that surrounded the house looked dry, as though the timber hadn't been oiled in ages. Now he was home, he would spruce the place up.

A figure appeared in the doorway distracting him from his makeover daydream. From under his broad-brimmed hat, he instantly recognised Nora. She seemed to have absorbed all the beauty that was missing from the lake: just sixteen years old, she looked like an angel. Even from a distance he could tell she was the loveliest woman he'd ever seen. His bruised, stubbled face cracked a smile despite the pain. As he walked closer he could see her eyes, the warmest brown, as she hesitatingly came towards him, not sure who he was. Her movements were subtle, graceful and girlish. She stopped, and shading her eyes from the sun, spoke in a clear, sublimely youthful voice.

"Hello!" she called. "Can I help you?"

Turk was mesmerized. Look at you Nora, he thought. All grown up. "I — I don't know," he said, tentatively. "Do you still remember me?"

Did she ever! On recognising his voice, she let out an earth-shattering scream and raced the five metres across the brown lawn like a woman possessed, leaping into his waiting arms as they laughed and cried together. Turk didn't even feel the pain.

Later, after he had cleaned up and changed his filthy clothes, after he'd treated his cuts and bruises, and after he'd related the terrible events at Reno's bar on the night before, Turk told Nora that he felt responsible for Elsa's body. He wanted to go to town to sort out a funeral. Nora wanted to accompany him, but he thought it unwise: the Rebels could still be around. But when she pointed out that she hadn't been expecting him, and there wasn't enough food in the house for them both, he reluctantly agreed to let her go along.

While Nora was in her room getting ready, Turk went outside to the garage. The cobwebs around the doorjamb showed that it hadn't been opened since he had left for the war. When he wrenched at the handle, the rusted old hinges gave way and the door ended up in his hands. He cast it aside and stepped into the dim light.

He found what he was looking for under a tarpaulin veiled with dust. Like a child unwrapping a gift, he gently raised one side of the tarp and caught a glimpse of metallic blue — his Holden Commodore SSV Redline, the very last Holden model produced in Australia before GMH closed in 2017. It was a classic. Memories flooded back: he was in the driver's seat, in his early twenties with a shock of curly brown hair. Reno was beside him, they were racing Jonno in his China-made Fu Xing and they'd left him for dead. Turk mumbled to himself, "The God of Happiness."

"I remember when you first got her," said Nora softly, behind him. "But I didn't know you called her that."

"What?"

"The God of Happiness."

"Oh! Nar, that was Jonno's car, the Fu Xing — the name translates in English to 'God of Happiness'."

"Ah, I see," she said, grinning cheekily. "You were having a little head-trip down memory lane, were you, old feller?"

"Old feller? I ought to spank your bum," he said playfully, and chased her out of the garage and over to the F-200. He caught her by the passenger-side-door and laughing, grabbed her in a bear hug and swung her round. It was almost like he'd never been away.

Suddenly Nora stopped laughing and locked eyes with her brother. Tears jewelled her eyelids. "I've missed you, big brother," she whispered, soberly.

He kissed the top of her head — something she'd only allow her big brother to do — as tears filled his blackened eyes. "I've missed you, too, little sister," he croaked. "Oh God, how I've missed you!"

They cried a little, locked in each other's arms, feeling the long years of loss, until Turk remembered they had business to complete.

"Okay, sis," he said, holding her at arm's length and looking seriously into her teary eyes. "Let's get these jobs done. But you stick real close to me in town, alright?"

He looked her over, shaking his head. It was difficult to get used to this blossoming young woman, especially when he remembered her as a dark-skinned flat-chested tomboy. He eyed her short blue skirt doubtfully. "Should you — er — should you maybe wear jeans or something?" he tried.

She stared at him in disbelief. "In this heat? I don't think so — Dad," she quipped.

Realising he was beaten, he shook his head and grinned. "Come on then," he said. "Let's hit the frog and toad."

On their way into Snake Ridge, silence distanced them. Turk guessed Nora was collecting her thoughts. She'd be wondering what to ask him about the war ... how to ask him, in fact. A lot had changed for them both over seven years. They'd have to get to know each other all over again. Finally, she worked up the courage to speak.

"I got the credits you sent every month," she said. "And I was so grateful. But I'd have traded them all for a word from you."

Turk posted his guilt through the driver's side window. "There was no way to correspond from the front line," he lied. "I thought — well, I thought that with credits coming every month, you'd know I was still alive."

"Jeez," pouted Nora. "Only you could think that way, Turk. That's not how it works for an adolescent girl left on her own."

"You had Aunt Dolly and Uncle Jack just up the road."

"Turk, they were so old! I had to care for them, not the other way round."

"Yeah, but they gave you a sense of family, didn't they?"

"Oh, sure," she said, sarcastically. "Especially when I had to bury both of them. Not the best way to spend my fourteenth birthday." She sniffed, dashing tears from her eyes with an impatient gesture.

"I'm sorry, Nors," he said. "But I lost control over my own life the moment I was conscripted. I'm only just now learning how to get it back. Hasn't exactly been a great start," he fell silent, remembering Elsa's face as she slid to the floor.

Nora gently took his free hand. "Don't worry, big brother," she said, warmly. "We made it, didn't we? We fought through all the slime. It won't be long until everything's right as rain again, just the way it's supposed to be."

"Now you sound like Dad," he chuckled, and they shared a smile. "But listen, tell me this. Elsa said credits aren't worth anything anymore. So how do we live?"

"You can still buy stuff with them," Nora said, "But Elsa is — was — right. We have to grow what we can't buy."

That was a harrowing thought for a guy not known for his green thumb. The only success he'd ever had when it came to horticulture was growing a dope plant when he was a teenager. Even his cacti had died. That didn't bode well for the farming life.

The conversation lapsed into silence again as they entered Snake Ridge. The town was desolate, no sign of the bikers, but Turk was determined to stay sharp. He had a feeling they were still around.

Angle-parking the F-200 beside a police car in front of Reno's Bar, he shook his head.

"I'm not looking forward to this," he admitted.

"What — talking to the sheriff?"

"Yeah. I've never got on with the law."

They found the local sheriff and his deputy inside the bar. A tall, thin man with a belligerent demeanour, the sheriff wore a big grey moustache that brought his skinny face and piercing eyes into even sharper focus. His dumpy deputy, on the other hand, sported a flabby face featuring a gape like someone had just pinched his lunch money. Unfortunately for Turk, his own appearance didn't seem to be doing him any favours. From the get-go, the sheriff was disinclined to be helpful.

After giving Turk a chance to tell his version of events, he announced, flatly: "I've questioned the witnesses here, and their story doesn't corroborate your version. They say there was a brawl, and Elsa's death was an accident."

"Mate," scoffed Turk, "Isn't it obvious the girls have been threatened? They've been told to zip up, so they made up this crap about a brawl."

"First, sir, I'm not your mate," the man fired back. "I've got no reason to doubt what I was told, which is that Elsa was trying to break up a melee between you and the Rebels, and got accidentally stabbed in the process."

"Yeah right," said Turk. "She had her throat cut accidentally. Next you'll be telling me she fell on the knife!"

"Don't get smart, fella!" snapped the deputy, chiming in.

"More than six witnesses told the same story," the sheriff said, dismissively. Turk knew further argument would be wasted. So he simply eyeballed the man and said, calmly but firmly: "No-one is safe while those bastards are out there, sheriff. No-one."

"That's your opinion," said the sheriff, "And it doesn't count for much. I think, to avoid any further trouble, you'd better hand over your weapons."

Turk glared at him long enough to make the man feel uneasy. Then, without unlocking his stare, he reluctantly surrendered his pistol.

Stepping back outside the bar, Turk and Nora were greeted by a hostile bunch of towns-folk. They'd heard the story, figured Turk was responsible for Elsa's death, and gathered to jeer.

Angry, Nora gave them a verbal spray. "You bunch of losers!" she yelled. "Turk's one of us! How dare you blame him? He grew up with Elsa, they've been friends longer than most of you fools have been alive!"

Taking Nora's arm, Turk kept walking to the F-200. "Leave it, sis," he said. "They won't believe you anyway, and there's no way that sheriff's going to bring Elsa's murderer to justice. He's shit-scared. They all are." He stopped and looked around. "I've gotta get hold of Reno," he added, loud enough for the crowd to hear. "And quick. We better get on our way."

"Turk, this is looking dangerous," said Nora. "Maybe you should just drop the whole thing?"

"I would," he said, passionately. "But it's Elsa."

She understood. The two of them sat solemnly in the F-200, waiting for the sheriff and deputy to leave the bar. Once the police car had driven off, Turk and Nora got out and sneaked back inside Reno's.

There was only one girl there from the previous night, and she almost fainted when she saw Turk. Nora stepped in behind him. She knew the girl, and couldn't resist giving her a spray too. "Serious, Terri?" she snarled. "I'd be sus too if I'd just fed a mountain of crap to the sheriff!"

"It wasn't me, Nora," pleaded the teenage girl. "Honest, it wasn't! It was the others!"

Nora walked up to the short blond as though she was going to bite her head off. "Yeah, right!" she growled.

In spite of everything, Turk had to smile. She was, in many ways, just like him.

"Listen, Terri," he said, understandingly, "I get why you told the sheriff that story. Nobody wants to get beat up — or worse. But just help me out a bit here, eh? I need to get hold of Reno."

Terri looked up at Turk, and saw nothing but kindness in his face. Her expression changed, from pleading to determination. She strode over to the front desk, ripped a page from a diary and jotted something down. Coming back over, she handed the slip of paper to Turk.

"Don't tell the others, all right?" she said. "It's Jonno's address in Angel City. He'll know where to find the boss."

"Thanks, Terri," Turk smiled warmly, then turned to his sister, who was still giving the girl the heaviest stink-eye she could muster. "Let's go, Nora," he said. Giving Terri one last up-and-down glare, Nora turned on her heel and strode out after her brother. Bitch wasn't worth more.

The two teenage boys from the night before were sitting in the gutter, messing with a bluetongue lizard. They looked up at Turk and Nora, who had been to the store and were now loading grocery bags into the F-200.

"Dad reckons Turk was the best fighter in Snake when he was young," said the first.

"Ah, bullcrap," said the other. "He couldn't've beat Reno."

"They say he did once — with one hand tied behind his back!"

"Seriously?"

"Can-oath."

As if he'd heard them, Turk looked over and waved from behind the wheel of the F-200. The lizard scarpered, forgotten, as the boys stared after the pick up as it backed out and headed down the road towards Blanket Bay.

Storm clouds had started gathering on the horizon. Turk looked up.

"Sky looks skuddox," he said. "It's gonna rain."

"That's inherited," Nora said.

"What is?"

"'Skuddox'," she said. "Dad always said it when he meant 'grim'. Remember?"

"Yeah, I guess, must be the Yuin language," he said, vaguely, bringing his attention back to the road.

"Turk?" said Nora, hesitantly, "In the war … Did you … Did you ever kill anyone?"

He glanced at his sister. He'd been dreading the question, and wasn't sure how to answer it. A strange, deep anxiety washed over him, and tinnitus built in his ears until it blocked out all other sound. Dizziness had him blinking, trying to maintain concentration on the road ahead; images were flashing through his mind at speed and he was struggling to make sense of them — were they memories? They couldn't be, he recognised none of them: a ferry at night, a submarine, a storm. A fist fight, glass shattering, and the gut feeling that he faced an enormous threat. There was a blond-haired woman beside him in the torrential rain and gusting wind. She was helping him. A voice yelled: "We've got to get to the bridge, Hope!"

"Turk? Turk!" Nora was shaking his arm, terrified. He realised the voice had been his own.

His sister was trembling as he blinked himself back into full consciousness. "I'm so sorry," she said, almost in tears. "I didn't think mentioning the war would—"

"It's all right, Nora," he cut her off. Pinching the bridge of his nose, battling to stop more foreign thoughts overtaking his consciousness, he managed a smile. "It's … it's probably just a flashback or something. The medics said that could happen. But it was weird — why was she was calling me Alice?"

"Who?"

"I don't know — this woman I've never met. It was all weird — flashes of stuff I never did … There was this a woman, and a boat—"

He sighed and shook his head, clearing it of the last strands of his peculiar vision. "Anyway," he said. "You wanted to know if I'd—"

"I don't want to cause you more pain," interrupted Nora. "Just forget it, it's … it's fine."

"No, seriously, it's all right," said Turk. "I'd ask too, if I was you." There was a pregnant pause while he considered his answer.

"I just did what I was ordered," he said. "Most of the time we were firing at gunshots — just muzzle flashes coming out of a blur. Self-preservation kicks in … you don't really think about the target as a person."

"What about hand to hand?"

"At the end of the first year overseas they chose a few of us for an SAS course. Being a six foot six monster, I was picked. They trained me in hand-to-hand combat and other stuff for black ops, you know — behind the enemy lines stuff."

"Did you ever get shot?"

Thunder sounded in the distance and, together with Nora's question, triggered another series of images in his mind's eye. This time he recognised them.

He remembered that night. A bomb had just exploded, he could feel the vibration in the earth through his boots. He was in the desert, looking at a distant Tabriz being relentlessly shelled by the allied forces. He'd learned a little of the city's history: a capital in the Iranian East Azerbaijan province, with a population of nearly four million. It was thought by some archaeologists to be the location of the Garden of Eden. He'd thought, then, that by the time they'd finished, it would be a garden of death, the ground planted with nothing but corpses.

It had been a stinking hot July night: over 40 degrees, and even hotter in his tiny foxhole. He was parched, his tongue feeling like the bottom of a parrot's cage. Sweating up a soup, he peered into the night sky, knowing the battle was being monitored by hundreds of small sensor drones overhead. When the bat-sized drones detected movement in their designated search arc, they relayed the coordinates to a larger, armed predator drone flying out of range of enemy fire. The remote operator would then determine if the movement was friend or foe. If they decided it was an enemy, they'd flick the switch that would unleash accurate ordnance to take them out. Turk imagined that to these kids, safely stashed somewhere on the west coast of the United States, remotes in hand, it felt like nothing more than a computer game. The only stakes were the score, not the lives and deaths of men like himself — on both sides.

Between the drones and the WarBots, he'd wondered why there was any need for humans at all. But that was up to the brass, located a safe distance from the action, probably on an aircraft carrier in the gulf, monitoring the live feed from their holographic projectors. He could visualize them, lounging in comfy chairs, sipping hot, fresh coffee, nibbling cakes. It gave a whole new meaning to the expression theatre of war.

Suddenly, the delayed crack of a fresh wave of drone attacks had shaken him from his reverie. He crouched lower in his foxhole to watch Tabriz light up from another barrage. The delayed percussive thumps of exploding ordnance followed, the pyrotechnic light show through his night-vision goggles sent a green-tinged chill through his nervous system. His heart was pumping hard — circulating the adrenalin that would get him through this ordeal. A dozen armoured personnel carriers thundered past in convoy, leaving a dust storm in their wake. Roaring fighter-bombers swooped from overhead to join the fray, dumping incendiaries on the besieged city then hitting the afterburners and thundering deafeningly skyward like a salvo of rockets, getting the hell out of Dodge.

Turk knew the black camouflaged APCs passing by were carrying WarBots: remote-controlled android monsters, half-human, half machine and programmed to take no prisoners. Better them than me, he'd thought. His job was to mop up after the 'bots had done their thing. That wasn't going to be pretty: the things had no soul, no fear, no guilt. Nothing but a programme to kill.

A red flare lit up the sky, and Turk's heads-up display came to life with coordinates. It was 'GO' time. He glanced at the desert surrounding him, and out of nowhere fifteen men rose from well-camouflaged foxholes and moved as one in the direction of the city, Turk with them.

As they'd reached an outlying suburb, they were met by resistance fire that forced them to hit the deck. One of Turk's platoon mates flopped down beside him. Turk recognised him through the black and olive green camouflage paint. "Hey, Jack," he rasped. "Looks like the 'bots are leaving the suburbs for us!"

Jack had the physique of an ex rugby player, scarred eyebrows, mandatory front rower's cauliflower ears and a nose that proved being a scrum hooker with your arms wrapped around your prop's shoulders meant you were unable to duck.

"Yeah, never a dull moment, eh?" The big Queenslander's gruff reply finished with a grin.

Then there came a sound. Thunk! Turk saw Jack's grin freeze, and a trickle of blood run from a neat hole in his forehead and down the bridge of his nose. He slumped, dead, shot by a sniper.

Before he could think, Turk got the order to move out. Driven by instinct, he leapt up and ran full tilt with the others towards the building the sniper's bullet had come from. Muzzle flashes were blinking from broken front windows of a building covered in battle-scarred yellow stucco. The sound of gunshots was masked by the overall cacophony of the battle for the city, and that meant Turk had to rely on savvy. He and his comrades opened fire on the run.

He'd made it to the building ahead of the others. With his back to the exterior wall, he took a cautious peek through a ground-floor window, saw movement and fired. His target took the full burst of his automatic weapon and was cut to pieces. Turk climbed in through the open window and opened fire inside the room, driven by hate, fear and a desire to avenge Jack's death.

He stopped firing. All went quiet, the darkness of the room killed every now and then by flashes from nearby explosions. A muffled underscore followed, cutting through the ringing in his ears. Several of his comrades entered the room, one brandishing a power light. He shone it around and lit up the six bodies Turk had cut down.

He turned away. The bodies lay on the sand-covered floor, twisted, riddled with bullet holes. The size of the wounds was vivid testimony to the hollow-tipped bullets he'd been equipped with — bullets that exploded once they entered a body, guaranteeing a kill. A few of the bodies had been shot in the face, heads all but blown off. Blood everywhere, soaking the floor, splattered on the white walls. They were all young girls, none older than fourteen. All armed, all front-line resistance fighters. He'd killed every one of them. And each one was someone's sister, like the girl who sat beside him now. Turk had doubled over and thrown up.

"So? Did you?" Nora repeated, her voice shocking him back to the present.

"What's that?" He looked at her, still momentarily disoriented.

"Did you ever get shot?"

"No ... No," he said, the sound of his own voice distant. He could still smell the stench of blood. A clap of distant thunder seemed to mock him, mimicking the horrific rumbling of exploding ordnance that would forever echo in the dark chambers buried in his mind.

Just before the turn-off to Blanket Bay, Turk sighted Rebels squatting round a campfire on the side of the road. They hadn't been there when he and Nora had passed earlier, so he guessed they must have just arrived. Now he was worried. They'd recognise the F-200. Silently, he cursed himself for bringing Nora with him.

Dropping the bottle of booze he'd been holding, one of the Rebels pointed to the F-200 and yelled something. The entire group ran to their choppers like scrambling fighter pilots. Turk checked his mirror and said, quietly but firmly, "Listen, sis, do exactly what I say.

Lay in the floor-well. If they pull us over just stay put. No matter what, stay put. You got me?"

Nora shot her brother a look of dread. She could tell the situation was dire. The girl squeezed into the floor-well to hide as Turk gunned the big vehicle. A bike was already closing on him, had to be doing near two hundred clicks to catch up. There was a hard left turn in the road ahead. Turk was going to have to slow down to make it, and the bike would catch up. As he braked, the Rebel behind took aim with a sawn-off shotgun. A thump rocked the cabin as a rear tyre exploded. Turk fought the pick-up to stop it rolling, broadsided to a stop and was enveloped by wall of red dust. When it cleared Rebel bikers had the truck surrounded.

"This is no good, Nors," he said, seriously. "Remember what I said … not a sound, no matter what happens. Damn that idiot sheriff for taking my gun!"

He swung the door open and stepped out, fingers laced behind his head in surrender. A big biker strode up and king hit him. Turk went down on one knee, blood streaming from his nose. He fought for consciousness ... he had to take the punishment to keep them away from Nora. He glared at the Rebels surrounding him. "Alright, boys," he said. "How about this: I'll take you all on, one at a time … You got the balls for that?"

The Rebel that had king hit him let fly with a kick, but Turk grabbed his foot before it connected. Still holding on, he leapt up and thrust the foot above his head, hurling the Rebel to the ground. Turk stood over him, still gripping his foot, his face completely calm. He twisted, stopping just before the ankle snapped. As the Rebel writhed in pain, he glared at the rest of them. "Get back on your bikes," he snarled, "Or I will break it."

Duke emerged from the back of the crowd. Chewing on a matchstick, he ambled up to Turk, drew his gun and fired. The bullet shattered Turk's left knee and he crumbled to the ground.

Huddled in the floor-well holding her breath, Nora flinched at the sound. Certain her brother had been shot, she felt sick to the core.

"I don't think so, soldier boy," the big man said, resting his smoking .45 calibre on his shoulder and grinning past the matchstick at Turk writhing on the ground. "We left you for dead last time, but oh no, you had to come back for more. Well, we're happy to accommodate you. Bring me a jerry can!" he ordered his men. "We'll torch the car first, then this brave soldier."

Horror broke into Turk's soul — Nora would be incinerated.

"No!" he groaned, through blinding pain. "Me! Finish me! Come on, get it over with!"

Nora wanted to scream, but knew what would happen if she did. She stuffed her fist into her mouth, biting down.

A half-balding biker in a sleeveless leather vest that revealed tattooed, well-muscled arms brought a jerry can for Duke.

Turk tried to think quick. Rising above his agony, he propped himself up on one elbow and challenged Duke. "What is it with you imbeciles?" he scoffed. "Two tries and you still can't kill me? Fricking morons, not one of you big enough to fight a bloke one on one!"

"You're full of it, soldier boy!" Duke growled, not a man to be intimidated. He snatched the jerry can from his henchman, flipped the lid, and, stepping over Turk, opened the car door. He lifted the can, but before he poured he looked back once more. "Don't worry, soldier boy," he grinned. "You'll get your chance. I'll burn you next."

As the first splash of gasoline hit the cabin he heard a whimper. "Ah!" he exclaimed. "What do have we here?" He reached inside, grabbed a fistful of Nora's hair and dragged her from the car.

"Leave her alone!" Turk yelled. "She's just a kid. Your score is with me!"

Nora screamed as Duke pushed her towards his men. He bent down beside Turk, flicked off his hat with the barrel of his gun, and peered into his panicked eyes. "Time to settle that score, soldier boy," he leered.

The storm broke as they attacked Nora like a pack of wolves.

Turk screamed and writhed, his shattered knee holding him helpless. He prayed for the savagery to end.

"That'll do, Spike!"

They stopped leaving Nora on the ground, motionless, only just breathing.

Turk, glaring at the eight men with tortured eyes, committed each face to memory. "On my word," he growled. "You better kill me. 'Cause if you don't, I'll hunt every one of you down."

Duke shrugged, picking up. "Seeing you fixed up one of my boys back in that excuse for a town, I reckon you should get a bit of your own back, abo soldier boy," he said, dousing Turk's legs with gasoline. "There you go, all gassed up ... a rare commodity these days. I seriously doubt you'll be hunting anyone down after this. Eh, fellers?"

They all grinned, anticipating the big moment. Thunder sounded again. The sky was growing darker by the minute, and Turk felt it closing in. Duke glanced up. "Huh," he said. "A southerly buster. Time we left, soldier boy!"

He strode back to his bike, trailing gasoline. He methodically packed the resealed can into his saddlebags, then took the match he'd been chewing, struck it on the sole of his boot and lit a cigar.

Turk knew his moment was coming. All he could do was close his eyes and wait for it.

Displaying the burning match for his mob, Duke turned his back on Turk and irreverently flicked it over his shoulder. It landed on the trail of gas, which ignited. The flame flew along the line towards Turk. As he exploded into flames the shock waves rocked his audience. Then, in unison, they shrieked their Rebel yell, hopped back on their bikes and thundered off, leaving Turk rolling agonisingly in the dust, desperately trying to put out the flames.

Seconds later, as though the gods had finally taken pity, the storm broke with an almighty clap of thunder and a deluge extinguished the flames consuming him. Turk and Nora, still unconscious, lay in the rain. Every breath felt corrupted by the stench of his own burnt flesh. Delirious with pain, he hallucinated a murder of crows settling on his charred legs, stripping off lumps of cooked flesh. He screamed ... but no-one heard.

CHAPTER 7
OBLIVION'S CURSE

SITTING UPRIGHT IN a hospital bed, bandaged like an Egyptian mummy and drip-fed through a small nasal tube, Turk peered through the narrow slits in his bandages, trying to focus but unable to escape the morphine-induced hallucinations.

Amidst a hazy swirl of distorted shapes and colours, the eight Rebels' faces laughed at him while he burned. The sheriff and his deputy were watching, laughing hysterically. Blackness descended once more.

When he opened his eyes again, a nurse was leaning over him, glowing like an angel and wearing a surgical mask. When she removed it he recognised Elsa. Then the phantom Elsa dissolved and was gone — darkness. He woke again — was he back to normal this time? Struggling from the hospital bed, he staggered to the en-suite. He looked in the mirror and stopped, mouth open in astonishment. That wasn't him! It was a face he didn't recognise. He watched as a shaky hand reached for the bar of soap and used it to scribble a phrase on the mirror: *Alice was here*. Then the miasma of the dreaming consumed him once again.

Turk had been lucky, in a way. The teenage boys from Snake Ridge, who'd been expecting him to return, happened to mention that he hadn't been seen. One of their fathers had set out to scope the road. He'd found Turk and Nora and called what still passed for the authorities. Now, months later, Turk struggled from the F-200, took a deep breath and limped along the garden path to his family home. He stopped at the door, turned and glanced up from the shadow of his broad-brimmed hat. The lake, the bush, the scent of jasmine raised no emotion. Nora wouldn't be coming out to greet him this time. Nothing left but memories too painful to dwell on. Even the sun felt different on his freshly-scarred face. His eyes were like those of a shark, reflecting nothing, no emotion, soulless and dead. He removed his hat, ran a hand over his clean-shaven head. The look made him appear meaner than hell. His entire demeanour had been transformed by the emptiness of hate. The scars weren't only on the surface of his skin — they went all the way down to the core.

As he stepped onto the porch, a middle-aged nurse in a white uniform wheeled Nora out to meet him. It was the first time he'd seen her since the attack. He'd thought he was prepared for it, but the shock still hit him like a left hook.

The brutal beating had taken a terrible toll, smashing fragments of bone into her temporal lobe, reducing the lively, happy, graceful girl to a lifeless husk, confined to a wheelchair for the rest of her life. The scars tracing a permanent grin across her face couldn't entirely obliterate her beauty, but her mind was gone. She stared mindlessly into oblivion, a string of saliva hanging in a long, thin dribble from the corner of her mouth to her chest.

Turk stared. After the first shock, he felt only numb. No sorrow, nothing … every ounce of his existence had been converted to hate. Nothing but hate eating his soul, and all of it reserved for one person. Duke.

The nurse said nothing. She knew there was nothing she could say. She simply applied the brakes to Nora's chair, and left them alone.

Turk took Nora's hand and tried to get her to look into his eyes. She didn't even register his presence. "I should never have taken you to town that day," he whispered, dully. "This is all my fault. The worst thing — the worst thing — is that there's nothing I can do to repair the damage. But I swear this to you, my Nora, my lovely sister: I will not rest until I've made them pay." He squeezed her delicate hand. "I promise you, sis," he added. "I promise it with everything I have left."

Under the back of the house, in a long-unused storeroom, Turk foraged through a dust-covered tea chest and came up with his Dad's .44 magnum. He strapped on the holster and, for the first time in a long while, felt complete. On his way back to the car, he stopped at the porch to kiss Nora goodbye on that special big-brother spot on the top of her head. The nurse called after him as he reached the F-200. "Sir? When will you be back?"

He couldn't answer. He just didn't know.

Turk limped into Reno's bar. As his eyes adjusted to the darkness, he saw a guy sitting alone at the bar, his back to the door. Turk paused and slowly moved his hand over the pistol holstered on his hip. "Can I help you?" the guy asked, without turning. When no reply came, he slowly rose to his feet and turned toward Turk. The two of them faced off for what seemed like an eternity, each searching the other for the boy they once knew. Then they silently stepped forward and embraced like long-lost brothers,

"I'm sorry, I'm so sorry," gasped Turk. "I couldn't help — I couldn't stop them..."

"I know, my friend," said Reno. "I know."

Turk studied his old friend. As always, Reno wore his brown hair long, but the natural curl kept it above his broad shoulders. The same height as Turk, Reno had a slighter build, but was no less formidable. At the same time, he had kind green eyes and, to Turk at least, the charisma and looks of a rock star. Turk could still recognise the boy in the man, and some feeling returned for the first time in what felt like forever — the love that can only come from years of mate-ship, even though the war had intervened."

"Sit down, mate," said Reno. "We'll drink to Elsa — and to old times." They pulled up stools at the bar, and Reno looked deeply into Turk's dark eyes. "There's only one story about that night that I believe," he said, "And that's yours. The girls were threatened, told what to say. I know that, same as you." With tears welling in his eyes, Reno reached out and grasped Turk by the back of the head, pulled him close and kissed his cheek. "It wasn't your fault, mate," he whispered. "There was nothing you could have done."

A girl Turk recognised as Jenny, the shy one cut by the Rebels on that terrible night, arrived with a tray of beers. She placed six bottles on the table in front of them, then shot Turk a sad, knowing smile. The scars on her face were deep and savage. There wasn't much left of her looks. Turk knew it wasn't pity showing in her young eyes. It was an acknowledgement of what they had in common — hatred for the bastards who had ruined their lives. He returned her smile in silence and watched her move off.

"They cut her bad," he said, morosely.

"You know the girls here aren't call girls, mate," said Reno. "Elsa and I took 'em in 'coz they'd lost their families during the war. We wanted to help 'em, stop 'em winding up as prostitutes. In here, all they have to do is share a few drinks with lonely guys. You know the drill. Elsa wouldn't have it any other way. They're all good kids. The kids we never had. Never got to have." He paused, looked Turk in the eye and said, solemnly: "Did she go quick?"

Turk was prepared for the question. Even so, it punctuated the conversation like the slash of a razor. He looked up at the ceiling fan, felt its cool breeze. "Yeah man," he said. "The blade found its mark. She didn't suffer." He chose to omit any grisly details. Reno didn't need to know.

"I'm going to miss her, man," Reno admitted. A sad, single tear traversed his stubbly cheek. "She was my right hand, you know."

"I know," said Turk, sympathetically. "Ever since you were kids."

Reno nodded, swiping away the tear. No dwelling on it for him, not his style. After a deep sigh, he sat back a little and surveyed his friend. "It's amazing you can still walk after—"

"Yeah," nodded Turk, who had no desire to go over the attack again. "And all it took was a stay in hospital, a mountain of drugs, some plastic skin, a Kevlar bionic knee, stacks of physio and enough motivation to last two lifetimes. But hey, yes, I can walk."

"Sorry I didn't visit mate. I just couldn't—"

"Say no more, buddy. Hospitals are a drag at the best of times."

"Dancing days over then?" Reno said, trying to lighten the mood a little.

"Dunno," Turk grinned in spite of himself. "Couldn't dance before. Maybe I can now!" He returned his friend's appraising look. Reno had once held a national kickboxing title. He might be in his thirties but he still trained and was well cut. "What about you?" Turk asked. "You look pretty lean and mean!"

"Yeah, I'm in decent shape," said his friend. "Ready for anything, me." He nodded. The shark look came back into Turk's eyes as he turned his focus to their joint task. "I reckon we'll need a team of six all in to track 'em down and kill 'em," he said. "But they'll need to be the best. This is not a mission for the faint-hearted."

Reno raised his beer. They drank to their mission, bound by friendship and a serious score to settle. "Listen," he said, "While you were in hospital, I got a lead. You know they came back to town after they... after? That's when they cut Jenny in front of the other girls to shut 'em up." Turk nodded knowingly.

"Then they went over to Voodoo and took four of their girls: all local. Families sent the sheriff after them. He tried to track them down but he was bloody useless."

"He's a piece of crap that bloke," said Turk. "Probably didn't even try."

"You've got his number, mate. Scared gutless. Anyhow, one of those girls has a teenage boyfriend in town. Name's Tatts. He wants his girl back, so he tracks the Rebels. Finds their hangout. Gets twenty shades of crap beaten out of him for doing so, but at least he finds them. Guess they thought he was dead, left him in the roadway. But he's not, and he made it back here.

"He says their garrison is about twenty strong, holed up in an old farmhouse in the bush about fifty clicks north. Right near the Tuross Falls … and, mate, it's fortified to the max."

Turk nodded slowly. "The Tuross Falls," he said, a smile breaking free in spite of itself. "Remember going there when we were kids? You tried to dive off the top and landed right on Jonno floating in the lagoon."

Reno laughed. "Yeah, the big porker probably saved my life. I reckon I wouldn't be here now if it wasn't for him and his whale impression. Would've broke me back!"

"Well, we'd better go get him then," Turk smiled. "He might have to break your fall again!"

Two days later, a big black and chrome Mack prime mover was powering up the Angel City highway. Inside the cabin, chewing gum at the wheel, Reno grinned at Turk.

"She's a beauty, isn't she?" he said, "me ole Betsy."

"She's a serious beast!" Turk agreed, appreciatively. "Hybrid for fuel efficiency — is she automaton?"

"Yeah, but I prefer to drive. Automaton was okay on the motorways, but they're gone. I needed a machine to outrun the cops, and Betsy was the number. Bought her when I got into the trucking game. Figured moving freight around during the war would be a winner. I'd no idea that the country would turn to crap within three years. Freight wasn't the issue — fuel became the currency. Everything totally stuffed up."

"Hard to believe you survived, with all the amenities gone and arseholes like Duke rough-riding you," said Turk. "We never heard anything about home over there, just the propaganda we were fed to keep us from wigging out."

"They say the robots did all the hard yards. Is that true?"

"Sort of, but that's not where the war was fought. It was occupying the towns after the bots had been through, that was the tough part. A media war," Turk spat. "They armed both sides then sold the news so the world could watch it live in 3-D from their lounge chairs. Trouble was they thought it was going to be a lay-down misère, but it escalated out of control when the other side used its nukes."

"Well, we sure lost everything we had," said Reno. "Literally, man. There's bugger all left."

"Hear, hear!"

"There were some crazy rumours," Reno added. "I've heard the war was backed by faceless men, bankers who had sold themselves to aliens called tall whites."

"Yeah, I heard that one too," grinned Turk. "Never saw any bloody aliens, though!"

"Nah, me either. Just gangs of fricking murderers roaming around the countryside taking what they want, when they want, no opposition. There's no law and order, it's all stuffed. Some of these gangs are better armed than the bastards you fought in the war. Cop that!"

"Sick!" Turk said.

"Wait and see! You know I had to pay two hundred credits each for a day visa to Angel City?"

"You've got to be kidding man! Why?"

"It's a protected compound."

"Protected by what?"

"The Zen Corporation. They run security for just about every compound in the country. A mega business."

"Zen? You mean Zen Corp?"

"Yeah, that's the crowd."

"Their logo — double pentagram, ten-pointed star — was on all our weapons and munitions. Actually, about two years into the war, we were occupying Tabriz. Found a huge cache of enemy weapons. Guess what?"

"Double pentagram?"

"Got it in one. We reported it to the brass. They closed it all off and did their thing. That was the last we ever heard of it."

"Covered up?"

Turk nodded. "Buried from the top down, I reckon. So the same crooks who were backing both sides in the war have set themselves up here as rulers?"

"Not just here bud. The States, the UK, Japan, Russia, China ... you name it. They're ubiquitous!"

"Who the hell are they?" Turk quizzed.

"No idea. Probably those damn aliens!"

Reno was still laughing as Turk sat up sharply. There was something on the road ahead.

"Pull over next to that burnt-out car, will you mate?" he said.

"Not a good idea bud," Reno answered. "Could be a trap."

"For what?"

"For our gas!"

"Look, pull over and cover me, alright?" Turk growled.

Reno did as he was told. There were burnt-out vehicles every fifty metres on this section of the highway — it was like a car graveyard.

"Why so many wrecks?" Turk asked, opening the door, pistol in hand.

Reno shrugged. "Guess they run out of gas here trying to get to Angel."

Turk walked over to the SUV and peered through the shattered driver's side window.

He looked back up at Reno. "I know this car," he yelled. "There are bullet holes, it's been attacked."

"Knocked over for the gas, mate. Look, the tank is open."

Turk had a hunch and walked into the nearby bush.

"Turk!" yelled Reno, alarmed. "Come on man, we need to get moving!"

Turk stopped when he found what he was looking for — human remains, withered and desiccated, but still bearing traces of long sandy hair and red nail polish on the bare, shrivelled toes. There was no doubting it was Rita. He knew she'd died hard, beaten before being shot through the right temple, the wound gaping blackly against the leatherized flesh on her skull. Squatting on his haunches, he took a strand of her hair betwesen his fingers. "Not how I wanted to meet you again," he whispered sadly. He made his way sadly back to Reno and their truck.

"Rita," he said, climbing in. "The girl who drove me to Snake when I first arrived. Looks like the Rebels found her."

Reno shook his head. "Another victim of the times, my friend," he said. "And another reason to hunt these mongrels down and kill them all." He slammed Betsy into gear and stamped on the gas.

Some things need to be said and some need to be understood. Turk was struggling with both. After fifteen minutes of silent stewing over Rita's senseless death, Reno broke the ice.

"Up ahead, mate," he said. "Angel City."

Turk gawked at the huge walls.

"Looks more like a prison than a city," he grunted.

Reno trod on the air brakes and the big truck hissed, decelerating from two hundred and sixty clicks an hour.

"It is a prison," he said. "We're paying to visit the inmates. Only one gate in and out. Weapons surrender on entry and if you get carded while you're there, you're never coming back."

"Carded?" asked Turk. "Sounds like a deadly version of a fricking football game."

"You can't use normal credits," said Reno. "You have to buy a Zencard. Tracks your movements in the city, and if you put a foot wrong…" He looked at Turk's expression. "Yeah," he added. "It's stuffed. Why do you think I live in Snake? It might be vulnerable to attacks, but at least for now I can more or less be free."

Reno pulled Betsy up to the big double-gated entrance to the massive complex.

"They're scanning my plate-chip," he grumbled. After a few moments, the massive gates swung open and he motored through.

He parked in an empty, cordoned-off parking area that backed onto what looked like abandoned warehouses. The sun was reflecting off the rooftops.

"Solar roofs?" Turk asked.

"Yeah, pretty much on every building," said Reno. "Battery power reigns."

"Not much life around. Now what?"

"See that monorail over there?" Reno pointed. There was a two-seater cart parked on a rail about a hundred metres away. "That's for us," said Reno, leading the way.

They climbed on board and sat together like a pair of kids on a theme park ride.

"It's a driverless taxi," Reno explained, pressing a button on the dashboard that sent them rolling towards the gatehouse. It stopped to allow Reno to pop his Zencard into a machine like an ATM, which beeped and spat it back out. A hatch slid open in the wall.

"Bung your weapons in there, mate," Reno said.

They loaded their weaponry into the hatch. After it closed, a red laser scanned them. As Turk watched the red line pass over his body he was reminded of laser sights from enemy weapons during the war. He shivered. If you were on the battlefield and saw a red bead on your body it was probably the last thing you'd ever see.

"Making sure we're not carrying," Reno said, noticing the uneasy look on Turk's face.

A second gate opened and the cab moved through. They entered the city.

"This is like some kind of weird bloody Disneyland," Turk said, dully.

"The cab will take us to Jonno's bar."

"How does it know where to go?"

"I had to submit a visiting plan before we left Snake. The fee got us a 24-hour visa and the programmed cab to take us wherever my plan designated."

"Unbelievable!" said Turk, astonished by the tightness of the security.

"The entire city is covered by CCTV as well."

"They're either totally paranoid or they've got something to hide," said Turk.

The cart motored silently through the city, and Turk saw, for the first time, what had become of the world in his absence.

"Where is everybody?" he asked, looking wonderingly at the desolation.

Angel was a large city. It should have had a population of at least a million people. But in the heat of the day it seemed empty. Dark, bleak and soulless.

"There aren't many here now," said Reno. "Some, live in compound shelters on the outskirts, some in the CBD — the Central Business District — and some in the old bar section where Jonno is. I nearly went into business with him just after you left. We were going to move here, but Elsa talked me out of it."

"How come?"

"Oh, I think she had an inkling it was going to end up like this. Great visionary, that girl."

"They started building Angel just before I left," said Turk. "Used to be Goulburn, right?"

"Yeah, but after Canberra got whacked a major effort went into relocating what was left of the population here."

"Is it always this bloody hot?" asked Turk, unbuttoning the front of his khaki army shirt.

"Crazy hot summers, freezing winters, violent storms out of nowhere — nothing's the same since the fallout," said Reno, as the cab began to slow. "Ah, here we are."

The cab pulled to a stop outside a dilapidated bar sporting a broken-down neon sign reading 'Headbangers Bar.'

Turk barked a laugh. "That sounds like Jonno!" he said.

Stepping out of the cart, Reno cased the street. "Business looks crook," he said. "All the other bars are shut."

"Well, it is morning," Turk reminded him.

"Huh — six months ago this place would have been crawling with punters at this time of day."

"Listen to that," Turk said, looking around.

"What? I can't hear anything," said Reno, confused.

"Exactly. Not a thing! No birds, no cars, no dogs, nothing except that generator over there and thunder from that storm coming in from the south."

Reno looked south, wondering how in hell Turk knew there was a storm coming, then noticed the thunderheads way in the distance.

He patted Turk on the back. "With the fallout after Sydney and Canberra got nuked, birds were dropping out of the sky dead as doornails," he said. "We spent seven months in underground fallout shelters. Sydney had the subway — probably the same in most big cities — though I heard New York and London were hit so hard there was nowhere to hide. They reckon none of us will make old bones, and we'll sure as hell never have kids. We're all gonna die of cancer from the radiation. So, we'd better get on with it, eh?"

Turk took a moment to answer. Things were dire indeed, even more than he'd realised.

"S'pose so," he said, taking off his black cowboy hat and scratching his head. "Yep. I s'pose so," he added forlornly.

CHAPTER 8
RAISING THE BAR

RENO LED TURK inside the ramshackle building. The bar was empty, without lights, no sign of life. The darkness had transformed the room into a cave. Poles hung from the false ceiling at two-metre intervals, like chrome stalactites supporting a long, elevated catwalk. Turk imagined what it would have looked like in its heyday, with scantily-clad dancers performing for the punters at their feet.

"Business looks crud," said Reno. "I was only here a few months back and there was at least a few punters then ... Cooee!" he bellowed.

After a moment, an irate reply cracked like thunder from a back room: "Whoever you are, nick off! I'm having a kip!"

"Get your butt out here, fatso!" yelled Reno. "That should get him," he muttered to Turk. "Get ready to duck."

A racket akin to a rhino charging exploded from the rear of the premises, followed by a huge hulk of a man, hostile as a swarm of hornets. That was until he recognised Reno, and stopped dead in his tracks.

"Reno!" he roared. "Yer big mug! What are you doing stuffing up my kip?"

A six-five, bearded muscular bruiser with tattoos covering every inch of his Popeye-like forearms, Jonno looked like a Santa who could bite your head off. But his close mates knew he was a gentle giant. His bulbous nose and tattooed head were not particularly reassuring, but the lines that creased his face had come from a lifetime of laughter. He thundered up to Reno and wrapped him in an inescapable bear hug, delighted to see his old buddy. When the dark stranger standing quietly by caught his eye, Jonno froze, waiting for his brain to match the face. Suddenly, the penny dropped. He let go of Reno and erupted with joy. "It's you! It's fricking you, ain't it Turk?"

Turk fired him a big cheesy grin.

"Goddamn! It sure is you!" the big man bellowed. "No-one else has a smile that could either mean 'I'm gonna kill you' or 'g'day, mate!'"

They hugged, laughing. "Let me look at yer!" Jonno held Turk at arm's-length and studied his battle-scarred face. "The world's knocked you round a bit old son," he said. "Head like a bashed crab. Get those scars in the war did ya?"

Turk's smile faded, hate filled his eyes. "No, my friend," he said. "I got them back here. Bastard Rebel bikers. Killed our Elsa and beat my Nora into a vegetable."

Jonno looked sadly at Reno. "Mongrel bastards!" he roared, and spat on the ground. "Never mind my sons," he went on, a massive arm around each of their shoulders. "You're here. And now we are three."

There was never any question about whether Jonno would join them — the bond of mateship had been unbreakable since they were kids. So the first order of business was a visit to a competitor's bar to meet some more potential recruits.

Downing shots at 'Bar Up', Turk, Jonno and Reno were idly ignoring the girls pole-dancing on the catwalk, only an arms' length away.

"Can't believe you blokes got into running bars," Turk said, shaking his head. "I leave the place straight as a gun barrel, and within a few years, it's turned into bar city, complete with dancing girls. It's like bloody Patpong before the war."

Reno licked a line of salt on the back of his hand, threw back a shot of Tequila and bit on a slice of lemon. Wincing, he said, "That's gone now, hasn't it?"

"Yeah," Jonno burped. "Bangkok was the first joint nuked."

"I was nearly in that one," nodded Turk. "Glad I missed it. The whole 4th AIF battalion went down."

"Heard there wasn't much left of the joint," Reno said.

"Mongrel towel-heads," Jonno cursed.

Turk leaned back in his chair "Yeah, well, we did the same to them," he said, dourly. "Levelled Tehran and Tabriz. Saw the results of that first hand."

"You went in?" Jonno asked, eagerly.

Turk answered without taking his eyes off the dancer now directly in front of him. "Yeah," he said. "Israel used a dirty bomb, minimal fallout, so they could pillage it. That was the year before the Yanks went in. We went after them. It was wrong," he said, bowing his head.

"Why?" said Reno, surprised by Turk's sympathy. "They were the enemy, right?"

"It was the disease, man," said Turk. "They'd been hit with chemicals. Then out allies went in and got stuck into the looting … had to be seen to be believed … They've got a lot to answer for in my book. And then it started."

"What started?" The two of them bleated simultaneously.

Turk seemed reticent. But knowing his friends wanted to hear, and that he needed to speak, he knocked back his drink and placed the glass on the bar.

"The bullcrap," he said, slowly. "The bullcrap started."

"What bullcrap?" Jonno demanded, scratching his head.

Turk leaned back in his chair again, eyes still directed at the dancer but seeing a very different image in his mind. "It was two years in when we hit Tabriz," he said. "That's when we discovered it was all crap. They had nothing. Just like in Iraq in the 1990s. No weapons of mass destruction. Bugger all."

"They had enough to nuke Bangkok, didn't they?" Jonno countered.

"That wasn't them, mate," said Turk, shaking his head. "Extremist radicals. Word is the nuke came from somewhere in Afghanistan."

"What about the nukes that hit New York, London, Sydney, Tokyo?" said Reno. Couldn't have been the Afghans — who was behind them?"

Turk shrugged. "They reckon it was some sort of fraternity, hell bent on culling the population," he said.

"Huh?" said Reno. "We're back to the aliens, or the Illuminati or something?"

"Dunno," Turk said, again shrugging his shoulders. "Zen Corp, maybe? Who knows? All I know it was incredibly well orchestrated. No way it came down to a bunch of dissidents with fifty-year-old automatic rifles."

Jonno was even more confused. "It's got me stuffed who the bad guys were," he said. "Who the hell were you fighting then? Who took out the satellites?"

"We might never know." Turk folded his arms defiantly. "Let me tell you boys, there were so many different factions over there, all with an axe to grind … It was a bit like being told to kill anyone who supports the Democrats — how could we pick one from the others?"

"Hmm, I guess you couldn't," Reno said frankly.

"Anyhow, there's no democrats anymore," Jonno threw in.

"He was using an analogy, Jonno."

"I had one of them once," hiccupped the big man. "Made me sneeze all bloody day."

Turk smiled at Jonno, poured another tequila and continued. "Eventually, after they'd robbed Tabriz of everything valuable, they sent in the WarBots for a dose of ethnic cleansing. That way no human could be blamed for what they did."

"Well yeah, but someone had to program them, right?" Reno observed.

"True," agreed Turk. "Apparently, they were operated via satellite from LA, using the military dark net. And guess who runs that? Zen Corp."

Reno chuckled incredulously. "What — the same Zen that issues our cards and now runs the—" He was interrupted by the arrival of the bar owner.

"Jonno, how goes it?" the man said, offering his hand.

"Frank," said Jonno, giving it a firm shake. "Good to see you, mate. Didn't expect to, heard you were crook."

"Yeah," said Frank, stoically. "Radiation sickness. Awful shit. Some days I'm okay, others I'm butcher's hook."

Turk studied Frank's badly scarred skin and was reminded of what he'd seen during the war: soldiers with their entire bodies covered in an angry red rash, skin peeling and flesh rotting.

"Meet me buddies, Turk and Reno," said Jonno, indicating his two friends. "We grew up together in Snake."

Frank held out a hand. "Don't worry, it's not catching," he quipped.

"Saw plenty of fellers with your condition during the war mate," said Turk, sympathetically. "We called it red wheel because of the patterns it leaves on your skin. Painful stuff."

"Yeah, I guess they might've had it worse than me, going in after dirty bombs and all," said Frank. "I got it from working on a high-rise the day Canberra got nuked by the aliens. We were up too high to get clear."

"Damn," Reno swore softly, imagining what it must've been like. "You were lucky not to get fried."

"Yeah well, the other eighty blokes on the job got cooked, but soon as I realised what was happening I climbed inside one of them big commercial air-conditioning units that was being installed. Thing saved me from getting done like fish 'n chips, but I got this bleedin' disease instead. I was lucky not to be blinded as well, fortunately the unit shielded me but I was deaf for a few days from the pressure wave.”

“What do you mean, nuked by aliens?” Turk asked.

“I dunno,” Frank replied. “Everyone has their idea of what happened, you know? Who was the real enemy? But I reckon it was aliens. Remember when that alien ship landed in Tokyo in ‘47? Could’ve been the start of it all. Maybe it’s always been their plan to turn us all against each other; get us to blow ourselves away. Let’s face it, all we needed was a good nudge.

“We all know the aliens are here,” he went on. “The Yanks even admitted it after the Ruskies pushed them seventy or so years ago — Roswell and all that. They claimed Tokyo first contact was a result of the Iran/Korean wars a few years earlier.”

All of this was extremely unsettling for Turk, who found himself questioning what he had fought for. It was giving strength to his doubts. “But what makes you certain it was them?” he asked.

“You’ll probably think I’m nuts,” said Frank. “But I swear I saw something in the sky that day.”

“A UFO?” Jonno asked, wide-eyed.

“I reckon. Everything had gone super quiet — no birds, no nothing, really, really eerie … I was fifty floors up in the air, looked up just in time to see something silver come out from behind a cloud. I reckon it fired a weapon, and that’s why there was no early warning — nothing saw the missile coming, ’cause there never bloody was one!”

“What?” roared Jonno. “You reckon the UFO dropped the nuke?”

“I know it did mate,” said Frank his voice radiating utter conviction.

“You know, that would explain a lot of stuff I saw during the war that no-one could set right,” Turk said.

“It sure would explain why places like America, with their defence systems, still got whacked!” added Reno. “Everyone wondered how they could’ve failed!”

"Maybe the Yanks rubbed the aliens up the wrong way or something," Jonno said.

Frank shook his head. "I guess we'll never know the answer," he said. "But if their plan was to take over the earth, they sure got what they wanted, I reckon."

"How's that?" Reno asked.

"We're all sterile mate … Zero population growth. Mankind's been halted in its tracks. They want to inherit the earth? All they need do is wait."

A chill went through the four men.

"D'you really believe that?" asked Reno.

"Look at me mate," said Frank, sadly. "You reckon I need to make up a story like that? I'll be dead in a couple of months."

The admission hit home hard.

"Anyhow, fellas, gotta go out back. Gotta bathe in oil six times a day to stop all me skin peeling off. Nice to meet you blokes," he went on, as they all shuddered. "Take it from me — enjoy your lives. Hey, Charlie!" he called to the bartender. "Give these mugs one on the house."

"Thanks mate," Jonno said, shaking his hand again.

"Say hi to Trixy for me," Frank said, a smile cracking his blistered face. He limped off, walking like his legs were only loosely attached.

"Poor bugger," muttered Jonno. "He's only thirty. Rotten way to go."

"Stuff me!" said Reno, shaking his head. "He looks ancient! Christ, what a way to die. No wonder they call it the creeping death…"

He was interrupted by a big, mean-looking dude thundering into the bar. Six foot six, broad shouldered, his big round head bald except for a long, plaited ponytail hanging from the nape of such neck as he had to speak of. A huge ginger beard draped to his chest, his mouth totally obscured by the thick ginger moustache that went with it. His matching eyebrows all but concealed his eyes, and a long, deep scar crossed his left cheek and eye. His huge, tattooed forearms made Jonno look like a wimpy kid.

The ten or so patrons scattered about the bar, and the dozen or so bargirls working the catwalk, all froze. The monster stopped just inside the door, silhouetted by the outside light, and checked each person in the place, one at a time, every one of them cringing when his eyes met theirs. Then he focused on Jonno, who was sitting with his back to him. Surprisingly silently for such a huge man, he stalked up behind Jonno. Turk kept a keen eye on him. He flinched when the big man took a swing. But you'd have to get up very early in the morning to catch Jonno out. He saw the man's move reflected in the chrome wall, snared his arm and threw him from the hip onto the deck, Koshi Waza Judo style. The attacker landed with a thump that shook the foundations, but kicked out like lightning, knocking Jonno's feet from under him. He too slammed down onto the deck.

Turk felt as if he was watching two heavyweight wrestlers. Thinking Jonno might be in trouble, he moved to help. Reno put out a hand and held him back. The two big men rolled on the floor, each seeking the advantage, until Jonno locked his opponent in a full Nelson that had him slapping the wooden floor with an open palm. To Turk's surprise, they then helped each other up, laughing like a pair of schoolboys. Puffing, Jonno threw his arm around the invisible neck of the big dude, and dragged him in a headlock over to Turk and Reno.

"Guys, this big fat bastard is my good mate Mad Dog," he said, grinning a big and mostly toothless smile. "Now we are four!"

After bonding over a drink or three, Turk and his companions cruised out of Bar-Up, bound back to Headbangers.

Out on the street, the stiflingly humid air enshrouded them like a thick, damp blanket. They headed down a dirt track, dodging dust devils swirling in the searing hot wind. Surrounded by desolate, dilapidated buildings, they looked as if they were on the set of a twentieth-century spaghetti western.

Suddenly, Turk stopped dead in his tracks. "Choppers!" he growled. He looked over at Reno.

"I can't hear any choppers!" he said. The sound of motorbike engines, and in particular the unique rumble of a Harley Davidson chopper, wasn't one he wanted to hear right now. Two tense minutes later, two choppers thundered up the street and stopped in front of them, trailing a wall of dust. One of the bikers lifted his goggles, revealing a face red with dust except for the circles around his eyes. "Hey, Jonno!" he shouted jovially. "You rang?"

Jonno grinned widely, checking Turk, Reno and Mad Dog. "This lunatic is Cutter, and his sidekick is Nerdo," he proclaimed. "Now we are six!"

The six of them were seated in Headbangers, getting acquainted over a drink. Jonno's wife Trixy, a small and jovial Filipina, served them Pica-pica — the Filipino version of tapas.

"Okay," said Turk, taking charge. "Let's sort out who does what. Mad Dog, you first. What's your skill-set?"

"Hmm," said the big man, apparently thinking deeply. "Oh, I know! I can down a can of piss in one swallow!"

That cracked them up. "Dunno if I can use that, buddy," said Turk with a wry smile. "What else you got?"

"Hey Trix," Mad Dog growled, "Chuck me that blade." Trixy handed over the carving knife and in the blink of an eye, Mad Dog had fired it through the air at Turk, who didn't budge as it hit the wooden post beside his ear with a thunk!

"Impressive," said Turk.

"He can do that just as accurately from twenty metres away," Jonno claimed. "Deadly."

Turk wrenched the blade from the post, felt the tip then, in a flash, hurled it back at Mad Dog. It sank into the wooden seat right between his legs, leaving very little margin for his family jewels. Mad Dog gulped.

Turk took a swig of his beer.

Mad Dog raised hands in surrender. "I'm impressed," he chortled.

Turk turned to the next man round the table, "Cutter?"

With his long curly black hair, moustache and goatee, the slightly-built Cutter could have been mistaken for one of the Three Musketeers. There was a suggestion of pent-up aggression about the young man, only softened by the vibrant blue eyes in his greyhound-thin face.

"Former SAS," he said, his gravelly voice not at all suited to his appearance. "Vehicles and munitions."

"Do the war?" asked Turk.

"Yeah. Discharged twelve months ago. Waste of fricking time. Should have been a mercenary, at least I would've come out of it with some credits. We were just making it easier for corporations and politicians to get even richer by exterminating their competitors."

Turk nodded. "You're not wrong, Cutter," he said, and glanced at the last man. A real odd-bod if Turk ever had seen one. Five-ten, skinny, almost effeminately built. The kid looked like a full-on geek, except for an unmistakable take-no-shit glint in two dark eyes. It was difficult to make out much more than that under a bulky military jacket two sizes too big, and a khaki baseball cap.

"I did time with Cutter in the SAS," said Nerdo, in answer to Turk's look. "My gig is computers. Anything with a circuit or that needs to be hacked."

Looking into those eyes, Turk said, nonchalantly: "Are you bonking Cutter?"

The question caused a unanimous raising of eyebrows.

"What you insinuating?" asked Jonno. But Turk's eyes hadn't strayed from Nerdo's. Suddenly, one corner of Nerdo's thin lips arched.

"Don't often get caught out," she said. "But no. I'm into other ladies."

"Well, I'll be stuffed!" Jonno exclaimed. "You're a chick? I've known you what, a year? I had no idea!"

"Don't let it get to you, Jonno," she said. "I still shower with the boys."

"Bulldust," said Cutter. "I've never seen you bollocky."

They all laughed. But now all of them, with the exception of Cutter, were looking at the sixth member of their team a little differently. She stood, whipped off her cap, took off her jacket and flexed her tattooed arms. Slim, yes, but wiry and strong, she cut a smart figure under her big, multi-pocketed, khaki jacket.

Cutter chipped in again. "Make no mistake, fellas, she's a bloody wizard," he said. "Show her anything that supposed to have current running through it and she'll fix it if it's stuffed or turn it into a weapon. She worked on the WarBots."

Turk grimaced, then eyeballed Nerdo. "What's er mob?"

Nerdo smiled knowingly, "The Yolngu people. You?"

"Yuin," Turk answered with a look reserved only for first nations folk.

Mad Dog looked hard at Reno. "What about you, buddy?" he asked. Reno leaned back in his chair. "Did the kickboxing circuit with Turk before the war, he said."

"And he's bloody lethal," Jonno added.

"Anyone Jonno gives the nod to is well cool by us," said Cutter, glancing at Nerdo. She nodded in accord.

"Well, know this," said Jonno, rising to his feet. "These guys, Turk and Reno, are top-shelf. I'd take a bullet for either of them. Turk gives the orders and Reno's his 2-IC. This is their gig. Alright?" He eyeballed them one at a time. They nodded their approval. "Any questions?"

Mad Dog wiped his bearded mouth with the back of his hand, "Yeah, um … What's in it for us who ain't after retribution?" he asked.

Jonno squared up to him. "The fricking thrill!" he barked.

"Plus whatever spoils we score," Turk put in. "I'm told these bastards have been robbing people 'round here for years. Should be some fair pickings in their camp, right? You can have the lot. The only thing I want is their nuts on a plate."

Mad Dog raised his bottle. "Alright," he said. "I'll drink to that."

The tension eased. "So, you did service, Turk?" Cutter asked. "What division?"

"SASR, one squadron," said Turk. Cutter whistled. The original Australian special air service squadron, formed in 1957, took only the best.

"Who dares wins," Nerdo said, trumpeting the SAS motto.

"TAG or Delta?" Cutter asked.

"What are they?" said Jonno.

"TAG is Tactical Assault Group. Delta is special ops," Cutter replied.

Turk nodded. "TAG, gauntlet five. Dishonourably discharged."

"Speak English, can't yer?" grumbled Jonno. "What's all that mean?"

"Gauntlet means he was land-based," said Nerdo. "Five means he did five years. Cutter and me got eight, starting in Sabre squadron. He ended up with OAT — that's offshore assault team. I did hot comms."

Jonno and Mad Dog, still wearing lost looks, brightened up as Trixy came over to the table with a tray of hot food.

"Mmmm, that smells happening!" said Mad Dog, grinning.

"Here we go fellers," Trixy announced, placing four big dishes on the table. "Home-cooked tucker."

"Thanks Trix," said Reno. "What have we got here?"

Mad Dog sniffed the fragrance. "Fish?" he questioned.

"Nar, that'd be Trixy," Jonno joked. "She hasn't had a bath for a few weeks." They all laughed. "Hey, water costs nearly as much as gas in Angel!" he added.

"You're kidding me!" Turk said, surprised.

"It's Zen," said Cutter, bitterly. "All the rivers are polluted, so they filter the sewerage systems and sell our own pee back to us as fresh water. Criminal. It's safer to drink Johnny Walker!"

"Who'd drink bloody water anyway?" Mad Dog quipped, and spat on the floor. "Fish crap in it!"

"Yeah, well," Trixy said, her faint Filipino accent tinged with regret. "No such thing as fish anymore, eh, Jonno? Fallout kill dem all."

"She'd know," said Jonno, ruefully. "Her grandfather wrapped up business as a fisherman back in two thousand and fifteen, after the government back then made fishing sanctuaries up and down the coast. Didn't matter in the end, pollution and fallout got the fish anyhow. I still remember when all them whales started beaching themselves up and down the coast. We didn't know then they were dying from fallout, just like the birds."

"Yeah," said Mad Dog, nodding along. "Dolphins and everything washed up, awful. Still a few carp about inland even they died out in the end. So, what is in this then, Trix? Tinned fish?"

"This, my friends, is one of Trix's specialities," he said. "La Cucaracha stew. And this one," he went on, dipping his finger into the sauce and tasting it, "Ah yes, rodent in ginger sauce. Real nice. Hunted the little buggers myself last night. Rats and cockroaches — that's all that's left fellas. Literally, the only game in town."

Next morning, Betsy led the two choppers out through the Angel City gates, en route back to Snake Ridge.

CHAPTER 9
DEVIL'S PACT

HONOR CHECKED HERSELF in the mirror, which was still misted after her shower. She sighed, looking at the dressings covering the burns she'd sustained on night of Alice's escape, caused by a red-hot, fusing robot. She gently peeled back the bandage on her left thigh and scowled at the wound underneath. Better not to look. Out of sight, out of mind.

Her phone implant rang. She answered. "Hello!" she snapped. "Yes, this is she. I zought I'd made myself clear," she spat, as the person on the other end explained the reason for their call. "I vanted text reports, not calls … Vhat?" She froze, suddenly furious. "Detain zem both!" she roared. "Now, damn it! Do not let zem out of your sight! I vill be zere in twenty minutes." She caught another glimpse of herself in the mirror. "Make zat twenty-five."

In fact, it was mid-morning by the time Honor and Karzoff stepped out of the black, Government-issue EV they'd driven to the Jones Bay Wharf car park. Four troopers were waiting to meet them.

"Right," barked Honor. "Lead ze vay."

Fifty metres away, a ferry was docked at the harbour — the same ferry Alice had disappeared from. On the wharf a mobile generator, with a long lead extending like an umbilical cord up to the bridge of the boat, rumbled loudly, breaking the surrounding serenity, void as it was of any other human activity.

They'd been able to see blue and white flashes of high-voltage arc light coming from the ferry even from their car. "Looks like they have their machine working already," Karzoff had said. Stamping along the wharf behind their escort, Honor was venting her displeasure. "I should haff been notified earlier," she growled. "Zese incompetent fools are incapable off effective surveillance — ve might be too late!" They hurried onto the gangway.

On the bridge, Secta and Hope were sheltering in an alcove to the side of the companionway, a safe distance from the sparking light show emanating from a large, clear plastic bubble. Two metres around, it only barely fitted the space. Wearing white Hazmat suits, protective goggles and headsets, Secta and Hope were shouting into their mikes to make themselves heard.

"It doesn't look good, Hope!" Secta yelled, peering at a remote control in his hand. "I think I'll have to—" But before he could finish, the cacophony suddenly ceased. "Huh? That's odd," he said. "Either we just blew a fuse, or somebody pulled the plug."

"Ze latter is quvite correct, Secta," bellowed Honor's unmelodious voice from the deck below.

Secta turned and peered down the companionway at Honor and Karzoff. He removed his goggles and pulled back the hood on his Hazmat suit. Hope did the same. "I see you brought your pet clown, Honor," said Secta, cynically. "I hope whoever turned off my generator was ticketed. The union can be touchy about demarcation you know..." He chuckled to himself.

"Shut up!" Honor bawled. "Troopers! Arrest Dr Hope! Immediately!"

They rushed up the companionway, pushed past Secta, and seized Hope, manhandling her back down to the lower deck. "Let go of me!" she demanded, struggling to pull her arms free.

Secta simply shook his head. "What is it this time, Honor?" he asked, sadly. "Why do you always have to be such a party pooper? Did you have an unhappy childhood or something? A dysfunctional family, perhaps? I need my sister to work on this experiment," he went on. "I have told you this before, Honor ... Would you prefer that I called the President?"

Honor remained silent, as Hope, still struggling, was dragged towards the waiting paddy wagon. She was tired of Secta threatening to use his relationship with the President whenever she had him on toast. She was determined that this time it would be different. A nod to Karzoff was his cue to approach their enemy.

"Dr Secta," the man said, diplomatically, "Let us sit down as civilized government servants, and discuss the matter at hand."

"Always the humourist, Honor," said Secta, brushing past Karzoff and making his way to the top of the companionway. Removing his thick rubber gloves and scanning the red-haired man as though studying a laboratory specimen, he went on: "As if this little clown could ever be a government servant. Hilarious! Although the uniform is quite good. He almost looks the part."

"Stop zis fooling around Secta. Now zit!"

"Zit?" Secta coolly replied. "I don't have any zits, Honor. Lost them with my virginity and my favourite teddy bear when I was twelve. Not necessarily in that order, of course."

"I imagine you lost your virginity viz your teddy," Honor spat, finally goaded into retaliation. "Surely not with anyzing human, or alive."

"You're the one who made it with a robot," Secta smirked. "Quite a hot little scene, I'm told."

Honor stiffened but this time bit her lip. There was no need to spar with the man. She gave Karzoff another nod. He got the message. Stepping forward, he took Secta by the arm and twisted, forcing him down into a seat.

"What is this?" Secta gasped. "Such unwonted physicality! Honor, I must protest…"

"Shut up!" she snapped. "Ze only zing you must do now is answer my quvestions. Vhat are you doing up there viz zat machine? On the ferry used for ze Octagon demonstration? Zat seems suspicious to me…"

"Ve just met and I vas asking it for a date, vhat do you think Honor?" he mocked.

"You listen to me," she said, in icy tones that matched her cold stare. "If you continue vis your childish antics, I vill have a cement block tied to your sister's feet and dump her off ze vharf! I trust I am making myself quvite clear?"

Secta swallowed. He'd pushed her far enough — now she meant business. Visibly shaken, he simply nodded.

Honor flashed a grim smile. "So, I vill ask you one more time," she said. "Vhat vere you doing on ze bridge?"

"In scientific jargon or layman's terms?" asked Secta, unable even with the threat against Hope to prevent himself.

Honor drew a deep breath and closed her eyes. "Just answer ze question, Dr Secta," she ground out through gritted teeth. "Use any vords you feel are necessary."

"Okay, okay," he grumbled. "Don't get your knickers in a knot. It's perfectly simple: we have constructed a cloud chamber — that is this big plastic bubble — containing helium. I will fire a number of different types of sub-atomic particles into the gas using a proton accelerator. When the gas and the particles within it are exposed to both an electromagnetic field and either neutrino or gamma rays, we expect a reaction. We can't tell which rays will work yet," he added, contemptuously, "Since our experiment was so rudely interrupted."

"Vy here?" asked Honor. "Vy on zis ferry, and not in your lab?"

Secta sighed his special professor-addressing-idiot-student sigh. "Because this is where Black Alice vanished," he said, as though it were patently clear. "I think he may have left a residual break in the fabric of time. That is what I am testing for — the way through."

Honor smiled, contentedly. Now she was getting somewhere. "And ze reaction?" she said. "It is used for vhat?"

"It will permit us to peer into that dimension, to try to locate an atomic marker I placed on a strand of Black Alice's DNA."

"For vhat purpose?" Honor demanded.

"So we can open a wormhole to him — perhaps. It's only a theory, Honor. It may not work."

She began to pace the deck. "And if it does?" she said. "Vill he be able come back through zis wormhole?"

"No," said Secta. "He wouldn't know how. He would have to be physically brought back."

"How? And vhy?"

"As to how, Honor, I simply have no idea. We first have to locate him. As for why—"

"Indeed!" she barked. "Zat is ze question, since it vas your job to lose him in ze first place — a job I seem to remember you assuring me had been done!"

"Senior Inspector," he said, using the woman's title for the first time. He'd judged it right. She was shocked into silence by this uncharacteristic display of respect. "Alice is extremely important, Senior Inspector," he said, desperately inventing, not wanting to disclose the truth. "Think about it for a moment. The very first human time traveller. And you could be the one to extract from him all the incredibly valuable information he must have…" He paused, seeing from her face that he'd touched the right nerve.

"Continue," she said, curtly.

Secta grinned. Once again, he had the floor. "Black Alice will be more important to history than the first man to walk on the moon!" he declaimed. "Why? Because he has travelled to other dimensions … imagine if one of them was the future! He would have knowledge about advanced technologies, weaponry, military tactics. He'll know who holds the power and why. He will have knowledge none of us could ever dream of! Think of it Honor," he said, throwing an expansive arm around the woman's shoulders and holding a dramatic hand out to the horizon across the bay. "He could provide our Government with an edge never held by any other. And you — along with the Great Grimalidi here — could bring it all to our President! Oh, the accolades! The fame! The honour, Honor!"

She stood in his grasp, transfixed, her unseeing eyes picturing a ticker-tape parade, medals, the admiration of the President. Power. "Is zis vhat your holographic experiment vas designed to do?" she asked, almost dreamily.

"Not originally, no!" cried Secta. "But it is now! With Black Alice having been to the future and back again, we may have invented a dimensional matter-transfer system!"

"But vill it vork, Secta? Can you retrieve him?"

"I will have to undergo the dematerialization process myself in order to find him," said Secta. "Once I have him, I'll need the means to bring us both back. If I succeed, we will have made history and proved my theory. If I fail, this world is still rid of Alice. And, Honor, it will be rid of me."

"Wait — just let me get this straight," Karzoff interrupted. "How are you going to find the means to come back? Is your plan to build it now, and find it again in the future?"

"Vat on Earth are you babbling about, Karzoff?" Honor growled.

"In fact, he's quite correct, Honor," said Secta. "Believe me, I'm as surprised as you. But we will indeed build a recovery machine in this timeline, and store it in a place secure enough that it will still be there in a future timeline."

Proud of himself, Karzoff nodded at Honor. Then his brow wrinkled. "Unless..." he said, "Unless Alice has gone into the past."

"That is possible, but it seems extremely unlikely," said Secta. "Quantum mechanics suggest that travelling backwards in time is implausible. Besides, if it were possible we'd probably know about it already, don't you think?"

There were a few moments of silence as Honor and Karzoff pondered all the pieces of this theoretical puzzle. Finally, they seemed to decide all of them would fit.

"I … I suppose it makes sense," said Honor, nodding her head slowly, thoughtfully. She turned on her heel and spoke to her implant. "Operator, zis is Senior Inspector Honor, 2-4-D Delta. Have ze troopers return Dr Hope to my current GPS. Yes, zat is correct." She cut the call off and turned back to the scientist. "Your sister vill be returned to help you viz ze experiment," she said. "You vill speak to no-one of zis, Secta. You vill report your progress to me, and to me only. I vill arrange for you to use ze ferry until you have succeeded. Guards vill be posted on ze wharf." She closed on him with a menacing stare. "Do not forget, Secta. Your sister can still be fitted for zose cement shoes. Get on viz it, Secta. Ve vill talk further soon." She gestured to Karzoff, and they walked onto the gangway. Honor stopped and turned once more before leaving. "Do not let me down, doctor," she said, treating him to an excessively long dose of stink-eye to stress the point.

Hope gave Honor and Karzoff a supercilious look as she passed them on the gangway. Once on the bridge deck, she flopped onto the bench seat beside her brother. Secta was silent, deep in thought. "Well, brother dear?" she asked. "How did you get me out of it this time?"

Secta stood up as the generator reactivated and answered with uncommon brusqueness. "Just my usual sweet talking, Hope," he said. "Come on, let's get on with the tests."

In the passenger seat beside Karzoff on the way back to Oceana SSD HQ, Honor looked at her red-haired second in command. "Zat vent vell, yes?" she said.

"You are a devil, are you not?" Karzoff responded, with an evil grimace.

"I like to zink I can close a deal ven it is necessary, yes." Smiling with grim satisfaction she added: "Do you zink zis is really as big a deal as Secta asserts?"

"No, Honor," smirked Karzoff, knowingly, "No, I believe it is even bigger!"

CHAPTER 10
iWISH

S NAKE RIDGE WAS deserted. The only indication the town was inhabited was the neon light casting flashing purple across the facade of Club Voodoo. The ghostly silence broke when ten choppers roared down the main street and parked in the glow.

The bikers dismounted. Duke led four of them into Reno's Bar. The remaining five went into Voodoo.

On their way back to Snake Ridge, Turk was lost in thought, the music playing on the sampler underscoring his vivid memories of war.

A fan of late 20th century music, especially heavy metal, Reno had programmed a compilation of his favourites. AC/DC's Let There Be Rock had just finished, and Sons of Steel by Black Alice was next. As the opening bars kicked in, Turk's mind reeled.

"There's something up ahead..." said Reno. "Turk? Turk!" he jostled his pal, trying to snap him out of his trance. He turned the music off to make sure he was being heard. Suddenly Turk's head snapped around.

"The ferry!" he yelled, in an odd voice. "We have to stop the ferry!"

"What? What are you talking about, man?" said Reno. "What bloody ferry?"

"Uh ... Sorry man, what did you say?" Turk mumbled, shaking his head clear.

"I was saying it looks like trouble up ahead."

They were close to Snake Ridge. Betsy's airbrakes hissed as Reno pulled her to a stop at a barricade of burnt out vehicles, stacked two high. They climbed down from the cabin as the others pulled up.

Turk squatted at the roadside, studying the pile up. Two dozen burnt out cars were stacked across the road, as though a giant had picked them up, piled them on top of one another and put them to the torch.

"Bottom one's a cop car," he said. "The sheriff's, I reckon. Torched at first light, by the smell of it."

Jonno joined them. "Someone's had a barbecue," he growled.

Turk rose to his feet. "Duke," he said, flatly.

Reno spat on the ground. "Not a good sign."

"Looks like he might be expecting us," added Jonno.

"I don't think so," said Turk. He walked to the sheriff's car and peered in through a shattered window. "It's a warning," he said. "Not for us, for anyone. It'll be worse in town. We leave our vehicles here. Arm up," he ordered, coldly. "We're going in."

A couple of minutes later he was leading them beyond the barricade along the main street of Snake.

"It's like a bloody ghost town," Mad Dog growled.

Each of them had their guns up, cocked, ready.

"Not a good silence," said Cutter, scanning the topography. "Feels like we're being watched."

"Keep your eyes peeled," said Reno, calmly. "Stay cool. It's probably just the locals. They'll be scared."

"Fan out around the next corner," said Turk, sharply. "But be careful — I can smell death."

To an old soldier the stench of death is unforgettable. Turk wasn't wrong. As they rounded the corner, they were stopped in their tracks by the sight of two men chained to separate streetlights.

"The sheriff and his deputy," Reno spat. "They've crucified 'em."

Some of the buildings had been torched and were still smouldering.

"What about these arseholes?" Mad Dog snarled. "They're a law unto themselves."

Reno walked over to his bar. It had been trashed. Turk saw movement in a second-storey apartment window above an old shop. "You're right Reno," he said, quietly. "The townsfolk are hiding."

Reno walked into the middle of the road. "It's me!" he shouted. "Reno! Come out — I want to know what happened here!"

Hearing his voice, the townsfolk slowly began emerging from the smouldering ruins, looking like frightened animals. Their spokesperson was a longhaired, scrawny, tough-looking teenager. His face bore the signs of a beating and the denim jacket, T-shirt and jeans he wore were ripped and covered in dust.

Recognizing Reno, he confronted him, brimming with spite. "Huh! Reno!" he spat. "Man, you can sure be relied on to not be around when it's needed!"

Reno eyeballed him but ignored his aggression.

"Tatts," he growled. "What happened here?"

A grizzled man covered in tattoos and sporting a beer belly came forward. "The girls from your bar have bailed, man," he said. "Those bastards took a couple of them, along with four girls from Voodoo. They tortured the sheriff and the deputy in front of us ... doused 'em with gas, strung 'em up on the poles and set 'em on fire! Anyone who said anything got the crap kicked out of 'em."

A dozen or so people in the crowd grumbled in agreement, half angrily, half ashamed.

"We want our girls back!" yelled Tatts, all fired up. "And we want Duke's head on a fricking spike!"

A ragged cheer came from his supporters.

"We're planning to hit their hideout tonight," he went on. "You with us or not?"

Reno wanted to placate him. He knew it would be a suicide mission. It would take a stronger force than these battered civilians to make a dent on the Rebels' stronghold.

"Settle down, son," he said, putting a not unsympathetic hand on his shoulder. "You can't just—"

Tatts pulled away sharply. "What would you know, man?" he was yelling to avoid sobbing, Turk and his friends could all see that. "They took my girl. They beat the crap outta me. They cut the deputy's fingers off one by one then strung him up with the sheriff. They … they..." his voice broke and he stopped, furious with himself.

Turk stepped up.

"I think Reno knows only too well what we're up against here," he said. "They killed his wife, remember? And I've got a score of my own to settle. So, let's cut the bravado and get this right. No-one goes anywhere near the Rebels' camp until we're good and ready."

Tatts, unable to contain his resentment, got in Turk's face.

"Just who voted you town mayor?" he demanded. "Who the hell are you?"

Turk shot the boy a glare intense enough to melt steel. "Name's Turk," he said, coolly.

Tatts backed down. He knew the name. Since Turk had burnt the biker outside Voodoo, the residents of Snake had elevated him to legendary status. Wind taken from his sails, Tatts simply nodded once, sharply, turned on his heel and strode defiantly strode off.

"I need a drink," Mad Dog groaned.

"Wisest thing I've heard all day," said Jonno.

They followed Reno into what was left of his bar.

With a sad look Reno scanned the interior.

Turk patted him on the back consolingly. "I'm so sorry mate," he said. "Feels like I brought all this down on you."

"Nah, mate," said Reno. "These bastards would have done this whether it was you or not. I just feel for the girls, you know? Elsa treated them like our own daughters. I'm worried for 'em, and that's the truth."

Jonno patted him consolingly on the back, almost sending him sprawling to the floor. "We'll get 'em back," he said, gruffly. "For Elsa, man. We'll get 'em all back."

"You can count on that," Turk agreed.

Reno nodded sorrowfully, tears in his eyes, then shook it off and made his way out back to the freezer. A few seconds later he called out, "Bastards aren't so smart as they think they are."

"Left us some weapons?" Mad Dog growled.

"Nah mate," said Reno. "Left us some beer."

It was midnight. The witching hour. Mad Dog lay snoring, sprawled like a beached whale on the three-legged pool table. Cutter was propped against the wall, chin on his chest and snoring. Nerdo was at the front desk, messing with the remains of the smashed sound system. Jonno, Turk and Reno occupied a dimly-lit cubicle, drinking. The whirring of the generator at the rear of the premises filled the background while they talked.

"You've gotta give it a try, man," said Jonno, enthusiastically but with a noticeable slur. "It'sh a sherious rush…"

"I dunno mate," Turk answered. "I can't get my head around having a plug in the back of my melon." He was watching his mate slide slowly into three versions of himself and back again.

"Your cereber-eberal cortexsh," Reno corrected, swaying gently to a tune only he could hear.

"Easy enough for you to say," hiccupped Turk. "But plugging meself into the A/C for a kick? Jesus H. Nelly! Not for me, thanksh. Could end up like a bleedin' WarBot…"

Jonno waved a hand expansively. "There's a credit-card-sized player that goes with the whole shebang, a whatchoucallit, an interface between the plug in your head and the AC. Means you can play stuff right into your noggin. Plus, plus, it does something to the power so your brain don't fry."

"Say … say you select classical piano tuition," said Reno. "You just whack in the right SIM, plug in, hit the DIGEST button and in seconds you're asleep. You wake up minutes later and you can play the piano like a bloody expert."

"Hell," said Turk. "You think I could learn to dance?"

"Sure, you could!" Jonno erupted.

"No way. I hate dancing," Turk scoffed.

They laughed.

"Problem was, the thing was abused," said Reno, with regret. He hauled himself up and over to Nerdo at the front desk.

"Yeah, it was used as a drug, trippin' on the multiple trance modes," said Jonno. "I tried trance three once, just to see what'd happen. Didn't know who I was when I woke up!"

"Thought you woke up like that all the time," Turk laughed.

"See, 'slike, it can access parts of your brain you never knew you had and fire 'em up," Jonno went on, ignoring the interruption "It can, like, bring out the worst or the best in people … or, sometimes, stuff in your head that you've, you know, repressed. No good for schizos!" he added with a grunt, taking another generous swig of Scotch.

"Yeah, eat your heart out folks with an MPD," said Reno, walking unsteadily back from the desk with an armful of electronic gadgetry. "Here." He dumped it all on the table in front of Turk. "A complete iWish kit!"

"Whoa!" said Jonno. "That's worth a bleedin' motzer, mate!"

Turk lifted the control box. "Ah, there's a familiar name," he said. "Our old friend, Zen Corp!"

"Yeah, they're into everything now," said Jonno. "The entire computer industry — for what that's worth these days."

"Come on then, Turk," said Reno. "Give it a try."

"I dunno…" Turk was doubtful. "There some stuff in my head I don't want to get out," he said.

"Tell you what," Reno proposed, keen for him to try. "I've got a program that teaches you to sing a song perfectly in just ten minutes."

"Oh yeah? Sounds mighty," said Turk. "Always fancied meself as a singer. Any side effects?"

"Only that you'll think you're a real singer and drive us all nuts with the one song you know," said Reno. "Look — you can even select the type of music," he added, milling through a bunch of iWish chips. "Ah, here's one! Good old heavy metal!"

"That's him!" hooted Jonno. "Turk's a closet headbanger if I've ever known one!"

"Some other time, guys," said Turk, dismissively, downing his Scotch.

"Hey, there might not be another time," said Reno, warmly but resolutely. "Tomorrow we go to war again. Our own war. Look, it's me, mate, Reno. You can trust me. You know I'd never put you in harm's way."

Turk looked long and hard at his friends. He relaxed. Reno was right. The battle against the Rebels could cost them their lives, and by now he should be able to trust his mates.

He caved in. "Righty-o," he said, slamming down the bottle. "Heavy metal it is!"

Reno rose from his seat, holding a device that looked like a cross between a stapler and a glue gun. "Right," he said to Turk. "Just bend your head down — that's it — I've got to line this feller up with your occipital protuberance."

"Never thought I'd be letting you handle any protuberance of mine," Turk joked, going along with it.

Reno placed the device against the base of the back of Turk's skull. There was a hiss, a tap, and the tiny plug was in position.

"There! Done," Reno grinned.

"Alright," said Turk. "What now?"

Reno held up a small jack. "I plug this into your port like … so … then activate the module … like … so… It's wireless," he said, as lights illuminated on the remote module in his hand. "Now we insert the SIM." He placed it into position and continued. "Sit back," he said. "When I hit DIGEST, you'll see a flash of light then it's off to slumber land. You'll wake up in ten minutes and sing to us like a rock star. But before that happens, we need to pick a song."

Turk nodded.

Reno inserted the SIM and a small screen on the module displayed a song list.

"How about this one, Jonno?" grinned Reno. "A real golden oldie."

Jonno checked the display, "Yeah, excellent choice!"

Reno put his finger on the DIGEST button, "Okay mate. Here we go."

A flash of light jolted Turk's head back. His eyes rolled, then closed.

"I picked that song coz I've got a karaoke version of it here somewhere," said Reno. "So he'll be able to sing along to the backtrack — oh wait! Crap! I forgot the sound system's stuffed"

"No it ain't," called Nerdo. "I fixed it. What track is it?"

"'Reck' by Black Alice," Reno replied.

"Killer," said Nerdo, as she nudged through the sample player's selection.

In Turk's mind's eye, he was shooting backwards through space. His body was shimmering in and out of visibility. His eyes shot open in a wide stare.

"Hey, Reno, something's wrong!" Jonno shouted. "His eyes shouldn't be open yet!"

"What the stuff's going on here?" said Turk, in a voice nothing like his own. He glared at Jonno like he didn't recognise him, then at Reno in the same way.

"Who the hell are you two?"

"It's all right, Turk, you're okay," said Reno, trying to placate him.

"Turk? Who's Turk?" said the voice, and suddenly Turk saw his reflection in a wall mirror. It visibly rocked him. He rose slowly to his feet, pointing. "Hey, that's not me!" he cried. "I'm Black Alice!" he felt a tug at the back of his head where the jack was connected, and grabbed at it. "What the stuff's this?" he yelled.

"No, mate! Don't pull that out!" Reno yelled.

Too late. Turk pulled the plug … and hit the floor.

CHAPTER 11
MORAL HAZARD

SECTA GAZED AT Hope over a steaming mug of fresh jungle-bean coffee. She looked tired. Café Epiphany was the right place for them to recuperate. They'd been working long hours, trying to solve the riddle of the cloud chamber. It seemed to Secta that there was a distant look in her eyes. She seemed to be staring at him, but her eyes were focused on something behind him. He swivelled around quickly to see what it was and found a surreal painting mounted on the café wall. A painting he'd never really noticed before.

"Hope?" he questioned, in an effort to snap her out of it. "Hope!" he said, more urgently. Her eyes suddenly switched to his.

"Sorry," she said. "Guess I was off with the pixies."

"Maybe we need a rest," he replied. "We've been at it for days without any sleep. You've got call-centre eyes."

"Call-centre eyes?" she questioned.

"Dark circles … it's what call-centre shift workers get from long hours. Look, it's half past tomorrow, and we're no closer to an answer than we were at half past yesterday."

She smiled, wearily. "At least we've eliminated some options, she said. So we're now down to—"

"Exactly," he said. "Down to what?" She'd gone back to staring at the painting again. "What is it with that painting?" he said.

Suddenly she lit up. "That's it!" she exclaimed. "Secta, the painting ... look at it. What do you see?"

He swivelled round and studied it. The artist's signature, 'Taj' was at the bottom in the right-hand corner. A small plaque underneath described it as the artist's surreal depiction of Sydney after an apocalypse. It dawned on Secta what Hope was excited about. In the painting, the landscape of Sydney had been reduced to the torso of a reclining female nude, a green growth sprouting from her navel.

He smiled. "It's not what's going in. It's what's coming out, isn't it?" He rose slowly to his feet.

"Exactly, Secta," she said. "But what is the formula?"

He drew a pen from his top pocket, sat back down and started scribbling on the paper placemat in front of him, mumbling like a man possessed.

"T equals two pi r over velocity which equals ... Hope, you're right! The cyclotron resonance frequency is wrong! We need a neutron gun not a proton gun — and we need to shoot through the ionizer into a velocity selector, just like a particle accelerator! It's the only way we'll get a positron reaction!"

"Holy mackerel," she grinned. "If that's the case we're going to need a lot of voltage. A hell of lot!"

Secta raised a finger, and accessed his implant, "Hello, operator. Secta, 17-7. Patch me through to Inspector Honor, please." Hope wrinkled her nose at the name. "Hello, Honor," Secta purred. "Yes, I know it's five a.m.," he grimaced at Hope, he'd had no idea of the time. "But this is important. We are very close to a result. However, I need a mobile radioactive generator. There's one at the Lucas Heights Nuclear Facility ... No, they don't hire it out! We'll need a special government requisition order ... No, it's the only way Honor. If this doesn't work it's all over. Okay. Get back to me. As quickly as possible, please." He terminated.

"Please?" questioned Hope.

"We need to keep her sweet," he shrugged.

He fixed his eyes on Hope's. She lazed back in her chair with folded arms. "Well?"

He held up five fingers, and began counting down. "Five … four … three … two…" his face lit up as he answered his implant. "Yes, Honor," he said, grinning triumphantly at his grumbling sister. "Good. This morning, eleven hundred hours. Understood." He terminated the call and smirked at Hope. "So, we'll have enough volts to fry a whale by eleven this morning," he said. "Good enough?"

"Brilliant!" Hope said as they high-fived. "She seems pretty keen to help you," she added. "What's in it for her?"

"I just think she just wants Black Alice back," said Secta. "Maybe she misses him."

"Be square with me, Secta. I know when you're feeding me crap. What deal did you cut?"

"Look," he said, wearily. "I just told her that Alice is her ticket. You know, it'll get her and her other half with the red hair a commendation. That did the trick."

"So, what, now Alice is back in the good books?"

"It bought us some time, alright? Now let's get back to work. It's only a few hours until the unit arrives."

"Why do I have the feeling you're not telling me everything, Secta?"

"Hope," he said as he stood to leave, "Sometimes the less you know the better, okay? Trust me. For once, just trust me."

"Trust you?" she mumbled, loud enough for him to hear. "That'll be the day, big brother."

Seated behind a gunmetal desk in her stark office, Honor looked up to see Karzoff entering.

He stopped and looked around. "Hmm," he said. "Your office is as grey, gloomy and humble as mine."

"I vould not haff put it so nicely, Karzoff. Haff you not been here before?"

"No, we mostly rendezvous in the conference room. I always presumed you had a plush office."

"I vill have before long, dear toad."

"Of that you can be certain," he said, encouragingly.

Honor produced a tablet, and peered at it intensely. "I haff received a note from Secta," she said. "It is a list of his latest requvirements for ze experiment. I vill copy you. Take a seat."

Karzoff sat and produced his own tablet from a pocket.

"I see," he said, reading the list Honor had sent. "What is this 'isotopic labelling detection device' — this ILDD?"

"Secta sent me an earlier note on that," she said, scrolling. "Here it is … an ILDD is a unit used for tracking ze passage of an isotope, or an atom viz a variation, through a reaction, metabolic pathway, or cell. It is apparently used in medicine for tracking radioactive isotopes used for ze treatment of tumours. He vill be using it to locate Black Alice, once he has found his signature in ze correct time zone."

"Ah, I understand. He must open the wormhole that connects to the dimension in which Alice is located. Then he will store that location information. Later he will demolecularize himself, so he can enter through the wormhole. Once there, he will find the hidden return mechanism and collect this ILDD detection device in order to locate Alice."

"Why does he not simply take ze ILDD viz him?"

"Because it is not organic. He cannot reduce and reconstitute it, like he can himself."

"So how vill he materialise in ze future?"

"I think he will send himself to a device hidden alongside the return mechanism, and use it to re-materialize."

He smiled, satisfied with his scientific acumen.

"You amaze me, dear toad," said Honor, and for once she actually seemed sincere.

"But what if he fails to come back?" Karzoff asked. "What if he goes and takes Hope with him? There goes your hostage."

"Do not underestimate me, dear toad, I haff an insurance scheme … Now. Get online and start ordering ze items on Secta's list. Ve must not cause any delays. Besides, my department budget is nearly exhausted, so ve had better spend it vhile we still haff it."

Honor received a priority call. Her face drained of colour. "Yes, I understand," she said. "Immediately. I am on my vay." She disconnected and looked at Karzoff. "I haff been summoned by ze President," she explained.

"Just explain the situation to him," said Karzoff. "You know he is a reasonable man."

Honor was already on her way out of the door. "But if I tell him vhat has happened and vhat ve are doing … and if ze experiment fails…" she chewed anxiously on her pinkie fingernail.

"Be sensible, Honor," her companion replied. "You have done your job. Black Alice has been liquidated. Now all you need do is explain how you — and I — have come up with what could be the greatest discovery in history — actual time travel! — and that it rests upon Secta's experiment. Remember, that buffoon is the President's favourite son, is he not? Worst case, the President doesn't buy into it and won't proceed. Then we simply leave Black Alice where he is — stuck in his alternative future." He dusted his hands together. "Job done."

She stopped and looked back. "You know vhat, my dear toad? Once again, you haff hit ze proverbial nail on ze head. I should be more positive. Ve succeeded in our mission, after all. Alice has been liquidated, and vizout a voice, Octagon is in disarray."

She brushed non-existent lint from the front of her uniform, checked her face in the desktop vanity mirror and touched up her red lips. Feeling a little more confident, she posed for Karzoff.

"How do I look?"

"Yummy," he said, with as much innuendo as he dared muster. It was wasted on her.

Honor entered the lobby of the President's penthouse and approached the receptionist.

"Miss Vallins," she nodded.

"Senior Inspector Honor. The President is waiting. Go right in."

Honor paused on the mark for a quick body scan, and a loud click sounded her permission to enter. She strode in, confident she had something the President would find appealing.

This time he was not behind his desk. He was seated in his armchair, reading a 3-D newspaper. Upon hearing her enter, he terminated the holographic image, and then peered at her under his black eyebrows.

"Ah, Inspector Honor … Please take a seat." Honor sat. "I have been receiving your reports, and I have a few queries."

Before he could finish, Miss Vallins interrupted, sashaying into the room with two mugs of steaming coffee and a plate of biscuits on a tray. Honor noticed a small shot-glass, too. The shapely woman placed the tray in front of the President, and passed him the shot glass.

"Your meds, sir."

"That time already? Thank you, Miss Vallins."

He downed the small quantity of medicine in a gulp and handed it back, watching the secretary hungrily as she wiggled back out of the room.

"Medicine, sir?" Honor enquired.

"Hmm? Oh, nanobots, Honor. Tiny, cell-sized, single-function robots: a veritable army of them. They go to work cleaning my liver."

"Amazing. How often do you…?"

"Oh, a few doses over the next six weeks. I have an unhappy liver, so Secta arranged a little housekeeping."

"Secta is your doctor then?"

"No, he built the nanobots. A brilliant man, our Secta. His inventions will make our country, and himself, very rich indeed. Not really someone susceptible to treason, Honor," he added, sharply, aware that Honor had interrogated both Secta and Hope under the charge. He took his coffee, and dunked a biscuit. He continued with his mouth full, "Do try a biscuit, Senior Inspector," he said. "They really are fantastic."

She couldn't stop herself. "Did Secta invent zese as vell as ze nanobots and ze programmable wallpaper?"

"Ha! That's funny, Honor," the man laughed. "I didn't realise you had a sense of humour. Aha! Indeed. Now," he said, as his smile switched off like a lamp. "To the matter at hand. What is the status of your operation? I have just been informed that you have requested further funds. I assumed the mission was over, now that Black Alice has gone. So why the need for funds?"

"Sir," she said, trying to show only absolute confidence, "I haff made a judgment call viz regard to Black Alice. It could be regarded as rash, but I zink in your visdom, you vill recognise ze incredible potential." The President's enormous eyebrows raised a fraction. "Do go on, Senior Inspector," he rumbled. "Do, please go on…"

On the bridge of the ferry, Secta turned to Hope and lifted his goggles. "It worked!" he screamed above the cacophony. His eyes were wide with excitement. He and Hope hugged, both of them thrilled to the core. The scientist held his sister at arm's length and looked seriously into her eyes.

"So, I guess this is the scary bit," he said. "I'm not looking forward to being de-molecularized. Tell me, why I am doing this again?"

She folded her arms and glared at him. "A number of reasons, dear brother," she said. "Firstly, you owe it to Alice for saving your life. Second, you created his condition in the first place. And third, because you want the experiment to succeed — you do want that Nobel prize, don't you?"

"Well yes, of course," he said. "But becoming a god particle in the process? That I'm not convinced, although, of course, it does seem somehow appropriate."

Hope grinned. "Sounds like a landslide in favour of going then."

A look of manic glee lit his eyes. "You know me so well," he agreed.

CHAPTER 12
THE REBEL STRONGHOLD

RENO PLACED A pot of hot coffee, cups, a jug of milk and some sweeteners on a table and announced, tunefully: "Wakey! Wakey! Rise and shine, get out of bed ... it's breakfast time!"

Unimpressed by his early morning lyricism, a chorus of groans, curses and epithets erupted from the newly-roused figures scattered around the room. Jonno appeared from the rear of the premises carrying a tray stacked with toast, a tub of butter, and a giant jar of Promite.

"Come on fellers, this'll put hair on your bums!" he roared. "You too Nerdo, although I'm sure your bum is fine as it is. I didn't know you could still get this stuff!" he added, delightedly.

"You old fox, that's my secret stash of Promite!" yelled Reno, jovially. "You absolutely can't get that any more, man. I traded a vibrator and a Led Zeppelin chip for that last year."

"Which album?" Jonno asked.

"Zep four."

"Man, 'Stairway to Heaven'? You was robbed!" Jonno moaned.

"That was Zep three," Mad Dog growled, as he rolled off the edge of the three-legged pool table and battled to stay upright.

"Nup, three was 'Immigrant Song'," Reno said.

"He's right, Mad Dog," Jonno allowed. "Has Turk come back to us yet?"

Reno went over to Turk, who was laid out in a cubicle, and gave him a nudge. "Turk?" he said, carefully. "You with us?"

"Careful doing that, man!" warned Jonno through a mouthful of toast. "He might clout you."

Reno heeded Jonno's caution and leaned back as Turk, sprawled across the cubicle table, stirred. Reno carefully stretched out an arm and gave him another, gentler nudge. "Turk!" he said, softly. "You with us?"

Then, as though someone had flicked a switch, Turk raised his head from the table and glared at Reno through one squinted eye. "What happened?" he croaked. "Thought I'd be able to sing?"

"That was hours ago my friend," Jonno scoffed. "You've been out cold. Come and get some caffeine and holy-ghost into ya."

"You all right?" Reno asked, genuinely concerned. "I think you had a bad reaction to the iWish."

Turk felt for the plug in the back of his head.

"I took it out," Reno said. "You scared the crap out of us. Told us you were Black Alice."

"That's the bloke who sang the song we uploaded for you," Jonno said.

"Wires must've got crossed," Reno laughed. "You didn't learn the song — you learned the singer!"

Turk poured himself a stiff black coffee, shaking his head.

"I remember Black Alice and that song," he managed. "Didn't something weird happen to that bloke?"

"Yeah," said Jonno, spraying crumbs. "Legend has it he just disappeared; vanished into thin air off the deck of a boat or something."

Pouring himself a coffee, Cutter hummed the theme to The Twilight Zone. "That's serious Rod Serling stuff," he said.

"What are you, like 300 years old?" teased Nerdo. Their bickering was interrupted when Tatts walked into the bar, alone. He stopped and eyeballed Reno. Everybody froze, not sure what to expect.

"I want in," the boy said brazenly.

Turk, Jonno and Reno exchanged looks.

"Sorry son," said Turk, casually. "You don't have the skills."

Tatts glared at Turk like he'd been slapped with a dead fish. "I know how to find the Rebels' camp," he said, defiantly. "Look, they've got my chick. Let me in or I go on my ace."

"Look, Tatts, I don't want to risk any more lives than I have to," said Turk. "We've already lost too many."

Tatts nodded sharply, then looked behind him and called out: "Debbie!"

A cute but rough-looking teenage girl entered, a baby nestling in her arms.

"This is my girl's sister," said Tatts. "Baby's mine. Rebels took her mother."

Turk stared at the sad little threesome for a long while. He'd as good as lost the one person left in the world who meant the most to him, and he had no doubt there were worse things than death. He knew how the lad felt. Jonno and Reno watched him intensely. They all understood the boy's feelings, and they couldn't help but respect him for having the guts to stand his ground. Finally, Turk spoke.

"Pour yourself a coffee, Tatts, and grab a round of toast. You'll be needing the sustenance." He cracked a smile. "And get that baby outta here!"

Tatts grinned. Now they were seven.

Alice is pacing the floor of the netherworld.

En-Ki's voice discharged from the orb. "These men have a serious fight on their hands. Even though it seems like vengeance, it has a greater purpose, does it not? This marks the beginning of a partnership between you and Turk in a far greater battle than you could ever have imagined at the time."

Alice paused his pacing and thought that over. Turned and faced the orb, its bright glow illuminating his face. "Yep, a top bloke Turk, a helluva warrior."

Light flashed in Alice's mind.

It would need military precision to take on the Rebels, and the team was satisfied Turk was the right man for the job. Jonno had repaired the pool table — it was now back on four legs and functioning as the planning table. Sitting under the low-hanging light, they listened to Turk's plan. Empty beer bottles on the table represented locations.

"Tatts, you'll guide Cutter and me to a recce of the Rebels' stronghold," said Turk. "Once we've got the layout, we'll come back here to devise our attack strategy. Nerdo, you've got the comms gig."

"Fine," she said. "I'll get started building." She went to the front desk, now littered with the gadgets and wires she'd collected. The rest of them stayed seated.

"Hey, Reno!" Nerdo hollered across the room, "Can I butcher your iWish unit for parts?"

"No way, man!" he replied. "You've already cannibalised everything else in the joint — you even nicked the guts out of me old credit-swipe!"

Nerdo wandered back over, carrying a bunch of electronic junk in her arms. "I've already built these miniature camera sets, fitted with night glasses," she said. I made them up from Turk's, Reno's and Jonno's sunnies."

"Hey, I only loaned you those sunnies!" said Turk, tongue in cheek. "I didn't say you could bugger them up!"

Nerdo threw her hands up in surrender. "Hey, a girl can only use what's at her disposal," she said.

"It's a wonder you haven't attacked my Handcom," Reno mumbled.

Her eyes lit up. "Is it a terabyte model or—"

"3T," Reno grinned, proud of his techno-bling.

"Cool, that's exactly what I need," she said. "It would let you guys transmit digital pictures back to HQ. And I'd be able to transmit a heads-up display back to you in the field. Bu-uuuuut—"

"Yeah, right ... something's missing, right?" Reno said.

"It won't work without a fast enough processor," she replied. "Faster than this, anyway." She dug into one of her deep pockets and produced a microprocessor, waving it at them with sad puppy-dog eyes.

"Okay, okay," said Reno. "You can have the handcom. Just leave my iWish alone."

A few hours later, the roof of Reno's bar had sprouted a parabolic reflector made from an old metal rubbish bin lid and a few dozen yards of wire.

Inside, Nerdo and the others were gathered around three monitors set up on the front desk. With her fingers on the keyboard that was all that remained of Reno's 3T-Handcom miniature computer, she spoke while she poked at the keys. "I've hacked into an old com-sat to set up an audio-visual link," she explained. "There."

Three monitors came online, displaying pictures and audio from the guys in the field. Nerdo plastered a label on each one, counting them off.

"One is Turk, two is Cutter, three's Tatts."

"Clever girl," Jonno grinned at Reno. "Told ya she's a fricking genius."

"Only because she used all my good stuff," Reno moaned in mock pain. "Probably all bloody useless now."

Nerdo looked up from the screens, "I can get the swipe working again if you need it," she laughed.

"Yeah, right," Reno whined. "Fat lot of good that'd do — even if credit cards were still a thing, there's no bloody customers to swipe!"

After driving along a bush track for an hour, Turk parked the F-200 near the Rebels' stronghold. He, Tatts and Cutter moved in on foot for a closer look-see. They were as close as they could get without being detected. Time to check the extent of the Rebels' security.

On first inspection, it looked to Turk like an impregnable fortress — it was clear that Duke was no mug when it came to strategy. Concealed in the bushes, a hundred metres from the big double wooden front gates, Turk described the set-up to HQ.

"What you can see is a six-metre rampart," he whispered. "It's like a bloody castle, got everything but a moat. Sentries in towers on either side of the gates. CCTV about every twenty metres along the bulwark. I'm guessing, but I reckon the front gates are the only way in."

Turk's observations were drowned out by the sound of approaching bikes. Looking sharply over his shoulder, he saw headlights cutting the night sky. "We've got incoming," he continued, unperturbed.

Six choppers drew up to the gates, where they idled like a pack of hungry wolves in front of their lair.

Turk turned to Cutter and Tatts. "Here's our chance," he whispered. "Let's go!"

The three men moved like greased lightning, covered by the dust screen the bikes had stirred up from the dirt road. On Turk's signal, they stopped with their backs to the wall beside the gates, out of reach of the overhead cameras. They waited for the gates to open.

Turk whispered into his mike, "They must be getting clearance to enter. Security's tight."

The gates swung open and the bikes thundered inside. All of a sudden Tatts took off, making a run for it.

"Tatts, no!" Turk called after him.

But the boy ignored him, slowing just enough to throw a thumbs-up as he slipped through the gates before they closed.

Turk and Cutter had no option but to retreat, and fast.

Later, back at the bar, they found everyone gloomy.

"Aw, shit," said Cutter. "Tatts?"

"I recorded his camera," said Nerdo, disconsolately. "You should probably check it out."

Jonno handed out beers, and they sat in front of the monitor designated to Tatts. Nerdo hit play. On screen, the camera was looking through a window. Tatts' voice was whispering: "This must be the main dormitory. It's too dark to see any — Wait!" A door opened on one side, and a scantily clad girl was led into the room on a leash.

"That's Julie!" Tatts' voice erupted.

"Oh no," Turk groaned, "his girl."

Unable to contain his fury, Tatts dived through the window and attacked the biker holding the lead. The signal went static.

"Damn you son!" Turk bellowed.

"Wait, Turk," said Mad Dog, glumly. "There's more."

Nerdo spoke up. "They took the camera off him. We get picture back in a few seconds."

The screen sputtered back into life, showing Tatts, gagged and bound to a chair facing the camera. His face carried the signs of a heavy beating.

"They've set the shot up for maximum effect," Reno said, venomously.

There was a vacant chair beside Tatts. A shadowy figure moved between the camera and the object, and sat in it. Before it became obvious to Cutter, Turk growled: "Duke."

Duke raised his head and looked at the camera, delight shining in his cold dark eyes. "G'day!" he said, cheerfully. "So, you thought you could send this little clown in to spy on me, eh?" He sat back in the chair, crossed his legs, struck a match and lit his stogie. Checking it was alight, he continued. "He says his name is Tatts, which stands to reason 'coz he's covered in 'em." He looked at Tatts and blew cigar smoke in his face. "Not the first time we've met is it, son? Make you feel tough, having tattoos? Hmm?" He grabbed Tatts by the chin and forced the boy to face him. "What's the matter, sonny, cat got your tongue?" he snarled. "Oh, no wait!" he said, opening his hand to the camera to show a bloody lump in his palm. "I've got it!"

"Bastard!" Jonno howled through clenched teeth.

Duke removed the gag from Tatts' mouth.

Blood gushed out as Tatts' coughed, spluttered, and retched.

"Spunk, come here!" called Duke, and a white pit bull came into shot. "Sit!" he ordered, and the dog obeyed. "Here," he said, throwing the bloody piece of flesh to the dog. "Have a tongue." The dog snatched it out of the air, downed it in one gulp. Duke leaned close to the camera, sporting an evil grin. "Hmm, yummy!" he said.

"Now, I don't know who you are. Tatts wouldn't say. Tough little bugger, I'll give him that. So, I took away any chance he had of saying anything. And now here's the deal.

"Give yourselves up by midday tomorrow or I'll go live, feeding more chunks of your chum to man's best friend here. I might carve his off tattoos one by one, depends how hungry Spunk gets.

"Got that?" he said, leaning even further in. "Midday tomorrow. Oh, and just to show I mean business…" he produced a knife, gripped Tatts by the hair and then hacked off his left ear before throwing it to the dog. Tatts hung almost motionless, nearly unconscious from agony as Duke laughed at the camera. The signal cut to static, but Duke's laugh continued resonating through Turk's mind. He'd heard it before, while he was rolling on the ground, kicking and screaming, his body ablaze.

"So that's the enemy," snarled Mad Dog. "One mean mother."

"He won't be mean much longer," Turk said in a tone that brooked no contradiction.

"So we hit 'em tomorrow?" Cutter asked.

The question was followed by a deathly silence.

"No," said Turk, eventually. "We'd be at a disadvantage. They're expecting us."

"What about Tatts?" Nerdo said.

"There's nothing we can do for him now," sighed Turk. "We can't let it distract us."

"Wait — Duke doesn't know who he's up against, does he, Tatts didn't talk?" said Nerdo. "All he knows is that we're using surveillance gear. We could just be folk from Snake, wanting their women back."

"How does he know anyone was watching?" Jonno wondered.

"He doesn't," said Mad Dog. "He's only guessing. Hoping someone will turn up tomorrow."

Turk stood. "Not likely," he said. "I know his kind. He doesn't expect anyone to turn up."

"So he's bluffing?" Cutter asked, hopefully.

"No," said Turk. "He'll torture Tatts alright. He's just making sure he'll get no more unexpected visitors."

"Right," Reno agreed.

"So we go in tomorrow night," said Turk. "That's our best chance. Cutter, you've got 'til then to armour Betsy up, and scrounge whatever you and Nerdo can stick together as attack vehicles.

"Mad Dog, go with Reno and dig up all the guns and ammo in Snake. Jonno, let's work on tactics. We're gonna need them."

CHAPTER 13
INSURANCE

HONOR WAS READY to leave the office for the day. She'd already collected her coat, but was waiting for Karzoff. He'd called earlier to say he had important news that could only be relayed face to face. She wondered if he was feeling under the weather as well. Who was it, she wondered idly, who had said if the day begins with a hangover, it can only improve? They were totally wrong, anyway. She was feeling done in.

In fact, Honor rarely drank, but on this occasion, she'd felt a celebration was in order. She'd pulled off a coup with the President, and her future looked pretty golden. Besides, the pub did a decent champagne, and she was partial to a drop of fizz now and then. Karzoff had seemed much more wobbly than her when they'd rolled out of the Fortune of War pub at the Rocks at two in the morning. Her brow furrowed for a moment. Did I walk home alone?

Karzoff entered, flustered from hurrying. "I, I am sorry for being late," he puffed. "It is just this: I have been informed that I am off the case!"

"Zat cannot be," said Honor. "Ze President knows you are vital to zis mission. It has been given priority. Ein moment—" She placed an implant call.

"Miss Vallins, zis is Senior Inspector Honor," she said. "I haff been informed zat Karzoff has been taken from … Oh? I see … It is

just zat as the senior officer, I zought I vould haff been informed …
I see. In zat case I fully understand … Zank you."

She disconnected and focused on Karzoff. "It is a subterfuge,"
she said. "Merely a pretence, to distance you from ze operation. A
direct order from ze President."

"But … I don't understand," he quavered. "Why?"

"Come," said Honor. "Valk me home, ve can talk on ze way. But
first — you haff news?"

"Oh, yes!" said Karzoff, eyes shining. "Yes — Secta has reported
a breakthrough!"

"Really? Tell me!" she urged, excited.

"Secta and Hope are back at their lab. They've found Alice's
signature. They know where he is!"

"Zat … Zat is excellent news!" she said, fervently. "So vhat comes
next?"

But the elevator doors had opened, revealing a packed interior.
Honor and Karzoff managed to squeeze in, much to the disgust, of
the other occupants. Silence prevailed — further explanations would
have to wait three floors. Honor was almost bursting by the time the
doors re-opened at ground level and the passengers filed out,
shuffling through the metal detector queue at the exit. Once through
and onto the heavy pedestrian traffic on Bridge Street, she felt it was
safe to continue. She turned to Karzoff, eyebrows raised.

"Secta is now preparing the de-molecularizer unit for his own
transport," he said. "Then he will need to have all his equipment
moved to a safe house."

"So, he can use it to return, yes?"

Karzoff nodded.

"And haff you found a safe house?"

"No," he said. "That's what I was doing when I was told I was off
the case."

"Vhat about ze hand device he wanted? Ze vun zat vill detect ze
dissident ven Secta gets zere?"

"The ILDD," said Karzoff. "It has been delivered and tested. Secta thinks it will work just fine."

"Good," said Honor.

"Under the circumstances, perhaps you should visit Secta as soon as possible?" suggested Karzoff. "If I can no longer—"

"You are not off ze case, Karzoff," she interrupted. You are now merely undercover. Your mission continues — you vill observe from a distance, and once Secta departs, you vill abduct Hope and detain her. This vill be outside of protocol, you understand? It vill ensure Secta hands Alice over ven he returns."

A huge grin broke on his usually comical face. "Yes," he said excitedly. "Yes, I understand. I will need to keep her drugged and tied up?"

"Yes, dear toad," Honor crooned. "But remember ze President does not vant to offend Secta. So, keep the abduction under wraps until the good doctor returns. Zis is important. Ze President specifically requested zat his most trusted agent should take charge of zis mission."

"And I am he," Karzoff said, proudly.

The thought of Hope being his hostage, totally at his mercy, was a warm and welcome bonus to his deviant mind.

"Exactly," Honor agreed. "Now, I vill tell Secta you are off ze case, and in ze meantime, you find a good place to keep her." They stopped walking, having reached her apartment block on Macquarie Street. "Somewhere nearby, private and comfortable … for you, of course."

She knew perfectly well what Karzoff would have in mind for Hope, and privately she relished the thought. If there was anyone she wished to see mistreated, it was Hope — for deserting Oceana in favour of the Octagon, for helping Alice escape, for thwarting her plans repeatedly. Once someone made an enemy of Honor, it was etched in stone.

"I will see to it immediately," Karzoff said eagerly. As Honor was about to enter her building, Karzoff stopped her and said, earnestly:

"You would not exclude me from the fortunes made on this case, would you Honor?"

She fixed her eyes on him. "Vhat makes you zink I would do zat, dear toad?"

"Like you say, Honor, it is good to have insurance. I'm just seeking a little of that."

Hope was mixing the green fluid that would be injected into Secta as a major component of the de-molecularization process.

"Once you've gone through this, you'll be no different from Alice," she said. "You'll only have a certain amount of time in any one dimension before you begin to destabilise."

Secta swivelled on his chair, smiling smugly. "I've stabilized the dose far more than the one I gave Alice," he said. "So that simply won't happen, Hope."

"And if you turn up in another person?" she asked.

"I won't."

"Why not?"

"Because little sister, I aim to appear exactly where I departed," he said, strolling to the chair he'd used to dispatch Alice. "Right here," he said, patting the seat. "I'll be de-molecularized right here, and appear right here in the future, no matter where the wormhole is opened."

"That's pretty clever," she said.

"Maybe, Hope. There's still some guesswork involved. I'd like more time."

"Unfortunately, that luxury isn't on tap," she said, rolling her eyes.

He filled the syringe with the green fluid, and then squirted it experimentally. "Good," he said. "Now I need to inject this into your armpit."

"My armpit?" she said, confused. "Like hell! What for? I'm not going anywhere!"

"This, Hope, contains a DNA marker like the one I gave Alice. With it I will be able to locate you when I return."

"Why will you need to find me?"

"Because they will probably kidnap you to ensure I turn Alice over. Call it insurance."

"And what's to stop them destroying the equipment in your absence, if they decide they don't want you back?"

"Oh, they might threaten that, but they want Alice," he said. "He's their ticket to ride, remember? Alice is the experiment. And besides, I'm the President's favourite son, remember?"

"Yes," she sighed. "You're probably right. So, I'm going to be kidnapped? You're basing this on your knowledge of their standard MO, of course."

"Indubitably Hope. They are nothing if not predictable," he replied. "And ... let's just say I have my sources," he grinned over at her.

"Okay," she groaned, raising an arm. "Shoot me up now, before I change my mind."

"Right, then you can do me. I replicated two isotopic detection devices based on the one we 'borrowed'. They'll work just fine — we just calibrate them to our isotopic signatures. Yours is 355, mine is 477. He jabbed the needle into her soft underarm.

"Ouch!" snapped Hope. "Jeez, take it easy with that thing." She stepped back, holding her sore flesh. "It's all very well knowing what's coming," she said. "But I think I'd better set a few traps of my own."

When Honor entered her apartment, she felt a sudden chill — a presence — somebody was there! She flicked the light switch but nothing happened. Out of the darkness swooped an arm that wound around her neck from behind. She felt the cold, razor-sharp edge of a blade pressed against her throat.

"Disconnect your implant or I'll cut you," growled her assailant.

"Okay! Okay! Just take it easy!" she appealed. "I need ze terminator remote to do zat. It is in my desk."

"Fine. Lead me there. One false move and I'll slice you from ear to ear. You hear me?"

"Absolutely!" she gasped.

She led her assailant into the drawing room, opened the desk drawer, took out a small remote and held it for him to see.

"Zis is it," she said. "I just need to press this button—"

"Wait! Once you terminate, how long before the troopers arrive?"

"I do not know," she said. He tightened his grip and pressed the blade a little harder against her throat. It drew a trickle of blood.

"How long?" he growled, angrily.

"A … About fifteen minutes," she stammered.

"Don't terminate it. Just pause operation."

"Okay! Okay! I just haff to input ze code!"

"What code?"

"Ze code to pause ze connection."

"You know what?" he said, "I don't trust you. Just drop the remote on the floor." She complied. "Now sit in that chair. Do anything I don't like, I'll kill you."

Complying with his demands gave Honor the chance to look her captor over. Dressed in black with a balaclava covering his face, he was tall, well built, she'd guess mid to late twenties. A shiver went down her spine.

"Are you going to torture me?" she asked.

"Hell, lady," he said. "What's with you?"

"No rape or robbery?"

"No."

"Zen vhat? Who are you?" she hissed.

"Look, just shut up. You're not in a position to ask questions. I'm here to deliver a message." He produced a slip of paper and thrust it at her. "Here," he said. "This is where to take Hope once Secta has gone."

She laughed once, scornfully. "And vhy should I do zat?"

"Because I know where you live. I know where you work. And I'm very good at tracking. So, do as I say or I'll hunt you down and slit your throat … You get that, Honor?"

"You are ze Octagon!" she growled.

"Got one thing right," he said, nodding grimly. "Alice travelling in time should benefit all humanity. And we want him back. So, the experiment must succeed."

"Vhat has Hope to do with zat? Vhy is she so important?"

"She can run the experiment."

"Ah, I see. Of course — you do not trust Secta."

"He doesn't have a reputation worth trusting … besides, he's on your side." As he spoke, he lifted a lamp from a nearby table and used the cord to bind Honor to her chair. That done, Mal Function sheathed his knife and slipped from the apartment as deftly as he had arrived.

Secta and Hope were calibrating their equipment when the door servo sounded and Honor strode in. "Gut morning," she snapped. "I understand you are almost ready to initiate proceedings."

"Nothing like a few morning pleasantries, a little small talk," muttered Secta. "But since you insist, Honor, no, I wouldn't quite put it like that. Once our equipment has been transported and installed at the safe house, however, yes, we can launch."

"Ah, ve refer to it as a 'launch'? Gut," she said. "I vill use ze correct vernacular."

"Takes a little more than that to be a scientist, Honor," Hope said, spitefully.

"Save your pettiness for ze playground, Hope," snarled Honor. "Vhen I require your opinion, I vill ask."

"Now, now, ladies, that's enough," said Secta. "Honor, if you would be so good as to expedite the transportation and installation of the necessary equipment, that would speed our preparations here," he added.

"Ve haff in fact arranged a suitable safe house," she said, smugly. "It is south of Sydney, in Avalon. Do you know ze place?"

"I've heard of it, yes," Secta replied. "Why there? It's a long way away."

"It is a decommissioned nuclear fallout shelter, perfect for your needs. It vill not matter if you go hundreds of years into ze future, it vill still be zere."

"Ah, I see," said Secta. "That does sound perfect, actually. Have you secured a nuclear power source?"

"It is being installed as ve speak. All ze equipment on your list vill be sent in by chopper as soon as you give ze go signal."

"And us?" Hope asked, sourly.

"Ze same goes for you, Hope. As soon as you are ready, you vill both be flown zere."

"And after Secta has departed? Will I be returned?"

"Vhat is worrying you, Hope?" she asked, smiling like a croc watching a baby buffalo wobble down to drink. Her encounter of the previous night didn't mean she couldn't have a little fun. "Do you not trust us? Naturally, we shall return you immediately. Ze chopper vill be vaiting for you."

"And your little sidekick, Honor?" asked Secta. "What's happened to him? I find I rather miss him," asked Secta, sarcasm rolling off his tongue.

"Oh, he is of no further concern to you," she said, dismissively. "He is officially off ze case. Now. I vill be on my way." She turned and headed back to the door. "Call me ven you are ready," she added as the servos hummed and she walked through.

Hope watched her leave. "There is nothing in this world that would make me believe anything that comes out of that bitch's gob," she said, eyes narrowed.

"A truer statement has never come out of your delightful gob, dear sister. Now, let's finish up here. I've built up enough courage to do this thing. So we'd better get rolling before I suddenly recover my senses."

CHAPTER 14
PROMISE OF THINGS

THE SOUND OF motorbikes woke Turk. He snapped into defence mode. "Wake up!" he yelled. "Come on! We have company!"

Moving quickly, he peered from the front window of Reno's bar onto the street.

"Four Rebels!" he hissed to the team. "You know what to do. Let's move."

He looked back and recognised the Rebel who had cut Nora's face. "Spike," he mouthed, as vivid memories flooded back. A look like thunder on his face, he snapped his seven-cartridge pump-action sawn-off shotgun shut and nodded at Jonno, who cocked his Glock 17 in response, ready for action. Reno palmed a clip into his Hesse carbon fibre AR pistol. Without a word, command active, Cutter, Nerdo and Mad Dog slipped silently out the back door.

The four Rebels were standing next to their Harleys outside Voodoo, talking, when Turk appeared at the front of Reno's Bar. They immediately braced for action, but before they could make a single move Turk propped, raised his shotgun, and pumped half a dozen shells into their bikes, drilling holes in three of the gas tanks. The bikers spun, watching the precious gas spraying from the punctured choppers. Leaving one Harley unscathed, Turk swung the gun on the Rebels. They'd drawn their weapons, ready to respond, but had been stopped dead when Jonno and Reno stepped from the bar and opened fire at their feet. Now, under three guns, three of them dropped their weapons and raised their hands. Not Spike. He kept his sawn-off steadily trained on Turk.

"On the deck with your hands behind your heads! Now!" commanded Jonno. Three obeyed.

Still Spike stood resolute. "No frickin' way," he said with a growl, and shucked his shotgun. From behind a hunting knife appeared at his throat. Mad Dog had slipped up back of him. The huge man now hauled the biker backwards and the shotgun fired impotently into the air as he thudded down onto the road. His head smacked the bitumen with a crack. Mad Dog stood over him and kicked the shotgun away from of his hands. He leaned down, pinned his knife under Spike's chin and grumbled, with murderous intent: "On your knees, scumbag, or I'll stick you like a pig."

Knowing he was done, Spike did exactly as he was told.

Three of the Rebels were lined up on the floor of the bar with their backs to the wall, gagged and hogtied. Turk was fastening Spike spread-eagled to the pool table. "Not so tough now, are you Spike?" he spat as he fastened the last of the cords with a vicious jerk.

"How d'you know me name?" Spike, still defiant, spat the question, struggling against the restraints.

Turk drew a flick knife and an oilstone from a pocket in his khakis. Leaning against the table, he stroked the blade on the stone, honing the cutting edge. Reno, Jonno and Mad Dog were seated in a cubicle, sipping beers and watching the show.

The sound of the knife being whetted was clearly having an effect on Spike's bravado. "What are you gonna do with that," he asked, trying to sound contemptuous. "Give me a shave?" The patina of sweat breaking out on his face showed his nerves.

Turk tested the edge of his blade on his thumb. Satisfied, he slipped the oilstone back into its pocket, grabbed the belt holding up Spike's leather pants and cut it through. The two halves of the thick leather sheared apart like they were made of butter.

"What's this?" Spike growled.

"I made you and your friends a promise," Turk said, quietly. "After you beat my sixteen-year-old sister into a vegetable. Remember that?"

"Dunno," Spike spat.

Turk nodded. "Well, maybe you remember Duke dousing me with gas and flicking me a lighted match?" He leaned closer. "And maybe you remember me yelling what I'd do if and when I run you down. Hmm?"

"Sure," said Spike, swallowing. "Yeah, I guess that rings a bell. But hey … you wouldn't really do that to a bloke. Would ya?'

Cutter and Nerdo were out back, working, the screams of Turk's victims providing a grisly soundtrack. They were fitting the final section of armour cladding to Betsy. "Sounds like they're having one heck of a time in there," Cutter joked.

On her knees on the ground, Nerdo welded the panel Cutter was holding in place. She lifted the visor of her improvised welding helmet — kindly donated by one of the captured bikers — extinguished the oxy, and sat back, looking at Cutter.

"Yeah," she said, and stood up. "We're done here," she added. The screams ceased as she spoke. She nodded at Reno's. "Sounds like Turk's done too." Walking to the shade of the porch, she squatted, removed the helmet and wiped the perspiration from her face. Cutter saw her face as though for the first time — devoid of sweetness or gentleness, but attractive with its sharp bone structure, big eyes, thin spare mouth and slightly pointed chin.

It wasn't a youthful face — it lacked the soft curves of cheek and temple belonging to youth. Maybe that softness had been planed away by the harshness of life. Lines caused by weather and the savagery of war were etched around her eyes, but they added to the straightforward, clean intelligence of her face, pure in its harshness. Suddenly Cutter felt conscious. He was invading something private, something personal. He took a step back and switched his attention to Betsy. With a dozen or so metal spikes welded at the front, and a strong coat of steel all round, she was looking awesome.

"Now that's a truck!" Cutter exclaimed, proud of their work. "Talk about a weapon of mass destruction!" He proudly patted the rusty armour panel they had just fitted. "Betsy, the Truck of Doom."

Nerdo nodded at the huge, spiked bull bar. "That'll take out those bloody doors," she said, then grinned. "Hey, I saw a few cans of black spray-paint in the garage," she said. Should we give her a coat? Make her look even more wicked?"

"Let's do it!" Cutter replied, enthusiastically.

They were just about to move when Turk came out of the back door and knelt next to the tap to rinse his knife and blood-drenched hands.

Nerdo and Cutter watched him, carefully.

Turk looked up. "Nice job," he said casually, glancing at Betsy.

The two comrades wondered at his cool.

"Thanks," said Cutter, a little uncertainly. "You all done in there?"

"Yeah," Turk didn't grin. It might have been better if he had. "What's next?" Turk asked, pulling off his shirt and holding it under the tap. Crimson water cascaded to the ground.

"Ah, thinkin' of sticking a gun turret in Betsy's sunroof," said Cutter. "What do you reckon, boss?"

"And we're gonna give her a coat of black paint," Nerdo added. "Make her look—"

"The turret, yeah, good idea," Turk cut in. "Elbow the paint job. We've got better things to do than tart her up." He stood up, wringing out his shirt, his musculature something to be admired. "What we got to use in this turret?"

"Mad Dog's got an antique AK-47," said Cutter. "Maybe we can convince him to donate it."

"Give him the gunner gig," said Turk. "Then he can take it with him."

"Hell!" Cutter declared. "We're gonna need a bigger chair, Dog's got a butt the size of Tasmania!" Laughing, they headed to the back door of Reno's. Just as they reached it, Turk stumbled. Cutter turned and grabbed him by the arm to stop him falling.

"You all right?" he said, slowly lowering Turk to the ground. But Turk just collapsed onto the gravel, eyes closed. Then he started convulsing.

"Damn!" said Nerdo, "He's having a seizure! Quick, turn him on his side. And get him something to bite down on." She prized open one of his eyes. "Oh hell," she added, "They're right back in his head. Move!"

Cutter ran into Reno's for help. Suddenly uncharacteristically feminine, Nerdo tenderly stroked the unconscious man's face. All at once, he stopped convulsing and his eyes opened wide. The look on his face startled Nerdo, and she flinched — there was something unfamiliar about him.

He pushed her aside and sat up sharply, glaring at her. "What the stuff's going on here?" he snapped. That wasn't Turk's voice. It didn't sound anything like the man she knew. She didn't frighten easily, but this was weird. Tentatively, she tried to placate him.

"Take it easy, Turk," she said. "You've had a seizure. Probably brought on by all the excitement."

"Turk? Who the hell's Turk?"

If she hadn't been looking at the man, she wouldn't have believed it was Turk speaking.

"I'm Alice," he went on. "Now help me up, dude, and tell me where I am."

Nerdo helped him to his feet, but as he straightened up his knees gave way. Nerdo grabbed him round the waist, but he was a big man, and her own knees were starting to buckle. He looked round at her.

"Hey, you're a chick!" he said, and his eyes rolled back again.

Just then, Jonno and Reno came rushing out.

Realising Nerdo was losing her grip, Jonno took Turk's weight. "Got him, Nerdo," he said. "It's cool, you can let him go."

Nerdo stood back, trembling. "Stuff!" she said. "That was weird!"

Jonno propped Turk against the wall. "He's out cold," he said.

"What was weird?" Reno asked her.

"That — there's no way that was Turk's voice," she said, shivering.

Jonno stood up. "Reckon it's a side effect from iWish?" he asked.

Reno did what Nerdo had done, and prized open one of Turk's closed lids. He peered in. "Looks like what Cutter said," he replied. "Seizure. Might be related to iWish, I guess..."

"I don't think so..." said Nerdo. "I'm telling you. That wasn't Turk."

They all turned to look at the unconscious man.

"Well, whoever her is, we'd better get him inside," said Reno.

Nerdo was sitting at her comms set-up at the front desk, cleaning under her fingernails with a Swiss army knife. Suddenly, one of the TV monitors flickered on. She swivelled the chair sharply to face the others. "Reno! Jonno!" she called, urgently. "We've got an incoming signal — here, quick!"

The two men rushed over. Nerdo's focus was fixed on the monitor marked Tatts.

CHAPTER 15
GOD PARTICLE

HOPE GAZED OUT of the window of the Eurocopter AS350 at the clouds below. Secta was seated beside her, eyes tightly closed.

"Are you asleep?" she said, smirking, well aware of his phobias.

"No," he said, brusquely.

"Does keeping your eyes shut reduce the vertigo?" she asked.

In spite of himself, he opened one eye and looked at her from under an arched eyebrow. "Acrophobia," he said.

"What?"

"Acrophobia, Hope, is the fear of heights. Vertigo is not a fear of heights. Vertigo is the sensation that one is spinning when one is not."

"Is that right?" she said, enjoying his discomfiture. "So, I've been using that word wrong all my life? Not that I've used it much, mind you."

"I guess you have," he said, closing his eye again.

The pitch of the helicopter engines changed, declaring it was about to begin its descent. The sudden change frightened Secta, who moved sharply to brace himself in his seat, white knuckled. The chopper hit a pocket of turbulence, and Secta's hand shot out and grabbed Hope's knee.

"Geez, Secta!" she yelped. "You just about gave me a heart attack! Settle down, would you? There's nothing to worry about…"

The pilot chose that exact moment to look back at them. "It's gonna be a bit bumpy," he said. "Gotta get her down through this soup."

Both of Secta's eyes opened wide. "Soup?" he said. "Soup? What are we talking about here? A light consommé or something with lumps in it?"

"Relax, Secta, it'll be all right," said Hope, glaring at the back of the pilot's neck. "The man knows what he's doing, alright? I'm sure he's done this dozens of times before."

"That's what I say when I'm completely stumped, Hope," he said, refusing to be cheered. "Don't worry, I know what I'm doing!"

He risked a glance out of the window, but there was so much cloud that down looked just like up. He shut his eyes tight. "If I was religious I'd pray," he mumbled.

"Well, you believe in the god particle," said Hope. "Pray to that."

The chopper dropped into the cloud and torrential rain pounded the windows. Wind gusts knocked them about and lightning flashed purple against the blue-back background that consumed them. It was like being in the belly of a whale, if whales had thunderstorms in their bellies. Secta was pretty sure there was one happening in his, so who was to say they didn't? The chopper bumped and thumped from air pocket to air pocket, the wind trying its elemental best to unnerve Secta. It succeeded.

"Remind me again that all this punishment I am putting myself through is for a worthy cause..." he groaned.

Hope leaned over and mouthed 'Nobel Priiiize'... By the time they dropped into clear air at about three thousand feet, Secta's face was blanched, bloodless and deathlike.

Soupy descent over, the chopper gently set down on a concrete helipad in the middle of an otherwise apparently empty field. After flicking a series of overhead switches, the pilot removed his helmet and turned to his passengers. "So sorry for the bumpy ride," he said in private schoolboy tones. "I've been ordered to wait here until you're ready to leave, Dr Hope. Agent Honor is awaiting you both below."

Secta peered out the window at nothing but a field, surrounded by distant forest.

Mystified, he asked: "Much as I hate to appear thick, where exactly would below be? This is just a cow paddock!"

"Gosh, ever so sorry," the pilot said. He picked up his helmet and spoke some gobbledygook into the microphone.

Hope looked from the window. "Well, look at that," she said. A slab of turf had opened about ten metres from the helipad.

"That's the bunker entrance," said the pilot.

Secta couldn't get out of the chopper quick enough. Hope stayed a few seconds longer to thank the handsome pilot.

Secta found a descending staircase at the entrance. He waited for Hope, then proceeded with her down a dozen concrete stairs to a small landing facing a closed elevator door. Secta pressed the call button and the door opened. There was only room inside for three people, and only one button to press. Secta hit it and the doors closed. The elevator made a whirring noise as it descended.

"Funny sound," Hope noted.

"It's the power supply," said Secta. "The turbine generating the electricity is nuclear, I'd say. Activates only when the switch is triggered. A neat waste prevention measure."

The elevator stopped with a jolt and the doors opened.

"About eight floors underground, I'd guess," Secta declared, stepping out into a large room gently illuminated by ambient lighting.

The immediate space was pretty much a replica of his own laboratory, all of his scientific equipment in position according to his instructions.

"Feels just like home," he said happily, strolling over to the de-molecularizer chair.

"Velcome!" Honor's unmelodious voice echoed flatly off the concrete walls as she appeared, spectre-like, from a dark corner of the cavernous room.

Unperturbed, Secta simply nodded and said: "Thank you. Is everything activated, or do we need to plug it all in?"

"Off course it is all active!" she snapped, striding to within a few inches, asserting some authority. "A dedicated crew spent hours setting it up, all in accordance to your specifications!"

"And the power source?" he queried.

"Nuclear, of course!" she snapped back. "Ze power cells could last a thousand years. Everzing vill be quvite safe here. Zis bunker was constructed in ze 1960s for leading government ministers as a precaution against nuclear or conventional attack. It is surrounded by two-foot-thick titanium outer valls, buried beneath vun hundred feet of steel-reinforced concrete. It could vizstand a direct thermonuclear hit." She walked off a little way, an arm sweeping round as she continued her spiel. "Zere are six offices over zere," she indicated the dark section of the room she'd stepped out of, "And ze entire shelter is fitted with sensor lighting, vhich helps ensure ve do not drain unnecessary energy. It is a space exactly suited to your needs."

"You are aware that when I depart, I expect to rematerialise right here in the future?" Secta said.

"You haff already told me zat. Vhat is your point?"

"I'm wondering how we can we be sure there won't be any buildings constructed over this site by then."

A look crossed Honor's face that could almost have been a smile. "I am vay ahead of you, Secta," she said. "Zis is government land. It has been zoned to remain parkland in perpetuity. Ze chances of anyzing being erected on it are sufficiently minimal as to present almost zero risk."

"Almost zero," he repeated. "As ever, you fill me with confidence, Honor."

"That's provided you materialize here, Secta," said Hope. "We still haven't resolved whether you'll need a host or not."

Secta waved off her question — he wasn't interested in such technicalities. He continued questioning Honor, not because he didn't know the answers, merely because he enjoyed it. "And how do I get the trapdoor to open, so I can get back down here?" he said.

"I anticipated zat question," she said. "Excuse me a moment..." Honor turned on her heel and strode back into the darkness. The clacking of her stilettos resonated from the walls. Suddenly the room flooded with light. Hope and Secta raised their eyebrows at its vast extent.

Honor was standing at a small metal box fixed halfway up a wall, right next to the first of several offices. Two illuminated buttons, one red and one green, were blinking on the front of the box.

"Here, Secta!" she commanded.

He shrugged and went over.

Honor produced a key inserted and turned it, then paused, a finger over the green button. "On ze count of three, nominate a verbal passkey," she said, pressing it. "Vun. Two. Three."

"Open, Sesame," said Secta, comically.

Honor merely rolled her eyes, and pressed the red button to lock the password in. "Ze entrance is now voice-activated," she said. "Only your voice vill open ze door. It automatically closes again after two minutes." She glanced at Hope, who was now busy calibrating equipment. She stepped a little closer and whispered: "A vord, Secta, if you please."

He followed her into the nearest office, lit by incandescent strips. They took chairs either side of a government-issue desk.

Hope kept a sly eye on them. When she was confident of being out of Honor's line of vision, she quickly concealed Secta's two ILDD DNA marker decoders, the size of television remotes, under the de-molecularizer chair. Unlike the unit supplied by Honor to locate Black Alice in the future, these were the ones programmed to help the two siblings find each other again once Secta had returned.

In the office, Honor glared at Secta across the desk. Without preamble, she said: "You haff sixty hours only to complete your mission."

He saw she was trying to intimidate him, but was not impressed. "And who, exactly, will be in the future to police that, Honor?" he replied, indifferently.

"I vill!" she declared, eyeballing him sharply. She took a small remote from her inside pocket and showed it him. "Zis detonates a very small explosive at ze core of ze bunker power source," she said. "I expect you know vhat zat wud mean?"

"Yes, Honor," he said, in a bored voice. "Everything that runs on electricity would cease to function."

"Correct."

"And what makes you think I'd stay in the future to warrant that?"

"It is a precaution, Secta."

"And Hope?" he asked. "What assurance will you give me that she will not be exploited as a precaution as well?"

Honor lifted one shoulder in a nonchalant shrug. "None."

Secta rose to his feet. "You would have made a good Nazi, Honor," he said. "You have the mind for it. Very well, we have an understanding. Now, if you're quite finished, I'd like to get on with my experiment."

"I haff one more concern," she growled. "Ze experiment is not ready."

Secta stopped in the doorway, turned and glared. "What makes you say that?" he asked.

"Hope. She has just said you are not certain of your destination point."

"Oh, if that's all," he said, turning to leave. "Don't let that worry you, Honor, just leave the science to me. Besides, what does it matter? I'm the one going, not you."

She stood called after him, intent on getting in the last word, "I vill be sticking around to see you off!"

"If you must, Honor," he called back. "But you're too late — I've been off for years! Haven't you noticed?"

He chuckled to himself as he traipsed over to the cloud chamber, now positioned in the centre of the room.

"Okay, Hope," he said. "Let's get this crazy show on the road!"

Hope stabbed a few buttons, and they watched the cloud chamber and its associated apparatus light up like a whole theatre full of science fiction movies.

"Set the de-molecularizer on standby," Secta ordered.

Hope moved to the control panel and made the appropriate adjustments.

"Done," she acknowledged.

Honor, now watching over her shoulder, said: "So — you are capable of operating zis apparatus vithout Secta."

"If that was a question, Honor," said Hope, bluntly, as she continued working, "Then yes."

The noise level was increasing. Honor raised her voice. "Run past me vat vill happen," she commanded. "In sequence, please."

It was an order, not a request. Hope chose to obey — no point in ruffling Honor's feathers at this stage.

"Secta will sit in the chair where he will be de-molecularized into the hologram unit," she said. "I will then transfer his atoms into a neutron gun, and fire it into the active cloud chamber. When the particles collide, they will cause a wormhole to open in the timeline we expect Black Alice is occupying. Secta will pass through the wormhole, and materialize in that timeline."

"So, he vill be like a digital upload," said Honor, nodding along.

"Similar," said Hope. "But with sub-atomic particles, rather than binary code. The destination point will be within a kilometre or so."

Secta sat in the chair, ready for activation, and looked proudly at them both.

"Yes, sub-atomic particles," he said. "God particles, if you will. That's what I'll be in a few seconds time — although in scientific reality that's what we all are, all the time. God particles," he added with a smile. "How very apt." He bowed his head for a moment, as though in prayer. Hope had to admire his sense of drama.

"Hope!" he cried, raising his eyes to hers, "I am ready! An audacious time traveller, prepared to create history — dispatch me into our destiny!"

CHAPTER 16
DEAD MAN'S SHADOW

RENO, NERDO AND Jonno stared at the live feed from the monitor.

"Is that it, Nerdo?" Reno asked. "An old house?"

"I saw a shadow move between the camera and the house," she said. "Probably setting the shot up."

"Wait a minute," Reno sounded troubled. "I think that's Turk's old house at Blanket Bay."

"Better get him," said Jonno. "Looks like it to me as well." He went over to where Turk lay in a cubicle, still unconscious. "Hey, Turk?" he said, tapping the man's foot. "Wake up, mate. It's Jonno."

Turk moaned, rolled over and faced the big man. The bright overhead light made him squint. "Who's that?" he groaned. Jonno offered him a hand. Turk took it and pulled himself up.

"Come and take a gander at this!" Reno called, his eyes fixed on the monitor.

Knuckling sleep from his eyes, Turk accompanied Jonno to the front desk.

Reno pointed at the screen. "That your old place, mate?"

Turk squinted to focus. "Nar," he growled.

There was movement in shot. A wheelchair containing a vacant-eyed figure in white came into view.

"Shit!" shouted Reno. "That's Nora! It is your house, man!"

Turk leaned for a closer look at the monitor. "Dunno," he yawned, vaguely.

Jonno and Reno exchanged glances. Something wasn't right. The chair advanced further into shot, and now they could see who was pushing it.

"Damn," said Jonno, softly. "Duke."

The camera was hand-held. It moved closer, then stopped with Duke and Nora in mid-shot.

"Hey, Turk!" the Rebel leader grinned. "Look who we found — your little sister, who we had so much fun with before! Though by the look of her now, she's not gonna be such a barrel of laughs this time round…"

Nerdo closed her eyes. Cutter put a hand on her shoulder.

"What's the bastard up to?" Reno growled.

Duke looked over his shoulder. "Bring him out!" he yelled.

Two Rebels manhandled Tatts out of the house and forced him to his knees beside Nora's chair.

"Tatts lost another ear before we figured what he'd been trying to tell us," said Duke. "Maybe I cut his tongue out too soon after all. Anyhow, we now know you're still alive, soldier boy, and hell-bent on attacking us with your bunch of goons."

There wasn't a sound in the bar.

"As entertaining as that sounds," Duke went on, "I reckon it would be better for your sister and your friend here if you all surrendered instead. So, instead of holing up there at Reno's bar — hi Reno, by the way, bad luck about the missus—"

"Bastard!" Reno spat.

"—I'll give you 'til sunset to get here. You don't make it by then, I'll go live with the cabbage patch doll here. Oh, and bring my men you're holding prisoner with you while you're about it." The man stepped forward, face right into the lens, grease and stubble filling the screen. "You hear that, Turk? Sunset." He nodded, and the picture cut to video noise.

They all turned to stare at Turk. At where Turk had been. Apparently totally unaffected, he'd turned his back on the monitor and walked away.

"What the— Turk!" called Reno. "What are you doing, man? Turk!"

But Turk ignored him, and kept walking. He wandered into the kitchen. There was the sound of rummaging, then a shout of: "Anything to eat in this joint?"

Reno stared at Jonno. "What got into him?" he said.

Nerdo swivelled angrily around in her chair. "I told you!" she said, her face scored with frustration and puzzlement. "That's not Turk! He's someone else — maybe this Black Alice geezer!"

"But ... but..." Jonno was shaking his head. "But that's preposterous," he said. "It can't be, the man would have died umpteen years ago if he hadn't vanished into thin air first..."

Turk ambled back into the room, tearing at a cooked chicken leg as if he hadn't eaten in months. "I'd kill for a pig's ear," he said, through a mouthful of food. "Where's the nearest pub?"

Jonno and Reno exchanged looks. "Haven't heard that expression since I was a kid," Jonno admitted.

"Yeah, me dad used to say that," said Reno. "Never heard Turk use it though. Besides, there's been no pubs here since way before the war... There's a few cold ones in the freezer, Turk!" he added, emphasizing the name, but there was no reaction. Turk just went back into the kitchen, returning moments later with a bottle of cold beer.

"So, in case it's escaped your notice, mate, we've got a serious problem that needs your attention," Reno barked at Turk, finally losing his rag.

Turk dawdled over to him, swigging beer and still chewing on the drumstick. "Dude, I don't know what you're going on about," he said. "Can't see how any of this applies to me. I don't even know who the stuff you are."

Nerdo took over. "Look, man, who are you?" she said.

He stopped chewing and grinned at her, bits of chicken still hanging from his lips. "You're having me on," he said. "I'm Black Alice! What, don't you dudes ever read the papers?"

Nerdo gave Reno an I-told-you-so look. Jonno went over to the wall, unhooked a bar mirror and carried it back. He held it up in front of Turk. "Yeah?" he growled. "Who's that then?"

Turk stared, apparently dumbstruck. His hand came up to his face, tracing its battered but still rugged contours like they were new to him. "I've ... I've got no idea," he said, slumping into a chair. "Ugly bugger, though."

Reno, Nerdo and Jonno went into a huddle. None of this was making sense.

"Look, I don't know what's happening here, but Nerdo's right," said Reno. "That's not Turk."

"Maybe it's some kind of a mental condition from the war?" Jonno guessed. "Soldiers went through some weird stuff out there. You know — chemicals, radiation, all that. What do you reckon? PTSD, maybe?"

"Look," said Nerdo, "Let's just talk to him. You never know, we might find something out."

The three nodded in unison. Reno and Jonno let her take the lead. She stepped up and sat down next to Alice-Turk. "Look, dude, we're going to try and help," she said, kindly. "Tell me the last thing you remember..."

He gazed at her with lost-puppy-dog eyes. "I was on the bridge of the ferry," he said, vaguely. "We'd missed the sub. Hope and Mal were talking to me..." Excitement broke on his face. "Yeah, that's right, she was saying not to forget who I am ... It was weird," he went on. "I looked at my hands, and they kept fading in and out ... I mean, like I could see them one minute and they were gone the next. Hope said something ... something about someone else's body, another time dimension..." He looked at Reno sharply. "Next thing I remember, there was a bloke cutting some chick's throat ... over there, right next to the pool table."

Reno glanced at Jonno. "Elsa," he said, sorrowfully.

"Then my legs were on fire … there was some poor girl…" Alice-Turk grimaced, reliving the memories. "Then, I dunno, a whole pile of stuff. Images and voices … some bastard laughing and laughing … seems like an album of still photographs in my head, dreams … not quite real."

"How did you feel when you saw that bloke on the monitor just then?" Nerdo asked.

"Felt like I hated him, now you mention it," said Alice-Turk. "Can't think why," he went on. "I mean, he's clearly a right bastard, but as far as I know he's never done anything to me."

Nerdo straightened up.

"This isn't a side-effect from iWish," she said. "This is something completely different."

"Like what?" Jonno queried.

"Like possession?" Reno proposed.

"What, demons?" Jonno reacted with a jolt.

"Cut it out!" Alice-Turk growled. "Demons…"

"No, it's more like some sort of split personality," said Nerdo. I bet the real Turk's still in there … He's just been sort of taken over by this other personality. You could be right, Reno. Maybe he was brainwashed during the war, or used in some sort of mind-control experiment."

"You people are off your faces," snarled Alice-Turk.

"What are we gonna do about it?" Jonno wondered.

"Nothing," said Reno, confidently. "Just keep on treating him like one of us, just bat on. Maybe Turk'll turn up, maybe he won't. Whatever happens, we've got a big problem on our plate and precious little time to solve it."

Cutter came in, followed by Mad Dog. "Gun turrets are done!" he announced, cheerfully. "Betsy's looking awesome!"

Mad Dog looked at Turk slumped in the chair with an uncharacteristic look of puzzlement and despair on his face. "What's up with you?" he said.

"Better sit down, guys," said Reno. "We've got to talk."

Mad Dog stared at the others. "To be honest," he said, "With Turk out of the show, this ain't what I signed up for. You know, this is his gig. He was at the helm, and now he isn't."

Cutter nodded. "I'm with you," he said. "I don't wanna risk my life going after an animal like Duke without him. None of us here have his savvy. Look at how he chopped up those Rebels ... that's the bloke I'll follow into battle. Not this dude!" They all looked at Alice-Turk, still slumped in his chair.

Reno chimed in.

"Look, this is as much my fight as it is Turk's," he said. "My wife was butchered by these bastards as well as Turk's sister. Maybe his leadership was the driving force, but I was second in command, and I'm still committed. After what he done to Elsa, Nora, Turk and now Tatts, I want that bugger's head on a stick more than ever."

Jonno nodded in agreement. "Hear! Hear!" he bawled. "But hey, if any of you wanna opt out, now's the time!" He eyeballed each of them, one at a time. "Nerdo?" he asked.

She sat back in her chair, picking a fingernail with a Swiss army knife. Then she stopped abruptly and returned Jonno's stare. "I'm still in," she said. "I trust you, Jonno."

"Dog?"

The big feller nodded his head slowly, "Yeah okay. I'll stick around."

"Cutter?"

Cutter held up his hands in surrender. "No point being the lone fish in the sea," he said. "'Sides, where she goes, I go. I'm in."

Jonno grinned. "Thought so," he said. So, Reno, what's the plan?"

Before Reno could open his mouth, Alice-Turk sat bolt upright in his chair. "So what's this?" he roared. "Don't I get a vote?" He clambered to his feet and prowled over to Reno, moving like a jaguar stalking its prey. Reno took a cautious step back. Turk had grace, but he didn't move like this.

"Seems you dudes are in the shit," Alice-Turk went on. "Well, let me tell you … this is nothing! Nothing! I've fought Government troopers, monsters and half the damn population of Sydney to get here — and look!" He paused, pointing at himself. "I'm still standing! You say this bloke Turk has balls?" He grabbed a fistful of crotch with one hand and eyeballed Mad Dog. "Well, they're my balls now!" He turned to each of them, still firmly gripping himself. "This Turk geezer might be gone for now," he went on, "But I'm his shadow and let me tell you, anything he could do, I can do too, and then some!" He prowled around them. "So let's get a plan together to nail this son-of-a-bitch Duke, 'coz if there's one thing I hate it's some pratt standing over the common folk. And it seems to me that when it comes to being a lowlife, this dude takes the cake!"

The others looked at each other. The dude might be batshit crazy, but Turk was in there somewhere, and besides, there was something in his tone, and the honesty in his furious eyes, that stifled any objections.

"O-kay," said Nerdo, cautiously, "I'll buy into the fact that you're on board with Turk's revenge. But how about telling us how and why you took him over?"

Alice stopped, scowling at her. Then his face softened. "I can only tell you what I think, alright?" he said. "Because honestly, I don't really know. Let's see. First, what year is this?"

"2087," answered Nerdo.

"Alright," he said. "I'm in the future. Again. My time is the early part of this century. Don't ask me how I'm here now, all I know is that some weirdo government scientist did something experimental that makes me slip into different times. And now, apparently, into different people, too."

"Sounds like science fiction to me," growled Mad Dog.

Alice eyeballed him. "Maybe so," he said. "But it's my personal nightmare!"

"Why are you so keen to take on someone else's fight?" asked Jonno. "Why risk being killed yourself?"

"Can't answer that," said Alice. "Maybe I just believe in standing up for the underdog. Maybe the vengeance driving this Turk has infected me as well. All I can tell you is that I usually play what's in front of me. And at this stage that's all I've got. That's who I am."

"Yeah?" said Mad Dog. "But who exactly are you?"

"I already told you that, dude. I'm Black Alice."

They exchanged looks.

"Alright — Alice," said Cutter. "What if the going gets too tough and you wanna quit? You're not a soldier. You're not Turk."

"See this?" said Alice, pointing to his head. They nodded, perplexed.

"Yeah," said Jonno. "Your head, so what?"

"No," said Alice, grinning. "It's Turk's head. Do I need to say any more? His brain, his body. I'm just driving it now, and let me tell you, I'm no quitter! You tell me, why the hell would I volunteer to buy into Turk's hassle unless I meant it? I'll tell you why. I believe in freedom. And I hate fascist governments, insurance companies, gluttonous banks, liars, cheats, bad music, poor acting and parking attendants. But most of all, I can't stand a bar of bloody stand-over merchants like Duke!"

Somehow, they were all on their feet, applauding this stranger in their friend's body, convinced of his integrity and his passion. The man from the past was living up to his legend. They were still a team.

While the others were catching a little shut-eye, Alice was wide awake, trying to come to terms with this latest life instalment. He headed towards the kitchen, catching sight of his reflection in a full-length wall mirror as he did so. There was just enough light for him to inspect his newly acquired body. Nice to have a bit of height — six four or more, maybe. He unbuttoned his army shirt and peeled it off. Biceps … not bad. Could do with some work. Deltoids … yeah, they'll do. He flexed his chest. Good pecs, nice obliques and a reasonable six pack — guess Turk works out. He moved closer to the mirror to study his face, and felt his chin. Got a good few scars there, fella. Coulda had a head like a bashed crab … but hey, just some happening scars, square jaw, cool vibe — looks like lady luck rolled for me on this one.

Half asleep and walking like a zombie on her way to the ladies', Nerdo caught sight of Alice. Knuckling her eyes, she watched him standing in front of the wall mirror, topless, posing like a contestant in a Mr Universe contest. "What's the story, there, pal?" she said, grinning.

He flexed again, trying to impress her. "Not often you get a shot at having a physical upgrade," he said. "I'm just checking it out."

"Yeah, good-o," she mumbled with a yawn and leaned tiredly against the wall. "Tell me," she said. "How does it work, travelling in time?"

"Well, you start in a special place with a weird seat that looks like a dentist's chair…"

"A what?"

"Ha! Yeah, you probably don't have those these days," he said. "Never mind — it's just a weird-looking chair-thingy, okay? Then you get jabbed in the throat with a great big hypodermic syringe full of green gunk, you spin out, the room rumbles and you magically wake up somewhere else … That's about it."

"Sounds like fun," Nerdo said, without a trace of irony.

"If that's your idea of a good time," he said, looking her meaningfully up and down. "It's not mine — although sometimes a good time can still be had…." He took another look.

"Whatever," she said, yawned again, and ambled off to the ladies.

Guess Turk's not a hit with the ladies after all, thought Alice.

CHAPTER 17
WAXING MOON

MORRIGAN HUD — known as Morri — had decided to spend her 18th birthday alone, and there was no better way to do that than on the highway. Speed was her drug. Others had guns, booze, uppers, downers or just plain old space-out sessions on iWish. She got her rush from pushing her British racing green Wilson-Kit J-car to the max. She'd assembled it herself — her father's well-equipped garage had been a playground for her, and the isolation of their small farm in Avalon meant she'd had little else to do but learn from him. No car enthusiast in the world would have imagined a Wilson J-Car hitting the sort of speeds she could pull out of hers.

Her father found it difficult to explain his daughter's extraordinary grasp of engines and mechanics — he had no idea where she got it from. He was a gifted amateur, but Morri totally absorbed everything and anything she learned, and her eidetic memory enabled her to recall every scrap in vivid detail. There was almost nothing on wheels she couldn't fix, customise, improve or, in extreme cases, create.

She managed to fit a particle engine into a Wilson J-Car body, and goose it up to pull three hundred clicks an hour — nothing short of an engineering marvel. Nobody else had been able to carry it off. And with gas rarer than hen's teeth, a car that could hit two hundred clicks without it was a valuable commodity and seriously sought after.

Morri loved driving manually, as opposed to auto-drive, and speeding with the roof down was her thing. Just her, the wind licking her long blond hair, tree shadows striping the road, the sun slicing between their boughs like a blade flickering over her, no other car on the road. No feeling like it.

The horror of the last few weeks was being left in her wake as she sped away from her bad memories. Her father's voice sounded in her head, reminding her to keep an eye on the gauges. Tears sprang to her eyes. She was angry. She hadn't been there when the gang had invaded her home and murdered both her parents.

So now she drove, no idea where she was heading. She'd loaded the trunk with everything she needed and taken to the highway. But there was one important stop to make before driving the unknown: Woodhenge in Avalon. A temple twenty kilometres away, it was where her parents had been married in an indigenous ceremony; where she'd been given her name. It was also where the family had attended regular worship before the war.

Morri turned the J-Car off the highway onto the dirt road to Woodhenge. A few minutes later she stopped at a chain-padlocked gate, which hung across a cattle grid. The sign read 'Government Heritage Park', along with a brief history of why Woodhenge had been created in the likeness of Stonehenge in England. She didn't need the sign — she could hear her father's deep voice saying: "The environmental minister for the old Oceana State Government, Walden Hart, was a good friend of mine — and an elder of our mob. He had this site erected as a place for us to worship the dreaming."

Morrigan lifted the gull-wing door and climbed out of the car, carrying the two small metal urns that contained her parents' ashes. She ducked under the fastened gate, then followed an overgrown track to Woodhenge, fifty metres away in the middle of the field.

Her crying had stopped. Woodhenge was filling her with positive energy, for the simple reason that it held so many wonderful memories. She spotted some honeysuckle growing wild, and stopped to pick a bunch. As she straightened with the flowers in her hand, she felt the midday sun burning her face … it seemed hotter than normal, uncomfortably so. Shielding her eyes, she looked skyward, sensing something amiss. Suddenly, overcome by dizziness and a loud, high-pitched whistle in both ears, she staggered and almost passed out. The flowers dropped from her hand, her arms fell limp and she watched the two urns drop in surreal slow motion from her grasp, landing on the ground and bouncing a little way. Her heart was pounding so hard she could see it hammering in her chest. In a desperate bid to stay conscious, she focused on Woodhenge, but it didn't help. Stars were flying across her vision, and the upright wooden pillars were shimmering like a mirage. She blacked out.

She woke at sunset. A waxing crescent moon hung in the darkening sky, and an eerie atmosphere pervaded the scene. The long shadows of the monument stretched like the withered fingers of a giant to her feet, almost as though they were beckoning her. The moon was in line with the Heel Stone, and a hot breeze was blowing through her long blond hair. She looked at the two urns on the ground, collected them and her dropped flowers, then stepped out of her shoes and walked barefoot towards the Heel Stone, determined to complete her quest.

As she poured the contents of the urns over the flowers on the Heel Stone, some of the ashes clung to her blue jeans. Brushing it off, she suddenly said out loud: "What on earth am I doing?" She looked down. "They're not my feet!" She patted her face, then her body, urgently. "Goodness, I've got tits!" she exclaimed. "Oh, well, that's a pleasant change."

She walked over to the northeast corner of a concrete pad that was partially overgrown with weeds, talking to herself. "Always wondered what it'd be like to be female," she said. "Oooh, my voice sounds so different! Nice though. Melodious." Standing on the pad, looking back to the monument in the centre of the field, she went on: "I warned you they might build something over the top of the bunker, Honor. Well, they sure have. Looks like a tree-hugger's version of Stonehenge!"

She stepped off the concrete pad into the long grass and began to hobble through it, but stopped sort with a sudden squeal. "Ouch!" Hopping on one leg, she checked the sole of her foot and found a prickle. "Oh, dear!" she said, extracting and studying the thorn. "Hmm, calotis cuneifolia — a nasty little prick!"

Unwilling to continue trudging through the grass for fear of more punctures, she cried: "Open, Sesame!" Nothing happened. "Damn, maybe it was over there," she muttered, turning in a new direction. Cupping her hands to her mouth, she tried again: "Open, Sesame!" Still nothing. She seemed to think for a moment, then tried again, this time in a much lower tone. "Open, Sesame!" To her relief, a trapdoor groaned as it opened, pushing back the grass only three metres away. A light blinked on within.

As she made for it she grumbled, "Ouch! Ouch! Why on earth is she barefooted, silly girl?"

She stopped just before the trapdoor, blinking. "I beg your pardon?" she said. "Who said that? Was it me?"

"Yes, it was," came the reply.

"Wait … what?" she said. "Is this some kind of spirit?"

"No, Morrigan. It's simply me."

"Okay … Fine. Now, just one question: who the hell is me?"

"Ah, of course. I apologise. My name is Secta … Doctor Secta, to be precise."

"A doctor?"

"Yes! Um, and I'm afraid I've taken over your body for a while."

"Like hell you are," said Morri. "This … this is me having a psychic breakdown or something. Hearing voices. I need to get help."

"No, Morrigan, you're not having a breakdown," said Secta. "And yes, you are hearing voices — one voice, anyway, but I advise you simply to treat me as an uninvited guest and let me run the show for the next sixty hours or so."

"Hell, no! Get out of my mind!"

"Calm down, please. Calm down, girl. Look, I just need your help for a little while. Just for a couple of days at the most."

"Oh yeah? And then what happens?" Morrigan enquired. "I wake up in the nearest loony bin, right?"

"No, my dear, I will simply evacuate and you'll be back to your old self. But first I have a mission, and I must complete it. My sister's life depends on it!" he added, dramatically.

"Okay. Let me get this straight," she folded her arms defiantly. "I'm not having a breakdown."

"No."

"But I am hearing voices."

"One voice, but yes."

"And I'm not talking to myself, I'm talking to this Dr Spectre."

"Dr Secta, dear. Yes, that's correct. I'm a doctor of science, not a medical practitioner."

"And you're on a mission."

"Indeed. My, we're quick on the uptake," Morri felt her own eyes start to roll.

"Alright, no need for that," she said. "It's a lot to take in, alright? Look, I grew up pagan. I can wrap my head around stuff like astral projection and I've got my own psychic abilities, so I think I can wrap my head around this — just about. But I have two quite big questions…"

Secta's voice sniggered. "Two quite big—"

"A mission for whom and how did you get inside my head?" she said, quickly cutting him off.

There was a psychic sigh. "Fine, I'll tell you the short version," Secta said. "But do you mind if we do our talking while we're walking? The clock is ticking, after all. I'm from the past," he went on, as she started down the concrete stairs. "I've been turned into atoms, transmitted through a time portal and into a host — you. My mission is to locate a man who has also travelled from the past to now, and to return him safely to his — and my — own time."

"Will he be happy to go, or will he resist?"

"Well, he knows me," answered Secta, leaving out the fact that he was the one who sent Alice there in the first place. "I've helped him before. He will not cause a problem — as least … I don't think he will."

"You don't think?"

"Well, I'm new to time travel. Anything could happen."

"Okay…" she said. "Okay. I'm going to go along with this. Either I'm having a breakdown, in which case it's not real so it won't matter, or this is real, and I'm about to have the adventure of my life." She felt Secta's approval, but continued before he could speak. "But there's one condition, doc: if I feel like things aren't going right, I reserve the right to take charge. Deal?" They stood in front of the elevator. She felt her hand trying to lift to press the button, but sternly resisted.

"Rights, rights…" grumbled Secta. "Why is everyone so obsessed with rights?"

"Look, it's my body," said Morri, firmly. "And I've got eighteen more years of experience in it than you. So I reckon I can take over if I really put my mind to it, and that leaves you, basically, up the creek. Okay?"

"Point taken," came the reply. "You might perhaps have phrased it more elegantly, but point taken … Okay, agreed. Let's move."

"Some birthday present," said Morri, allowing her hand to press the button.

"Oh? Is it your — or perhaps our — birthday?"

"Mine," she said, grimly. "Not yours." The elevator doors slid open, and they stepped inside. "What is this place doing under Woodhenge?"

"I'll explain later."

"This is just too weird."

"What's weird?"

"Not having full control of my body."

"Don't worry. It's not like you're going to pee in your pants or something."

"Well that's ... reassuring..." She cleared her throat. Weird reference. "So," she said, changing the subject: "When are you from?"

"The early 21st century."

"What, the time of Oceana State Government? Wow, that's way before the war."

"There's been a war? Gosh. What year is it now?"

"2087. The Cyberwars started in 2080 and lasted seven years. Nothing will ever be the same."

The elevator door opened, and a light blinked on to reveal Secta's laboratory, still in pristine condition.

"Wow," said Morri, wide-eyed. "Check out all the gadgetry!"

"That is not gadgetry, young lady," said Secta, disapprovingly. "That is top-of-the-line scientific equipment."

He walked her over to the de-molecularizer chair, reached down underneath and came up with the two devices hidden there by Hope.

"Good girl," he said. "They're still here."

"Are you talking to me?"

"No, to my sister."

"Aw geez, don't tell me there are more of us in here?"

"Ha! I'm glad you have a sense of humour, Morrigan. Or... Morri? Do you mind if I call you that?"

"Sure," she said. "That's what most people call me."

He was inspecting the ILDD devices to discern which carried Hope and Alice's codes. "Is that what your parents called you?"

"Yes," she choked, brought up short by a wave of grief. "I was bringing their ashes to Woodhenge when ... well, when this happened."

"I'm sorry for your loss," he said. "I can feel how much you loved them."

"You can feel what I feel?"

"Yes. It's terrible."

"Sit down," she said. "You might as well know it all. Here's a replay of my most recent memories."

She sank into a brief meditation. Within minutes, tears were streaming down her cheeks. She could feel a sense of puzzlement, or unfamiliarity, alongside her grief.

"I'm … I … That was terrible, Morri," came Secta's hesitant voice. "I'm genuinely sorry. Gosh," he added. "I actually am. It's most unlike me, but I really feel quite dreadful about it."

"You know, it's weirdly comforting to be sharing my memories with someone," said Morri. "Even if that someone is me — sort of."

"That's extremely Freudian," said Secta, and she could imagine him smiling now. "Now…" he flicked on the ILDD and checked the dial. "Hmm, no reading. That would be the poor reception down here."

"How come there's still power down here?"

"Oh, it runs on a small nuclear cell … Look, we better go back up top. How did you get here?"

"My car."

"Excellent."

Back up top, Secta held the ILDD at arm's length, searching for Alice's signal, turning in a slow arc until it registered. Behind them, the trapdoor closed of its own accord.

"What is that thing?" Morri asked.

"A marker detection device — an ILDD, as it's affectionately known. It locates atomic DNA markers. I placed one in Alice's DNA."

"Alice? I thought you said we were looking for a he?"

"Black Alice is a he … and there he is!" said Secta. "He's about seventy kilometres away in that direction," he pointed east.

"Hmm, Snake Ridge I guess."

"How long to get there?"

"Oh, an hour or so, maybe. It depends."

"Depends on what?"

"On who's driving and what obstacles are in the way." They walked on towards the gate, with Morri in a thoughtful mood. "Say, you'll need to be careful, won't you, while you're here? I mean, not to do anything that might alter the timeline? Like, say if you fathered a baby, and then went back to your own time. The baby would have a father who'd was also its great-great-grandfather or something."

"Um, I don't know if you've noticed, but I don't really have a body," said Secta. "So I don't think I'll be fathering children anytime soon."

"Oh, yeah!" she laughed. "Lucky you didn't arrive in your own body then. Could you have?" she went on, ducking under the gate.

"I thought I was going to," he said. "Maybe this is Mother Nature's way of keeping the timeline in check."

"Yeah," said Morri. "She's pretty powerful, at that. It might well be."

"What is that?" asked Secta, pointing forwards.

"The field?"

"No, imbecile. That vehicle."

The moon was reflected in the shiny green paintwork of Morri's car, making it look unreal, magical.

"Lovely, isn't she?" she said. "That's my Wilson Kit J-Car." She ran a tender hand over the bonnet.

"She truly is," said Secta, his voice warm. "What's under the hood?"

Morri tapped the hood with her fingers. It popped open and she raised it to reveal the gleaming mechanism inside.

"Particle engine," she said, proudly. "450 horse power at 9,000 rpm, no fuel required."

"No. No, I'm sorry, but that's impossible," Secta giggled.

"Guess you didn't have particle technology in your day."

"We do not. Please, explain."

"A particle engine runs on nuclear energy. The source is a tiny, permanently sealed capsule containing nuclear beads — particles. It provides an unlimited power source."

"It's a miniature reactor?"

"Exactly! The rest is gearing."

"It's hard to imagine how you could get an engine like that to deliver so much power…"

"Well, let's hop in and I'll show you," she said. "Just tap on the car. My print will register and open her up."

Secta reached out and touched the paintwork. The driver's-side door lifted, and they climbed into the bucket seat. The headlights illuminated automatically and the engine started, purring like a big cat: quiet but awe-inspiring.

"You can select automaton or manual."

"Self-driving? No thanks, way too scary."

"You don't trust technology?"

"Only if I made it," said Secta. "Even then, things can go wrong … look at me. I'm female. I rest my case."

"Alright, back off a little then. I'll drive."

Morri felt the resistance that came from sharing her body lift suddenly. She executed a U-turn, and motored slowly along the dirt road back to the highway, where she gunned it and the machine shot off like a bullet.

"Morri," squealed a clearly delighted Secta, "you are a genius!"

"Guess you're not alone then, eh?" she laughed. "This is going to be one hell of a ride. But look, we've got an hour or so to kill. So why not tell me about things in your time?"

"There's not much to tell," said Secta. "It's a world of career politicians, motivated purely by self-interest. Personal gain is the only true priority, the rest is building walls to keep the truth at bay.

"Mine is a time in which people are obsessed with political correctness, where a plethora of 'alternative facts' simply generates the chaos that comes from too many points of view. Money rules, liars win, bigotry abounds; there are too many guns and too many laws. It's a breeding ground for paranoia, which is the only real illness left. Social media and the worldwide web long ago destroyed any kind of original thinking, and we've developed even more ways to connect, to avoid reality, to numb our bodies and brains.

"But it's also a time of incredible advances," he went on. "Take genetics, for example. We've been able for the first time to merge the biological and digital transmutation processes, creating proto-androids that could become the most important servants mankind has ever known."

"They won't though," said Morri, sadly. "Let me tell you about my time. Let me tell you about the Cyberwars…"

CHAPTER 18
CONVOY OF DOOM

IT WAS NIGHT by the time Jonno pulled Betsy out onto the highway, flicked on the running lights, and gunned her. The big prime mover thundered into the dark, with the light from the waxing moon glinting on the nightmarish spikes on her big bull bar. Following behind was the F-200 with Reno at the wheel, then Nerdo and Cutter on their choppers. A convoy of doom, armed to the teeth.

Unsure how to take Black Alice, now they were alone in the car, Reno opened the conversation. "When I was a kid, they taught us at school you were the leader of the Octagon Peace Movement," he said.

"Yep," Alice nodded.

"A pacifist."

"Yep."

"Um ... how can I put this?" said Reno.

"I know," said Alice. "But my philosophy is that sometimes you have to fight for peace. Some arseholes just need to be taken out if we're going to achieve it. This mongrel Duke is one of them."

"Plenty more just like him."

"Yeah? Well, one at a time."

"IIow long can you stay   you know, inside Turk?"

"Dunno," said Alice. "Haven't done this before. First time round I was in my own body. Turned up in a future that had been totally stuffed by a nuclear accident — same deal as this in a way. The survivors there were bikers as well. Bastards must be like cockroaches. Seems like they survive anything."

They both grinned.

"Anyhow, once I made it back, I had to stop the accident that destroyed everything — turns out it was me own group's protest. We were on a ferry, protesting against a US nuclear sub in Sydney Harbour. In the future timeline, the two collided, everything went up in smoke. So I had to change the timeline. Nothin' to it, right?" He grinned at Reno again. "Long story short, mate, we got that done, next thing I know I'm here. One minute on the ferry, celebrating saving the world, next minute in this poor bugger's head. So, in answer to your question, I honestly haven't got a clue."

"Well, in any case, we're glad to have you aboard, Alice," said Reno. "You're literally a living legend, you know that?"

Alice was not at all averse to having his ego stroked.

"A legend, eh?" he said, smiling broadly. "Wish that showed in me bank account or the amount of music downloads I'm sellin'."

"Downloads?" said Reno, frowning. "Oh, wait, I remember! That's how people used to buy music!" Reno said.

"Yeah, back when 'losing a bit of weight' meant having a haircut," laughed Alice. "So, how do you buy music now?"

"Well you can't since the fricking war. But before that you got everything through your implant."

"Your implant? What the hell's that?"

"At three years old everyone got an organic, cochlear stem-cell implant."

"You mean like a phone implant? We have those. Is it some kind of extension of that?"

"Not really," said Reno. "Your OSCI sends data directly to your five senses: sight, hearing, touch, smell and taste."

"So it can send you food then?"

"Nar, just the synthesized smell and taste."

"Bloody hell! That's amazing. So is it like a chip?"

"No, it's organic. They used your own stem cells to grow nerve links that connected to the sensory areas in your brain."

"Unbelievable," said Alice. "So you were all online then, like, it uses the Internet?"

"Yeah, sort of … the country had total open Wi-Fi capability before the war, so everyone was permanently connected."

"Did that cost?"

"Yeah, a monthly subscription credit was deducted from your account. Not for the implant, just for the service provider."

"Wow. So you got your music delivered directly into your head?"

"Pretty well," said Reno. "You just needed to think 'music', the OSCI would snag it, log you onto a music register, then you just thought of the artist or song you wanted to hear. A credit would come off your account automatically — guess it was paid as a royalty to the performer or composer."

"Ever hear my stuff?" Alice asked.

"Sure," said Reno, grinning, "Although Jonno's the real fan. I've heard the Sons of Steel album, Endangered Species, Knightmare … the World album At War With The Great Unknown, brilliant."

"Cool, I'm impressed," said Alice. "Must be a stack of my money somewhere that some mug has collected on my behalf, 'coz I've seen none of it."

"Pity it's disconnected. I could have checked for you."

"Disconnected, how come?" Alice queried.

"Whole reason for the Cyberwars, mate. Communications satellites shut down, even the nano-satellites. That took the early detection umbrella down, as well as the electricity grid and every other utility we depended on."

"Who started it?"

"Jury's out on that one. Best ask Turk, he was on the front line, right behind the WarBots."

"WarBots? What the stuff are those?"

"Robots that look like people," said Reno. "cyborgs, controlled by a military version of OSCI."

"You're kiddin' me! Robots?" Alice exclaimed.

"Imagine a bionic soldier with no guilt, no fear and no pain. They could be remotely controlled from anywhere in the world. Supposed to be the perfect weapon, the weapon to end all weapons. Supposed to prevent war. Guess they got that wrong."

"Typical. Bloody governments," spat Alice. "I guess that's the danger of messin' with the brain … reminds me of that lunatic Secta." He flashed back on the scientist who had interfered with his grey matter and growled. "Man, if I could get my hands on him … Anyway. So, everybody's wired up then? Could your implant be reactivated?"

"Yeah, I guess," Reno said, wondering where the conversation was heading.

"So, if some evil bludger hacked into one of those satellites up there, he could turn everyone into these WarBots?"

"I s'pose so. But why would they?" Reno questioned.

"Control," said Alice, grimly. "That's what every government since the Romans has been hell-bent on. Maybe after all this is over with, you blokes should look into knocking out all them satellites, just to make sure."

"Ha, we'd need a mad scientist to do that."

"Funny, I know just the guy … Unfortunately, he's in the wrong time."

Suddenly Betsy's hazard lights lit up and the convoy pulled over to the side of the road. Reno got out and walked up to the cab of the killer Mack.

Jonno leaned out of the driver's side window and said: "Turn off is on the right, just ahead."

Alice, Cutter and Nerdo joined them.

"Take the lead as planned, Jonno. No lights," said Reno, looking up at the turret. "Don't start shooting till we're through, Dog."

Mad Dog gave Reno the thumbs up.

"Any questions?" Alice asked. None came. "Good, let's do this. Stick to the game plan. See you all on the other side."

They returned to their respective machines. This was the big moment: they were going into battle against a formidable foe.

Jonno cranked Betsy and pulled her out to lead the way. Stealthily, lights out, she crept along the dirt road toward the Rebel stronghold.

Mad Dog strapped himself into his seat in the turret, cocked his AK-47 and sat with trigger finger itching, ready for anything.

As Betsy rounded a bend and the gates came into view, Jonno pulled her to a stop.

Twenty metres behind, Alice eased the F-200 to a halt.

"He's going to gun it," said Reno.

A telltale puff of smoke shot from the two chrome exhaust stacks either side of Betsy's cabin — Jonno had planted his foot. Betsy roared as she hurtled towards the big wooden gates. She was doing eighty when she hit the barricade, splintering it like matchwood and ploughing right through. Jonno slammed on the airbrakes and Betsy skidded to a dust-filled stop in the courtyard. Gunfire hailed down on them but Mad Dog was already swivelling the turret to fire at the muzzle flashes from the battlements either side of the ruined gateway behind them, letting loose with a barrage of fire. Lumps of concrete flew from the AK rounds as they blasted the gun emplacements. The firing stopped, but was quickly replaced by gunners from a vantage point atop the main building. Mad Dog swung the turret around and unleashed another volley.

The F-200 powered into the courtyard and skidded broadside to a stop. Dust from the skid provided cover for Nerdo and Cutter to enter on their bikes. Within seconds, Alice's team had quit their vehicles and split into two groups, taking cover left and right of the main building.

But Jonno hadn't finished. He revved Betsy and drove, full tilt, right in through the main door, obliterating the entranceway in an awesome mess of busted concrete and timber. Still the gunfire blazed from left and right. Noticing now that Mad Dog wasn't retuning fire, Jonno stood up to check on him. The big man had been hit, his left shoulder blown clean off. Blood had sprayed all over the turret, and was now pumping weakly from the wound.

Dog smirked at his old mate with a toothless grin. "Always the fricking party-pooper, ain't I?" he growled, before slumping forward, still strapped to his seat.

Enraged, Jonno dragged the AK-47 from its mounting and manoeuvred it and himself outside. Crouching beside the driver's side door, he let loose a hail of fire at the muzzle flashes. The bullets found their mark, and two Rebels pitched forward, slid down the sloping iron roof and landed with a thump on the ground. Jonno riddled the bodies with more fire, just to make sure. He only then noticed the bullets ricocheting off Betsy and zinging past his ears, spun on his heel and let go in the direction of fire.

He heard a thump and felt a dull pain in his thigh. He'd been hit, but kept on firing. And then he ran out of ammo.

Alice saw Jonno was in trouble. Without a second's thought, he backed over to Betsy, an automatic pistol in each hand, blazing at the rooftop targets to give the man time to limp to cover. Realising return fire had ceased, Alice stopped firing too. All went quiet. Moving like a marine, Alice dashed to Jonno's side and found him sitting on the ground, his hand covering a thigh wound that was gushing blood in pulses.

Jonno was in serious trouble. He was trying to keep pressure on the wound, but blood was pumping between his fingers. Alice dropped his guns, slipped off his belt and tightened it around Jonno's leg.

"This'll do the trick, mate," he said through clenched teeth as he tightened the belt as hard as it would go. The bleeding slowed, stopped.

"Thanks," croaked Jonno. "Got carried away back there." He hung his head. "They killed Mad Dog."

"Would have done the same thing myself," Alice replied, handing over a pistol. "Here," he said. "Hang on to this and stay put. We'll carry on."

Jonno looked at his leg. "Don't worry," he said, managing a smile. "I won't be going anywhere."

Alice heard a whistle and looked up — Reno was waving at him. He picked up the other pistol, nodded at Jonno, and dashed over.

"They alright?" Reno asked.

"No. Jonno took a bad one in the thigh and they got Dog. What's the scoop here?"

"All quiet. I don't think there'll be any more opposition out here."

"Did you expect more?"

"Yeah."

"How many with Duke then?"

"I reckon four or five, but there might be more."

"Only one way to find out," said Alice, waving a signal at Cutter and Nerdo. "Let's go!"

Moving as one, the four remaining warriors stormed the main building.

CHAPTER 19
CRITICAL CONVERGENCE

IT **WAS DARK** by the time Morri pulled up outside Club Voodoo, the only joint in the street with lights on. Secta checked the ILDD.

"He's within a few kilometres," he said.

"How accurate is that thing?" asked Morri. "Because from here on, I'm lost."

"If you're asking whether it can guide us to him like a GPS, no. It only gives a general reading."

"So, what's next then?"

"Well, if I calibrate it like so…" He punched some numbers into the unit's small keypad. "It should read remnants."

"Remnants?" Morri queried.

"Artefacts … a signature, if you like. It can detect minute traces of radiation residue and it's found some in that place right over there. Reno's Bar."

Morri walked towards Reno's, holding the ILDD in front of them.

"He's definitely been here," said Secta, as they entered the bar.

She was instantly drawn to a pile of electronic equipment on the reception desk.

"Can't you use these psychic powers you say you have?"

"I don't say I have them," she snapped. "They're real. But … I'm not so in control of them. They tend only to kick in under … certain conditions."

"Like what … a trance?"

"Something like that," she mumbled. "Look, it's personal."

"Just tell me," said Secta. "There's no place for modesty here — we are, after all, rooming together."

"I only see things when I … Well, when I…."

"Ah. When you orgasm."

"Yes," she said, face scarlet. She sat down in a chair in front of a monitor array.

"Yes, well actually that makes kind of sense … the oxytocin release would impact the brain quite profoundly. Interesting. So what happens during these psychic episodes?"

"Sometimes it's a series of quick images, like flipping through photographs," she said. "Other times it's more connected, like a short film. If my mum had lived she would have taught me how to interpret the visions properly, but—"

"Have any of them been realised?" Secta asked.

"Yes," she said. "I saw my parents being attacked while I was … with someone." Tears threatened, and she quickly changed the subject. "What's this oxypotion stuff you're on about?"

"Oxytocin," he said, with a sigh. "It's a hormone released by the pituitary gland and believed to also affect the pineal gland. It's associated with social bonding, childbirth, nursing and — importantly — sexual activity. Interestingly, practitioners of transcendental meditation use it to achieve 'Turiya', or the fourth state.

"You may have enlarged pituitary and pineal glands, which would allow you to release more of the hormone than an average person — that would explain the intensity of your visions."

"Wow," she said. "You're like a walking encyclopaedia. Or you would be, if it was you doing the walking. So are you saying that my ability to have visions is physical, not supernatural?"

"Yes, but that's not to say you don't have other powers of perception. Ooh, I know, let's have an orgasm now so you can demonstrate!"

"Geez, Secta, no!" she exclaimed "I will not be sharing that experience with you!" He was about to argue, when a monitor in front of them, bearing the label 'Tatts' booted up and interrupted. It showed a large, filthy, hairy man in biker's leathers sitting in a big lounge chair. Morri leaned forward, spotted a 'record' button, and hit it.

The man grinned menacingly at the camera. "One of my boys just arrived to tell me you were making a mess of my place," he said. "He ducked out the back while you were coming in the front. Tut tut, Turkie! I expected better than that from you, soldier boy! Charge in, guns blazing, and you don't always get what you want.

"Those guards you killed? Not my men. They was the girls from Reno's and Voodoo. Funny isn't it? Give 'em a gun, aim one at them, and tell them to shoot or be shot. So you killed your own girls. And my lads? Got away so quick you didn't even notice them leave. Oh dear, abo soldier boy.

"As for young Nora, I've decided to take her and your little chum Tatts to visit my friends at Zen back in Angel City. Nora's nurse, though … She's gonna hang around." The camera panned slowly to show a bloody body hanging by the neck from a light fitting in the ceiling. "Hey, someone tuck her tongue back in," came the evil voice. "No need to be rude!"

The camera turned back and the big man continued: "If you want us, soldier boy, you know where to find us. Bye-bye for now!" The monitor faded to video noise.

"Who on earth was that horrible character?" said Secta. "And what did he do to that poor woman? Who's he talking about — Turk? Nora? Tatts? And what in the world is Zen? He doesn't seem the peaceful type to me!"

"Zen is the corporation that governs everything," said Morri. "And I reckon that was the bastard who killed my parents. Same malice. Same evil. I could feel it."

"Actually, yes, I felt it as well," Secta agreed. "But what can we do? This isn't my mission — unless Black Alice is somehow involved..."

"What's the matter, Secta," scoffed Morri. "Scared of a fight?"

"That's not the point," he replied, irritably. "The point is that I don't need anything more complicated than simply getting Alice back to Woodhenge and into his right time. Time! I'm running out of damn time!"

"You have a limit?"

"Yes. Sixty hours."

"And if you exceed it?"

"Oh, I don't know. There are some terrible people running the operation back where I come from. They've threatened to kill my sister if I don't return by their deadline."

"We'd better get on with it, then," she said. "Let's stock up with some grub and water, if we can find any in this place, and get on with it."

They walked into the kitchen. "Freezer over there," she said. "Might be something we can take along."

She opened the door and saw a plastic bag. "Meat," she said. "No good, we'd need to cook it." She picked up the bag to move it aside, and stopped.

"Is that what I think it is?"

"Good Lord! That's disgusting!" Secta cried. "It can't be sanitary to keep those in there!"

Alice was pushing the F-200 hard, back to Reno's bar. They needed to get help for Jonno, and fast. He looked across at Reno. "This bastard's one step ahead."

Booted feet on the dashboard, Reno yawned in reply: "Yeah, he's playing games alright."

Alice looked at Betsy's headlights in the rear-vision mirror. "Jonno's no use with his leg stuffed. Dog's gone. That leaves four of us. You reckon that's enough to take this on?"

"No," said Reno, flatly. "But he killed my wife, ruined Turk's sister, destroyed Turk's knee and set him on fire and mutilated Tatts, among other things. Now we've lost Mad Dog as well. In my book that means taking him on anyway."

"You're not wrong," said Alice. "But unless we can find an army in a hurry, we don't stand a chance in hell."

Headlights cut through a wall of billowing dust as the convoy pulled into the car park out back of Reno's.

Morri, sitting at a cubicle chewing on a chicken leg, heard the sound of an engine and jumped up. "We've got company," she said.

"Well finish the drumstick before you do anything else," he replied. "I'm still hungry."

Alice and Reno entered, deep in conversation, and stopped dead in their tracks at the sight of a pretty young blonde, alone in the middle of the room, holding a drumstick.

"Er ... to what do we owe this pleasure?" Reno enquired.

"Hi," she said. "I'm Morrigan Hud. I came in here cause I didn't fancy that dump over the road. I was looking for food — sort of like Goldilocks, I guess!"

"Oh well done, girl, that should do the trick," said Secta, with silent sarcasm.

Unconcerned, the two men approached her. "Glad you found something," said Reno. "I thought he'd polished it all off." He nodded accusingly at Turk.

"Well, the bag of second-hand body parts in the freezer didn't appeal," she said. "Were you saving them for a special occasion?"

"Oh them," said Reno, screwing his nose up. "Yes. Well. Not a very pleasant sight for a young lady, I imagine."

"Especially if she's hungry," said Secta, facetiously.

Alice shot Morri a look. "Do I know you?" he asked.

Morri glanced at the ILDD. It was registering maximum signal. One of these men was Alice. "I don't think so," she said. "What's your name?"

"I'm Reno, this is my bar. And this ..." he jerked a thumb at Turk, "Is..."

"Turk," said Alice, quickly. "Name's Turk."

"Oh. You're Turk. There's ... a message for you. Over there," said Morri, pointing at the monitors.

"Right," said Alice. "Just gotta take care of my buddy here."

Cutter and Nerdo had entered, acting as human crutches for Jonno. Reno rushed over to give them a hand.

"What happened to him?" Morri asked.

"An accident," said Alice, gruffly.

Reno helped the big man into a cubicle. Jonno looked pale. He'd lost a lot of blood.

"I'll see if I can get hold of old Doc Dan," Reno told him. "Remember him? He still lives a couple of doors up."

"Yeah, thought the old bugger would be dead," said Jonno, trying to grin.

"I'll be back in a minute," said Reno to Alice. "Keep an eye on him." He ducked out the front door.

"Looks bad," said Morri.

"Yeah. We need to get the bullet out," said Alice, without thinking.

"Oh, that kind of accident!" said Secta. Alice shot Morri another look.

"Yeah, yeah, he got shot, okay?" he said. "Just ... don't ask."

Morri nodded.

Nerdo, meanwhile, had cruised over to her communications equipment and found Secta's ILDD. "What's this?" she said, holding it up.

Morri took it from her, "Oh, just my ILDD," said Secta. Before Nerdo could ask any more questions, he added: "Um, when we — I got here the TV came on. It looked important, so I recorded it."

Nerdo pulled a quizzical face. "What's a TV?"

"Oops," thought Secta in Morri's head. "I guess that doesn't mean anything here, except to antique dealers. If there's any of them left…"

"Sorry," said Morri, quickly. "The monitor. I meant to say monitor."

"Better check it out," Alice said, regarding her with a cool stare.

"I'm on it," Nerdo replied. Before she could hit the button, Reno returned with a decrepit old man. If it wasn't for the doctor's bag he carried, Alice would have mistaken him for a fisherman.

"Over here, Doc," Reno said, guiding the man over to Jonno.

"Well, well," he said. "If it isn't little Jonno. You've grown a bit, son!"

"Always had the good bedside manner, Doc Dan," said Jonno, teeth gritted. "Glad to see you. You must be the only old bloke left in Australia."

"A survivor, that's me! Not really sure why I bother, mind you. Now, let me take a look at this." He busied himself cutting open Jonno's trouser leg to get a look at the wound.

"Reno, there's a message here from Duke," called Nerdo.

Later, after Doc Dan had patched up Jonno and left, the rest of them gathered around the pool table to discuss Duke's gruesome message.

"He's a fricking animal," said Nerdo, bitterly. They all nodded.

"Tell me more about this Zen," said Alice, throwing out the question for anyone to answer.

"They virtually run the country," said Reno. "In fact, they pretty much run the world right now. They've got regional HQ in Angel City. But I've no idea why they'd have anything to do with the likes of Duke."

He looked forlornly at Jonno, sprawled out and sedated in a cubicle.

"Maybe it's not just Duke," Cutter suggested. "Maybe it's all the Rebels. Duke is only a small chapter member. The Rebels are a national body with serious muscle. If Zen owns the buildings, it's the Rebels that own the streets."

"That's just organized crime!" Alice spat.

"Sure," said Nerdo. "Zen's the law and the Rebels give the orders."

"My father knew one of the Zen executives," said Morri. "He'd still be there, I think."

"Now, that could be helpful," Reno said.

"I can probably get a list," Nerdo offered.

"How?" Cutter asked.

"I'll hack into the Zen database using an old comms satellite," she said. "I did it before when we were looking for secret fuel dumps. Remember?"

"Oh yeah ... hey it worked as well, we got heaps of gas!" Cutter said.

"How can you get an uplink without a server?" Secta asked. As he did every time Secta spoke, Alice looked carefully at Morri.

"I use an old early telecommunications link called Telstra," Nerdo was explaining. "Even though it's been shut down for decades, it sends regular time pulses to a com sat. I can piggyback that."

"Brilliant," said Alice, still staring at Morri. "Get onto it."

Morri was staring back at Alice. Secta spoke in her head. "I feel something vibrating," he smirked. "You're actually attracted to that big oaf, aren't you?"

"Stop it, Secta," Morri thought back. "That's hardly important right now, is it?"

"I'll get us passes for Angel City," said Reno. "How many will we need?"

"Me, Cutter, Nerdo, you..." Alice began.

"And Jonno," added Reno. "We can drop him Headbangers for Trixy to take care of."

"Me too!" said Morri, eagerly.

"This isn't your fight, Morrigan," Reno observed.

"Oh yeah? Look, I think Duke murdered my parents. Crucified them on the front door of my house, then set them on fire."

"Yeah ... that's his form all right," snarled Reno.

"I've got a score to settle too," she said.

"Shut up, girl!" snapped Secta, in her mind. "Now you've put us in it!"

Reno looked over at Alice. He hadn't broken his stare. Sending Reno's question, he replied with a nod.

"Six passes it is!" Reno concluded.

Later that evening, while the others were resting, Morri, guided by Secta, went out front. She found Alice on the veranda, gazing up at the vast canopy of stars, and sat down beside him. It was still stiflingly humid.

"Quite a few up there," Secta said.

"Sure are," Alice replied.

He seemed distant. "What are you thinking about?" asked Secta, carefully. "You're miles away."

"Oh, another place — another time, trying to hear space," he said, dreamily.

"It's not you listening to space Alice, it's space listening to you," Secta said profoundly.

"That's a bit deep."

"Can't sleep?"

"No."

"Me neither. Tell you what: let's play a game…"

"A game? What for?" Al said, a little grumpily.

"Take our minds off things. Maybe help us get some shut-eye."

"Worth a shot, I s'pose. Go on then," Alice said, without enthusiasm.

"Alright. I'll give you a word, and you say the first thing that pops into your mind. Here we go … Bastard."

"Secta," Alice said without thinking.

"Bitch."

"Secta."

"Clown."

"Karzoff."

"Freedom."

"Hope."

"Malfunction."

"You cheated," Alice complained.

"How's that?" Secta asked.

"Mal — Function. Two words … and the answer is 'Octagon'. So, I'm fresh out of showing surprise. How did you figure it out?"

"Because I'm Secta."

"What?" Alice erupted, rocketing to his feet. "What do you mean, you're bloody Secta?"

"I'm not bloody Secta, I am Secta," the scientist complained. "Look, Alice, I've come to help. I've come to take you back. I can stabilize you so you won't slip out of phase any more — unless you want to, that is." He backed away, hands raised against the look of fury in Alice's eyes.

"Oh, really?" yelled Alice. "Well, tell someone who cares!" He grabbed Morri by the lapels and eyeballing her with all the ferocity he could muster.

She let out a yelp. "I'm in here too, don't forget!"

"Good job for you, Secta," he growled. "I'm not about to punch that pretty face. But you'd better get explaining, or I'll…" Inspiration struck. "I'll hand her over to Nerdo!"

"Hope came to me after you vanished from the ferry," babbled Secta, quickly. "You remember that, don't you?"

Alice let Morri go. Rubbing hia bald head, the anger on his face turned to despair. "Yeah, I remember," he grumbled. "But it's all hazy." He leaned against the wall, swept away for a moment by regret, and a terrible, unsupportable sadness. His harsh face softened. "It's all too hazy…"

"Look, we — Hope and I — figured out how I could come after you, and help you come back," said Secta. "I basically went through the same process as you did. Although at least you're in the body of a man!"

"Hey!" said Morri, fiercely.

"I wouldn't be complaining if I was you Secta," said Alice, cracking a feeble joke. "She's a damn sight prettier than you are."

"Thank you for that, Alice. Anyway, never mind that. All we have to do now is get to where my equipment is hidden, and we can both go back."

"What makes you think I'd trust you, idiot?" Alice snapped back.

"Er … I thought you said this guy was going to be friendly," Morri interrupted.

"I don't know how to convince you, Alice, other than to say that I would hardly risk my own life for this if my intentions weren't honourable."

"And Honor? That bitch is involved in this somewhere!"

"Well, yes, I hate to admit it, but yes. She helped me to get here."

"And why would she do that?" Alice thundered.

"Because the President wants you back," Secta answered, simply.

"Yeah, for sure!"

"You wouldn't want to stay here, would you? At least in my laboratory I'll be able to work on stabilizing your condition. Here you could dematerialize at any moment!"

"You've gotta be kidding! No matter what you say, I can't trust you, man. You're the bastard who infected me with this bloody virus or whatever it is in the first place. I ought to rip you frickin' eyeball out and eat it!" he growled, hands clawed.

Morri backed off, eyes tightly closed. There was a pregnant pause, in which Alice breathed deeply and Secta considered his options.

Alice broke the silence. "Hear this loud and clear, Secta," he said. "Even if I did consider coming back with you, I'm not going anywhere till I've finished what we've started here!"

"But this isn't your fight, Alice," Secta moaned.

"Don't listen to him, Alice!" Morri cut in. "It's as much my battle as it is Turk's, and I know he'd want to see it through, too!"

"Shut up, Morri!" Secta scolded.

Suddenly the penny dropped for Alice. "Hey, wait, I've just realised something…"

"Wait a second, Alice — Morri, kindly stop interrupting, this is important!"

"No, hold on, Secta. Morri's still there, and you can talk to her."

"Yes, in the same way you can talk to Turk."

"I think I'd like to try talking to Turk," added Morri. "This guy's way too aggressive."

"Nar, that's impossible," Alice growled. "There's only me in here."

"Turk's still in there, Alice," said Morri, stepping closer. "Try this: close your eyes."

"No way man. Last time I closed my eyes around Secta I wound up in a stuffed future surrounded by barbarian holocaust survivors with bad breath."

"Never mind him, Alice," Morri said. "Trust me."

Reluctantly, Alice closed his eyes.

"Now concentrate. Picture a white circle, filled in with black. Can you see it?

"Yeah," he mumbled.

"Good. Now fill the circle with grey … done it?"

"Yeah."

"Okay. Keep the circle in your mind, and reach out to Turk."

"How can I reach out in my bloody mind, you goose?"

"Just think about him, Alice. You'll feel him, you'll feel another presence," she persisted.

"Wait – yeah!" said Alice. "There's someone here!"

"Okay … now, can you imagine moving over in your mind to give him room? Just … make some mental space for him," Morri continued, her voice soft. "That's it … yes, he's getting through Alice, I can feel it," she said.

"Oxycontiiiinnn …" sang Secta, in her mind. She ignored him.

"Alice," said a male voice. It wasn't Alice's. Turk was back. "I would have made the same mistake as you, mate. I'd have ambushed the Rebel stronghold." Morri — and Secta — stared at him. "It wasn't your fault those young girls died," Turk went on. "But I know you feel bad about it. I'm feeling it, too, man. But we've gotta bat on. We've gotta nail Duke."

"You're right, man," said Alice. "Good to meetcha, by the way,"

Turk grinned.

"Scum like Duke can't get away with murder," Alice went on. "We'll finish this together. Secta?"

"Yes, Alice?"

"I'll come back with you. After the four of us have put an end to what we've started here. Got that?"

"You give me little choice but to agree," said Secta, huffily. "I'm hardly in a position to strongarm you. But let me tell you this: if I'm not back inside fifty-two hours, Honor will blow my lab and my equipment. Then we're both stuck — I'll be inside Morri forever and you'll eventually phase on to somewhere else."

"Can't be helped," said Alice. "We're in this mess now."

"Yeah, and I started it," said Turk glad to have his voice back. "I'm committed to finishing it. But I'm also going to help you get back to your own time. I reckon you've already earned that, Alice."

"Hear! Hear!" Morri cried.

"There's a joke in all this about crazy people talking to themselves," said Alice. "But for the life of me I can't think what it is."

CHAPTER 20
ZENOPHOBIA

THE NEXT DAY, as pale blue light washed over the hills to the west of Reno's bar, rolling back the night, Turk took a deep breath of fresh country air and ambled back inside for breakfast. It was going to be a big day.

Nerdo was flat out on her back, snoring: she'd been up all night hacking, and it took a shake from Cutter to wake her. Reno and Morri were in the kitchen, making coffee and pancakes.

Alice sang out loud with his powerful heavy-metal voice: "Wakey wakey, rise and shine, get out of bed, kids, it's breakfast time!"

Moans and groans from the bar were his response.

Chuckling to himself, Alice headed for the kitchen, attracted by the aroma of cooking.

"Hey, there's still that bag of goodies in the fridge," he joked. "Might be good with some fried onions!"

The thought caused Morri to dry retch. "Ew!" she coughed.

"I know," said Secta. "Without eggs? That'd be ghastly."

"You're sick," Reno chuckled. "All of you," he added. "I know you're laughing too, Turk." Alice, Turk, Morri and Secta had already briefed the rest of the team on their almost-unique situations.

"Gonna be tough to know which of you is talking," Reno said. "Secta and Morri sound like Morri, Alice and Turk sound like Turk."

"Nah, there's a difference," said Alice. "Turk sounds like he eats babies for breakfast."

"Yeah," said Turk. "And Alice sounds like he's spent years gargling rocks."

"Secta definitely sounds more slippery than me," laughed Morri, joining in.

"How dare can you sssay sssuch a thing!" hissed Secta. "Ah," he added. "I see what you mean."

"Anyway, you'll just have to handle it," Alice finished. "We can't keep introducing ourselves all the time, and code would be too complicated."

"Yeah," agreed Turk. "The last thing we need is more complications."

"I still think that now Turk is back we could go back to our own time," said Secta. "That would simplify things, would it not?"

"For the last time, Secta, no," said Alice, all trace of humour gone. "I'll explain it once more so it sinks into your thick head. I'm not leaving until these folk are free of Duke and Turk has his sister back."

"But..."

"There is no 'but', Secta, got it?"

"Fine," sighed Secta. "But you realise it's your messiah complex I've got to buy into, and it's making me feel uncomfortable."

"Oh, shut up, Secta," Morri complained.

"What the stuff is a messiah complex?" asked Turk.

"The habit of trying to save the world," explained Morri." Don't be offended, Alice. Sometimes the world needs to be saved and an old-fashioned hero is just what it needs."

"Old-fashioned?" Alice exclaimed, with a look of pretend horror, as they all laughed.

"Right, that's settled," said Turk. "Now, first order of business: what do we do with our Rebel eunuchs out back?"

"Got something in mind?" Reno asked.

"How about we GPS Spike's chopper and send him back to Duke?" Turk said.

"I can see why you bloke's chose to support Turk," said Alice. "Brilliant idea. Hey, Nerdo!" he called. "Can you hook up a GPS?"

"Yeah, probably," she called back. The team exchanged nods.

"What'll we do with the rest of them?" asked Reno

"Give 'em a gun with three bullets, let them decide what to do with it," said Turk, showing no mercy.

Cutter and Nerdo joined them around the kitchen table for a cup of mud. Nerdo's puffy eyes bore testament to a long night of hacking as she handed Morri a slip of paper. "Any of these names ring a bell?" she asked. Morri looked them over.

"Yes, that's him," she said. "Gorrick Khan. He's a Brit — used to go pig hunting with my dad. From memory, he's a really strange dude."

"Your dad a hunter then?" Cutter said.

Morri smiled, "Comes with being an Elder,"

"Elder?" asked Nerdo.

"Our Morri here is a pagan," said Secta. "Her dad was the elder of her mob."

"That we have in common, my dad was an Elder as well," Nerdo admitted. "Well, according to what I found, your dad's buddy is the head honcho of Zen. You know, they've actually got communications up and running? Internet, cell phones — all of it, running off an old military satellite they've commandeered. Looks like it's a walled garden, only accessible by Zen, and there are over five thousand of them globally."

"Five thousand be blowed!" roared Alice. "These bastards are running the world!"

"You're not wrong," said Nerdo. "The Zen head office is like the Pentagon was in the US years ago. And get this — the European HQ is Buckingham Palace, traditional seat of the English throne!"

Alice couldn't believe it. "What?" he queried. "So there are no Royals anymore? No King. No US president? This Zen mob really are running the world?"

Turk took over. "Alice, I heard a lot of stories during the war," he said. "Zen Corp started the war, Zen Corp is owned by aliens … What I do know is that Zen invented WarBots and the mind-control system that operates them. But first they invented these implants and popped them into everyone's heads at a young age — apparently some kind of global connectivity thing that would benefit all mankind.

"Then there was iWish, allegedly a gaming and leisure system, but it sure seems like mind control to me. Zen are mind-control experts — so I reckon they purposely stuffed the world up, so they could pick up the pieces afterwards without political or military opposition."

"So they were the real enemy in the Cyberwars?" Reno asked.

Turk nodded. "I reckon they played all sides against each another," he said. "It suited their stratagem."

"Ugh, Big Brother!" said Secta. "Orwell's 1984, only it's 21st century digital dystopia … madness!"

"Yeah well, say what you like," said Reno, grinning amiably, "But if wasn't for iWish, Alice, you'd still be locked in Turk's mind."

"Ah, so that's how you gained consciousness," said Secta. "This iWish device is intriguing. May I see it?"

Reno retrieved it from the front desk and handed it over. "I see …" said Secta. "It's a mind hacker — an evolution of the iBrain, developed by neuroscientists earlier this century. They were working on brain cloning, but were in two minds about it. Ha! Two minds!" He looked at their disapproving stares. "Ahem. Well, you might be wrong about Zen's alien technology," he went on.

"It works on the Alpha zone and theta waves," said Nerdo. "Lifts the high-performance modes of the brain."

"You sound like you know your zeroes and ones, young lady!" said Secta, approvingly. "I'd say it uses a laser optical pulse to stimulate designated sections of the brain for data input through the visual cortex." Secta hypothesized. "And this is a game machine?"

"Yeah, you could say that," Nerdo replied. "Basically, you plug that part there into an implant in your occipital lobe, then download the programs you want from organo-digital software … Learn piano, languages … anything, really."

"Interesting…" said Secta. "But surely seriously addictive?"

"How so?" Nerdo asked.

"Because it would need to manipulate hypnotic elements of the thought process and neurotransmitters. In doing so, it would leave artefacts in axons for later activation — which would be useful if the regulator had designs on mass mind control…"

"There you go," Reno growled. "Zen are mind hackers!" He irreverently snatched the iWish from Morri and dumped it in a trash bin. "Good riddance!" he barked.

Nerdo cast it a longing glance.

"Leave it," he growled.

She left it.

While the others were outside preparing to leave, Nerdo picked her moment to quiz Secta about the time travel-process from a scientific perspective.

"I could do with a more scientific explanation of how you and Alice managed to possess your hosts," she said.

"Good question," said Morri. "He promised me an explanation ages ago, but I'm still waiting!"

She gestured for Nerdo to sit opposite her. Nerdo watched, fascinated, the slight change of expression that came over her youthful face as Secta's personality took over.

"Well, I'm always amenable to talking about myself," he chortled. "Essentially, it's all the result of a formula I developed, which temporarily unbinds the organic molecules that fasten us together at a sub-atomic level. Are you following me?"

Nerdo nodded.

"I can then focus the particles to pass through an open wormhole."

"You invented this process in the past, but we don't have it now," said Nerdo. "What happened to it?"

"Hmm, that's an interesting question," Secta replied. "I really have no idea."

"Alright, we'll get back to that," said Nerdo. "Tell me how you opened the wormhole," she went on.

Secta paced the floor as he continued his lecture.

"A wormhole is a tiny crack in the fabric of time," he said. "I used particle-collider technology in a cloud chamber to open one through which I could send the particle packet."

"Brilliant, like sending a binary data stream?"

"Yes, but I failed to envisage how the form would be reconstructed at the other end of the wormhole. In both our cases, we failed to reform into our bodies and instead entered hosts."

"Like possession?" Nerdo said.

"Yes, you could say that."

"I'm sure any religious fundamentalist would have called it demonic possession and had you exorcised," Morri added.

"So, was Alice your first test subject?" Nerdo asked.

"I suppose you could call him that," said Secta, "Though he might beg to differ. The problem with Alice is that the decay rate of the process wasn't stabilized when he was processed. He was de-molecularized with an imperfect formula and wasn't originally transported through a wormhole. Instead he was contained in a holographic projector from which he was accidentally released in the future."

"But you sent him to this time, didn't you?" Nerdo queried.

"No," said Secta. "He somehow managed to return from the future to our time, but within hours, he began to dematerialize again. There just happened to be a wormhole where he was at that point, which had been opened by extreme atmospheric conditions. When he dematerialized, he was sucked through it to this time, where he wound up possessing Turk. He needs to be stabilized, or it will keep happening. I'm here to take him back and stabilize him."

"You and he could evaporate any moment?" Morri exclaimed.

"Yes, I expect so."

Keen to hear more, Nerdo pressed: "How did you manage to track him to this time and place?"

"I had purposely placed a radioactive marker in his DNA," said Secta. "It was in the original formula. That allowed us to track the marker by following its residue. Once we had the marker coordinates, I took the formula myself and was projected through a wormhole to those coordinates."

"We?" Morri queried.

"My sister Hope is a physicist; she developed the process with me."

"You took a mega risk trying to track him. It could have gone wrong. You had no certainties," Nerdo said.

"Yes, you're right," said Secta. "But I was obligated to try, because I had injected him with an imperfect formula in the first place."

"I see. So, Alice's involvement in your experiment wasn't voluntary then?"

Morri stopped pacing and, sporting a guilty expression, sat back down opposite Nerdo.

"No," he admitted. "The President of Oceana had declared Alice a dissident. He ordered him disposed of. We, or I should say I, needed a candidate to test my theory, and the government gave me Alice."

"Ah," said Morri. "That explains a lot."

"Yes, I suppose I'd be angry too, in his shoes," said Secta. "Look. I admit I did the wrong thing. My sister knew it, but I was blinded by eagerness. I could say I was only obeying orders but in actuality I lost the bearings on my moral compass. So I owe Alice. I took the risk to find him. Besides, the government now wants him back."

"Why?" Nerdo asked.

"He's the world's first, time traveller. I convinced them he's a valuable asset."

"You did what?" Morri shouted, angered by Secta's apparent repeat of untrustworthiness. "So this is all in league with them? You'll hand Alice over like a lab rat?"

"No!" squealed Secta. "I had to say that, it was the only way to save him! Otherwise they wouldn't have approved the mission, and left him here to die!"

"So you're not working for them?" Morri asked.

"No! I'm truly on Alice's side. As I said … I owe him. Believe me, I'm almost as surprised as you are."

"What will happen to him when he returns?" Nerdo asked.

"I won't be handing him over to the government, if that's what you mean."

"Good, I figured you were a better person than that … Well, at least Morri is."

"Thanks, Nerdo. Secta, does Alice know all this?" Morri asked.

"He will in time. I don't want to rile him up right now — as you've seen, he can be a bit reactive. Slowly, slowly catch the monkey, as the saying goes … Now. You tell me something. What happened to the Oceana State Government?"

"They were brought down," said Nerdo. "It became a quasi-socialist democracy."

"A socialist democracy?" laughed Secta. "That's a quite the contradiction!"

"Not really," said Morri. "It worked right up until 2037, when all governments everywhere introduced the OSCI network. In effect, that gave the power back to the people. But at the same time, it set the stage for most government tasks to be sub-contracted out. Hence the rise of Zen." Morri said.

"You're hip to social history, Morri," Nerdo said with a smile.

"Not just a pretty face, our Morri," Secta joked. "Did the names Black Alice or Secta ever come up in your studies?".

"No never."

"Oh," Secta said, glumly.

"Why?"

"Well if my mission here was a success, I'd have expected history to reflect it."

"Maybe you don't make it back!" said Nerdo with a smirk, leaving pondering the possibility of Secta as a permanent resident. Neither of them fancied the idea.

"Well," said Secta. "Maybe that history is still being written."

Within the hour, they were ready to get on the road. Nerdo had successfully created and concealed a GPS in Spike's chopper, and Jonno had been comfortably laid out in Betsy.

As first light, with shadows stretching due west, Turk strode up to the garage door, a pistol in his hand. Reno followed, fumbling through a wad of keys for the one that secured the side door. While Turk covered him, Reno unfastened the padlock, opened the door and quickly stood back.

Turk called instructions into the dark room, "Spike! Walk out slowly with your arms folded behind your head. The rest of you, stay put."

"There is no 'rest of you!'" came Spike's voice, heavy with hate. "They're all dead. Bled out after your surgical handiwork!"

He appeared in the doorway, arms folded behind his head as ordered.

"Shame," said Turk. "How come you're alive?"

Spike studied Turk with a hateful smirk on his heavily bearded and tattooed face.

"Just for the hope of killing you!" he snarled, and spat brazenly on Turk's boots.

Aside from the dried blood that covered his jeans and boots, Spike initially appeared unaffected by his wounds. It became more apparent that this was not the case when Turk made him walk from the garage to his chopper, still parked in the yard. He stumbled along like Boris Karloff's Frankenstein's monster; stiff-legged, obviously in agony. He stopped at his bike.

Turk pointed the pistol at Spike's left knee. "Tell Duke I'm coming for him," he barked. "Now, get on your bike and piss off before I'm tempted to kneecap you just for the hell of it."

Spike moved to mount his bike, but paused when he noticed Jonno propped up in Betsy.

"Looks like Duke's whittling you down," he sneered. A groan of agony escaped his lips as he threw his leg over his bike and slowly brought himself down onto the seat. Even Reno, standing watching with his arms folded, winced.

Spike hit the ignition and his powerful bike thundered to life. With one last disdainful bow-finger to Turk and his colleagues, he motored off.

"Phew!" exhaled Reno. "Say whatever else you like about him, but that is one hell of a tough mother!"

Turk nodded. "Yeah," he said. "Gotta give him that. Right, let's douse the bodies with gas, give 'em a light and get out of Dodge. I want Duke's head more than ever." He strolled back to the bar, whistling as he went.

Reno smiled to himself. Whistling was one thing that made it easy to distinguish Turk and Alice. Turk didn't whistle.

Turk was driving Betsy. Secta was bored, and trying to start small talk with anyone who'd listen. No-one, however, was in the mood. After his third attempt to start a game of I-Spy, Turk's arm jerked and the big truck almost swerved off the road. "Oi!" Turk complained.

"Sorry," said Alice. "But I just remembered something. Secta, I was asking the guys if someone could reactivate that organic chip thing they have in their heads. You know about that?"

"Yes, a little," Secta replied. "Morri's had one since she was three."

"That's right," said Morri. "An organic stem cell implant — OSCI for short. Anyone under the age of 30 would have got one automatically. Folks born before they were invented could opt in."

"Yeah, that's right," said Alice. "Well, what if this Zen mob suddenly decides to reboot everyone? Turn the entire population into an army of WarBots?"

"Hmm, how Orwellian," said Secta. "Reminds me of the voice-of-God experiment by the CIA in the 1970s. They found a way to beam voices directly into people's minds."

"Mind control?" Morri said.

"Yes. From memory, the project was called something like MK-Ultra – anyhow, it worked."

"Well, the guys said it'd take a mad scientist to stop that happening," said Alice. "And before you turned up, I told 'em I knew just the right ratbag for the gig, but that he was in another time."

"Me? Why, how nice of you, Alice. I consider the mad scientist title a badge of honour. Ratbag, admittedly, less so. However. I see the potential issue here. But why bring it up now?"

"So you've got something to occupy your mind with, you bloody pest!"

"Oh," said Secta. "Oh, I see. That's really rather clever." Blessed silence fell over the truck, as Secta lapsed into contemplation.

It was close to midday by the time they'd got through the rigmarole of entering Angel City and managed to manhandle Jonno onto the monorail transport cart. Doc Dan had left them with a few morphine gas injectors to block the pain, but it was still difficult to position him in such a small space without causing agony. With the five of them eventually packed onto the four-seat cart like sardines, it travelled at a snail's pace towards Headbangers.

"D'you think Betsy will be safe in the car park, Reno?" said Cutter.

"She was last time we were here," Reno replied.

"Maybe, but she didn't look like the awesome beast she is now."

"True. Then again, would you risk being pounded by someone who owned something like her?"

Trixy was waiting outside Headbangers when they arrived. She let out a muffled scream when she saw her husband, and rushed up to embrace him.

"Don't fuss, Trix," Jonno groaned. "I'm okay, thanks to these guys."

Through teary eyes, she tried to find the words to thank them. With Jonno's mighty bulk leaning on her small frame, they turned and walked into the bar.

Later, after a bite to eat — courtesy of Trixy's culinary skills — everyone except Jonno and Trixy were sitting around a table. Morri was on a flexible smart-band phone, trying to get hold of Gorrick Khan at Zen HQ.

"Yes, I'll hold ... thank you," she said, politely.

"Zen HQ occupies the old FRT," Reno was saying.

"FRT?"

"Sorry, Alice, keep forgetting you're not Turk," he said. "FRT — Fast Rail Terminal. It was the preferred way to travel from Angel to Sydney before the war. Took just twenty minutes, reached Melbourne in forty. But like everything else, it went down second year into the war."

"How come?" Alice asked.

Reno shrugged. "Good question."

"Who owned it?"

"Government," Nerdo said, shortly.

"And ... what happened to the government?"

"After Sydney and Canberra were nuked, it declared a state of martial law," she replied. "Zen Security was given control."

"Alright. So then what happened to the military and the cops?"

"I can answer that," Cutter chimed in. "There was no police force like back in your day. Before the war the entire country — every house, street, office, road, no matter where — was CCTV monitored 24/7. Made police enforcement obsolete. Zen had the surveillance gig. If a problem was detected, anything from driving violations to robberies to murders, Zen took care of it.

"As for the military — well, the war left it in tatters. Too many regulars killed overseas. Besides, after Zen took control with the WarBots, the military were basically redundant. No pay packet, no forces."

"Yeah. I'll never get what I'm owed," said Turk.

"Us neither," said Cutter, nodding to Nerdo.

"So it all comes back to freaking Zen," said Alice. "So, who are they? Someone must be the top knob?"

"No-one knows," Cutter replied.

"Good hacking exercise," said Reno. "What d'you reckon, Nerdo?"

"I'll see if Jonno's got a computer," she said, getting up.

"So, basically, at this stage, Zen have inherited," Alice said.

"Not much to inherit," said Reno. "Bombs flattened everything, bushfires burnt everything else to a cinder. And once this generation has gone, no more people."

"Why's that?" Alice queried.

"Fallout," Reno said, wiggling his fingers in the air to imitate falling rain.

"Everyone's sterile," Cutter explained.

"What about sperm banks and in-vitro stuff, all that. Wouldn't that be safe?" Alice asked.

Morri was hanging on the phone but listening in, so Secta added: "As soon as a frozen embryo, egg or sperm was exposed to a radioactive atmosphere it would be rendered inert."

"Obviously, they chose not to tell us that while we were fighting their war for them," said Turk, cynically.

"Surely science has progressed past that by now?" Alice growled, finding it difficult to accept the lack of scientific advancement over the last seventy years. "You got your stem cells, your DNA — hey, they were nearly cloning people back in my day!"

"Yeah, but most of the progress was stymied by the war," said Nerdo. "The world as a whole was a much better place during your time."

Further discussion was cut off by Morri waving her hand about.

"Is that you Gorrick?" she was saying. "Yes, it has been a long time. No, sadly I lost them both earlier this year … Thank you … I'm all right I guess. Look, I'm calling because I'm in Angel with a friend. I'd love to see you … Yes, fifteen hundred hours today…" She looked at Turk with raised eyebrows. He fired a thumbs-up. "Yes, that will be fine. Two of us okay? Great. Meet you at Zen … FRT. Thanks Gorrick. It'll be great to see you. Bye!"

She terminated the call and punched the air. "Yes!"

"Well done, Morri!" Alice was pleased.

"Admission for two into Zen!" she said, proudly.

Turk got to his feet, "Okay, it's you and me, Morri. Plus our invisible mates. This is the breakthrough we were hoping for."

CHAPTER 21
Wi-Fi WOES

RENO SIGNALLED THUMBS up to Turk and Morri, and watched their cart move silently away, bound for Zen HQ.

"I guess Gorrick had the cart reprogrammed to take us to Zen?" Turk commented.

"Well, they run the show," said Morri, "I expect that was a piece of cake for him."

"You know, last time I was in the future or whatever it was," said Alice, "It had a bunch of barbarians in it too. I guess that's what you'd call them — they were the survivors of biker gangs like the Rebels. Ruled the roost the same way, too."

"What are you saying, Alice?" asked Secta.

"I dunno, Secta, you understand all this time-travel crap better than me ... But that future, with the bikers and all ... What if it was caused by what's going on in this time, with the biker gangs gaining so much power? Maybe the future has to happen the way I found it?"

"Like it's meant to happen, no matter what?"

"Yeah, I guess so."

"There was a history of trouble with biker gangs even before the war," said Morri. "Ever since the 2030 revolt. At that point they'd been infiltrated by middle-eastern religious extremists hell-bent on creating rebellion. They were running the illegal drug trade, so when OSCI became mandatory and Zen introduced iWish, they were set to lose everything. Zen didn't want a war with them, so they reached a deal."

"I think I'm getting the picture," Alice said. "Explains how they've achieved so much power. Doesn't explain whether it can be prevented or not."

"Alice," Secta posed, tentatively. "You can't continue to take on the woes of the world like they're your own personal problem — you, you just won't survive: these issues are far larger than you…"

"Size doesn't matter Secta, it's all about having the guts to take on the challenge."

Secta knew there was no argument against the bloke's bravado.

The cart plunged into a dimly lit subway tunnel that seemed to go on forever, but they were too deeply engaged in conversation to notice.

"It's only an urban myth," said Morri, "But some people reckon the bikers were given the means to disengage their OSCIs as a trade-off for losing their drug trade."

"Yes, I remember hearing that," said Turk. "And it adds weight to what Alice was saying about Zen planning to use everyone's OSCI to program a new race of WarBots."

"It does seem a likely scenario," Secta put in… "A race of programmable zombies, at Zen's beck and call: a new world order perhaps?"

"But what'd be the point?" asked Alice. "With the population dying out, it'd be nothing but a waste of time. Who's gonna be left to rule over?"

"I think the answer lies with the WarBots," Secta proposed. "Maybe Zen is intent on creating an entirely new population: a race of AI androids totally under their control."

"Doesn't it remind you of the Renken Tabs fiasco, Turk?" Morri asked.

"Yeah: 'the promise for the future'. That was their slogan. 2077, wasn't it? I didn't need them, but old people went nuts over them."

"Renken Tabs?" Secta asked.

"Sorry, I keep forgetting you and Alice don't know some of this stuff," said Turk. "A genetic modifier. You might remember that after society in 2020 had accepted mRNA modifying vaccinations against the SARS virus or COVID, that helped cull the population over the following twenty years ... then Renken Tabs were issued, supposed to target the age gene in people over sixty, eradicating Alzheimer's and dementia, claimed take twenty years off their age, physically and mentally. Well, it actually did the opposite."

"No wonder!" said Secta, quite gobsmacked. "A modifier like that, in the same way as the mRNA vaccines, would have serious side effects — even more so!"

"You're not kidding," said Turk. "Haven't you noticed that as well as no kids, we've got no old people? After six months from taking it the drug caused massive internal haemorrhaging. Poor old bastards just bled to death from the inside out."

"By the time the Cyberwars were declared in 2080, the senior population globally had been almost exterminated," said Morri. "We thought it was another terrible virus at first. We only discovered the truth after it was too late."

"I'll be stuffed," said Alice. "Bloody genocide!"

Suddenly the cart popped out of the dark tunnel. They had entered the central business district.

"Check it out," said Alice. "All these high-rise buildings and not a sign of life anywhere."

Morri noticed a gargantuan mushroom-shaped metal tower they were about to pass. The structure intrigued Secta. "Look at that," he said. "What is its purpose?"

"I think they call it the Tesla Tower," said Morri.

"Named for Nikola Tesla, no doubt," said Secta. "A brilliant man. Best known for his contributions to the design of the modern alternating current electricity supply system. He built the Tesla Tower to broadcast free electricity, something his adopted country — the US — didn't like. Land of the free," he scoffed. "Fine, as long as people are paying for it. I wonder what this tower broadcasted?"

"Who knows?" Morri replied.

"I'll take a guess," said Alice. "Zen built it to broadcast OSCI signals."

"You know, you have an exceptional mind — for a rock singer." Secta said.

As they passed the tower, the cart plunged into another tunnel. Seconds later they pulled up at a disused Fast Train Terminus and clambered out.

Though in a state of disrepair, to Alice the station looked familiar. An elegant, low-slung structure of grey stone and concrete, it was designed in a modern, minimalist style, with a facade gracefully devoid of signage except for one symbol: the winged letters FRT — obviously the logo of the once-proud railway system.

Morri found the elevators nearby. They entered one and pressed the button marked reception. "They still have buttons," Alice mused. "Thought things might have moved on a bit."

When the doors reopened, for the first time since they had left Headbangers, they saw people — and each and every one was dressed in an identical uniform. Alice and Secta were immediately reminded of the Oceana SSD livery: black with red piping, though these featured a Mandarin collar on the tight-fitting jacket, and shoes built in to the legs of the skin-tight trousers. Alice admired how the uniform accentuated the women's figures.

"Nice to finally get a look at the local talent!" he said cheekily to a young female passer-by. The girl ignored him completely.

"That's enough out of you, Alice," Morri scolded, jokingly.

"There must be a couple of hundred people here, and none of them over the age of thirty," Alice replied.

The four walked to another set of elevators, waiting with twenty or so Zen employees for the next available ride. The lack of chatter was noticeable, the only sound being the clatter of footsteps echoing off the black, mirror-finish marble floor. The occasion brought out the larrikin in him and he squeezed out a resounding fart.

Heads turned sharply in his direction only to be greeted by a cheeky grin. Morri gazed at the floor, trying hard not to crack up. Even Turk had to stifle a grin. Just then their elevator arrived and they stepped inside, accompanied by six office workers. There were no buttons to press this time, Alice noticed, wondering how the elevator knew when to stop. Finding the silence unnerving, he started to whistle.

After several stops along the way, the elevator finally reached the top floor. Morri and Turk were the only passengers remaining. They stepped out, and were immediately overwhelmed by the majestic view through the massive windows of the penthouse suite. Below them, Angel City radiated in a planned circle around a park and a stadium, with the whole lot ringed by thick eucalypt forest. Alice was reminded of pictures he'd seen of the ancient Mayan cities of the Yucatan Peninsula. It was breathtaking. But they didn't have time to dwell on it, as the moment was broken by the sound of a youthful female voice.

"Morrigan Hud?"

To their astonishment, Morri had been summoned by a hologram that looked human. The twenty-something young woman had materialised out of nowhere, dressed in a uniform slightly different than those they'd seen previously. Her jet-black hair was up in a bun, and she looked the picture of elegance and sophistication in her knee-length black skirt, matching jacket and black pumps.

"That's me," Morri replied, trying to look unperturbed.

"I am Cindy," she said, with a warm and extremely human voice. "I welcome you to Zen HQ. Please proceed to the double doors: they will open for you once you have passed the security check."

She then silently dissolved.

"Glad I didn't get a gig like that while I was a hologram, Secta," Alice muttered.

Secta raised Morri's eyebrows in reply.

They walked up to a pair of huge, polished timber doors that stretched at least ten metres from floor to ceiling.

"Those doors would have cost heaps," Alice said, peering at them. "Top woodwork."

Suddenly, a red laser descended from a point high above and scanned them from head to toe. It then retracted and a noticeable click sounded as the doors began to swing open. They entered the boardroom.

A tall, refined-looking man with striking, close-cropped white hair stood at the head of a long mahogany table polished to a mirror finish. This immaculately-dressed personage opened his arms and proclaimed in a deep, husky voice: "Well, if it isn't my little Morri."

She went up to the six-foot-six man, and they embraced.

"Gorrick," she said warmly.

He held her at arm's length and studied her. "I'm so sorry for your loss, my dear,' he said genuinely, in slight British accent. "Rowena and Dylan were very special people."

"He's lying," thought Morri, and felt Secta pick it up.

They stared at one another deeply, then Morri said, "I'd like you to meet—"

Gorrick didn't give her the chance to finish the introduction. "Turk, I believe," he bellowed, walking forward with his hand extended.

Turk walked a few paces to take it, looking at the man doubtfully.

"Sit down, sit down, make yourselves comfortable," said Gorrick, cordially. They obliged.

"I need your help, Gorrick," said Morri. "My parents didn't die … they were brutally tortured and murdered. I won't be able to rest until the murderers have paid. The only organization left with the power to help me is Zen."

"I empathise with you, Morri," said Gorrick, "And I, personally, would not hesitate to bring those bastards to justice. But as a corporation, we simply do not have the capability to make that happen."

Morri simply stared. "Mr Khan," Turk started.

"Gorrick, please."

"Gorrick, then. Look, I know the kind of capability Zen has. I fought—"

"Excuse me for interrupting, Turk," said Gorrick, "But I already know. You fought in the war, you had some trouble when you returned to Snake Ridge, and you too are seeking retribution. Unfortunately, this is something we just cannot help with."

"Yeah, well pardon me for interrupting you but Zen is charged with maintaining law and order, is it not?"

Alice whispered in the back of Turk's mind: "Good! Keep winding him up, he'll get angry and spill the beans ... notice he doesn't blink?"

"No, Turk," said the man, infuriatingly calmly. "That is not our job."

"Then whose freaking job is it?" Turk barked back.

"No need to raise your voice, Turk, and certainly no need for profanity," said Gorrick. "I'm sure we can all keep our cool and talk this through in a civilized manner."

"Talk this through. Alright," said Turk. "Let's start with how you know my name and so much about me."

"Your OSCI," he said calmly. "Most people fail to realise it is permanently active. It emits a pulse signal that the appropriate detection device can read. Information such as your full name, DOB, security number; in your case your enlistment ID, service records and other information."

"Wait a minute," Turk said. "How...?"

"It's organically-based, son. It melds with your own brain. So everything you know about you, we know about you too. Knew it before you even stepped into this building."

"You got that information from my Angel entry visa, don't feed me rubbish," Turk snapped.

Gorrick remained cool, "No, that only provided your name and registered address. Both could easily have been false. Look, we created the OSCI system, so we can activate, deactivate and reactivate it when we want to. It really is as simple as that. Now," he leaned forward, locked eyes with Turk, and said quietly. "I think it would be best if you curbed your attitude, son. I am not your enemy."

Turk leaned even closer to him and returned his tone. "I'm not your son, Gorrick," he said. "And I'll decide who my enemies are."

Gorrick sat back. He was tall even while seated. His forehead was high, crowned with his white, short-cropped hair, and deep lines curved around his sharp, hard nose, giving him a cruel, sullen look even behind his phony smile. His mouth was large and well formed, though once again marred by harsh lines suggestive of cruelty and capriciousness. The eyes that were hungrily regarding Turk were fine, intelligent, and steady, a strange colour and as Alice had noticed, unblinking.

"He looks like one of those tall Nordic aliens that UFOlogists talk about," thought Alice.

"Maybe he is," Turk thought back. "Let's see."

"You know, there are people out there who think all of you are aliens, out to take over the planet," he said out loud. "What do you say to that?"

The man's smile never faltered. "I would say that is a load of hyperbole," he answered, lightly. "And I would say you are a dangerous man, Turk. A violent man. You did time for stepping out of line in the forces. If you do not watch your step, you will be doing time again. Here."

"Didn't I just hear you say Zen doesn't meddle in domestic strife?"

Gorrick ignored the question. Morri, who had been listening to her inner Secta, then piped up. "How come you have satellite communications up and running when no-one else has?" she asked.

"That is an odd question from my little girl," he answered, still with that same patient smile. "But I will tell you this, Morrigan. Zen is rebuilding our world. There are things we need to do to achieve our aims that can easily be misunderstood."

Alice couldn't help himself. He jumped in. "Exactly who issued you the damn right to rebuild the world?" he snarled. "Why is it that all through history there have been jerks like you, trying to suppress people and dictate what to do? You're nothing but a frigging cheap stand-over man!"

Gorrick, fortunately, seemed not to see the changes that indicated Alice, and not Turk, was talking.

"You, are out of line, Mr Turk," he said, a warning note entering his voice.

"You just told us that Zen can activate everyone's OSCI," Alice snapped back. "Planning to turn people into mindless zombies, like your precious WarBots? Now that you've made mankind sterile, you'll replace them with robots, will you?"

Gorrick seemed genuinely taken aback. "Obviously you have been reading too much science-fiction, son," he said, trying to recover his smooth manner, but showing the struggle for patience for the first time.

"I'd say you've already registered Zen's intentions by reactivating my OSCI for your use without my permission," said Turk. "That's a breach of my civil rights."

"There is no such thing as civil rights, Turk. Not any more. Look," he added, in a more conciliatory tone. "You are entitled to your opinion. I know war was a bad experience. Many returned soldiers have been left similarly confused. It is difficult to reconcile fighting for your life and your country, when you return home and find it changed for the worst. But it was a necessary war. The population needed to be culled. The world was suffocating. The war reduced that problem by several billon."

"A necessary war?" Turk growled.

"Culled?" said Morri.

"A necessity, Morrigan, to give our race the chance to rebuild."

"And who made Zen god?" raged Alice. "You're full of nothing but head-noise, man!"

"Head noise?" said Gorrick, one eyebrow raised in polite enquiry. Alice realised he'd lost his grip on current vernacular. Turk agreed.

"I mean that you're full of crap!" he clarified.

"Listen, both of you," said Gorrick, still apparently completely calm. "By the twenty-second century the world would have been drained of resources. By that I mean food, clean water, fertile land, even fresh air. Earth would have choked to death from our pollution. It would no longer have been able to sustain a population of over 11 billion people. But now we have a chance."

"A chance?" spat Turk. "You know what I think? I think you're a megalomaniac. You've marginalised those members of society with better standards of living, only to imprison them. You're nothing but a despot."

"History is littered with maniacs like you..." Alice picked up the thread. "You think of yourself as righteous, but you're a poor excuse for humanity! Just a new-world-order freak!"

Morri chimed in. "First we had iWish, designed for addiction. Then Renken Tabs to eradicate the old. Then the Cyberwars. Add the total sterilization of the population and the ruination of this planet, and you've got what Zen is guilty of. Genocide on a global scale."

Gorrick rose from his chair, visibly unsettled for the first time. His voice, however, remained calm, as he said: "You cannot blame Zen for all of that. We lived in volatile times, with virulent viruses before the war. Many unscrupulous profit makers, like drug companies, provided dangerous, irresponsible science. It was mad science that created Renken Tabs, not Zen."

"As a mad scientist, I take exception to that," Secta whispered in Morri's mind.

"You're nothing but a bloody corrupt security company!" said Turk.

"We started out in surveillance, that is quite correct," said Gorrick. "And in a way, we are still doing that, only on a much larger scale. Allow me to prove my point. Cindy?" There was a second's pause while the hologram appeared. "Show Mr Hiyak in, please."

Reno was sitting on the front porch of Headbangers, flicking through a magazine. Cutter was beside him, drinking a beer and appreciating the sun's rays filtering through the shade of the buildings. Flicking through the on-screen pages, Reno stopped at Miss November. Touching the picture with his finger caused it to jump into holographic life, and strike some intriguing poses.

Nerdo came out, leaned against the wall, and looked at them. Reno made an instinctive move to shut down the picture, then realised she probably appreciated it just as much as they did.

"Sorry to interrupt, fellers," she said. "I've got some bad news."

That distracted them from Miss November. Reno closed the mag and got to his feet.

"What is it?"

"I used Jonno's old Ulink computer to hack back into the Zen database," she said. "Got pretty deep inside Zen before I hit a firewall I couldn't bust through. Not with this tech, anyway," she qualified, hurriedly. "But I did find an interesting-looking cloud. So I opened it, and guess what was inside?"

"No clue," Reno admitted.

"A direct connection between this guy Gorrick Khan and the Rebels. Correspondence between Gorrick and some dude called Abdul Hiyak at Rebel HQ about Zen gifting them a WarBot."

"Hell, Turk and Morri are in serious danger!" Reno said. "The Rebels and Zen are in cahoots? We need to get them out of there, it's a bloody trap!"

Cutter's face had turned ashen. "A WarBot?" he said. "They're giving the Rebels a WarBot?"

"Look, I know it's bad, man, but ... What?" Reno asked. "Cutter, what is it?"

Cutter had his head in his hands, shaking, staring unseeing at the table. "Nerdo and me saw what WarBots are capable of at the battle of Gonabad, up near the Afghan border," he said. "She worked on 'em. If the Rebels get one — that's it. The game is up, man!"

Reno ran his fingers through his hair. "Damn, this actually makes sense," he said. "Zen arms the bikers, the bikers take control of everywhere outside the cities."

"And you know what's worse?" said Nerdo, gravely.

Reno and Cutter shook their heads. They couldn't think of anything that might be worse.

"This is conformation that Alice was right," she said. "They must be able to reactivate the OSCI network, or they wouldn't be able to operate WarBots."

They exchanged looks full of sombre apprehension. They knew they couldn't fight a weapon like that. It would give the Rebels unequivocal dominance. Resistance to the new tyranny, even if it was possible, would also be futile.

Turk and Morri's attention was focused on the big boardroom doors as they began to swing open.

"So, who's this guy then?" asked Alice.

"A colleague who will put our debate to rest," said Gorrick.

A big man in a smart black suit stepped in, and Gorrick gestured to him. "Meet our head of domestic security," he said. "Mr Abdul Hiyak."

Striding confidently into the room, Hiyak stopped short of the board table and fixed his eyes on Turk, who stood, transfixed, before growling: "Duke!"

CHAPTER 22
CHECKMATE

KARZOFF WAS ENJOYING his new gig. He had Hope stripped down to her underwear and suspended by her wrists from a pull bar atop a stand-alone home gym set. She was gagged, her ankles strapped to the floor supports on either side of the bench seat. The unit stood in the middle of a large room, bare except for a single lounge chair directly in front of the apparatus. Karzoff was seated in it, with his legs crossed.

"You look quite comfortable there, Hope," he said, greasily. "Don't worry, I will not inflict any pain on you. You may wonder why I'm doing this?" he paused, while she simply glared blackly at him from behind her gag. "Well," he went on, "You are simply our insurance — a guarantee that we will get Black Alice back..."

Hope knew screams and struggles would be useless. She was entirely at Karzoff's mercy.

It was late afternoon by the time Honor called it a day. Wary of a repeat attack from the Octagon, she'd requisitioned a bodyguard to meet her outside SSD HQ. Her intention was to visit Karzoff and grill Hope, as much for her own pleasure as for any reassurance it might offer. Secta had been gone for a little over thirteen hours, and her nerves were feeling strained. She wasn't the type to relinquish control to anyone, let alone someone as mercurial as Secta. She needed someone to take her anxiety out on. And who knew, Hope might even be able to offer some scientific assurance that Secta had made it to the other dimension, and had enough time to accomplish his mission. Honor shivered. She'd staked her reputation on a man she didn't trust.

She met her assigned bodyguard at HQ front entrance. Without a word, the big plain-clothes guard walked her to a EV-taxi, which he had waiting. It was safer than an agency car: there was less likelihood of being tailed.

It was a sunny, midweek autumn afternoon with little traffic to affect their progress. Driving south on Anzac Parade they headed for Maroubra Beach in the Eastern suburbs, and as they were passing the newly renamed Zen Sydney Football Stadium, Honor noticed a billboard promoting a coming rugby test: the Wallabies versus Japan. Zen Corporation was billed as the major sponsor.

"Vhat happened to our sponsorship of ze stadium?" she asked the guard indignantly. "I rather enjoyed ze complimentary tickets to ze rugby." She looked at the big, scarred man sitting beside her, taking up most of the rear bench. He looked like an ex-rugby player himself, his face marked by too many scrums and even more brawls.

"Zen is a new IT company with plenty of money," he said in a deep monotone that sent vibrations along the seat. "I guess they offered more than us for the naming rights."

'Humph. Zey already haff a stadium named after zem,' she complained.

He was thinking she was a skinny, pretentious rat.

"By ze size of your thighs, you are some kind of athlete, yes?" she asked.

"I was a Wallaby for three years," he replied disinterested, and turned his gaze out the window.

The taxi arrived at its destination, a modern, twenty-story apartment complex at South Maroubra, one of Sydney's premiere beaches. Honor stepped from the cab and waited for the bodyguard to pay. She was feeling grumpy, irritated by being shunned. When he joined her, she spun on her heel and defiantly strode towards the apartment block, causing him to hurry to catch up. She stopped at the entrance, folded her arms and impatiently tapped her foot, waiting for him to lead her to the elevator.

The penthouse door buzzed and opened. "Guard the door," she snapped at her chaperone.

As she entered the apartment, the bodyguard looked skyward for heavenly support, shaking his head. "What a pain," he muttered, under his breath.

Honor entered the living room and stopped to acknowledge the view of the beach through the French doors opening onto a small balcony. Then she turned her attention on Hope, still tied to the apparatus.

Ignoring the intrusion, Karzoff remained reclining in a lounge chair.

Hope let out a muffled groan.

"Having fun?" Honor purred, walking around Hope as though inspecting something on sale whose only appeal was that it was cheap.

"This is far more enjoyable than field work," Karzoff claimed.

"I vonder who has been haffing ze most fun — you or ze doctor here?"

Karzoff rose from the armchair and assumed a deferential crouch. "Just doing as ordered, Honor," he said.

Honor fired him a knowing glare. "They say 'sweets for ze sweet' — it seems your taste for ze extreme is just as random."

"If I did not know you better Honor, I would have thought you just made a joke," Karzoff said, giggling nervously.

"Save your asinine discourse for your friends, Karzoff!" she snapped, suddenly. "How do you expect to get her to admit anyzing viz her mouth gagged, imbecile?"

"I, I … did not think … I…," he stuttered, hating how Honor stood over him.

Hope let out a single muffled sob, exhausted physically and emotionally by the humiliation as much as the torture.

Shaking her head, Honor collected Hope's clothes from the floor and covered her. "Zere," she said. "Now, get her a glass of water, Karzoff."

Hope licked her parched lips. She knew she wasn't getting the water as an act of kindness. Honor was totally incapable of doing anything humane. She removed the gag. Hope tried to speak, but it came out as a croak.

While Karzoff went to the kitchen, Honor leaned close and whispered in her ear. "Karzoff's little games vill become increasingly perverted, perhaps even violent as time goes by," she said. "If you vant him to stop, give me ze complete formula for ze experiment, and you may go free."

Hope drew a deep breath. "Is that what this is about?" she replied, in a shaky voice. "I don't know the complete formula, Honor!"

"I do not believe you, Hope!" the woman spat in reply. "I know you can run ze experiment on your own, so you must know ze formula!"

"Even if I did, Honor," Hope said, "I wouldn't give it to you in a fit of madness!"

A glass of water was handed to Honor from behind Hope. Honor took it and placed the glass to the parched lips, but before her captive could get the longed-for relief, she pulled it away. She smiled cruelly, pleased with her sense of power.

"No, no, no," she said, with mock gentleness. "On second thoughts, you do not need a drink. I zink it best for Karzoff to continue overnight. Maybe by tomorrow you vill be more cooperative."

As Honor was about to move to the chair, she felt the blade of a knife at her throat.

"I don't know about that, Honor," snarled a deep voice. "I think you might be the one in an odd mood by tomorrow."

Relief broke out on Hope's haggard face. "Mal!" she gasped.

"Unfasten her!" Mal ordered.

Honor, as she went to comply, asked: "How did you get rid of ze guard?"

"What guard?" said Mal, grinning.

As soon as the last restraint was free, Hope staggered from the improvised torture rack, grabbed the glass of water and drank it down. Then she gathered her clothes and began dressing.

"Took you long enough," she rasped.

"Sorry," said Mal. "I've never been a punctual kind of guy." He grabbed Honor and started strapping her into the equipment.

"You can do vhatever you like to me, I vill enjoy it!" Honor snarled, defiantly.

"That doesn't surprise me, Honor," he replied. "The best way to torture you is to do nothing at all. And that really isn't difficult," he added, stepping back from his handiwork and looking her over. "Wait a minute," he said, noticing her silver-painted nails. "How about, just for the sake of it, I take off the first joint of your left pinkie?"

"Now zat vould be stretching a friendship," said Honor. "I suggest you zink about payback, Mr Function. Zat is somezing you need carefully to avoid. You vill not be able to hide from us, and ze consequences of your actions vill be diabolical."

"You ready, Hope?" he said, over his shoulder. "I'm so over this bitch."

"Yep," she said, buttoning up her white blouse. "It's been fun, Honor," she went on, crisply. "Do give Karzoff my best regards — when he comes round." For the first time, Honor noticed the slumped form of Karzoff, unconscious and bound on the floor.

"Bloody Octagon!" she snarled. "You mark my vords, Hope, and you too, Function! Zere is no place for you to hide! No place! I vill get you! Zat is a promise!"

"A little melodramatic, Honor," Hope said drily, shoving in the gag.

There was no bodyguard standing at the front door. Mal had also played rugby for the Wallabies. The bodyguard had been one of his teammates.

A surge of adrenaline rushed through Turk at the sight of their enemy, Duke. Yet no-one moved.

"Hit him mate!" Alice bellowed savagely in their shared mind-space.

"It seems the arrival of my friend here has sated your appetite for argument, Turk," Gorrick said, sarcastically. But before anyone could react, Turk dived across the table and grabbed his enemy by the throat. The force of the attack knocked the besuited biker backwards in his chair, and both men tumbled onto the floor. Turk struggled up on top, and let rip with a fierce flurry of blows. Both men were of a similar build, but Duke was more ripped, and had it all over Turk when it came to sheer muscle.

He blocked Turk's blows with his forearms until the ominous click of a trigger being cocked sounded in Turk's left ear and he registered the touch of cold steel on his temple. He froze. Fist poised to deliver a killer blow to Duke's exposed throat, Turk peered at the barrel from the corner of his eye.

"That is enough!" commanded Gorrick. "Get up, please, nice and slowly, and sit back down. Believe me, I will not hesitate to shoot you here and now if you fail to comply."

Turk's expression cleared into something emotionless. Gorrick recognised the warrior for the fearless fighter he was, and it worried him. The pistol was trembling in his hand. Turk knew a shaking hand was more likely to pull the trigger. Without looking at the man, he stood up and calmly moved around the table to sit beside Morri.

Gorrick offered Duke a hand up.

Through a bleeding eyebrow Duke scowled at Turk, then jeered: "Nice try, soldier boy, but the odds were never in your favour."

"Your choice of friends is disappointing, Gorrick," was all Turk said.

"What … not happy to see me, Turkie?" said Duke. "I guess I can understand that. But I'm hurt — last time we met, after all, I gave you a light!"

"Where is my sister?" Turk said, in a low, dangerous voice.

"Somewhere safe," said Duke, casually, then cast a grubby smirk at Morri. "Who's this tart?"

"Oh, how rude of me," said Gorrick, who had resumed his seat. "This is Morrigan Hud. I have known her since she was a child."

"You murdered my parents, you freaking pig!" Morri yelled at Duke.

"More flattery!" he said, smugly. "But what makes you think so, blondie?"

"Your MO was all over that scene. You crucified them on their front veranda, then incinerated them — remember?"

"Ah," said Duke. "But if they were incinerated, how do you know they were your parents?" He locked his dead fish eyes on her.

"You must admit, Morri, he has a point," said Gorrick, pocketing his pistol.

"Maybe what you found were decoys, a couple of charred red herrings," Duke went on. "Maybe your parents are still alive. Maybe, in fact, they're right here at Zen," he teased.

"Stop this!" snarled Turk. "What've you got to gain from this bullcrap? Why torture the girl? Your beef's with me!"

"Ah, well, that's where you're wrong," Duke sneered. "Such a narcissist, Turk … what the stuff would we want with you? Our little encounter was just some playing around, just my lads blowing off a little steam. Just a little payback for being a nosey parker. No, Turk. We're not interested in you at all." His gaze shifted to Morri, who was sitting transfixed.

"Now, Morrigan here," said Gorrick, stepping back in, "Well, we want Morri for her outstanding psychic abilities. You and your little team of brigands are simply in our way," he added. "I think we can dispense with them now?" he said to Duke.

The big biker stood. "Checkmate, soldier boy!" he growled, turned on his heel and strode out of the room.

"Why, Gorrick?" whispered Morri. "Why?" Her blue eyes were filled with abject sorrow.

"To make a better world, Morri," said Gorrick, patiently. "That is why."

"Well, stuff me!" said Alice, savagely. "How frigging noble of you!"

Reno, Jonno, Trixy, Cutter and Nerdo were sitting round a table in Headbangers. "It's fair to assume they won't be back," said Reno. "We knew that. So me and Turk made a backup plan. "I've got his and Morri's OSCI logons," he went on. "Remember how Alice reckoned our implants are still operative, and that Zen's gonna reactivate them? Turk figured Nerdo might be able to beat them to it in his or Morri's case. If you can do that, Nerdo, we can communicate with 'em, find out what's going on at Zen HQ. What d'you reckon?"

"I mean, I'll deffo give it a shot," Nerdo said, "But I'm certain Zen will jam me as soon as I get through. We'll only have a few minutes to talk to them at best."

"A few minutes might buy us just enough time," said Cutter.

Nerdo nodded. "I'll get right on it."

"Good-o," Reno said, lifting his beer. He turned to Jonno. "How's the leg, old son?"

"Still attached," said Jonno with a grin. "I can even walk on it now."

Two heavily armed guards towered over Morri as they escorted her and Turk to a cell in the basement of the building. It was a small cubicle with a bunk bed, a washbasin and a toilet. Once they'd been shoved inside, a guard activated a laser bulwark to contain them, and their escort stomped off. Morri flopped onto the bottom bunk, head in her hands.

"Hey, we're not dead yet," Turk said, his voice unusually kind.

"Yeah, I know," she said. "It's just what they said about my folks."

"They were messing with your head, kiddo," Alice piped up. "Sounds like they've got something big planned for you — maybe they're trying to break down your resistance by playing mind games."

"Well that's a pathetic plan," Morri snorted. "If that's their level of intelligence we don't need to worry about being outsmarted, at least. They should know that being psychic means I can tell if my folks are dead or alive."

Turk sat beside her. After a few seconds, he placed an arm around her shoulders.

"We have to stay strong, Morri," he said, gently. "I think it's going to get tougher before we can make things better."

"Well I don't like it!" Secta announced, his angst-ridden whine shattering the intimate moment. "I'm running out of time here! If I don't get back, with Alice, within the next twenty-four hours, they'll destroy my equipment and I'll be stuck here forever. Oh, and they might hurt Hope, too."

"How come every time you open her mouth, you come out with something that's all about you, Secta?" Alice complained. "Just shut up and hang in there, will ya? We'll think of something."

Turk saw a tear drop down Morri's cheek. "Want to talk about it?" he asked.

"I'll never forget seeing them," she wailed, bursting into sobs. "The bastard nailed them to the front of the house and set them on fire! And I ... I wasn't even there to help them!"

Turk wrapped her in a hug. "Sshh, nothing you could have done," he said. "I've seen these guys in action. You'd have been killed too, most likely. There's no point beating yourself up over it."

"You don't understand," she said. "I'd been in Avalon — with a guy. I'd stayed longer than I should've. All I could think was how they were gonna yell at me — and then ... then I saw them! I saw it happen while I was with him, Turk. I could never see him again after that. Sometimes I wish I had been killed alongside them."

"You can't blame yourself, Morri," Turk said again, then suddenly stood up as if bitten by a spider, a look of amazement on his face. "Hello?" he said, "Nerdo, is that you?"

Nerdo was sitting at Jonno's computer in the back office of Headbangers, the others standing around her. "Turk, yeah, it's me!" she said. "I've got a GPS fix on you through your OSCI. You okay?" she asked.

"Yes. Well, they've got us both in jail, but we're not hurt. Nerdo, tell the guys — Duke's here! He's in cahoots with bloody Gorrick and Zen!"

"Listen mate, I can't stay on. If they find this link we're cooked. I'll log off and we'll talk early in the morning, alright? Bear up mate, we're on this!" She disconnected.

Turk cracked a big grin at the still-sniffling Morri. "Nerdo," he said. "She hacked my OSCI. They know where we are, Morri. They'll get us out!"

The girl smiled, but she was still distraught. Silently, he gathered her into his arms, holding her like a child, frightened by the dark. They lay down together on the bunk and drifted off to sleep. It had been a rough day.

Morri saw a crowd of people standing and staring. They all wore Zen uniforms and looked exactly the same, not male, not female, androgynous. Sexless. Even more bizarre, they moved as one, identical in every way, like pre-programmed clones. It was daytime, the sun glaring directly above. She looked at her bare feet and suddenly realized she was hovering about six metres in the air above a platform that the uniformed crowd had encircled. There was a feeling of anticipation, excitement — they were anxiously waiting for something to happen.

She saw Gorrick sitting among the crowd with Duke at his side, and then, to her horror, she recognised the person beside Duke — herself, dressed in a Zen uniform. How can that be? she thought. What is this? Then Duke stood and the crowd cheered. He motioned for quiet and at once it became so silent you could have heard a pin drop. Duke was making an announcement, but his words were unintelligible, as though he spoke in some alien tongue. The clunk of a door opening below echoed in the air, and a murmur of fear erupted from the audience. She looked down at her feet to see a seven-foot cyborg standing on the platform holding a long-handled, double-headed axe. A roar went up from the crowd as the guards pushed four men alongside it. Morri recognised them: Jonno, Reno, Turk and Tatts.

It suddenly dawned on her that this was an execution. The cyborg was going to behead her friends. She had to stop it, but no matter how hard she tried she couldn't do more than hover in the air as a disembodied consciousness — a watcher.

She looked back at Duke. Still standing, he raised his thumb and then, to the roar of the audience, turned it down. It was the signal for the cyborg executioner to act. The uniformed Morri jumped to her feet beside Duke and screamed, but no sound came. No matter how she tried, not a sound came from her mouth.

Floating Morri looked back down. The cyborg gabbed Tatts, pushed him to his knees and beheaded him with one mighty swing, one single blow. The severed head bounced along the ground and into a basket — a loud ding sounded and the number one lit up on a digital scoreboard. The crowd cheered their approval.

She had to avert her eyes from the execution. To raucous cheers the scoreboard sounded a second ding, then a third; she'd lost two more friends. She looked back at that other Morri, in her seat with her head in her hands, sobbing. She knew Turk would be last to be executed. Suddenly uniform Morri looked sharply up and then slowly, with a look of determination, rose to her feet. This time she would be heard. But just then Gorrick jumped up, grasped his left ear, and peeled the skin off his face! Now his real face was revealed, alien and bizarre. He raised the ghastly mask in the air. The crowd followed suit, every one of them, save Duke, peeling off their faces and holding up the masks in silent reverence. This time Morri's scream echoed loud and clear.

Duke turned to Morri, laughed out loud, and shouted to the cyborg below: "Kill Turk!"

Morri screamed. "No! Turk! Turk!"

Jolted awake by Morri's cry, Turk sat bolt upright to find Duke leering at them from the other side of the laser barrier.

Morri stirred, awakened from her nightmare.

"Oh, what a lovely couple," the biker said facetiously. "It'll be a crying shame to split you up. But, hey, I've got a friend here to brighten your day, and he's real keen to see you." He whistled, as if calling a dog. Spike stepped out of the shadows.

CHAPTER 23
DARK ANGEL

NIGHT HAD FALLEN and Jonno was standing at the door of Headbangers, seeing off Reno, Nerdo and Cutter. "Damn it guys," he groaned, despondently, "I should be going with you."

Reno offered him a hand.

"There's no-one else I'd rather have at my side, mate, but we've gotta go on foot," he replied. "There's no cart and you know how tough that'd be with a crook leg."

"Even tougher trying to dodge Zen-CCTV," Nerdo added.

"I know, I know," said Jonno, still mournful. "Sometimes stuff just doesn't turn out the way you expect, eh?"

Jonno and Reno shook hands. Reno pulled him close and slapped his back affectionately. They'd been best mates for a long time. They both knew the danger of the mission.

"You come back, my friend, and bring our mates with you," Jonno whispered. "We didn't do all that growing up together for it to end bad, you hear me?"

"You broke my fall once, mate," said Reno, with smiling eyes. "You'll do it again, if I have anything to do with it."

Trixy appeared at Jonno's side, and together they watched the dark curtains of night close behind their friends.

"Hope they'll be all right," Jonno said, loathing the fact that he could not be with them.

"Feels like you can't be certain of anything anymore," Trixy replied, throwing an affectionate arm around her husband's waist.

After twenty minutes of navigating through a dark alley in the old red-light district of Angel City, Reno, Nerdo and Cutter arrived at the border of the Angel City CBD. Nerdo broke out a handheld Ulink computer she'd borrowed from Trixy, and checked a map.

"How do you get all this stuff without the internet?" asked Cutter.

"I carry this with me," she said, showing him a small clear plastic container the size of a matchbox. "The little round things in there are microdots — miniature cell drives. Each one is a specialized app. My favourite uses any computer Wi-Fi scanner to find more than just Wi-Fi — like microwaves, radio frequencies loads of wave lengths that organizations like Zen secretly use for their comms. I can piggyback them to get into their servers and hack their intranet. Got the microdots courtesy of the army," she added, with a chuckle. "They don't know I pinched them, of course!"

Reno was listening. "Might need to hack Morri's OSCI as well," he said. "She and Turk could be in different locations now."

"Yeah. When we get closer to Zen I'll do a locate ping on both of 'em. That's a different microdot, locks me into a com-sat. I've got Zen's IP protocol now, so I can log on to both their OSCI codes. Might only get one more shot before they jam me though."

"Cool, you're a genius!" Reno replied, rubbing his hands together to warm them up. The night had brought a stiff cool south west breeze, a sharp contrast to the blistering hot day.

"Yeah, it's cold," said Nerdo. "We'll need to get undercover soon or we'll freeze to death." She was only half joking. They weren't likely to freeze, but the cold could be mighty unpleasant.

"How far to Zen?" Cutter asked.

"About twenty minutes away, maybe thirty as the crow flies, but it's difficult to set up a route to avoid their CCTV network. It'll probably take us a few hours." said Nerdo. I reckon I've got it mapped, but there's one dud spot close to Zen where it'll get tricky."

"How would they recognise us on CCTV in the dark?" Reno asked.

"Eight thousand mega pixels, man," said Nerdo. "It's like a camera zooming from a satellite to count the hairs on your chin. Day or night, doesn't matter. Got the picture? Coz they sure will." She smiled.

"Let's get moving then," said Reno. "Sun's up in a few hours and we still need the cover of darkness, no matter how many mega pixels they've got!"

They moved off, sticking to the darkest shadows, like thieves in the night. Leading the way, Nerdo stopped periodically to refer to her Ulink, navigating around the cameras. They were just about to cross Federation Drive, the main street of the business area, when she signalled for them to stop.

"What's up?" Reno asked.

Peering intensely at the Ulink, Nerdo fumbled through her deep pockets and came up with a pair of sunglasses. She put them on, and peered into the distance. Cutter recognised them as army infrared glasses, designed for scanning for laser detectors.

"Thought so," Nerdo said, fixed on something a short distance away. "The city is wired with laser banding. These bastards are paranoid!"

"Maybe they're trying to protect something," Cutter said, turning to Reno who was looking over Nerdo's shoulder at the Ulink display. "We're lucky to have the military's number one hacker on our side, don't you reckon, mate?"

Reno nodded in agreement. "Reckon," he said. "So how are we going to get around the banding?"

"Take a look," said Nerdo, handing the glasses to Reno.

As he put them on, the black and white cityscape lit up with thin, red crisscrossing lasers, aimed from various vantage points high up in buildings down into the streets below. The streets were covered by them.

"Damn! "How we going to get through that mess?" Reno questioned, feeling the obstacles could put an end to the mission.

"We're not," Nerdo said, tapping Reno on the shoulder to get the glasses back. "We're going through the buildings. All we need do is get into the first building. See that?" She pointed at the Ulink screen. "Because they get unpredictable weather here, there's a subterranean shopping mall that connects all the buildings. From what I can see, it extends all the way to the car park and cart terminal under Zen HQ. I just need to find an access point."

"The subway!" suggested Reno, excitedly.

"Of course!" Nerdo agreed. "Brilliant ... and there it is, just two blocks from here. Corner of Federation Drive and Coalition Street."

"Yep, Fed Station, caught trains from there myself," Reno said.

"Let's move," said Nerdo, sharply. She led the way, carefully monitoring the Ulink for lasers. Moving slowly, they reached the subway entrance, only to find it barricaded. "Stuff it!" Nerdo cursed. "No — wait. There's a service entrance. Follow me."

They slipped silently into a narrow alleyway at the side of the entrance and stopped at a doorway. Nerdo could see laser banding intersecting it through her glasses. Once more, she fumbled in a pocket and produced a make-up compact.

Reno and Cutter exchanged raised eyebrows. Cutter nudged Reno. "What's up, Nerdo?" he whispered, "Think you might meet the girl of your dreams in there?"

Nerdo didn't reply — there was no time for jokes, as far as she was concerned. Ignoring the two men, she sprawled on the ground and carefully placed her compact on the footpath near the door. She lined it up with the laser and, quick as a flash, pushed the mirror into place. It intercepted the beam neatly, deflecting it without setting off an alarm. The move left a gap in the grid large enough for her to squeeze through. She sat back and took a deep breath, content.

"How'd it go?" Cutter asked.

"Well, no bells and whistles, no army — I guess it worked!" she said, taking Cutter's hand to get to her feet. "The trick will be getting through the door without touching a laser. I'll go first, then hand you back the glasses."

"Rad," Reno muttered, as he and Cutter stood back to give her room.

Nerdo had a lot of work to do to get through the small window she'd created in the cross-crossing laser grid. First, she reached a hand through to test if the door was open on the other side. She was in luck, but that was understandable; the door was effectively locked by the lasers. Next, she studied the grid. She'd have to step over one laser while ducking under another, keeping her arms tight by her sides to avoid other beams. She steadied herself, tucked her coat into her dungarees, pulled her baseball cap tighter and stepped through. Perfect. Gingerly, she handed the glasses back to Reno.

Like Nerdo, he tucked in everything that was loose, then put on the glasses.

"Damn!" he exclaimed. "It's a pretty small window, Nerdo!"

Being much larger than Nerdo, he had a narrower margin for error. But he was fit and flexible. He made it through.

"Phew, that was tough," he gasped. "Hope you've got a bit of contortionist in you, mate," he said to Cutter.

Cutter, being smaller and slighter than Reno, also proved equal to the task. He soon joined them on the other side. Now they could forget about the approach of daylight and laser banding — the rest of the journey would be underground.

Nerdo checked through the glasses.

"Anything?" Cutter asked.

"Hope not. A girl only carries one compact!" she joked. "Nar, nothing, but I'll keep the glasses on, just in case."

It was pitch black, apart from the light from Nerdo's Ulink. She led them into the gloomy, half-demolished world of subterranean Angel City.

"I'm gonna enjoy killing you," Spike said, leering at Turk through the laser bars. Turk ignored him, but Alice followed through. "Shut your face, no nuts, no-one cares. Besides, nothing's gonna bring back your balls. And that's a win for us, no matter what."

"Couldn't have said it better myself," Secta muttered. "Annoying degenerate."

"Okay, Spike, outside," said Duke, before the man could react. "Don't worry. You'll get your chance to get square."

Spike eyeballed Turk. "Mongrel," he growled, turning to walk away.

"Rather be a mongrel than a gelding," Alice snapped back.

"Soldier boy!" Duke held up a small remote. "When the grid turns green, step through. Bitch, you stay put."

"Turk," said Morri, urgently, grabbing his arm. "I had a premonition in my sleep. It wasn't good, we—"

"Shut it Blondie," snarled Duke. "Not another word. Now wait here like a good girl 'til we're good and ready for you."

He pressed the remote. The vertical laser bars changed to green, allowing Turk to pass and reverting to red as soon as hc passed through.

"Let's smack the bastard, take the remote and bail!" thought Alice. But Duke was, as ever, one step ahead. He pointed to Spike, still standing in the corridor, a gun trained on Turk.

"Wouldn't even think about it, soldier boy," Duke sneered. "He doesn't need an excuse to drill you. How's that knee of yours, anyway? Thought I heard it squeak!" Laughing at his own joke, he pushed Turk hard along the corridor towards the elevator.

Morri sank back onto the bunk.

"Must be almost time to panic," Secta suggested.

"Wc just have to sit tight," she said. "Turk says the cavalry's on their way, and I have a feeling he's right."

"I know…" said Secta, insinuatingly. "We could try for another vision … I'd very much like to experience that."

"In your dreams, Secta," Morri snapped. "There'll be no crossing that line."

"The last one was interesting, though" he whined.

"Yeah. And scary."

"I'll grant you that, but the question is, was it a metaphor or were you really seeing the future?" he said. "I mean, I would argue that inducing another vision right now would be both therapeutic and strategic. It could even help us save Turk and Alice."

"Secta, even if I was in the mood to gratify your sick little desires, which I'm not, this is hardly the place," she said. "End of story," she added, feeling him about to argue. "I'm going to try to sleep."

"Fine," sighed Secta. "You do that." But as she nodded off again, Secta had other ideas.

The darkness made it difficult to find a clear passage over the rubble and debris in the aisles and corridors of the underground mall. All the shops had been looted long ago, and most of the construction materials plundered. It was dark, dangerous and eerie … so dark that Nerdo was holding up the Ulink as a torch. In spite of the obstacles, they were making reasonable time, but Nerdo was becoming more vigilant as they neared Zen. She expected security to pick them up soon: it was only a matter of time.

She stopped abruptly. "We're close," she said. "It's the next station."

"Why are we stopping?" Reno asked.

"There'll be different security measures at that station, as well as CCTV," she said. I have no idea what could be waiting."

"Let's walk up the train lines," said Cutter. "Probably less security there."

"Good thinking," Nerdo agreed.

After about one hundred and fifty metres, Nerdo stopped them again. "I think we should get a GPS on Turk and Morri now," she said. "I've got a gut feeling it'll be the last chance we'll get."

"You won't get a signal down here," Reno said.

"Watch her," said Cutter, knowingly.

Both of them watched with interest as Nerdo opened the box containing the microdots, selected a green one the size of a sequin, and pressed a button on the side of the Ulink. A tiny yellow dot appeared from an almost invisible slit, which she removed and replaced with the green dot. Digging deep in her apparently endless pockets, she came up with a lead, which she plugged it into one of the Ulink's ports.

"What's that?" Reno asked.

Ignoring him, Nerdo bent down and touched the jack of the lead to the train track.

"Got it!" Cutter said. "She's using the metal as an aerial. Clever."

Nerdo hit keys on the Ulink so fast her fingers were a blur.

"I'm in!" she declared, punching in more numbers. "Got a fix on Turk — I'll just save the coordinates. Alright, wait … yes! There's Morri. We're done."

"Can we talk to—" Reno was saying, when Nerdo cut him off. "Signal's gone. They're onto us!" she said, gravely, gathering up the aerial cable. She looked at Cutter, concerned. "I wonder how they'll respond?"

"Better get moving," was the only reply.

The three jogged the final fifty metres to the FRT platform. Reno was just reaching down to give Nerdo a hand up when they heard Cutter hiss a warning. They froze as he took cover behind a platform bench, pistol up.

Reno pulled Nerdo up the two-metre rise in silence, and they joined him. Crouched, scanning the platform, for what he'd spotted, Cutter pointed towards the distant end of the platform. "There's someone there," he whispered. "I saw movement."

There was a bright flash of blinding light. As her eyes recovered, Morri realised she was alone in the confines of a small concrete room. No Turk, no Alice, no Secta. The light revealed that she was standing at the foot of a set of stairs. A rustle came from above, and she looked up — someone was climbing the staircase ahead of her. She followed and emerged onto a small platform beside him. Even in the inky darkness that followed the light, she could tell it was Turk.

Without looking at her, he reached for her hand.

The air was thick with dust, making it difficult to breathe. There was a deathly silence. The smell of cordite hung in the air. Her eyes, growing accustomed to the dark, peered down. They were four metres or so above the ground, in the middle of a charred crater on top of a strange concrete obelisk. There had clearly been a massive explosion. Beyond the rim of the crater stretched a blackened field, littered with small burning fires. It was like looking at the aftermath of a battle, and she wondered: is this the end of the world?

Nerdo produced a pair of night-vision thermal imaging glasses. Reno and Cutter held their breath while she scoured the platform. Her body stiffened.

Reno and Cutter tensed beside her. "What is it?" said Cutter.

"Hell!" Nerdo's curse was a harsh whisper.

Reno wasn't expecting that.

"It's an RF-2," she said, quietly. Her voice sounded dead.

"A what?"

"An early model WarBot," said Cutter. "Dangerous as hell."

"A robot?" Reno said, a little too loudly.

"Shhh!" Cutter signalled. "It's got better hearing than a bat!" he snapped in a hoarse whisper.

Nerdo was desperately tapping keys with lightning speed.

"If she can't hack it and pull it up, we're in serious trouble," said Cutter, taking the night glasses from Nerdo and training his gun on the target.

Reno stared at the platform. "Can't see anything for the life of me," he murmured.

Then he heard footsteps — jogging footsteps — resonating from the tunnel walls and getting closer. Then, out of the darkness he began to distinguish the runner's form. Even from a distance and in the dark, Reno could tell this guy was built like a mountain.

Cutter steadied himself for a shot.

"You'll only irritate it," said Nerdo, still hacking furiously. "You know you can't kill it."

Reno nervously watched Cutter's finger tighten on the trigger.

"Knees," he said, teeth clenched. "It's a two — the knees are vulnerable, remember?

Nerdo nodded. "Keep a bead on it," she said. "I'm almost there."

Despite their apparent calm, Reno could feel the tension. His heart was beating like a drum. The monster stopped running. It was only twenty metres away.

"What's it doing?" Reno asked, a tremor in his voice.

Nerdo took a quick glance. "It's receiving instructions," she said, her voice still curiously expressionless.

The pause gave Reno a moment to study the creature. He'd heard of WarBots, plenty of times, but never seen one. It was at least six feet eight, big square jaw, pallid skin, and built like the winner of a Mr Universe competition. Going by the bulkiness of its shoulders, chest, forearms and thighs, Reno figured it was also dressed in bulletproof armour, an assortment of weapons were attached to a thick black waist belt. A matt-black, tight-fitting metal skullcap topped it all off. As it stood, frozen, he could even make out the chromium caps fitted over its eyes, carrying what he knew was a heads up display with thermal and other wavelength imaging. In spite of everything, there were elements of humanity still in its austere face.

"Looks like a guy," he said. "Where do they get the ... the parts?"

"Some say body parts of fatally wounded military personnel, others say death-row prisoners," said Cutter.

"It's neither," said Nerdo, still keying. "They're reanimated soldiers. They have their own life force, cloned from the minds of elite soldiers."

The thought sent a chill through Reno. "Hell, I didn't know they could clone minds." He shuddered. "Are they sentient?"

"No, they're fricking zombies, man," said Cutter, darkly. "Less than fifty percent human. Human's, just the hard drive, the underlying system."

"Can they speak?"

"No. Their brains are holographic processors — these bastards have plenty of system faults and they can be compromised, but it's not easy. Nerdo worked on them big time, much more than me. She knows their flaws."

While Reno was absorbing that, the cyborg moved.

CHAPTER 24
SYNTHETIC IQ

THE OPERATOR PICKED up an incoming call. "Operator? Zis is Honor, 2-4-D, Delta. I need immediate assistance. Yes, zat is ze correct address. No injuries. How long? Four minutes. Good. Zank you." Honor had worked her gag free, but her hands were still suspended overhead, her legs lashed to the base of the gym gear. "Karzoff!" she cried out, "Karzoff, can you hear me? Help is on ze vay!"

At the wheel of his extensively customized, late model V8 Holden Commodore Ute in a serious shade of purple, Mal turned to Hope. "Listen, we didn't get off to a great start back on the ferry," he said. "I hope you understand. I didn't know you and Alice were trying to prevent a collision. I thought you'd turned him, that you were both SSD."

"It's okay, Mal," Hope said. "I wouldn't have asked you for help if I'd thought we were on opposite sides. I don't trust many people," she added. "But I trust you, and I trust Alice. Don't ask me why. Gut feel, I guess."

"Cool," he said, smiling. "Glad that's sorted. So, where to?"

"We don't have any option really," replied Hope. "We need to be close to the Avalon bunker to help Secta and Alice when they arrive back. There's no way to be sure they'll arrive exactly there, so I'll need to retrieve a device I've hidden there to detect Secta, wherever he might materialize."

"The narks are sure to be waiting for us there," said Mal. "You heard what she said — she'll do anything to get even. She's not fond of being humiliated."

"I guess you're right, but it's a risk we'll have to take."

"But can you be sure Secta is on our side? Like, we're risking our butts with these freaks … If the plan goes tits up and we don't get Alice back—"

"You have my word, Secta is on our side. He's my brother. And he's a lot of things, but there are two things about him you can always count on. One: he has an ego the size of Nebraska. And two: he has an ego the size of Nebraska!"

"Huh?" said Mal, while Hope laughed.

"He can't stand to fail," she explained. "His ego won't allow it. So when he commits to something, he sees it through. Look, I've risked everything too. My work, my life — everything — on getting Alice back. Believe me, it'll happen."

"Yeah, well, that's the part that puzzles me," said Mal. "Why would you give everything up for Alice? You barely know him."

"True, but he's connected to — part of — the work my brother and I do. And that's far too important to be compromised by a government with evil intentions."

Mal navigated the car through traffic.

"So it's a moral issue, is it?"

"Isn't it?"

He shrugged. "I guess," he said. "We're all about overthrowing a corrupt government to find peace. I guess that is a moral issue at that. So how long is this gonna take?"

"Honor gave Secta sixty hours."

"What — to find Alice in the future, convince him he's on his side now, then work out a way to bring him back? Wow. That's not much time, considering Alice wouldn't be likely to believe him. He doesn't change his mind easily. Have you forgotten how much he hates your brother?"

"I hear you," said Hope, gravely. "But what we think has little to do with what needs to be done. We've already lost almost half our time."

"Do you think time is the same where they are?"

"Of course — time is time."

"No, I mean — say, if an hour for us is like a day to them?"

"You should study quantum mechanics, Mal," she smiled. "That's quite a thought, and I can't answer it."

He grinned. "Alright," he said. "We'd better get a move on, just in case I'm wrong. Avalon's a bit of a drive from here, and you look tired. Get some kip."

"Yes, the old nervous system could do with a little time out," she admitted, curling up in the big leather bucket seat.

Mal glanced at her. Gorgeous, but a lot of what she said went way over his head. He triggered some soothing music and relaxed into driving. After a few minutes, he turned onto the Federal Freeway, entered the fast lane, and accelerated.

On the rear seat of an agency car, still decidedly dishevelled, Honor glanced over at Karzoff. A cut eyebrow was seeping blood. She pulled a tissue from her sleeve and handed it to him.

"Here, use zis," she said. "You are still bleeding."

"I will no doubt have a black eye tomorrow," huffed Karzoff. "I should receive workers' compensation for this injury."

"Fill out ze appropriate forms back at ze office," said Honor. "And do not vorry about vhat happened, it will not reflect on us." She sounded almost sympathetic. "But ve do need to find zem — and quvickly."

"Was he Octagon?"

"Absolutely."

"So do you expect to find them?"

"Vell, dear toad, zat is vhy I am senior inspector and you are not — listen, and learn." She made an implant call. After confirming their rescue and informing the operator that Karzoff has received a minor injury, she said:

"I vant to see CCTV road surveillance footage for the five-kilometre radius around ze safe house. Yes, road only. Ve are looking for an escape vehicle." She disconnected at Karzoff with a raised eyebrow. "Zere, dear toad," she said, smugly. "Your claim to compensation established, and our vay to finding — and punishing — zose responsible for your injuries. You see how it is done?"

Karzoff nodded, silently hating her for her never-ending arrogance and conceit.

If Secta double-crossed her, Hope was Honor's only chance. And she wasn't prepared to risk everything by betting on Secta's traitorous, unpredictable predisposition. If he failed to show up within the deadline, she had to have Hope, with her knowledge of the experiment, to dispatch Karzoff into the future after him.

Hope, however, was an even more able opponent now she had the backing of Mal Function and, by extension, The Octagon. They could conceivably grab Alice as soon as he arrived back, and that would spell disaster for all of them. Hope was the backup, potentially the key to Honor's entire plan, but the Octagon stood between them. Mal Function, she concluded, not without an element of personal satisfaction, had to be eliminated.

Turk was alone in pitch-black darkness. His hands and feet were tied, and he was bound to some sort of setup that creaked — metal against metal — when he moved. It felt like some kind of operating table, lying at a slight angle.

"Well, this brings back happy memories," Alice thought, facetiously.

"Yeah. Reminds me of solitary confinement."

"Not the dark," thought Alice. "The table! Seems like every time I get attached to something like this, it has some diabolical use. Hell, it's dark in here," he added. "I hate the dark."

Turk's eyes were suddenly blinded as an overhead light flicked on. Squinting, he made out a large room with a high ceiling, overlooked by a glassed-in mezzanine observation floor. It reminded Turk of an autopsy room.

"I hope this isn't what you think it is," Alice said, alarmed. Then he noticed movement on the mezzanine. There were people up there and he was, indeed, on a surgical table. He tried to raise his head, but he was securely fastened down across the chest and forehead. His wrists were attached to side rails, as were his feet. Scientific-looking machines were positioned around the room and a weird, alien-looking automaton, with a number of limbs sporting scientific instruments, was parked at his feet. He felt a chill, and realised he was naked. That made him conscious of the watchers, especially as one of them appeared to be a woman.

The lighting changed to a cool blue and the automaton at his feet sprang to life.

"That can't be good," thought Alice. "I don't like the look of that thing."

With a loud snap, a claw-like clamp extended from beneath Turk's head and tethered his neck. He couldn't move even a fraction.

Reality dawned. "This is a fricking WarBot lab!" he thought, desperately. "They're going to turn me into a cyborg!"

"What do you mean me?" moaned Alice. "There's two of us in here!"

"Hey! You up there!" he yelled to the watchers. "I'm not Turk! My name is Black Alice! Turk's my host for the moment, you dig? Two people, one mind?"

Regardless, a servo sounded and the automaton surgeon moved towards Turk's head, a set of ominous-looking instruments attached to its limbs. It was like a giant — and terrifying — Swiss army knife.

"It's the truth!" Turk yelled, hoping they'd register his different voice. "He's on a mission from the past! Get online and look him up —Black Alice. He was the leader of the Octagon peace movement in the first half of this century — Black Alice!" he ended on a strangled squawk as the neck restraint bit in. Above them, the woman's mouth was moving, but they had no way to tell what she was saying.

"Let's hope she buys it," said Alice. The automaton was still moving towards them. "Almost time to panic, do you think?" he added as the thing extended a limb holding a surgical saw. A thin laser fired from one of its arms onto Turk's forehead, creating a cutting guide, and the saw kicked into action — zzzzzzzz! They both flinched at the horrible, dentist-drill noise.

"I'd say that's a yes, Alice," said Turk. "Panic whenever you like."

The cyborg just stood there, face shrouded in shadow, motionless. It was enormous, blotting out any other sights on the platform, not that there were many. The chromium orbs of its eyes looked cold-blooded and cruel. Reno thought it was the most evil-looking thing he'd ever seen. A big man himself, he was a runt by comparison. Suddenly, clearly finished downloading its instructions, it turned towards them and started to move. Reno backpedalled, shoulders pressed against the subway wall. He slid past Cutter who held his position on one knee, pistol up, trained on the cyborg.

"It's going for its gun!" Reno yelled.

"Come on, Nerdo!" Cutter appealed urgently, through clenched teeth. "It's got a fricking laser-sight pistol."

Nerdo was like a woman possessed. Reno could barely see her fingers move. Teeth gritted, sweat pouring from her brow, veins were standing out on her forehead as she focused every ounce of herself into her task.

"I'm taking a shot!" Cutter warned.

Fifteen paces away…

"Nerdo, I'm going to fire!"

Ten paces away ... The Bot raised its pistol. A laser bead appeared on Cutter's forehead. Then, nothing. The cyborg froze.

"Don't shoot!" Nerdo cried. "I've got him!"

Cutter rose slowly, pistol still trained on the cyborg.

"You sure?" he said. Nerdo nodded.

"Girl," he sighed, "That was really going down to the wire."

"Look at that," Reno said, displaying a trembling hand. "I haven't shaken this much since I made the best man's speech at Jonno's wedding!"

The three of them collapsed into relieved laughter, releasing the extraordinary tension they'd been under.

Nerdo looked up at the cyborg. "Real glad you're not an RF-7, mate," she said, "Or it wouldn't be us doing the laughing."

Reno joined her to take a closer look at the monster and said, "Imagine a football team of 'em!"

Cutter joined him and holstered his pistol.

"Funny you should say that," he said. "They reckon Zen originally designed the RF-2 as rugby players."

"You're having me on!" Reno gasped.

"It's true. Zen owned the rights to a game called Cyberball — heavy-duty rugby with cyborg players — planned to take it global. Even set up plants to build players under sponsored franchises in Japan, the USA and the UK. They were cloning the minds of famous footballers to use as the system drives. Some Kiwi dude came up with the original idea."

"Trust the Kiwis," Reno laughed. "Always so passionate about their rugby!"

"But things changed," Cutter went on. "They diverted the cyborg technology into more profitable games: security, then war."

The two men stood silent, looking at the inactive killing machine in front of them. "Let's move," said Nerdo, breaking the spell. "They'll be working their butts off back at Zen, trying to reactivate it," Nerdo urged them.

"It won't get far if I shoot its knees out!" Cutter reckoned.

"While it's alive it's deadly, knees or not," Nerdo warned.

Reno jumped back from the cyborg. "You sayin' it could still come after us?"

"Yep," said Nerdo. "So let's go."

"Wait a second," Reno said. "We leave that thing there in working order, it'll be just another obstacle to get by on our way back. Can't we immobilize it or something? Like, totally?"

Nerdo thought about it. "You're right," she said, looking at Cutter. "Hey, remember how the Noogs used to knock the two over?"

Cutter smiled. "Yep, sure do. Wouldn't work on a seven, but it was the reason they retired the twos."

"Come on then," said Nerdo. "We better do it quickly."

They approached the RF-2, still standing like a statue. In one quick movement, Cutter hit the deck, twisted onto his back and kicked, sliding along the platform, gun raised, towards its parted legs. There was a warning hum from a cyborg servo. "It's reactivating!" yelled Reno, just as the monster looked down.

It was just in time to see Cutter arrive between its legs. The former soldier grinned, pressed the barrel of his Glock against its crotch, and fired. The bullet blew the metal skullcap clean off the top of its head. Brain matter, blood and muck painted the platform wall scarlet as the cyborg fell forward: terminated.

"Holy mackerel," said Cutter's voice from behind the ruined robot. "That was close!"

"The Noogs would bury themselves in the sand and shoot up at them when they went over," said Nerdo.

"Noogs?" Reno queried.

"The enemy. Any enemy," she replied.

"Pretty efficient," said Cutter, re-holstering his weapon as he moved past them towards the exit, casually brushing fragments of departed cyborg from his sleeves.

"Yeah," said Reno, turning to walk away. "Mind blowing, really."

On the edge of the cell bunk, Morri was having a conversation with herself.

"We had a dream last night, do you remember?" Secta asked.

"Yes," she said. "It was horrific."

"Dream, or premonition?"

"Pretty sure it was a dream," said Morri.

"Why? Because there was no orgasm?"

"Something like that," she snapped. "Let's just change the subject."

Secta sighed. "Sometimes I feel my not-so-honourable past deeds catching up with me," he said.

"Karma?" Morri suggested.

"You could call it that, I suppose."

"So, you're worried about it?"

"Not the past, so much." Secta admitted, "but the future? Yes, that worries me. It's never worried me before."

"Is this because you weren't in the premonition?" asked Morri. "That just suggests you got back to your own time, does it not?"

"I suppose so," he said, glumly. "But it doesn't tell me what happens to the rest of you. I don't know what's got into me. I usually don't care."

Morri was silent. There wasn't much she could say. Secta silently blamed his female body. "Hormones, and suchlike," he thought to himself. "Nurturing instincts, all that nonsense. God help me, maybe I'm evolving emotionally."

A shadow moved behind the laser light. "Step over to the wall," it commanded. "When it changes to green, step through."

Morri obeyed.

The guard walked her along the corridor to the elevator door.

"Where are we going?" Secta wondered, in her head. She didn't answer. She didn't know.

This elevator was different from the others they had taken — it moved sideways. The doors opened at a huge atrium with a high-domed ceiling, panelled with opaque sensor glass that provided a gently bright ambience, no matter the weather conditions outside. Uniformed Zen personnel crisscrossed the vast, black, polished marble floor. To Morri, they all looked bored.

The guard led her through an automated glass sliding door. She was outside. It felt like ages since she'd felt sunlight. Instinctively, she raised her face to it, taking a simple pleasure in the feeling. Suddenly, she was struck by a psychic thought: I will be asked to do something and I shouldn't refuse.

She felt Secta take a mental step back. "That was weird," he said.

"A revelation," she silently replied. "I get them sometimes. Mum said it was a gift of the dreaming."

"It's seriously creepy. So, you're First Nations by descent then," said Secta. "That explains a little but I'm not sure I like the way a thought can just fly into your head out of nowhere and completely take over."

They came to a park bench in a beautiful flower garden, an oasis between the glass towers. Gorrick was seated on the bench, peering at a handheld device. "Here's trouble!" thought Morri.

Without looking up, Gorrick dismissed the guard. "Leave her," he barked. "Sit down, Morrigan," he added, more politely. Morri obediently sat on the bench, but maintained a safe distance between them.

Gorrick noticed. "I am m not your enemy," he said, smiling gently. "And you are not an enemy of Zen, unlike your friends. I know you are not one of them. Because of that, and because I care for you, I would like to offer you a proposition."

"Do you often put the people you care about in jail, Gorrick?" Morri asked.

"Only when they align themselves with radicals, Morrigan," came the calm reply. "It was for your own protection." He took a deep breath. "My dear, in life we have choices. Either we run with the sheep, lead the herd or buck the system. I chose to lead the pack. I think you have been gifted with the intelligence and powers to do the same. Do you follow me?"

"I do," she said. "And I'm not your 'dear'."

"Quite right, Morri," thought Secta. "Don't let him patronise us."

"Very well," he sighed, patiently. "I have convinced my people that we can use your remote-viewing abilities. They are prepared to set you free, with the proviso you comply with certain conditions."

"And those are?"

"We will reactivate your OSCI, as a security measure, which will give us access to your visions and memories. You will be trained by our Psychic OSCI Interface division to use your psychic abilities to directly control artificially intelligent machines.

"This is cutting-edge technology, Morri, exciting stuff. We believe it will shape the future of mankind. Think of it. We could ultimately send intelligent machines on distant space missions at speeds that would kill human beings. They could survive in the most hazardous, the most toxic environments. They could explore without impediment, entirely controlled from Earth. You could be one of those explorers, Morrigan."

"Wow. That's actually quite the opportunity," said the voice of Secta in her head. "I actually feel quite tempted."

Morri, again, ignored him. "Are my parents dead?" she snapped.

"No, Morrigan," said Gorrick, smooth as butter. "They are already working in the AI division. I know they were taken from you in a terrible manner, but we had to leave cover. This mission is entirely secret. Had you been there, you would have been taken too, and spared much suffering. That you were not, I am truly sorry."

"That doesn't exonerate you collaborating with scum like Duke and the Rebels," said Morri. "They're animals. Worse than that … Monsters."

"Duke and his men are merely our arms and legs," said Gorrick. "They seek out people with psychic abilities for the AI program. They are excellent cover — and we must execute this as a clandestine operation. Post war has made things more difficult, because no-one is trusted anymore. But that will change when the world accepts the benefits Zen will provide."

"My, he's quite the zealot," thought Secta. "I say we accept his offer. The alternative would be bad for our health!"

"No," Morri answered. "He's full of crap. My parents are dead, and if I agree to OSCI activation, it gives them control over my mind. It also gives up the others."

"Not with me in here. OSCI can only take them so far while I'm holding the mental fort."

Morri spoke aloud. "Before I answer you, Gorrick, why is Zen still building cyborgs if the war is over?"

"Quite simple, my dear," he responded. "My vision — or, I should say, Zen's vision — is to take the first step in a natural evolution towards a non-biological life form for humanity. That first step is a sentient cyborg.

"It is the only way to save our kind. It has been achieved before, on other worlds. In fact, mankind on Earth was seeded by a civilization that had mastered the process. What we are offering you, Morrigan, is nothing more nor less than a role in the future of humanity."

She looked at the ground for a few moments, apparently deep in thought. Finally she sighed, squared her shoulders and looked at him. "Okay," she said. "You've got a deal. When do we start?"

He stood up and held out his arms. Seeing her refusal to step into them, he changed that to an extended hand. She got to her feet and took it.

"Effective immediately!" he said.

CHAPTER 25
ALTERED STAKES

HONOR WAS SITTING at her desk, peering at her tablet. "Zere zey are!" she exclaimed.

"Yes, yes, you can clearly see them both in the car!" said Karzoff, squinting at the surveillance video through the monocle screwed over his left eye. Honor was already making a call.

"Ve haff reviewed ze CCTV," she was saying. "Order a track on zis license plate: Foxtrot, Uniform, November, Charlie, Tango, India, Oscar, November."

She tapped her fingernails impatiently, waiting for the results.

"Vell yes, ve know ze owner is Malcolm Function ... and? Ah, ze Federal freeway towards Canberra. Excellent! I vant a chopper for pursuit. Excuse me? Vhat do you mean zere is none available? Very vell," she continued, closing her eyes in exasperation. "A car vill haff to do. Make sure it is fast, and get it here now!" She disconnected and jumped up, visibly irritated. "Humph!" she declared. "You vould zink ve vould haff priority over bloody visiting dignitaries!"

"Well, no, I wouldn't expect..." Karzoff began, but as usual she wasn't listening.

"Come!" she commanded. "Ve must get out of here. Zere vill be a car vaiting for us outside. I vill arrange for it to be armed. You vill drive."

Mal approached his purple Commodore, waving a motel key. He opened the driver's side door and stuck his head in. "Shall we retire to our room, madam?" he asked.

"Hop in, Mal," she said, pretending not to see his disappointed expression. "There's still an hour to kill before sunset. Plenty of time to get what I need from the bunker."

It took only ten minutes to reach the bunker site. Mal stopped the car next to the padlocked gates and said, waggishly, "I don't want to seem dumb or anything, but all I see is a cow paddock."

Hope didn't bother commenting. She simply got out of the car, ducked under the chain in front of the gates, and slipped through the gap between them. Thirty or so metres in, she reached the concrete pad in the middle of open field, Mal mooching along behind her.

"Hmm," he said, tapping the concrete with his boot. Helipad, I reckon. Something underneath?"

Getting a kick out of keeping him guessing, Hope strode onto the grass, deepened her voice and called: "Open, sesame!" hoping she sounded enough like Secta...

Mal cracked up. "Ah, come on!" he choked. "You're having me on!"

The look on his face was transformed into one of amazement as a trapdoor opened in the turf. "I'll be stuffed!" he bellowed, running up to Hope.

She had already skipped down the steps into the dark. Mal followed.

After a quick descent in the elevator, the doors opened to a dimly illuminated laboratory.

"What about this place?" Mal exclaimed, turning in big circles, arms open wide and mouth agape. "It's like something out of an old Bond movie."

Hope made a beeline for the chair, knelt, reached underneath and withdrew a small device. "Excellent," she muttered to herself. The other device was still there too — Secta would be able to find it in the future, and that caused her to smile.

"Alright, run it by me," said Mal. "What's that for?"

"It'll help me find Secta and Alice," she said. "Like I said before, they might not turn up right here. We want to find and secure them both before the narks do, right? So, this will help."

"You're more than just a pretty face, aren't you?" he smiled.

"Good of you to notice," she said, rolling her eyes.

Fettered to the surgeon's table, Turk could see the woman on the mezzanine was talking animatedly to the man beside her. The saw was getting closer to his forehead, the whirring sound drowning out everything else — then suddenly the automaton powered down. The blue lights overhead reverted to blinding yellow.

Turk let out a loud sigh. "Whew!"

"I get the feeling our fate is still being debated," Alice muttered.

"Yeah, we're not clear yet," agreed Turk. "Got any more bright ideas?"

"Nar," said Alice. "I think we're about to cash our chips."

Gorrick led Morri through a set of doors marked Theatre A. When they entered the room, a debonair-looking woman was talking excitedly to a man in uniform who, on seeing Gorrick immediately excused himself and left.

"Morrigan Hud, this is Dr Ursula Mennis," said Gorrick. "She is the department head of our Artificial Intelligence Development program."

Morri shook the tall, elegant woman's extended hand. She didn't seem to fit the bored, passive archetype of the average Zen employee.

She was about thirty, pretty, with a good figure, short black hair and pale but perfect skin. Sensual, mobile lips were painted cherry red, big almond-shaped eyes outlined with grey kohl. Long, shapely legs extended from her crisp black Zen uniform.

"I have been told you are psychic, yes?" she said. Her English perfect but distinctly accented, probably eastern European, thought Morri. Despite her looks, there was something icy about her. Morri nodded in answer to her question.

"We will be testing to determine the extent of your abilities," the woman went on, brusquely. "As well as being an AI psychologist, I have developed tests to determine psychic proficiency."

"She reminds me of Honor," Secta noted.

"There's nothing that suggests anything honourable to me," Morri returned. "But let's hope you're right. We may get lucky."

Secta didn't bother to squash that hope. There seemed little point.

"This is one of our labs," Mennis continued. "From here I control an automaton surgeon, as you can see below. We have an operation in progress."

She walked Morri to the large glass partition and they looked down. Morri caught her breath. "That's Turk!" she gasped, looking at Gorrick.

"Yes," he replied, smoothly. "So it is."

Morri eyeballed him. "A little item you failed to mention in your preamble," she snapped.

Gorrick had finally lost patience. "Activate both," he fired at Mennis. "Now!"

Ursula double-clicked a small remote, and Morri immediately felt the dizzying effects of OSCI activation. She steadied herself by grasping the window rail. Fighting to stay conscious, she focused on Turk.

Looking up, Turk shouted: "That's Morri up there!" He watched helplessly as she slumped against the window and slipped to the floor, unconscious. He opened his mouth to call her name when his OSCI activated and he too blacked out.

The sun was setting by the time Karzoff drove into the parking area of the Avalon Motor Inn.

"What if they are staying here?" he queried Honor.

"Zat vill only make it easier for us to follow zem, dear toad," she said, rolling her eyes. "Check ze register ven you sign us in."

Karzoff left her in the car. She just had time to refresh her makeup when he came running back over, waving frantically and pointing upstairs. She got out of the car. "Zey are staying here?" she asked.

"Yes!" he panted. "Yes— but they are not here now."

"Very vell," said Honor. "Let us get to our room before zey return."

Karzoff led the way. Minutes later, Honor was looking around, saying: "A king-size bed! Very nice. And where vill you be sleeping, toad?"

"I … I thought perhaps … we could…" Honor rolled her eyes.

"You vill sleep on ze sofa," she said, firmly. "I do not copulate with colleagues. Are we clear on this issue?"

"Well, yes, I suppose so," said Karzoff, huffily.

"Now, I am going to shower. Find ze room service menu and order us some food."

Karzoff, muttering, found the menu and picked up the phone.

Hope and Mal stepped out of the ute and made their way to their room. Hope looked around. "King-size bed," she said. "Nice. So where are you sleeping?" She sat on the edge of the bed and bounced a little, smirking cheekily.

"Tell you what," she grinned. "You order us some food while I take a shower. She hopped up and cruised into the bathroom.

"How about a sausage sandwich?" he called after her.

Jonno woke and sat bolt upright in bed. Trixy stirred beside him.

"Ssh!" he whispered sharply. "There's someone in the club! It might be the guys, but I'm not taking any chances. Get my Roscoe, honey."

Trixy got up, and quietly opened a bureau drawer to fetch Jonno his pistol. Jonno struggled to get out of the bed, his large frame and still-painful leg making it difficult to move quickly. He pulled on a pair of shorts, took the gun from Trixy, and gave her a peck on the cheek. "Stay here," he whispered. "I'll be back in a tick."

"Be careful love," she whispered, half petrified.

Jonno nodded and snuck from the bedroom, gun cocked. Trixy waited uneasily, listening intently to every sound, expecting at any moment to hear a scuffle or a shot. When nothing came, she became even more anxious.

Suddenly the frame of a large man appeared in the bedroom doorway. Trixy only had time to see a glint from the edge of the knife before it zipped through the air and sank deeply into her shoulder. She sat, frozen with shock and terror, pinned to the bed head. Spike leaned over her, glared into her eyes, and slowly twisted the knife as he withdrew it, inflicting as much pain as possible.

Jonno was on his knees on the front veranda, head bowed, a pistol pressed hard against each temple. The two Rebels behind the pistols were waiting for Spike. After a few minutes Spike emerged from the bar, hands, arms, and chest drenched in blood.

A pistol cracked Jonno over the back of the head and the lights went out.

Ursula woke Morri by stimulating her implant with a revival code. She opened her eyes and looked about, bewildered. "You're in my office, Morri," the doctor snapped. "Sit up!"

Morri sat up like a student reprimanded by her teacher.

"You there, Secta?" she checked, mentally.

"Yes, although I didn't see that coming. Got us both!"

"You won't win any friends here if you continue to behave like you just did, young lady," Mennis observed. "You are already on your last chance with Gorrick. He does not have unlimited patience, you know."

"He didn't tell me what he was doing to my friend," said Morri, irritably.

Mennis fired her a smug glare. "You are his prisoner, Morri," she said. "We do not have to tell prisoners anything. Now, I have installed the AI tech on your OSCI. You can access it through DS-4-AI. If you need visual access, I'll fit you with heads-up shells."

"Not necessary," Morri said. "I read it while you were talking. All looks pretty straightforward."

"Hmph," grunted Mennis. "You are a fine specimen. Eidetic memory? Total recall?"

"If that means being able to commit up to a hundred pages of text to memory, then yes."

"Very impressive indeed. Are you GM?"

"Genetically modified?" Morri said, taken aback. "I doubt it..." In fact, she'd never considered it.

Ursula took a passive laser pen from her desktop and approached Morri. "Let's check, shall we?" she said. "Lean your head back and look at the ceiling. Try not to blink. This will not hurt."

Morri did as instructed and Ursula aimed the penlight at her left eye. It bounced a thin red laser off the optic nerve.

"Optogenetics," Secta thought to Morri.

"Yes," Ursula mumbled like a doctor, moving to her desk, where she sat to read the holographic projection from the end of the pen. "E-7-14ZB. Yes, you were genetically modified as an embryo, a First Nations embryo in fact."

Morri was shocked.

"So my parents lied to me? I didn't inherit my psychic abilities?"

"No," Mennis replied. "Your psychic abilities were certainly inherited, but the instant recall, no. Your memory has been artificially enhanced."

Morri flopped back in her chair, trying to accept the revelation. "What else did they modify?" Secta prompted.

"What else did they modify?" Morri asked, automatically.

"Not much, I'd say. Eye colour, sex..."

"Sex?"

"Yes. They made sure you were female. Blue eyes, blonde hair, pale skin, memory enhancement and standard cancer prevention. Not bad things, I'm sure you'll agree, and commonly done for little cost before the war."

So she was, for the most part, natural. Morri felt a little better. Then she spotted Mennis's computer screen. It showed a schematic of the worldwide grid.

"Is that a grid map?" she asked.

"How perceptive of you. It will soon be our OSCI operations grid."

"But you'd need a functioning satellite system to cover the entire world, right?" Morri said.

"Watch," said Mennis, and punched a twenty-five-digit code into her computer. Dozens, hundreds of lines immediately criss-crossed the map.

Morri and Secta were shocked.

"You've activated the dormant telecommunication satellites or Starlink!" Secta said. Mennis was too busy looking at the screen to notice the subtly different voice.

"Yes," she said. "And some military nano-satellites, which most of the old governments didn't know existed. Some of them are no larger than 10x10 centimetres — it's incredible technology." Clearly feeling she'd shown Morri enough for the time, she shut the computer down.

"You will see more when you have begun your work here," she said. "Once I am convinced you can be trusted."

"You should know that already," she said. "I assume you've mined my memories?" Secta shifted uneasily at the back of her mind.

"In fact, I don't know," said Mennis. "Gorrick has ordered it done, but he will only reveal to me anything he thinks I should know. After all," she went on, "I have no wish to go through your angsty teenage years or your first love. There is little room in my life for such drama."

"Will my memories reveal you, Secta?" Morri asked her passenger.

"Eventually," he replied. "But they'll have a lot of mental junk to wade through first. There's nothing we can do about it now, in any case." Morri nodded, once.

"What's going to happen to Turk?" she asked.

Ursula looked up, sharply. "He is an interesting case," she said. "We had planned to make a cyborg of him." Morri's face blanched. "Oh, don't worry — for now," the woman added, smiling cruelly. "He suddenly exhibited signs of a dual personality. That merits further study, although whether it will leave him better off is open to question."

"Why do you say that?" Morri asked.

"Because he is bound for the ring on Anzac Day."

"The ring?"

"Yes. Gorrick likes to celebrate Anzac Day with a tournament."

"What, like a boxing match?"

The doctor laughed coldly. "Sort of," she said. "Anyhow, that is not until tomorrow. Plenty of time for further study."

"It's true, you know," said Secta. "He does have a very strange personality disorder."

That got her attention. "Oh? What do you mean?"

"What did he tell you?" Secta asked, unwilling to commit.

"He said he had been possessed by a person from the past — a person with an important mission. He said a name, but it eludes me for now."

"Was it Alice? Black Alice?"

"Yes, that is it — he said I should research the name."

"And have you?"

"No," she said, abruptly. "And it matters not, right now! We have a new unit coming in for conversion, and you will be observing. And this time, you will not complain about anything at all. Is that absolutely clear?"

"Yes," said Morri, meekly, feeling that she'd reached the woman's limits for the time being.

Secta growled at the back of her mind. Ursula felt like a carbon copy of Honor, right down to her stupid accent. "Bag head," he thought.

From behind a gate locked with a chain, Cutter scanned the street. He reported in a whisper loud enough for Reno and Nerdo to hear: "It'll be light in a while … loads of CCTV in the park opposite … no signs of life."

Nerdo and Reno crouched behind him.

"They'll know the two has been terminated," said Nerdo. "They'll have a trap set somewhere, for sure."

"I don't like it," Reno said. "This place gives me the creeps."

Cutter turned back to them. "If they suss out who we are, they'll be able activate our OSCI's and knock us out without a fight," he said. "Especially now we're inside the Zen Wi-Fi zone."

"Do they know who you are from your visas?" Reno asked.

"Nah," Nerdo smiled. "We gave you bum names and false security numbers."

"She doesn't trust anybody," Cutter said, with a devilish grin.

"I don't blame her," said Reno, wryly. "How d'you know we're in their Wi-Fi zone?"

"Because the two was functioning," she replied.

"Ah."

"They'd need a Wi-Fi connection to control it," she went on. "Little microdots like mine wouldn't be powerful or fast enough."

Reno nodded.

"Huddle up fells, here's what we need to do," Nerdo said. "We go back beyond the Wi-Fi field and try to get a heads up to Turk or Morri."

"How far back is that?" Reno queried.

"At least to the last hack on the train tracks," Nerdo replied.

"Reno should stay here to guard the entrance while we get that done," Cutter said.

Nerdo foraged in her everlasting pockets and came up with two matchbox-sized items fastened with a rubber band. She freed one and handed it to Reno.

"Here," she said. "Once we're done, I'll beep you. Meet us by the knocked-out two. Okay?" she said. He nodded. "Good," she said. "Now test it. Just press that button right there."

Reno pressed, and the unit in Nerdo's hand sounded a beep.

"If you get into trouble, beep twice and we'll come running. We'll do the same. Cool?"

"Yeah," said Reno. "As long as I don't see one of those RF monsters coming at me. Can't see a beep being much use then."

Cutter gave him a thumbs-up and Reno watched them take off on the double, dissolving into the darkness of the subway.

Duke turned from the big window, faced Gorrick at his desk, and read from the Ulink in his hand. "There are two of them," he said.

"OPPS got their OSCI numbers, but before we could act they dropped off line."

"They terminated a two…" Gorrick scowled, irritated. "How the hell did they do that?"

"One of them was a high-ranking officer in charge of programming 2s and 6s during the war," said Duke. "Her name is Diamantina Parkes, nicknamed Nerdo. Born in Arnhem Land, graduate of the Royal Military College Duntroon, before Canberra got turned to soot."

"She must be smart," Gorrick said. "We could use a head like that. Make sure she is left in one piece. And the other?"

"Wilson Burt, nicknamed Cutter, Quilpie Queensland, discharged arms specialist. Did the full seven. Three bravery commendations, has form for being rebellious. I could use him."

"They are both keepers," agreed Gorrick. "Best if we can knock them out, rather than killing them. Set something up to lure them into Wi-Fi range."

"OPPS reckons they can punch up the Wi-Fi when I give the order. That should do the trick. Right now they're probably hanging just out of range."

"Clever. But send in backup. Make a moral of it, Duke. I don't want any more foul-ups."

CHAPTER 26
HACK ATTACK

MORRI WAS IN an elevator with Ursula when Nerdo hacked her OSCI. She blinked. Thinking on her feet, she said: "I need to go to the ladies."

"First door on your right," said Mennis, coldly. "I'll be in the lab."

The elevator door opened and Morri hurried to the loo. Inside, she turned on a faucet to mask her voice and spoke in a harsh whisper.

"Nerdo? You there?" Hearing the other woman's voice, she went on: "Look, they're putting Turk in the arena tomorrow at midday for what they call the Anzac Day fight. I don't know what that is but it's not likely to be good, is it? Yeah, we're all right, but they got at my memory through my OSCI. You guys okay? Good. Okay, yeah, I'll make sure I'm there. Got to go — bye!"

At that moment, a young uniformed woman entered the room and, without acknowledging her, stepped into a cubicle.

"Guess they're human after all," Morri muttered to herself.

"An Anzac Day fight," Nerdo told Cutter. "We'll need to get a fix on this arena. But if they got Morri's memory they'll know who we are. They've probably already got our OSCI codes."

"It was only a matter of time," she said.

"Can they bump up the Wi-Fi range?"

"Damn right they can. But I've got an idea. Let's go." She beeped Reno and they raced back up the train line towards the platform.

Reno was waiting beside the RF-2, still lying face down on the platform.

"How'd you go?" he asked.

Nerdo was busy on her device, so Cutter answered for her.

"Turk's fighting in some arena or other at midday tomorrow. She's getting a fix on it now."

"What do you mean, fighting?"

"Some sort of sketchy Anzac Day tourney."

"Sounds like the sort of crap Duke would dream up," Reno growled.

Nerdo looked up from the Ulink. "Got it. Listen up. They're gonna knock Cutter and me out through our OSCI's for sure. I can counter it by keeping my hack codes in the Ulink memory and blocking them each time, but that'll only do it for one of us. We need to cut out the Bot's OSCI, then I can use it to create an interface that'll block the other one."

"What do you need?" Cutter asked.

"Just its head. We'll retreat well past Wi-Fi range and I'll operate on you."

"It's head?" Reno said, looking at the massive neck.

Nerdo ignored him. "We have to wait till just before midday tomorrow, anyhow."

Reno couldn't believe what he was hearing. "Are you serious? Cut off its head?"

Cutter drew a bayonet out of his boot and gave Reno a terrifying smile. "She sure is," he said. "Push it over."

Reno moved reluctantly to the cyborg and gave it a hard shove. It slid round until the neck was next to Cutter, who immediately went to work, hacking through tissue, sinew and bone. After much sawing and grunting, the head finally came free. Cutter tucked it under his arm like it was a rugby ball, and took off up the platform onto the train tracks, Reno, Nerdo and a bloody mess trailing behind him.

Turk woke in a prison cell, sat up on the bunk and knuckled his eyes. "Hey, we're still alive!" Alice said. "Turk? You there?" But Turk had been suppressed by the OSCI. Alice got up and stretched. "Looks like I'm on my ace for a change."

He heard footsteps approaching.

Duke entered and leered at him through the red laser bars. "Hey, soldier boy," he mocked. "I'm looking forward to seeing you fight in the ring tomorrow."

"I'm sure you are, you fat-arsed pig," said Alice.

Duke just grinned. "We'll see how wide you can be tomorrow, soldier boy! If I'm right, you'll be wider than you've ever been before..." Duke chuckled, and turned to leave.

"Hey!"

"What?"

"Am I fighting you? Hope so. I'll kick your teeth so far down your throat you'll need to shove your toothbrush up your butt to brush!" Alice growled.

"That'll be the day, soldier boy," Duke chuckled, striding off down the corridor. "That'll be the day!"

"Turk," thought Alice, desperately, "Where the stuff are you? I'm going to need your black belt, son!"

He sat on the bunk with his head in his hands. "How the stuff you going to get out of this mess, Alice?" he said. "How is it all I ever do is buy into trouble? Why can't life be freaking simple for a change?"

Cutter was just about to leap from the station platform when his legs gave way under him and he hit the deck, out cold. The cyborg head rolled from his grasp and stopped on the platform, dead chromium eyes staring up at Reno. Nerdo knew immediately what had happened and quickly entered her own code into the Ulink.

"Reno! They've jammed him! I'm ... I..." she was losing it. Desperately, she hit send. Just in time.

Reno was watching wide-eyed.

"Damn," she panted. "That was close! Quick, grab his bayonet," Nerdo ordered. "There's still a chance!"

Reno drew the blade out of Cutter's boot.

Nerdo retrieved the severed head. "Right," she said. "Hold the head next to Cutter's and give me the blade."

Reno did so. She hacked into the mastoid bone behind the cyborg's ear, digging deep with the bayonet tip until she unearthed a wire.

"There it is," she said. She pushed the knifepoint deeper, and twisted. A crack made Reno shudder, and a queasy feeling hit his gut as the mastoid bone split. "Right," said Nerdo. "Tug the wire and ... got it!"

A thin metal disk popped out.

"Can you remove Cutter's OSCI completely?" Reno asked.

"Nah," she replied. "If I sever the nerves that connect the OSCI to his sense synapses, I'll render them useless. He'd be a zombie. It's actually part of the cyborg creation process." She sliced through a few last sinews to free the device from the cyborg's head. "Done," she said, and then moved over to Cutter. "Right. Now hold his head the same way ... keep very still..."

Reno, sweating, took hold of Cutter's head, willing himself to stay absolutely still.

"Good," Nerdo said, and Reno grimaced as she performed the same operation, only with considerably more delicacy. Once she had the surgical wire in Cutter's mastoid exposed, she spliced it with the wire from the cyborg implant. Then, with bloodied fingers, she punched a series of complicated codes into the Ulink. Finally, after sticking everything back together with strips of plaster from her never-failing pockets, she wiped her brow, leaned against the wall and sighed deeply. "Come on!" she urged, willing Cutter back to consciousness. There was a long couple of minutes. Then her friend's eyes flickered open, one at a time.

"We have ignition!" Reno said with a grin.

Nerdo struggled to her feet and looked down at her comrade. "There you are!" she joked. "Took you bloody long enough!"

Cutter grinned at her, sat up and scratched his head. When he felt behind his left ear he said, "How'd you know it was the left side?"

"Coz you're left-handed—der!"

"Then how'd you know Mr No-body there was right handed?"

She looked at the cyborg head and shrugged her shoulders. "Just a lucky hunch, I guess."

"What do you mean, it failed?" Duke was bellowing at the head of Zen OPPS. His tirade had reduced the plump young woman to a trembling mess. They were the only ones standing in the open-plan centre, twenty operators glued to their heads-up display windows around them.

"Sir, we had Cutter on line," she said. "But … but somehow he dropped out."

"What about the other one?" Duke snarled.

"She … out-coded us."

"Out-coded? What? You telling me she hacked all of this?" He made a grandiose, all-embracing gesture with his right arm, signifying all the equipment in the room. "And succeeded? I want her working for me. She's better than the lot of you put together! You hear me? You all hear me?

"Now, you listen to me fatso," he went on, poking her left breast. "Find-a-way! Copy that?" Not waiting for a reply, he strode out of the room.

The girl flopped into a chair, gasping for breath. A female co-worker picked up a plastic folder from a desktop and feverishly fanned her sweet but chubby face. All the operators were sympathetic — none of them liked Duke.

"So has this piece of scrap metal gotta hang out of my head for the remainder of the mission?" Cutter groaned.

"Think of it like an earring," she said.

"I don't wear bloody earrings!" he growled.

"You're wearing one now," she grinned. She was right, his ear was a bloody mess. "Here," she said, producing a baseball cap from a pocket. "Tuck it up under the cap, it'll be fine. Believe me, the alternative is worse."

He knew she was right.

"What else have you got in those pockets, Nerdo?" Reno joked. "You're like a magician. Next thing you'll be pulling out a rabbit!"

"Don't tempt her," Cutter said. "How long is this gonna work for?" he asked.

"Long enough get you out of here," she said. "Now, let's get on with the mission."

Cutter looked downhearted; he figured his mission was over for him.

"It's near dark," said Reno. "A good time to move nearer the arena?"

"I'll need to keep hacking all night," said Nerdo. "If I let my guard down once, they'll nail me for sure."

"I'll see you to the exit," Cutter said gloomily.

As they entered the tunnel, a chilling spectre stopped them in their tracks. Backlit by the setting sun, an even bigger cyborg blocked the way out.

"It's another two," whispered Nerdo. "But I won't be able to jam this one. If I try to hack it, they'll get through to me. We're stuffed."

"I'll distract it," said Cutter. "You slip past."

"You're no match for it, mate," she pleaded.

Cutter grabbed her and pulled her close. He looked into her startled eyes for a moment, then planted a kiss on her lips. She stiffened, then relaxed, returning the kiss with apparent enthusiasm. Reno looked away.

Cutter stepped back. Holding Nerdo by the shoulders he said: "There, never let it be said I don't like you. Now, get set to run."

What is this, a Greek tragedy?" she spat back at him. "You kiss the girl, tell her you care for her, then head off to fight the monster and die?"

The cyborg started walking.

"Um … it's coming our way," Reno nervously said.

The two friends continued to stare at each other.

"Yeah, guess that's about it," Cutter replied.

"It's getting closer!" Reno sang.

"Well, stuff you, man!" Nerdo yelled, and shoved Cutter in the chest.

"Hey, I'm only trying to—"

The cyborg raised a high-calibre pistol and fired a round. The shot echoed loudly and took a huge chunk out of the wall right beside Reno's head. "Will you two shut up and listen to me?" he screamed.

Cutter unlocked his eyes from Nerdo's, drew his pistol and charged the cyborg, yelling, "Go! Go! Go!"

Nerdo's battle instincts cut in. She took off after Cutter, determined to distract the big machine.

Reno hesitated, shook his head, grimaced and followed.

The cyborg changed its aim to Nerdo, allowing Cutter to reach it safely. As before, he hit the deck, flipped and slid along the dusty floor, gun extended, ready for his shot. Reno and Nerdo, both running frantically to draw its attention, heard the bang, felt the foul soup of blood and brain matter spray their faces. It didn't deter them, it just meant Cutter had succeeded.

The big cyborg rocked back and forth. Unlike its fallen comrade, though, it didn't tip forwards. Instead, it collapsed like a ton of bricks, pinning Cutter under it. He screamed as the weight snapped his leg with a loud crack, just above the left ankle.

Nerdo and Reno skidded to a halt then backtracked at speed.

After a struggle, they managed to roll the massive carcass off Cutter.

"Shit!" Nerdo exclaimed, staring at the broken bone sticking through Cutter's leg. "Now look what you've done, you silly bugger!"

"Got anything in those pockets that'll fix this?" he managed through his agony.

"Can't fix it, but..." She rummages, and came up with a small black case from which she took a gas syringe.

"Morphine," she said. "It'll last about twelve hours. Give me your belt, Reno, we need a tourniquet." She pulled the cover off the gas injector then jabbed it into Cutter's thigh.

Reno had his belt off in a flash and tightened it just above Cutter's knee.

"Good, now make a crutch out of the cyborg's armour. But hurry, they'll try and lock onto me again once they know it's down."

Reno got to work, tearing pieces off the fallen cyborg.

Cutter calmed as the sedation kicked in. Nerdo tightened the belt another notch. He smiled at her, soppily. "You crazy bastard," she said, grabbing his bearded chin. "Why did you have to go and do that? I could have lost you." His grin widened as the morphine hit home.

Reno had lashed chunks of cyborg armour and kit together to create a makeshift crutch.

"This do?"

"Great. Now let's get him on his feet."

She took Cutter's arm, Reno gripped the other, and they carefully raised him onto his one good leg. Reno fitted the crutch under his armpit.

Cutter tentatively tested his weight. "Good one, mate," he said, groggily. "Should do the trick."

"Now listen to me," Nerdo said, locking eyes with him. "You're out of it on morphine, because you've got a badly broken leg. You hear me, mate?"

"Yep, copy that," he said. "Broken leg, and I'm definitely out of it. Wheeee!"

"We'll get you to the rail tracks, then you need to go as far as you can out of Wi-Fi range … got that? Reno, give him your beeper," she said.

"Yup," Cutter nodded. "Get outta Wi-Fi range, hahaha. Get outta Dodge. Get outta it. Hooray!"

Reno tucked the beeper into his shirt's breast pocket, looking at Nerdo. Her focus didn't waver.

"I'll beep you when we get back to the platform," she said. "Listen, Cutter! If you don't get a beep by fifteen hundred tomorrow, head up the tunnel back to Headbangers. All right?"

He looked at her, suddenly serious.

"Copy that," he grinned, wobbling unsteadily on the crutch.

CHAPTER 27
ANZAC DAY GAMES

MORRI STEPPED OUT of the shower and stood in front of the fogged up bathroom mirror. She wiped it clear then stepped back. "Will you stop ogling me, she snapped, as she felt Secta's appreciation. "You're making me feel self-conscious." Secta merely turned side-on so he could admire her further.

"I've spent the majority of my life ignoring the mirror," he said. "Allow me to enjoy what I'm seeing for once."

"Are you ugly or something?"

"Quite the contrary, my dear. It's simply that flattering my own vanity has never been high on my list of priorities."

"So now that you have breasts and no old-fella, vanity is back on the list is it?"

Their conversation was interrupted by a monotone female voice over the intercom.

"Assemble midday tomorrow at Zen Arena for Anzac Day Games."

"Good grief," said Secta. "The walls not only have ears, they have a voice as well!"

Morri wrapped herself in a towel and walked into the bedroom of the small high-rise apartment she'd been billeted in. The bedside clock showed eleven p.m. "At least this's a comfy bed," she said, sleepily. "That prison bunk was awful." She stepped out of the towel and slipped between the clean, crisp sheets. "Lights out!" She commanded, and the lights obliged.

"Good night, Morri."

"Good night, Secta."

"We both have the same dreams you know," Secta reminded her.

"I expect so."

Nerdo and Reno were in the deserted streets of Angel City, trying to find their way to the Zen Arena without getting caught on CCTV or blundering into laser banding. They kept to the shadows, avoiding moonlight and open spaces. There were no neon signs, streetlights, billboards or traffic lights. No humans. If it hadn't been for the high-rise buildings, it would be difficult to tell they were in the business district of a city at all.

Reno was leading, because Nerdo had to constantly monitor the Ulink for the location of CCTV cameras, and to block Zen's random attempts to lock on to her OSCI, which meant periodically she had to stop and frantically hack to block them.

"So far, so good," she said, quietly, consulting the Ulink map. "The Arena is on the other side of Central Park, which starts at the end of this street."

"All this stalking about is making me hungry," Reno replied.

"Hang on," Nerdo stopped. "I've got a bar, I think."

She started searching her pockets.

"D'you ever think what you might have done if there'd been no war?" asked Reno, randomly.

"Oh, I probably would have stayed working for a tech company in Darwin," she said. "You?"

"I dunno. I guess I'd still have my wife. Maybe we'd have taken up coaching on the kickboxing circuit."

"Here," she said, handing him a protein bar.

He took it, unwrapped it, snapped it in two and handed half back to her. As she reached out a hand to take it, Nerdo fumbled the Ulink. It clattered to the road.

"Shit!" she exclaimed, scrabbling after it. Her worst fear was realised: the screen was blank. The Ulink was broken. She sank to the ground. "For the sake of half a protein bar," she groaned. "Frig! How could I be so stupid?"

"It was my fault," said Reno. "I distracted you, I shouldn't have—"

"You didn't drop it, mate," she said, cutting him off. "Well, we're in trouble now, or at least I am. You'd better scram. They'll probably zap me in the next few minutes. No good you being caught as well. One of us has to keep—"

Her eyes glazed over, her head rolled back and she slumped — out cold. She'd gone.

Reno looked at her for a moment, reached down and patted her affectionately on the cheek. Then he took the other half of the protein bar from her unconscious hand and polished it off in one bite. He was just going to have to do the best he could alone. He propped her up against the wall.

Alice had just finished the slop the guards had served under the guise of breakfast when two heavily-armed wardens appeared on the other side of the bars. He still hadn't been able to reach Turk.

"Stand and face us at the laser grid," one of the wardens intoned. "When it changes to green, step through. Acknowledge."

Alice casually got to his feet. "Yeah, I know the drill," he said abrasively. "Light goes green, I step through. You sound like a message bank, dude!"

When the lights turned green he hopped through playfully and landed on the other side, balanced on one foot with his arms outstretched.

"So what next, fellas," he said, grinning cheekily. "Am I free to go?"

Unwilling to take any attitude, one of the guards hit his forearm with an electric prodder.

"Ouch! Cut it out!" Alice snapped.

"Move!" the guard growled, pushing him down the corridor to the waiting elevator.

"Tough crowd," muttered Alice.

Half a dozen floors down, the elevator doors opened at a cart terminus. They ushered him into a waiting cart, then bookended him. The cart was substantially different to the one that had brought him to Zen. One of the guards flicked a switch and a Plexiglas canopy closed overhead. The cart moved off — silently, but much faster than the standard public model.

"You know, I hate the way these things move," Alice observed, to no-one in particular. "You need a bit of grunt in your car, mate, not this rubbish. Listen to it. It's pathetic. Sounds like a golf cart. And you know what's wrong with that? I hate golf!"

He looked from side to side for some kind of reaction, but got none. The guards simply stared straight ahead, like a pair of shop dummies. He wondered what they'd do if he made a break for it, but decided not to find out.

Minutes later, they'd emerged outdoors and were travelling along a plastic track elevated above street level. The view was spectacular, even under the less-than-ideal circumstances. Dawn was breaking, fingers of red light filtering through the city streets, beneath a sky rising through shimmering shades of pink, orange and gold into aquamarine, cerulean and sapphire. Alice could see hundreds of bikers garbed in chapter colours gathering in Central Park. It appeared like it was a dawn service. The morning light was so clear he could make out individual chapter names on the backs of their leather jackets: Comanches, Rat Finks, Avengers, Bandits, Notors, Nomadics and — outnumbering the rest — Rebels.

"What's happening down there?" he wondered, not expecting an answer.

"Anzac Day service," said one of the guards, unexpectedly.

"Cut it out," said Alice. "Why would they give a rat's arse about Anzac Day?"

"Not their call," snapped the guard. "Zen's. Now shut up!"

Reno heard a whooshing overhead and looked up sharply to see a bullet-shaped cart glide past along on the monorail. Instinctively, he slipped behind a tree to avoid detection. The dawn light may have been incredible to look at, but it was already beginning to cause him problems. He needed to get to the arena before day broke completely, so he decided to take a shortcut through the Park. Using the shrubbery for cover, he made a dash as far as the high hedge border. Squatting behind it, he heard voices and parted the branches for a look-see. A sea of bikers broke in front of him. He was in serious trouble. The sun seemed to be rising quicker than it ever had in his life, there were CCTV cameras galore behind him, and no Nerdo to keep him right. He was thinking over what to do when a big mitt descended on him from behind and pulled him over backwards. He looked up and into the barrel of a Mossberg SA-20 tactical shotgun. At the trigger end was a big, bearded biker covered in tattoos, with four more evil-looking dudes alongside him. One of them had a baseball bat in his hand. The biker raised it, and Reno's world went dark.

She was standing alone with the soft orange glow of dawn licking her face. There was nothing soft about what she was staring at, other than skeins of mist drifting as though on gossamer wings through the valley. But the mist was not natural, it was the aftermath of battle. Within it were intermittent, explosive red flashes from detonating ordnance. Morri looked down at her toes, overhanging the cliff edge upon which she stood. Her bare feet were cut, sore and bleeding from the manic climb she'd just completed. In her frantic escape, the thorny strands of blackberry bushes had whipped at her relentlessly, tearing her jeans to shreds and lacerating any bare flesh. Hands on her hips, she inhaled deeply in a desperate effort to regain her breath. The smell of gunpowder, fires and death was thick in the air.

Peering over the ridge, she was overcome by a terrible sense of loss. The cyborg army had routed the people's militia and were finishing off the prisoners and the wounded with single bullets to the head. The militia had been up against impossible odds — more than a hundred relentless, merciless, soulless, remote-controlled soldiers, various generations of the RF series, designed and constructed by Zen. In a matter of only a few days they had virtually annihilated the militia, together with the civilian population. What made it even more horrific was that Zen hadn't risked a single human life on their side — the entire massacre had been stage-managed by the psychics under Gorrick's instruction, from the comfort of plush offices in Angel City.

From her vantage point, Morri could see the blood spray from every headshot and hear the delayed sound each time a bullet was fired. The cyborgs' prey were lined up like sheep at an abattoir, forced to their knees, then shot. As she turned away, a voice startled her.

"We're as good as done now." It was Turk, a gun held limply at his side. His stubbly face was cut and bleeding, his bare forearms were lacerated. His body showed the all the scars and signs of a life spent dealing with traumatic injury. But even in his battered condition, Morri marvelled at his athletic body and the rugged beauty of his honest, caring face. His bloodied shirt was shredded, she could see the strong, hard body underneath. And despite everything, he still had that look in his eyes that she cherished; the one that made her feel safe and secure. He strode over to her and took her in his strong arms. She melted into him, thinking why does it always have to be like this? Why is there never time for us? A tear tracked down her sullied cheek. She closed her eyes, savouring for a moment his powerful embrace.

He pushed her back to arm's length. "It's only a matter of time before they find us," he said. We need to make a run for it. Our child must be born."

She managed to squeeze out a smile as she put a hand protectively to her already slightly rounded pregnant belly. Turk was right — her safety was all that mattered now. She was, after all, the first person on Earth to carry a child since the Cyberwars.

They both took a last, despondent look at the panorama of devastation. Black columns of smoke rose into the air for far as the eye could see, all the way to the horizon. Towns Zen had put to the torch and in them the incinerated corpses of the innocents they had tried so desperately to defend. Zen had won.

The cart arrived at a platform marked 'Zen Arena'. It was busy — uniformed Zen workers were arriving. This station was different to the FRT. Ultra-modern. Clean. Busy. Seeing the uniforms, Alice was oddly reminded of lemmings charging towards the precipice from which they would plunge.

His guards shepherded him through the crowds, over the platform and through an open door to a waiting service elevator. A brief journey downwards and they were in the basement. Alice had seen plenty of those in his gigging days and this one was no different: unpainted, grey concrete walls, minimal lighting, dark corridors and alcoves shooting off this way and that. He had only a few seconds to take it all in before one of the guards pushed him into a dark, narrow corridor. They bustled him along to a metal door, which the guard opened, before shoving him inside. The door slammed and, with a clunk, locked shut. Alice listened to their heavy, steady footsteps as they strode off.

"Pair of cruds!" he growled loudly after them.

"I'd call them something worse than that, buddy."

He turned sharply. "Jonno!" he raced across the room and embraced the big man.

"Great to see you, Turk!"

"No, mate, Turk ain't home. It's Alice. They stuffed with his implant and he's gone."

"Ah, they must've reactivated it. They can knock someone out, even put them in an artificial coma, so I've heard."

"How did they get you?"

"Our friend Spike turned up at Headbangers with a couple of his goons. I was no match for 'em in this condition," he added, nodding at his still-bandaged leg.

"And Trixy?"

Jonno looked at the floor, face still. Alice put a hand on his shoulder. "I'm sorry, mate," he said, quietly. Jonno nodded. Alice turned and walked to the door. "Where've they brought us, mate?"

"We're under Zen arena," said Jonno. "It's where they hold fights and events. Take a gander." He pointed at the far wall, which was made up of horizontal metal slats. Turk peered through. He was looking into an arena about the size of a basketball court but circular, with a dirt floor. It was enclosed in what looked like a massive metal tank, open to the sky. Around the top, tiers of seats. Alice couldn't make any sense of it. He turned back to Jonno.

"I don't know either mate," Jonno said, seeing his puzzled expression. "I've been sitting here scratching my head over it since they dumped me here last night."

Alice sat on the wet floor beside his friend, gazing at the mildew on the slimy walls.

"You know," said Jonno, quietly, "I've been thinking about what Frank told us in his bar that day."

"Frank?" Alice queried.

"Oh yeah, it wasn't you — it was Turk. I keep forgetting. Anyway, Frank's a mate of mine, owns a bar near Headbangers. He was there when the nuke took out Canberra. Thirty-something floors up on scaffolding at the time. Saw the flash, and ducked inside an air con unit. Saved him from frying, but not the radiation. Poor bugger's only got a few months left.

"Anyway. He told us that, just before the explosion, he saw some kind of craft duck out from behind a cloud and fire a weapon at the city. He reckons aliens were behind the Cyberwars."

"Aliens? Really?"

"Yeah … Anyhow, I was wondering … What if that's what Zen are?"

Alice thought about it. "You saying that Zen could be run by aliens trying to take over the world? You might be right at that, mate. It would explain a hell of a lot about that bastard Gorrick, for a start."

Morri was at the vanity table in her Zen apartment, doing a terrible job of putting on lipstick. "This would go better if you'd stop interfering, Secta," she complained.

"But it's so fascinating," he said. "I haven't worn lipstick since dressing in drag for the Sydney Gay and Lesbian Mardi Gras. That must be twenty years ago — in my time, that is. It'd be seventy years ago here."

"Are you gay?" she asked, surprised.

"Only when I laugh," he quipped. "Sometimes I think maybe I am, maybe a switch-hitter. I have to say, that day in drag was a most wonderful day."

"What was the Gay and Lesbian Mardi Gras? I've never heard of that."

"Oh, it was an opportunity for LGBTQ plus people to celebrate themselves without harassment," he said. "However, I believe you are discussing this with me because you want to avoid discussing the dream we had last night."

"You're right," said Morri, flatly.

"Don't be like that Morri," he said, soothingly. "I can understand your attraction for Turk. He's a handsome man, despite the scars and lack of personality, and of course there is the age difference."

"I'm not talking about that," she snapped. "I just find it extremely uncomfortable to share such … intimate thoughts and experiences with a stranger."

"I'm hardly a stranger Morri, am I?" he asked. "I mean, I know we haven't known each other long, but it has been rather intense."

Morri's face reddened. She was getting ready to deliver a tirade, when Secta went on: "But look, none of that matters, I share your memories anyhow. The vision is what's important. And the thing that stood out for me was that neither Alice nor I appeared to be in it. Which means it's after…"

"That would be the thing you'd notice," she said, stiffly. "I'm more spun-out by how horrific it was. And how could I possibly be pregnant? You know the war made us all sterile…"

A knock at the door interrupted them. She wiped off the mess of lipstick, stood up and straightened her Zen Uniform.

"You look fine," said Secta, as she glanced in the mirror.

"I don't think so," she sulked.

"Now what's the problem?"

"Seriously? My hair looks dreadful and I can't put on makeup with you getting in the way." She turned on her heel and strode for the door.

"Women!" Secta barked.

Nerdo woke on a cell bunk and quickly slid off, only to stand gaping at the red laser bars.

"Oh, great!" she groaned, then looked around desperately. She had been stripped of her coat of many pockets, and that made her feel more vulnerable than if she'd been left naked. She made up her mind. "I'm not going to just sit here and grow older," she muttered to herself. Spotting a camera on the wall, she looked into it and waved. "Hello?" she said. "Could I speak to whoever's in charge, please?"

It wasn't long before two guards arrived. Shortly afterwards, she was sitting outside an office several floors above the jail. The door opened and Duke led out six big, unshaven bikers dressed in leathers. Nerdo noted the insignias on the back of their jackets: all the major gangs were represented and of course, even though Duke was in civvies, she knew he was president of the Rebels. "Why are they all here?" she wondered. "What's the connection between Duke and Zen?"

"Okay, see you at the games," said Duke, acting the Grand Pooh Bah. "Should be a killer."

Laughing, the bikers stomped off in an overpowering fog of stale sweat and old leather. Duke's expression changed as he leered at Nerdo. "Bring her in," he ordered.

Once they'd shut the door behind them, he spoke up. "Quite the clever clogs, aren't you?" he said. Nerdo shrugged her shoulders in response. Duke moved closer and looked her over like he was thinking of buying her as a slave. "Skinny, nothing of you," he said. "You a diesel dyke? Well, I'm gonna make you an offer, Diesel."

"Name's Nerdo," she growled.

"Okay, Nerdo," he sneered. Here's your choice: work for me, or die."

"You call that a choice?"

Duke shrugged, "Nah. Just life," he said. "Or death, as the case may be." He paused, looking at her quizzically, then spun and walked back to his desk. "I'm not getting any younger here," he said. "Make the call."

"What's the job?"

"Working on RF-8s."

Nerdo gasped. "There's no such thing," she said.

"Yeah. That's why we need to work on 'em, see?"

"My God," she said. "Is that what this is all about? Zen's working on an eight, and you and the other gangs will get them!"

"See?" he said again. "Clever clogs. So, what'll it be?"

"Don't see that I've got much choice," she said. "And I gotta admit, the idea of developing an eight is interesting…" The words came reluctantly, but for now the only plan Nerdo had was to stay alive until she came up with a better one.

"Fine," he said, standing. "We'll get you into a uniform, then you'll come with me to the games."

CHAPTER 28
DEATHBALL

ALICE WAS PEERING through the slats at the arena when the door opened behind him. Two guards barged in and dragged Jonno from of the cell. He managed a quick look back before they slammed the door shut behind them.

Alice knew the look was goodbye. "Chaa, mate!" he mumbled sadly, knowing there was nothing he could do. He went back to peering through the slats. The floor of the arena was a circle, about 20 or so metres across. The sides sloped at twenty degrees, ramping up another twenty metres from the floor, until they reached a vertical section that extended a further five metres to the top. There was a single basketball hoop positioned three metres up the sloping wall from the floor. The whole thing looked deathly ominous. The tiered balcony seats were full of Zen workers and bikers, and when a horn blast sounded the waiting crowd erupted with a loud cheer.

Suddenly the crowd's attention was diverted. A figure was gradually rising from a trapdoor in the centre of the arena, which Alice hadn't noticed before. As Duke rose into the arena, the crowd went ballistic.

He stood dead centre, like a circus ringmaster, arms extended wide, circling to take in all the applause. As it began to subside, he announced: "Welcome, workers of Zen, bikers, associates, dignitaries and guests!"

His amplified voice caused an even louder roar.

Alice was chomping at the bit to get at him. He grabbed the slats, white knuckled. Sweat raced down his cheeks. "You piece of crap, Duke!" he shouted, fiercely. But Duke was oblivious.

"Like last year, we bring you the spectacle of the Anzac Day Games!" he went on, and the crowd roared again. He held up a hand to quieten them. "Our champions from last year —Slasher from the Comanches and Flaps from the Avengers — will take on the best opposition in the land! Blood will be spilled!" he screamed, as the crowd exploded with savage joy. After a few moments, he again raised a hand for quiet.

"The rules!" he declared. "Two bikers, Slasher and Flaps, form the black team! Two fighters, on foot, the red team! One ball, one goal, one objective — three baskets to win freedom! I give you ... Deathball!"

The arena erupted. Alice understood what he'd been looking at: the set-up of a murderous game. A wall of death, once a sideshow feature at carnivals and shows, now a macabre scene of entertainment. Filled with terror, rage and disgust, Alice continued to watch.

Duke's trapdoor descended, and a door swung shut to seal the hole. The crowd reached a new crescendo as a door in the sloped wall opened and Slasher and Flaps, clad head to toe in leathers, roared into the ring on vintage TM 450 E motocross bikes. They cruised around the ring, waving at the crowd. The mob commenced a slow handclap, which motivated the riders to speed up. They ascended the slope, eventually slipping smoothly onto the vertical wall and thundering around it, close to the top, ninety degrees to the ground at breakneck speed. As the two bikes roared past the audience went ballistic, thrilled by their daredevil display. After a dozen dizzying laps, the bikers descended to ground level, where they stopped, dismounted, and raised their arms to wild applause. The sloped door opened again, and a biker entered carrying a pair of two-metre long wooden lances. He handed one to each biker and exited.

Duke and Gorrick were by now sitting in the commentary box at the centre of the balcony seating. They were accompanied by the six Chapter presidents, Ursula and Morri and, at Duke's side, Nerdo. An electronic scoreboard was just below the box. It lit up:

BLACK - 0. RED - 0.

Then, for the third time, the door opened to reveal a lone figure carrying a basketball: Jonno.

Alice watched his mate through the slats. "This is your chance, Jonno!" he screamed. "Do this for Trixy!"

By some miracle, Jonno heard him. He looked over to where he knew Alice was watching, and grinned. At that moment, a second man appeared at the entrance. Tatts, almost unrecognisable after months of extreme torture, staggered out to stand beside Jonno. Despite his battered condition, he stood tall, ready to fight to the death. He and Jonno shook hands warmly, and took up their positions, back to back.

In the box, Morri sat stunned, watching these people she knew prepare to die. She risked a glance at Nerdo, looking odd but elegant and strangely feminine in her uniform. Without looking at Morri, Nerdo offered the smallest shake of her head. Morri sat back. Nerdo was still on side.

Aware of Morri's glance, Duke turned to Nerdo. "Plenty of time for a reunion later," he scoffed. "She made the same choice you did. Now you both work for us. S'pose you could say the same for your buddies in the ring." Chortling, he jumped up, silenced the audience with a hand signal, and nodded at Gorrick. The tall, white-haired Englishman rose slowly to his feet, glanced imperiously around the audience, and raised a thumb.

Slasher and Flaps kick-started their bikes and moved off. Menacingly, they circled Jonno and Tatts who stood their ground. The bikers flashed past them, stabbing teasingly with their spears. The two men tried to position themselves for a shot at a basket. Jonno ducked under a spear as it passed and flicked the ball to Tatts, who had managed a run of ten metres or so and was closer to the hoop.

Tatts caught the ball and, being the fitter of the two, ran flat out to try for a shot. As he steadied himself to throw, he heard the roar of a bike coming up behind and quickly passed back to Jonno. He turned sharply to face the oncoming biker. As Flaps lunged at him with the spear, Tatts grabbed it, leapt, swung and landed on the back of the bike.

The crowd erupted in approval as Flaps hit the accelerator and took to the wall, Tatts clinging to his back. Meantime, Jonno had again dodged his opponent, made a limping run and was ready to take a shot.

When Jonno scored, both Nerdo and Morri leapt to their feet and cheered. A snarl from Duke made them sink back down, but it couldn't kill their elation.

As Jonno retrieved the ball, Slasher made a move. Jonno spun to face him and as Slasher drove at him, spear aimed to kill, he fired the ball into the oncoming biker's face. The instinctive flinch, together with the impact from Jonno's mighty throw, was enough. Slasher fell, bike on top, pinned. That brought the audience to their feet, but they weren't cheering.

In his cell, Alice punched the air. "Yes!" he bellowed. "Go, Jonno!"

Still clinging to Flaps' jacket, Tatts brought a vicious elbow down on the back of the man's neck. Flaps, however, risked losing one arm and returned the elbow, catching Tatts in the face. The teenager went backwards off the bike and dropped vertically. His trajectory angled so that he hit the wall and slid, rather than hitting the deck fifteen metres below, but the steep slide still resulted in a sickening crack as hit the ground. The audience cheered wildly. Tatts tried to get back to his feet, but one arm hung useless and his ankle was broken. He wasn't going anywhere.

Alice looked away. Tatts … Tatts wasn't going to make it.

Flaps seized his opportunity. Speeding down the wall, spear raised, he caught Tatts full in the chest. Jonno, enraged, rushed Flaps, shoulder-charging him off his bike. As Flaps hit the deck, the spear jolted from his grasp and they both lunged for it. Slasher saw his partner in trouble and his struggles to get out from under his bike increased.

Jonno crash-tackled Flaps again. Holding him down, a knee across his throat, he bent down, bit, and spat an ear onto the ground.

Alice belted the slats with both hands, screaming at the top of his voice. "Yeah, Jonno! Yeah!"

Jonno kicked the fallen biker, who rolled onto all fours, stunned, trying to get up. Jonno picked up the spear. With all his might, he rammed into the biker. Rising through the man's gut, chest and throat, the tip came out of his mouth. Impaled, eyes rolled back in his head, Flaps gurgled, spewing blood. Jonno wasn't about to show mercy. He rolled the stricken man onto his back, took a wide back swing, and kicked him so hard in the mouth that the spearhead snapped off and the man's jaw all but came off.

Slasher had broken out from under his bike, dragged it upright, and was once again charging at Jonno. The big man, hearing the engine, grabbed the mangled corpse, hefted it above his head and flung it at the oncoming biker. It landed just in front of the bike. Slasher, forced to swerve violently, managed to stay on, but was visibly rattled. He retreated to the side of the ring, watching Jonno, bike idling.

Making use of the moment, Jonno hobbled to the body and, with a mighty jerk, tugged the spear free. He collected the basketball, tucked it under his arm and limped slowly towards the hoop. The audience was up, clapping in unison. Their tide had turned. They wanted Jonno to score.

Duke and Gorrick exchanged worried looks. Gorrick wasn't impressed — the visitors were supposed to lose.

Alice was hanging from the slats, screaming at Jonno. "Go on mate, go! Do it!"

Slasher watched, revving his bike, waiting for his moment. The crowd fell silent. Slasher was going to charge Jonno like a jousting knight. He knew Jonno would have to turn his back to take his shot at the hoop, and that would be his cue. Jonno steadied for the throw. Slasher lowered his spear. The crowd stared, wide-eyed. Jonno's arms drew back, he turned, and the biker began to roll forward lance up.

Jonno made the basket just as Slasher arrived. With surprising dexterity, he grabbed his own spear, dodged the biker's thrust, whirled and broke his spear across the back of Slasher's head. The force knocked the man off his bike, which belted into the wall with a tremendous crash. The crowd jumped up but stayed silent, watching with bated breath.

Jonno glanced at the scoreboard:

RED - 2. BLACK - 0.

One more basket would buy him freedom. He hobbled over to the ball and picked it up.

Alice was holding the slats so hard they were cutting Turk's fingers. "You can do it, mate!" he roared. "Take the shot! Take the shot!"

Nerdo and Morri were out of their seats, wringing their hands, ignoring orders to sit down.

Jonno staggered over to take his shot. Behind him, the stunned biker was feebly reaching for his spear. Jonno made his throw. Slasher, finding some remaining reserve of strength, launched — and impaled Jonno through the back. He staggered, spear protruding from his chest, watching the flight of the ball with the rest of the crowd. It seemed to move in surreal slow motion. The ball hit the hoop, did one agonizingly slow roll around the rim, then dropped through the basket. Jonno raised an arm in the air, victorious.

The only sound came from Alice's cell. "Yes, Jonno!" he screamed, tears almost blinding him. "Yes!"

Jonno turned to Alice with huge smile. He stood for a second, then the lights went out in his eyes. He sank backwards and was held upright, propped by the spear that had killed him. Even in death, they couldn't put him down. The crowd erupted with cheers. Nerdo and Morri flopped back in their seats, exhausted, tears streaming.

Duke got to his feet.

"The red team has won!" he declaimed. "They are free to go!" There was a brief pause. "Too bad they're dead!" he yelled.

"Oh, I say," said Secta to Morri, as the crowd roared, torn between approval and disapproval. "That's bad taste, surely? Even I wouldn't have cracked that joke."

The cell door opened behind Alice — his turn had come. Two guards grabbed him and brutally cuffed him. "You're a mob of gutless bastards!" he snarled. "Send an unarmed bloke to fight an armed opponent?" He struggled, getting in the face of one of the guards. "You're nothing!" he spat. "Nothing, compared to him! You hear me? Freakin' nothing!" He snapped his teeth, trying to bite, but the other guard let fly three rapid-fire kidney punches that knocked the wind out of him. They dragged him up the dark corridor to the door leading into the arena. Halfway there, he found his legs. Violently shrugging off the guards, he walked to his destiny with pride.

Duke stood from his seat in the imperial box and waved a hand to calm the audience. "It is time for the main event ... our feature contest!" he roared. He paused, allowing the excitement to build. "Presenting ... former SAS dissident, and now leader of the red team ... Turk!"

The guards removed his cuffs. He glared at them contemptuously, and stalked out to centre ring. He grinned. It was like walking onto the stage at a gig. He raised an arm to the crowd and turned in a slow circle, giving everyone in the stadium a good look. Seeing Duke and Gorrick in the main box he stopped, gave Duke the evil eye, and held up both hands, bow fingers extended. The crowd roared their approval.

Duke chuckled at Turk's arrogance. "What about this soldier boy?" he growled to Gorrick. "He's about to die and he's still cocky as hell." Gorrick simply shook his head.

Nerdo fired Morri a surreptitious wink — she was backing Turk. Secta, on the other hand, was panicking. "If Turk loses, I lose too!" he said in her head. "Alice is dead, I'm stuck here, and Hope will probably die…"

"Don't underestimate him, Secta," said Morri, softly, watching Turk's strong form performing Alice's antics. "They threw away the cast when he was made."

Duke, meanwhile, was continuing his rant. "And now, the second member of the red team…" he said. "Another dissident, and, fittingly, another of Turk's best friends, from Snake Ridge … Reno!"

Alice turned sharply to see Reno striding towards him. They embraced in the centre of the circus.

"Turk," said Reno. "I guess we get to make a final stand together."

"Sorry to disappoint you buddy," said Alice. "Turk's not here. Bloody wish he was."

"No worries," grinned Reno. "You're a mate too. Let's just try to stop these bastards, alright?"

"Introducing the black team!" Duke bellowed. "Led by last year's champion, from the Rebels, it is … Spike!"

The crowd jeered, some booed — Spike was far from being a crowd favourite.

"And he is partnered by another champion: from the Bandits … Drill!"

The crowd stamped their feet in support. They liked Drill.

The two bikers thundered into the ring, spears up.

Duke motioned the crowd quiet. "Same rules," he said. "First team to three baskets wins. Gorrick?"

Gorrick stood, and was handed a basketball. He raised it over his head, to wild cheers from the audience, then cast it down to the red team with a loud shout: "Let's play!"

CHAPTER 29
HELL HATH NO FURY

ALICE PICKED UP the ball and sprinted to one end of the arena while Reno scurried to the other. With his back hugging the wall to prevent the bikers from getting behind him, he ran crabwise, displaying amazing dexterity, making his way towards the hoop. These two weren't injured like Jonno and Tatts were, this wasn't going to be a one-sided fight.

Before Spike and Drill could do more than reach him, Alice took a shot and scored. The crowd went insane. Again, Gorrick fired Duke a contemptuous glare.

Dodging the two bikers, who'd managed to entangle their spears in their rush to reach him, he grabbed the ball and drop-kicked it to Reno. With the two bikers still following Alice, Reno was free to make a dash to the hoop and take a shot. Barely two minutes in, and the score was already two-nil to the Reds. It was everything the crowd had hoped for. The underdogs were getting on top, and they lustily cheered them on.

Reno retrieved the ball and punted it back to Alice, but this time it was intercepted by Drill. Now it was on. Reno and Alice raced back to centre ring and stood back-to-back, waiting for the bikers to come at them. The black team circled for what seemed like forever, far too long at any rate for the audience, who were getting restless, and letting the black team know it. Neither biker seemed to want to make the first move. They propped, one at each end of the arena, and turned to face their opponents, lances raised, preparing to make a simultaneous charge. They revved their engines ... and launched at speed.

It was a clumsy move, and Reno and Alice easily dodged it. Cursing and frustrated by the jeering of the crowd, Spike and Drill repositioned for another assault. Unbeknown to them, Alice and Reno had agreed on a plan, their words masked by the cacophony of the crowd and the roaring of the bikes.

With a nod, Reno and Alice positioned themselves. As the bikers closed in, each dived at his opponent's spear. Travelling too fast to do more than avoid collision, the bikers could only watch as their spears were torn from their grasp. The black team was in real trouble. So too, by the look of it, was Duke. Gorrick was not pleased.

Alice raced over to the wall and waited. Reno waved cheekily at Drill, challenging him to charge. The ploy worked. Drill drove at Reno who, waiting until the very last second, flung his spear. It glanced off the biker's helmet. Drill fishtailed sideways then turned one-eighty degrees on a dime. There was no doubt the man could ride.

Reno ran to retrieve the spear, but Drill charged again. Reno realised the danger too late, and though he tried to dodge, the bike caught him in a vicious collision that smashed his arm. He staggered to his feet, clinging to the spear in his right hand, for the moment oblivious to the jagged radius protruding through the meat of his left forearm. Blood gushed from the wound, streaming down his useless arm and dripping into a gory puddle at his feet. Reno was in bad shape.

Seeing his chance, Drill turned his bike for another charge, intent on going in for the kill.

Determined to help, Alice leapt from the wall and fired his spear at Drill. The missile sank deep into Drill's back, but couldn't stop him hitting Reno full-bore. The collision was horrific, even the maddened crowd gasped. The three figures, a terrible tangle of man and metal, tumbled over and over in the dust. Alice saw Spike start after him and raced back to the wall. Reno, if he'd survived, would have to fend for himself for the moment.

Drill struggled to his feet and tried to reach the spear in his back, but couldn't quite grasp the shaft. Miraculously, Reno struggled to his feet behind him. Alice watched him battling to press on, despite what must have been overwhelming pain. His grit was awe-inspiring.

Alice couldn't stop himself. "Do it for Elsa, mate!" he screamed. "Do it!"

Reno, with a look of grim resolve, picked up the bike's front fork, which had detached in the wreck. Carrying it in his good hand, he staggered to his enemy, still struggling to extract the spear from his back. Reno struck the biker across the side of the head as hard as could. The force knocked Drill's helmet off and he dropped to one knee, stunned. Mustering his last ounce of strength, Reno swung again at Drill's head. The blow smashed into the man's skull, tearing apart skin and bone, all but cleaving his head in half. Drill's legs buckled under him and he collapsed on the deck, dead meat. Reno was spent. The fork dropped from his limp hand into the blood at his feet as he staggered dizzily, wavering in and out of consciousness. He was barely hanging on.

Spike knew Reno was done for, and turned his attention to finishing him off. He drove over, stopped, dismounted and put down the ball. Snapping off a chunk of the spear still protruding from Drill's back, he walked over to Reno and stabbed it into his left eye. To calls of 'finish him, finish him, finish him,' from the crowd, baying for more blood, Spike pushed it deeper into Reno's brain.

Nerdo and Morri buried their faces in their hands, unable to watch. Gorrick was finally smiling.

While Spike was focused on ravaging Reno's body, Alice slipped up behind him and commandeered his bike. Face set, he revved the big 450, hit the gas and raised the front wheel then cannoned off, climbing the wall at speed. He drove higher and faster than anyone had ever done before, driving the crowd wild. Duke alone seemed unimpressed.

Spike, alone in the middle of the ring with blood-drenched hands, could only waiting for the man on the bike to make his move.

Alice descended. As he reached Spike, he leapt, flying through the air to crash-tackle the big Rebel to the ground. Even at his size, Spike was no match for Alice, who was almost on fire with fury. The singer pinned the big biker beneath him and lashed out, but powerful as his blows were, they were ill directed, deflected by Spike's helmet. Alice wasn't the fighter Turk was. He jumped off Spike and let then man struggle to his feet, then let go with a power kick to the head. The blow connected, finally knocking the helmet off. Breaking away, Alice raced for the ball, his mission now to end the game.

Spike staggered to his bike, stood it up and mounted. He kicked it over, once, twice, then it fired and he roared after Alice who, ball in hand, was running full-tilt for the hoop. Spike was closing, and Alice knew it.

Morri and Nerdo were on their feet again, screaming. "Turk!" they yelled. "Behind you! He's right behind you!"

Mennis grabbed Morri's arm and dragged her back into her seat.

As Spike got to him, Alice spun on one leg and with a huge roundhouse, kicked him clean off his bike. Spike flew backwards and hit the deck hard, stunned. Alice took a shot at the hoop but missed.

Spike struggled to his feet.

The President of the Comanches reached past Duke and handed Gorrick a chrome bike chain. Gorrick nodded his thanks, took the chain, and threw it down to Spike. The crowd booed.

Spike rushed to the chain and picked it up. Whirling it overhead, he came at Alice. Whack! He whipped the metal across his opponent's face, opening up his cheek. He hit him again, hard, and the blow dropped Alice to one knee. Spike laid into him with the chain. Alice could only raise his arms to deflect the blows.

"Turk!" he screamed, mentally, "Where the hell are you, man? Spike's gonna win!" Suddenly, he felt a massive surge of power. "Oh, thank Christ!" he said. "We're getting beaten to a pulp here!"

Turk rose slowly to his feet. He squared, dodged Spike's cartwheeling chain, and bolted, straight for the bike. Spike stood his ground, a huge grin on his ugly face, spinning the chain.

"Come on, soldier boy Abo!" he spat, defiantly racist.

It was the wrong thing to say to Turk. The bike started. Revving the engine, he lined it up for a run at Spike.

The crowd fell silent, only the sound of the engine echoing around the arena. On the edge of their seats, they waited for Turk to make his move. He hit the throttle and the bike leapt towards Spike who stood unwavering, swinging the chain. Just before he reached his enemy, Turk wrenched the throttle all the way open and whipped the bike onto its back wheel. Caught off guard, Spike lashed out. The chain missed its target, but wrapped around the foot peg of the bike where it locked on, jammed. Turk brought the bike down and accelerated again. The chain, wound around Spike's wrist, hauled him off his feet. Turk drove flat out around the circus, dragging the biker behind him, tearing chunks from every bit of exposed flesh as he bounced behind the speeding bike.

Purposely aiming for Reno's dead body, Turk dragged Spike right over the top of it. The spear still protruding from Reno's eye caught Spike in the stomach, tore open his leathers and hooked into flesh, opening his gut. The point snagged entrails, unravelling them into a long, slippery rope. Spike was being towed behind the bike, his own entrails dragging Reno's body behind him. Realising what had happened, Turk came to a stop. Spike, somehow, struggled to his feet, trying to clutch at his innards with both hands. They slid through his fingers like some obscene umbilical cord binding him to Reno. The man screamed as the gruesome rope, already desperately damaged, finally snapped, leaving him sagging to his knees in the centre of the circus, with a great, bloody cavity where his digestive tract should have been.

Turk stepped off the bike and strode over. He kicked the man backwards, then stamped a boot across his throat. He held it there, seeking the approval of the crowd. But the crowd had fallen silent. Turk sought out Duke.

"Watch this, you freaking imbecile!" he roared, and rammed his foot down on Spike's throat. The loud crack as the spine snapped echoed around the stunned arena. A deathly silence fell. Turk walked over to the ball, picked it up and headed for the hoop.

Gorrick was livid. Turk was about to win.

"Do something you big oaf," he snarled to Duke. "Can't you see he'll be a hero? It'll make a mockery of us!"

Duke wasn't impressed. It was an insult to be ridiculed in front of the other biker presidents. He glared at Gorrick, then sprang to his feet and yelled.

"Turk! I'll free Nora too! But only if you can score the third basket against me — no holds barred!"

The crowd roared their approval.

Turk froze near the hoop.

The audience began a slow-hand clap.

"Okay mate," said Turk to Alice, "We can just crack on, score and leave … or we can get Nora back. If I die, you die. So what will it be?"

There wasn't even a second of hesitation. "Let's kill the prick!"

"Thought you'd say that," he smiled.

Turk glared up at Duke. "Not just Nora," he called. "Nerdo and Morri, too. And I want confirmation from Gorrick that the offer is legit. If I win, we all go free."

"There's no negotiation here, Turk!" Duke roared back, so vehemently he sprayed the people in the seats below him with spittle. "Nora only!"

"I'm not asking you!" yelled Alice. "Gorrick! Answer me now, in front of everyone here!"

Gorrick slowly rose to his feet. He paused for a moment, then said: "Done!"

Duke stared daggers at him. "What?" he snarled.

Ignoring him, Gorrick announced, loudly: "I agree! Beat Duke and you, Nerdo, Morrigan and Nora walk free!"

"Nora won't be walking anywhere," sneered Duke. "She's dead."

"All the more incentive for you to beat him then!" Gorrick answered, in evident distaste.

The cheer that erupted when Duke strode centre court did nothing to damage his immense ego. He'd changed from his tailored suit into leathers, a sleeveless leather vest showing off his muscular, tattooed arms and powerful pecs.

Turk marched up, grim savagery burning in his eyes.

"You dirt bag," he said, quietly. "You're not walking out of this ring."

Duke spat at Turk's feet. "Do your worst, soldier boy Abo," he replied.

Turk turned his back and strode over to the ball. As he bent to collect it, Duke struck him from behind with a massive kidney punch. The ball flew from Turk's grip as Duke tried to press his advantage, but Turk whirled and met him face on. Toe to toe, the two men exchanged a flurry of heavy blows. Duke soon realised that, however hard he hit, he would never match Turk's fighting finesse. His opponent was getting the better of him. Duke grinned, and pulled a blade.

Unimpressed, the crowd booed.

Turk raised an arm in defence, and the blade cut deep. He stepped back, considering his next move, and Duke took the opportunity to goad him, hoping to enrage him.

"Maybe you and Nora can have matching wheelchairs after this," he jeered. Turk reacted as he had hoped, with a wild lunge, but so quickly that the knife missed his heart and plunged into his shoulder instead.

Morri let out an earth-shattering scream.

"Turk! get it together!" Alice yelled.

Duke stood back, grinning. The man was clearly struggling, yelling to himself that way. He spotted the basketball and retrieved it — then stuck in his knife. "Try to win now, soldier boy!" he sneered, throwing the deflated ball at Turk's feet.

Blood streamed from Turk's shoulder wound, his nose, forearm, eyebrows and split lips. But he did not look like a beaten man. Duke hesitated, just for a second, and that was enough. A high-speed, precision roundhouse smacked the blade out of his hand and before he could react, Turk was on him, pent-up hate pouring out in a barrage of punches and kicks so brutal even the crowd was stunned into silence. Voiceless, they watched as Duke was pulverized.

Panting, Turk stood back. Duke lay half-conscious on the ground. Turning, Turk limped over to the smashed remains of the bike that had run Reno down, and tore off the front mudguard. The crowd murmured, confused. Carrying the twisted metal back to his fallen nemesis, Turk stood over him, shark eyes staring down blankly. Duke opened his remaining eye and peered up at him. Arrogance undiminished, he smirked. "Nora's dead," he spluttered, through a mouth filled with blood and broken teeth. "She didn't even make here," he coughed a laugh. "She's nothing but bleached bones, lying by the side of some road..."

Turk, still blank-eyed, raised the mudguard above his head. He drove it down on Duke's exposed throat with all his might. The metal, sharpened before the fight and honed still further by its mangled condition, cleaved the man's head from his body. The audience, stunned, remained silent. Even Gorrick seemed frozen to the spot. Morri and Nerdo were on their feet, aghast.

Turk grabbed Duke's head by the hair, and started a halting, painful walk towards the hoop. Aware of what he was about to do, the crowd rose as one.

Morri and Nerdo started a chant, subdued at first: "Turk ... Turk ... Turk..." One by one the audience joined in, "Turk, Turk, Turk!", until it built to a thundering tribute to this champion of champions. By the time Turk stopped and steadied for his shot, everyone in the audience, with the exception of Gorrick and the biker presidents, was on their feet, screaming the gore-covered gladiator's name. "Turk! Turk! Turk!"

Gorrick couldn't take anymore. He got up and stormed out, the disgruntled biker leaders following. Mennis stayed in her seat, apparently unaffected, watching with cool interest. Nerdo and Morri were jumping up and down, cheering wildly, as if they'd won a war.

Turk raised Duke's severed head. Blood dribbled from the ragged neck and down his arm. The crowd fell silent. He took his shot. Duke's head didn't even touch the sides. It hit the net and lodged, eyes staring wide in deadly disbelief. The scoreboard ticked over:

RED - 3. BLACK - 0.

The crowd were beyond applause. They simply stood, watching Turk in silent awe, as he hobbled back to centre court. When he stopped, a dropped pin would have sounded like a girder crashing from a great height. Ignoring the pain from his wounds, he raised his arms in the air. Then the crowd went ballistic.

Amid the cacophony, Secta whispered: "We live again."

CHAPTER 30
NO WARNING

TURK WAS MARCHED into Gorrick's office. Although patched up, he still looked considerably the worse for wear. Once the two guards had gone, Turk waited for Gorrick to turn and face him, but he didn't.

"You acquitted yourself admirably, Turk," he said slowly, deliberately. "Few thought you capable of defeating Duke. He was a hard man."

"He was a vicious psychopath," Turk spat.

Gorrick turned slowly. "Perhaps you're right," he said. "I admit, I had occasional doubts about him."

"He's full of it," said Alice's voice at the back of his mind.

"How's the shoulder?" Gorrick asked.

"Your medics did a decent job. I'm grateful for that much at least."

"Good," said Gorrick, sitting behind his desk and motioning to Turk to sit.

"I'll stand," said Turk.

"Please yourself," Gorrick shrugged. "So. What now?"

"Why the allegiance with the biker gangs?" Turk asked.

"Simple. Zen is the new law. They will be the new order."

"They're nothing but thugs! My friends died in the ring!"

"Tough times require firm control," said Gorrick, his face expressionless. "Without that the country will decline into chaos."

"You and your sick corporation have already caused chaos," said Turk. "I witnessed plenty of that during the war. The results were not pretty."

"That was then, Turk," Gorrick replied. "This is now. And any rate, Zen's involvement in the war was minimal."

"Rubbish," said Turk, speaking ominously quietly. "It was you. It was all you."

"How ... insightful of you," Gorrick smiled.

"The Zen brand was on the weapons ... all of the weapons," said Turk. "Every WarBot was manufactured by Zen. You're building your own private empire, Gorrick. You're taking over the world."

Gorrick sat back in his chair and folded his arms. "You are entitled to your opinion, Turk," he said, calmly. "But the fact remains, people like you must be controlled, or you will simply run riot. Your poor disciplinary record is testament to that. You are no better than those fools who babble about aliens," he added dismissively.

"People like me believe in freedom and human dignity," said Turk. "And that's what you and your organization are trying to take away."

"Hear, hear!" Alice silently agreed.

Their debate was cut short by a beep that told Gorrick someone had been cleared to enter. Rising, he pressed a button concealed below his desktop. The door opened and Mennis, accompanied by two guards, led in Nerdo and Morri. Turk gave the two women a broad, battered smile.

Gorrick nodded to the guards, who wheeled about and left.

Mennis joined Gorrick on his side of the desk. Morri ran to Turk and threw her arms around him. Nerdo watched, one eyebrow raised, amused in spite of everything.

"Looking good, Turk, all things considered," she said.

"Yeah," he answered. "A new shoulder would be nice, though." He grimaced as he tried to return Morri's embrace.

"At least you're in one piece," Morri said, touching the stitches on his cheek.

"She's got the hots for us," Alice whispered playfully.

"Not sure about those uniforms," Turk said, looking at both women. "They don't suit you one bit."

Nerdo shrugged. "Very smart and all that," she said, "But I'll take my jungle greens any day."

"Are you certain you won't change your mind, Morri?" Ursula asked, blandly. "You could have an exceptional future here with Zen, you know."

"Good heavens, she has all the personality of a biker's armpit!" thought Secta.

"Absolutely," she replied. "I never wanted to be here in the first place. You know that," she added, looking at Gorrick. The other two also turned their gazes on the tall, apparently unflappable man.

"Will you keep your word?" said Turk.

"Of course," said Gorrick, smoothly. "You have accused me of many things, but I am, if nothing else, a man of my word."

"He's lying!" thought Morri.

"How do you know?" replied Secta.

"I'm psychic? Remember?"

"Oh, yes. Wait — why aren't I psychic too? I'm in here as well!"

"Why should we believe you?" she said.

It was Mennis who answered. "Talents such as yours are too valuable to waste," she said. "Here, we would nurture and develop them. Out there, you will have nothing. The time may yet come when you will change your minds."

"Not a chance, love," Alice broke through. "Not in the slightest bit interested. There's nothing for us here except imprisonment and slavery. Now, I think we've got a cart to catch?"

There was a moment's silence, the three prisoners waiting tensely for the verdict.

"So be it," said Gorrick brusquely.

"And you'll turn off our OSCIs," said Nerdo.

"Good thinking, Nerdo," said Turk. "Yes," he went on, glaring at Gorrick. "Call it a demonstration of good faith."

Gorrick glanced at Mennis. After a long pause, he gave her a reluctant nod.

She spoke through her implant, barking the order. "Done," she said, glaring at Nerdo.

"You say it's done," Morri said. "But we have no assurance it won't be reactivated as soon as we walk out the door. I want your word, Gorrick. And you know — you both know — I can tell when you're lying." She stood resolute, hands on hips, giving Gorrick some serious stink eye.

Holding her stare, he said: "You have my word, Morrigan."

She nodded, and the three companions turned as one and walked to the door. Gorrick hit the switch to unlatch it. "Goodbye, Morrigan," he said, with what might have been a hint of sentimentality.

Morri stopped, turned back and speared him with a look. "When Duke butchered my parents," she said, her voice laced with malice, "He did it on your orders."

"Duke told you they were alive," he replied.

"I'm psychic, you fool." She turned her back and strode defiantly out the door, leaving the last shred of their relationship behind.

As the door closed behind them, Ursula leaned on Gorrick's desk, her hand on his. "You're not going to let them get away, are you?" she said. "They know too much."

He removed his hand from under hers, strolled over to the window and gazed out into the rain punishing the parched city outside.

"Hardly," he said, quietly. "Perhaps this would be the perfect opportunity to give our R-8s their first test run."

"Perfect," she smiled. "I'll get on it right away."

He stopped her on her way out. "Wait," he said. "I'm meeting the chapter presidents in half an hour to elect a new Grand Master.

I want a progress report on the eights at the conclusion of that meeting. And Mennis — make it convincing."

"Roger that," she responded, and saw herself out.

Guards escorted Turk, Nerdo and Morri to the Zen HQ platform, where a cart was waiting. Nerdo and Morri were back in civvies, Nerdo reunited with her beloved coat.

Groaning, Turk clambered into the cart and helped the others on board.

The two guards didn't wait around.

As soon as Nerdo sat down she began ferreting through her pockets. She was not happy. "They've pinched heaps of stuff," she groaned.

"Don't worry," said Turk, smiling. "First pile of junk we come to, you'll be able to replace it all."

"Junk!" Nerdo exclaimed. "Well, I guess one person's junk is another person's treasure, that's all."

Morri placed the flat of each hand on Turk's broad shoulders. Closing her eyes, she sank into the dreaming, meditating while droning ancient words of healing.

"That feels incredible," he said, softly. He felt invigorated. His aching muscles were soothed and re-energized. The throbbing and stinging from his many wounds settled. Even his mind felt soothed.

As the cart pulled away from the platform Nerdo pulled something from a hidden pocket with a shout. "Got it!" she said, triumphantly, brandishing a small remote. "At least they didn't find this!" She hit a button.

"What is it, Nerdo?" Morri asked, releasing Turk's shoulders.

"Remote signal," she said. "I sent a beep to Cutter. If he's still alive he'll be there meet us just past the Fed platform. We'll have to get off this thing, it's programmed to take us back to Headbangers."

"You know, that reminds me," said Morri, slyly, reaching into a pocket of her own. "Here, I nicked this for you." She handed Nerdo an Ulink portable computer.

"Mate!" Nerdo gasped. "You're a diamond! Whose is it?"

"Secta pinched it from Ursula."

"Oh, of course, blame me," said Secta, clearly delighted with himself. "I just thought it might contain some interesting data, that's all."

"How long do we have left on your mission, dude?" asked Alice.

"Twelve hours," was the gloomy reply.

"I must admit, Cutter and I had our doubts about this possession gig," said Nerdo. "But after everything we've been through ... Well, it's been quite a privilege."

"I second that," grinned Turk. "Sharing my body with the legendary Black Alice? What a trip!" Turk admitted.

"Why the stuff would you have any doubts, Nerdo?" Alice replied. "It was only your friend and leader being possessed by someone from another time. That stuff happens every day! And besides," he threw in, as they all laughed, "It ain't over yet!"

Nerdo keying joyfully into the Ulink said: "Okay, we need to jump ship just up ahead on the bend."

"Fine," confirmed Turk, as the bend approached. "Let's do it!" The three of them jumped blindly into the rain.

Turk rolled when he landed and got up, groaning. "You all right?" said Morri, putting a concerned hand on his arm.

"Just battered and bruised," he said. "Secta, why is it only I get to feel the pain and Alice doesn't?"

"Actually, the truth of it is, Alice could feel your pain if he tuned in to it," Secta answered. "I mean, I can certainly feel Morri's emotions."

"Saying no more on that subject would be best for your health, Secta," Morri warned.

Nerdo, once more glued to her stolen Ulink, swore. "Damn! They're tracking us through your OSCIs!"

"I knew we couldn't trust Gorrick," Morri sighed. "He was lying through his teeth."

"They could zap the three of us any time they want," said Nerdo. "So why haven't they? We need to get out of range, and quick!"

"They want us dead, that's why," said Secta. "We know too much."

"This way, everyone. Fed's about ten minutes from here," said Nerdo, leading them into a side-tunnel and along rusty, disused tracks.

"Somewhere the wolves are howling, life's last breath is a sigh, when the hunter becomes the hunted, they're scowling like metal on ice! No warning, no warning, ooo!" Sprawled next to the train tracks in a tunnel, a hundred metres or so from the Fed platform, Cutter had his busted leg propped up on an old four-litre drum and was singing to keep himself company in the dim light. "No warning, no warning," he squealed, enjoying the tunnel's reverb.

Nerdo stopped dead as she heard distant wailing in the dark. "Wait!" she snapped. "What's that?"

They all listened intently.

"No warning, no warning…" It echoed then faded.

Alice took over: "Then spit in your eye, to draw out the flame that burns like a knife in my chest!" The entire subway reverberated to his operatically metal tones.

A grin broke on Nerdo's face. "That's Cutter's favourite song," she said, cupping a hand to her ear. There was a slight delay, but then: "No warning, no warning…."

"An excellent song, if I don't mind saying so myself," said Alice with playful arrogance.

"Oh, you know it?" Nerdo asked, tongue in cheek.

"Should do — I wrote it!" Alice laughed. "Pity I'm not getting any royalties from the sucker."

"I guess the iWish worked," Turk quipped. "I can sing just like Black Alice."

"Yeah right," Alice grinned. "Don't give up your day job."

Nerdo led them past the decapitated body of the RF-2. Morri looked away.

"Your handiwork, Nerdo?" Alice asked.

"Yep, harvested for parts," she grinned.

"Why didn't you take its weapons?"

"Wouldn't work," she replied. "They're personalized: sensors recognise the 'Bot they've been assigned to."

They leapt down onto the train tracks and found Cutter sitting with a broad grin on his face. "Welcome, guys!" he said. "What took you so long? Hey, where's old Reno?"

"He didn't make it," Turk said, sorrowfully.

"Damn!" Cutter said, slapping his injured leg. "Ouch! Sorry mate. You okay? You look like you've been in the wars."

"Tell you all about it later," Turk replied. "We need to get moving."

Turk helped Cutter up and the four of them started along the tracks.

"There's a service alcove with an old pump trolley up ahead," said Cutter. "I did a bit of exploring. Could be just what the doctor ordered."

"Good job," said Turk. "And that's clearly a good crutch."

"Yeah, Reno made it out of the RF-2 armour," said Cutter. "He was a good bloke. Sorry we've lost him."

"We've lost three of them," said Turk, quietly. "Jonno and Tatt's gone as well. They were good mates, the best. But, hey, they went down fighting, and they took some scum with them. Couldn't ask for a better way to go than that."

They soon came to where the tracks split from the main line to a siding.

"There's a manual switch for the tracks over there," Cutter said, pointing. Sure enough, Turk found a lever and, after a bit of effort, managed to lock the siding to the main track. It took three of them to wheel the heavy pump trolley from where it had clearly been stored for donkey's years.

"How old is this thing?" Alice complained.

"About as old as you, Alice, I reckon," Cutter said, chuckling.

They manhandled it onto the main track and climbed aboard. Turk and Nerdo took an end of the handle each and, Turk hissing through his teeth with every push, got it rolling.

"Hey, Nerdo, can I yank this goddamned cyborg thingy out of my head now?" Cutter said.

"Not yet," Nerdo said. "They're still tracking us. Besides, we might need it."

"See?" said Turk, grinning, "There you go collecting junk again."

"Yeah, well," she said, with a smile. "You never know when it might come in handy."

The Presidents of the six national biker chapters were seated around a large mahogany table in the Zen HQ boardroom. At its head sat Gorrick, body language boasting authority.

"The vote is unanimous," he said stiffly. "Animal, as he's known by the local chapter of the Rebels, is your new Grand Master."

All of them, with the exception of Animal, applauded. Gorrick motioned for the new Grand Master to speak. Animal rose to his feet. He was even bigger, more bestial and intimidating than his predecessor. Six feet six, straight-backed with dark brown hair in a long ponytail, he weighed in at around 125 kilos. Animal was a giant. A former soldier with a chiselled face and a tight, lipless mouth indicating cold cruelty, he delivered his acceptance speech.

"I'm not one for formalities," he said. "But I will say this ... Duke was a mate and a Rebel, and I don't think I need your approval to find his killer and make a trophy of his head." The five presidents rose to their feet as one.

Animal led them in the Rebel yell. "Fight to the death!" he howled. Punching the air, they all picked up the chant: "Super charged, programmed to kill, we'll cut you down to get our thrill — Victims bleed in twisted wrecks, we'll run you down. Fight to the death!" They roared approval at the end of their chant and retook their seats.

Gorrick continued in a slow handclap until he got their attention. Then he stopped, leaned casually back and announced, with menace: "That won't be necessary."

A dozen eyes narrowed as they focused on him. But before anyone could interject, the oak doors parted and Mennis strode in. Gorrick gestured for attention.

She stopped short of the board table and stood to attention. All eyes diverted to her.

"I am Dr Mennis," she said, briskly. "Gorrick asked me to report to this meeting on the progress of the RF-7WB. But I'm not going to do that." She paused, watching their eyes widen slightly at her apparent insubordination. "Instead," she said, her voice growing louder, "I give you … the RF-8!"

Jaws dropped as a man-shaped creature bigger than Animal and twice the build strode into the room. Mennis stepped aside to allow it to pass. Gigantic, armour clad, it strode up to the board table, stopped at the far end, reached out and gripped it in one hand. Then it lifted the entire thing like a matchstick — and held it without so much as a tremor. As it lowered the table effortlessly back down, the bikers applauded. Suddenly, the cyborg brought its big fist round in a burst of power that smashed the table in half. The presidents jumped back from the wreckage and the RF-8 lunged for Animal, grasping a shoulder in one hand. It squeezed, forcing the mountainous biker to his knees.

Gorrick was enjoying the demonstration. He fired Mennis a congratulatory nod. Infuriated, Animal threw a massive punch into the machine's solar plexus. It didn't so much as flinch. Deathly silence shrouded the room as the bikers watched the creature increase the pressure until it forced a howl of pain from Animal's throat.

"Thank you, eight," said Gorrick, cool as a cucumber. "You may release him."

The cyborg obeyed immediately.

"I believe our demonstration has proved that avenging Duke's death is well in hand," Gorrick said, smugly.

Mennis applauded.

Exchanging looks of trepidation, the presidents rose one by one and joined in. Even Animal, struggling to his feet, joined in. There was no denying it — the eight was one hell of a killing machine.

CHAPTER 31
BLADE OF SLAUGHTER

T HE SUNLIGHT FELT good on their faces as they emerged from the tunnel. The rain had passed, leaving the air thick with humidity.

Nerdo checked the Ulink map.

"Turk, we should get off," she said. "There's CCTV up ahead."

"Can we avoid it to reach the front gates?" Turk asked.

"Most of it, I think," she said. "But it's bloody everywhere!"

Turk was near to exhaustion. "Is there another way out?" asked Alice. "Turk's stuffed, he needs a break."

"There's a camera up ahead, so let's stop for a minute," Nerdo said, studying the Ulink. "Wait! Yeah! We're pretty close to Betsy, let's go for her. She'll bash those bloody gates down, cameras or not!"

"Great thinking," said Cutter. "Plus we've got a load of weapons planted on board."

Turk thought. There was no point in going to Headbangers, the enemy would be waiting in ambush there. While they stayed in Angel, they were sitting ducks. Betsy as a battering ram wasn't just their best hope — she was their only option. He looked at Nerdo and nodded.

"I've found a back route that shouldn't have CCTV coverage," she said. "We need to get off at that ramp up ahead."

They all looked. The jump from the ramp was to a service platform tower, from which a metal ladder led to an alleyway twenty metres below. Morri looked at Cutter. "He's not going to make that, not in his condition," she said.

Turk looked up. "Alright, stop a minute," he said. He'd seen another ladder nearby, fixed to a pole connecting overhead power lines. "Those lines still live?" he asked.

"Not likely," said Nerdo. "The power for the carts is in the tracks."

Turk nodded. Jumping to the tracks, he jogged to the ladder. They watched him painfully hauling himself up until he reached the power line. Getting a firm grip on the rungs, he grabbed a handful of cable, then yanked. It took several painful pulls, but eventually the cable came free of its coupling. Coiling it around one shoulder. Turk started back down.

"Geez, he's a smart cookie!" Cutter said, chuckling.

Turk threaded the power line through the railing at the side of the track, then lowered the end into the alleyway.

"There you go, Cutter," he said, sweating. "You did a bit of rappelling in your SAS days, didn't you?" Cutter grinned and nodded. "Nerdo, you go down first," Turk commanded. "Steady the line for him to slip down."

Nerdo pocketed the Ulink and leapt into action.

In no time flat, they were all in the alleyway.

Crammed into the small CCTV monitoring room, the six biker presidents watched Mennis and four operators searching for Turk and his friends. Mennis was losing patience.

"If you can't give me their co-ordinates, I can't send in my forces," she snapped, lips set in a thin, uncompromising line.

"They're avoiding our cameras, ma'am," a young operator behind a monitor said, apologetically.

"Let's take a step back here," said Animal. "Forget CCTV for the moment. Where would you go if you thought we were coming after you?" He glared at the bikers for an answer.

The chief of the Comanches spoke. "I'd be making for the front gate," he rasped. "They gotta have vehicles, right? That's where they'll be headed."

"There you go," said Animal. "You have your answer."

"The car park is three blocks from here," said Nerdo, as they headed down an alley flanked by old, beaten warehouses. "We need to cross a main street to get to it, and there's CCTV everywhere."

Turk stopped them, peering over Nerdo's shoulder at the Ulink.

"What's that there?" he pointed at the screen. "That corner building? It's huge."

Nerdo zoomed in on the map. "It's an old jail," she said.

"Right. That was before Angel became a city," said Cutter. "What was it called again? Goulburn?"

"Ha!" laughed Alice, startling them all. "Sorry ... it's just — Goulburn Jail! Half of my band have been in there. Back in the day, that is." He shot them a devilish grin.

"They got CCTV in there. Nerdo?" asked Turk.

"Not that I can see," she said. "Not operational, anyway."

"Excellent. Can we get to it through one of these old warehouses?"

"Yeah, there's a way through that one," Nerdo said, pointing at one directly ahead. "But we have to get over a drain or something. See it?"

"Yeah," said Alice, peering over Nerdo's shoulder again. "And it'll take longer — but it looks a hell of a lot safer," he decided.

They continued towards the dilapidated warehouse, and soon came to the watercourse Nerdo had seen on the map. A deep, concrete storm-water channel, it was ten metres across and contained only a thin, trickling stream.

Gorrick entered the CCTV operations room as Animal was leading Mennis and the rest of the bikers out. "What is going on?" he asked, flatly. "Have you located them yet?"

"No, sir," said Mennis solemnly. "They are avoiding our CCTV network."

"What was your last fix on them?" he snapped, unimpressed.

"Never mind that," said Animal. "They're heading for the front gates. That's where their vehicle will be. They're making a run for it."

"Seems a logical assumption," Gorrick agreed, opening the door to the operations room. He stuck in his head and barked an order: "Richards, get onto HQ and have an armed drone launched to the car park. We will monitor it from HQ comms!" He glanced back confidently at Mennis and the six bikers. "That should do the trick," he said, confidently. "If they are above ground, it will find them. Follow me."

Karzoff left the breakfast buffet, plate stacked high, and sat down at the window opposite Honor. She looked distastefully at him over her cup.

"Karzoff, zat is your second helping," she grimaced. "Vhere on Earth do you put it all?"

Before he could answer, he saw something outside.

"Car," he answered vaguely, mouth full.

"Don't be ridiculous, Karzoff," she snapped.

"No!" he managed, and pointed. "Car!"

Honor turned sharply in time to see Hope and Mal Function getting into their car.

"Don't look now," said Mal, "But the bookends are having breakfast in the restaurant."

Hope sank in her seat. "Too late doc," he said, as Honor flung down her coffee cup and fled. Karzoff paused only long enough to grab a handful of bacon before flying after her.

"We've been spotted," Mal groaned, backing the car out and screeching out of the car park. "We need to get away from here fast."

"Head for Goulburn," said Hope. "It's only a few clicks away, it'll give us a bit of cover."

"What's there?" he said.

"Wait, I'll check the SatNav," Hope said, stabbing at the GPS unit. "Here we go ... The Big Merino, some wineries, Wombeyan Caves and Goulburn Jail, built in 1830. Sounds like fun!" she finished, playfully.

"Well, I don't know about you, but the Big Merino is a selfie must and we've gotta catch the jail!" Mal said, laughing.

"Okay," she joined in the joke. "Then lunch and a gurgle at the winery. That should keep us going until Secta's deadline. 5 a.m. tomorrow," she finished. "All we need to do is avoid the ugly twins until then."

As Karzoff powered their car from the car park, Honor produced her tablet and checked local maps.

"Goulburn," she said. "It's ze nearest big town to here. Zat's vere zey vill be headed."

"Ooh, there is loads to see there," said Karzoff, munching bacon. "The Big Merino, Wombeyan Caves—

"Shut up, fool!" she snapped. "Ze only zing you will be doing vhen ve find zem is killing ze singing peace activist and taking Hope prisoner."

"Kill him?" he choked "Me? I mean, I have no problem taking Hope but ... but ... I have no experience in—"

"Vipe your mouth," said Honor, stony-faced. "You are spraying bacon everyvhere. Get zis right, and you vill be able to do both. Get rid of Function, and Hope vill be all yours."

"Yes, but I ... But he…" stammered, Karzoff. Mal was a big bloke. Karzoff didn't fancy trying to take him on, especially after last time.

"Good," snapped Honor. "Zen it is settled. Now. I see here zat ze gallows at Goulburn Jail vere built in 1832, and floggings zere vere commonplace." She looked up at the horizon, where Goulburn showed as a dark smudge. "Zounds like my kind of town."

"Is this the only place we can cross?" Turk asked.

"There's a bridge over yonder," said Nerdo. "But it's—"

"Covered by CCTV," he finished with her. "Fine. We'll have to cross here."

Cutter checked the steep descent. "Easy for you to say."

Turk climbed the hip-high fence and stood on the edge of the concrete wall that sloped ten metres down to the water.

"Prop your butt on the fence, mate," he said. "I'll lift your legs over." On the other side of the fence, Morri and Nerdo helped Cutter onto Turk's back. A little slipping and sliding down the sloping embankment later, they were standing on the flat area at the bottom. The others joined them.

"You right, Cutter?" Turk asked.

"Yeah. You make a good pack horse."

"Don't rest easy yet. We've still got to get up the other side."

"Hang on!" said Nerdo, staring anxiously at her Ulink. "They're up to something. Another satellite's just came on line. And — listen!" she said, looking sharply at the sky. "I know that sound!"

"Me too," said Turk. "Drone. Those things are lethal — take cover!"

"Where?" said Morri, desperately. There was nowhere to hide.

"There!" Cutter shouted, balancing on his crutch and pointing eastward.

The drone was flying just above the buildings, coming their way.

In the state-of-the-art HQ comms centre, monitors glowed as technicians worked at more than a dozen consoles. The main monitor used fogscreen mid-air display technology: lasers providing 3-D visuals that floated in the centre of the circular room. Gorrick was at the operations console, Mennis and Animal on either side. Like magic, a 3D display hologram materialized in mid-air, showing a vista of warehouses — and the outlines of four figures standing in a deep storm channel.

"Just as I thought," Gorrick said smugly, pointing at the hologram. "They are in the channel. Arm the drone."

"Autofire enabled, sir?"

They could see the figures start to run.

"Yes," Gorrick growled.

Nerdo's wartime experience kicked in. "Wait!" she yelled. "These things have movement sensors, not eyes. Hit the deck, roll away from where you land, and stay absolutely still. It'll take its mark from your last movement. Go!"

As if on cue, the drone descended at speed. They hit the deck, Cutter rolling from Turks' back, and lay still. The drone opened fire.

"5.56 mm small calibre mini-gun," yelled Cutter, face down on the ground. "Watch out for ricochets!"

Bullets pinged all around them, but as Nerdo had said, in spots where the drone had last detected movement. Cutter was also right. The ricochet was as dangerous as the initial shot, bullets and flying shrapnel zinged all around them.

The hologram POV from the drone showed the targets disappearing. "Dammit!" snapped Gorrick. "They have out-foxed us again. Operator two," he said, icily, "Open the floodgates to ... what section is this?"

"177, sir!" operator two responded.

"Fine. Open them.

"Sir, the drone?"

"Disarm and circle!"

"Quick, get to cover before the next pass!" Turk shouted.

"No!" Nerdo countered, studying the drone. "It's ascending. It won't attack from up there."

"That was too close," said Alice. "Everyone alright?"

"Hush!" said Secta, suddenly. "What's that sound?"

Morri looked about sharply. "Sounds like ... a door opening?" she said. "Is that likely?"

Back on their feet, they all glanced in the direction of the sound.

Turk helped Cutter up. "They're opening the floodgates," he said. "We need to move. Now!"

About a hundred metres along the culvert, a pair of rusted metal floodgates was creaking open, immense volumes of water already coming through. He hoisted Cutter once more and they all raced for the other side. The roar of rushing water filled the air as Turk got to the wall but the weight of Cutter on his back and the steep gradient made the climb incredibly hard. He was almost at the top when he started to slide.

"Hold on!" Nerdo yelled, "I'll get up and give you a hand!"

Turk scrabbled with fingers and toes, stopping his slide almost by sheer willpower alone.

Nerdo scrambled up the slope, nimble as a monkey going after bananas. Gripping the rail, she reached for Turk with her free hand. They came up short. "Move!" yelled Cutter. "Get yourself and Morri out of here!" But Nerdo wasn't done. Shrugging out of her coat, she grabbed the tails and threw it down. Turk grabbed hold. Nerdo gritted her teeth, using all her strength to anchor herself and the coat while Turk started hauling himself and Cutter back up the steep wall.

The water was coming down in a torrent now, and rising.

Turk was still struggling. Thinking on her feet, Morri whipped off her belt, looped it through the buckle and lowered it to Cutter, who slipped his wrist through the loop and steadied himself for the wave.

"Hold on!" Nerdo yelled, still gripping the coat.

"I've got you, Cutter!" screamed Morri, hanging onto the belt for grim death.

The passage of time seemed to slow for Turk — then the water struck. It lifted him high, allowing him to buck Cutter off his back. Cutter was level with the fence. Grabbing it, he swung himself onto the top of the wall beside Nerdo and Morri. But Nerdo's coat was simply flapping uselessly in the torrent. Turk had disappeared into the boiling flood.

"No!" screamed Nerdo, trying to catch sight of him, but he'd gone. Clinging together, the surviving three saw the initial rage of the flood subside, and it settled into a fast, steady flow, dropping a little as it did so. Soaking wet, lucky to be alive, they watched the floodgates close, staring blankly at the water, speechless, in shock. They watched the brown waters below, willing Turk to bob to the surface like a cork. But with every second that ticked away, it became more and more unlikely.

"I let him go," Nerdo sobbed. "I can't believe I let him go…"

"Don't," said Cutter. "Don't do that to yourself. It wasn't your fault." He passed a hand over his own eyes as he placed a wet but consoling arm around her shoulders.

"There ends my mission," said Secta, dejectedly, still watching the raging waters.

"He's not dead," said Morri, in a small voice.

"What?" said Nerdo, disbelievingly. "Morri, we all want that to be true. But—"

"I can feel him."

Cutter raised his head. "Really?" he said.

"Really," she nodded. "I don't know where he is, but he's not dead. Not yet."

"Well then," said Cutter, pragmatically, "We'd better get off our arses and find him, hadn't we?"

"That drone is still up there," said Secta. "And goodness only knows what else. Perhaps we should wait here for Turk and Alice to return."

"Trouble is, if we hang around, we're sitting ducks," said Cutter. "We need to keep moving."

"Cutter's right," said Nerdo. "Who knows what else they've got to throw at us. We need to move."

"Turk knows where we were headed," said Morri, firmly. "He'd tell us to keep moving. I know he would. He'll catch us up."

"Seems like I'm arguing against myself," Secta said.

With as much of a sprint as they could muster, the two women supporting Cutter between them, raced for the cool, dark shadows between the buildings, where a drone would find it harder to spot them.

They reached another derelict warehouse, where they stopped for a breather while Nerdo cased for an entrance.

"It's so bloody hot," Cutter complained. "I can hardly breathe."

"Entrance up ahead." Nerdo looked up from her Ulink and pointed. "There."

Cutter hobbled over. A dilapidated door, barely hanging from its rusted hinges, crashed easily open. They went to step through, but he stopped them abruptly. "Wait!" he barked. "There's footprints in the dust!"

"Fresh?" Nerdo asked.

"Pretty fresh, I'd say." He drew his pistol.

"You're kidding," said Secta. "We're not going in there, are we? Are we?"

No-one bothered to answer him as they stepped inside.

As the gloom closed around them, a whistle echoed around the walls, followed by a voice: "A quick dip is a top way to start the day…"

Cutter holstered his pistol, recognising the whistle and the tune.

"Alright, mates?" said Alice.

Relief broke out on Cutter's face as he saw Turk sitting on the dusty floor in a huge puddle of water. He climbed to his feet as Morri reached him and wrapped him in a hug. "I knew you were all right," she said, teary eyed nonetheless.

"A bit of a frantic swim," Turk grinned. "Not easy with a crook shoulder. Good job I had Alice along."

"Cut my teeth body-surfing Cottesloe Beach in bigger rips than that!" Alice grinned.

"Well, my friend," Secta said. "I really feared that one was the end of you."

"Nar, mate," said Alice. "Alice á la Turk is stronger than that!"

Making his way to a broken window, Turk checked the street outside. It was clear and desolate, but he had a gut feeling that experience had taught him never to ignore.

Nerdo joined him at the window. "All quiet?"

"I'm not so sure," Turk said, scanning the street. "Something feels wrong."

"You're right," Morri agreed. "Something's very wrong. My mind's reeling."

Cutter was checking the hundreds of forty-four-gallon drums stacked against the side wall. "Hey!" he yelled, "These are all full! What a cache of gas — worth a fortune! Must be hundreds of 'em!"

he hobbled over to Turk, who was still peering out of the window. "Worried about the drone?" he asked.

Nerdo, back in her sodden coat, tapped at the Ulink. "Drone's gone," she said. "And we're right opposite to the old jail. No CCTV in the street, and Betsy's parked in the courtyard on the other side of it."

Turk turned his back on the window and slid down the wall to rest his weary body on the cold concrete floor. "I don't know, Nerdo," he sighed. "My head says 'go for it' but my gut is screaming 'trap!' And Morri's sixth sense says my gut's got it right."

"Yeah, well, we can't just sit on our butts, can we?" said Alice. "How about I go and check it out on my own? If it's clear, I'll give you a signal." Alice proposed.

"Sounds like a plan," said Turk, grinning in spite of himself. "Can I come too?"

"What if you run into another RF-2?" Cutter demanded.

"Run like hell," said Nerdo. "You know the drill, Turk, you were in the war."

"Excuse me, but I don't know the drill," Alice said.

Morri joined them at the window. "Do try not to get yourself killed, Alice," said Secta, before she could speak. "After all we've been through, I'd be rather sorry to see you go. And remember, we're due to get out of here in the morning."

"Yeah, got that," Alice grunted. But there might be a bit of crap to deal with between what we're due to do and what we can do."

"Tell me, Alice," Secta said, after a pause. "Have you ever given any thought to religion?"

"Religion?" said Alice. "What's that got to do with anything? I haven't thought about it at all. Why, Secta?" he grinned. "You losing your scientific perspective?"

"Well, you know, here we are," said Secta. "In another time, odds against us, both reduced to atoms and manifested in other bodies. Makes one think, that's all."

Alice laughed. "I'll tell you this much, Secta," he said, "I can believe in a lot of things. But big old beardies in the sky, controlling the fates of men? Nah. There I'm drawing a line."

"Hmm," Secta said. "A compelling point of view. However, if we make it out of this alive, I may change my opinion."

Opposite the window, Cutter lowered himself to rest against one of the gas drums. Nerdo ambled over to him. Morri, who was idly watching them while listening to Secta's conversation with Alice, was horrified to see him draw a bayonet from his boot and hurl it at Turk.

She screamed as it sank with a loud *thunk* into the wooden beam beside Turk's cheek. He coolly retrieved it. "Thanks mate," he said.

"You want the Roscoe?" Cutter asked, grinning at Morri's outraged expression and holding up the pistol.

Turk slid the bayonet into his boot-top, then tucked his pants leg over it. "Nah," he said. "The blade'll be fine. You hang onto it." He got up and headed for the exit.

"Wait!" called Morri, jumping up and rushing after him. She grabbed his arm, and he turned to face her. Taking his face in her hands, she stood on tiptoe, bent his head down and kissed him gently on the lips. "Be careful," she said. "Both of you."

"Will do. He turned to walk away, but paused. Without looking back, he said: "That was you, right Morri?"

"Cut it out," Secta chortled. "I'm a better kisser than that!"

Turk shot back a smile and disappeared through the double doors into the street. Morri went to the window to watch him go. A terrible feeling of dread, which she could not shake, took hold. Nerdo helped Cutter to his feet and they joined her.

Turk scurried along the deserted street, noting that most of the buildings bore signs of looting. He came to the weather-beaten front doors of the prison administration building. The colonial façade, astonishingly still in place, was almost entirely taken up by a portico of four columns and a gaping bronze door. The sculptured relief above the doorway said 'Erected 1883'. "What a shame," he said. In a strange way, the once majestic old building reminded him of the stinking dead kangaroo he'd come across on the highway at the start of his journey. Both seemed like symbols of his country's decay. Thinking no more of it, he callously kicked one of the doors, which obligingly fell off its hinges.

"He's in!" Nerdo announced, relieved. Morri looked away, her pretty face filled with concern. "God, I hope he'll be all right," she said.

"God?" Secta said, quizzically. "Has my conversation with Alice converted you? I thought you were a pagan."

"I am," said Morri. "And that means, in a sense, that everything is god in my view. Even you, Secta."

"Why thank you," said Secta, drily. "I don't mind admitting, it's not the first time I've been described as divine."

Turk was jogging along the corridor when he was struck by an ear-piercing squeal inside his head. He skidded to a halt and covered his ears with his hands. "Argh! Alice … they're jamming my OSCI—"

In a flash, he'd gone, disappeared like someone had simply flicked a switch. Which, Alice supposed, was pretty much the case. "Bugger," he groaned, leaning glumly against the corridor wall. "On my own again. That's what I get for having a go at the gods!"

Back in the warehouse, Morri too had grabbed her ears. "No!" she screamed, once, then dropped to the floor.

Secta tried to summon her. "Morri?" he said, anxiously. "Morri?" he looked up at Nerdo from Morri's recumbent position. "I've lost her!" he gasped.

Nerdo looked grim. "They've got that satellite link working," she said. "They've jammed her OSCI." She sat on the floor and began battering computer keys. "Yep, they're using the bird," she confirmed. "Now we're in serious trouble. They've probably knocked Turk out as well. I can only hold them off for so long. Just as well you kept that implant, Cutter," she smiled, feebly. "Otherwise they'd have us all."

Alice had no option but to forge on. He jumped up and continued down the dimly lit corridor. When he arrived at the end, he saw a large, open courtyard leading to the veranda of a building on the other side. Beyond that was the car park and, hopefully, Betsy. "…This reeks of ambush," he thought. But there was no choice — he had to get to Betsy. If she was even still there. He mustered his courage, took a deep breath and launched himself across the courtyard as fast as his legs would carry him.

Halfway across the cloister he heard a bullet ricochet, then another, and another. Head down, he kept going, full tilt. He made it to the veranda, but there was no reprieve. Looking back, he saw a monster cyborg step out of the shadows, aiming a pistol at him. It dwarfed the robot he'd fought back in his own time to escape SSD HQ. This thing was one serious mother. "It must be one of those RF-2 things, like Cutter fought in the subway," he thought. "Now, how did he say he killed the freaking thing? Dammit, I should've taken the Roscoe."

Ping! A bullet deflected off the paver right next to his foot. "Whoa!" he bellowed. "I'm outta here!" He bolted towards the car park. The cyborg followed.

CHAPTER 32
PSYCHOLOGICAL OBSOLESCENCE

N ERDO, MAKING USE of the time until Alice came back, had re-set Cutter's leg, stitched his wound and constructed a makeshift splint. Secta had been too squeamish to watch and was gloomily staring out of the window. Cutter was grinning widely, having been administered Nerdo's remaining syringe of morphine.

"The gunshots have stopped," said Secta. "I hope Alice is okay."

"Well, if nothing else, our OSCI blocks are holding," Nerdo said, packing away her tools and going back to the Ulink.

"Have you finished torturing me?" Cutter quipped.

"Haven't even started," she sniped back, without looking away from the screen.

"He should've taken the gun," Secta grumbled.

"Stop moaning, Secta," snapped Nerdo, losing patience. "It ain't gonna help, alright?"

"I guess you're right," Secta said morosely. "But I still wish he'd taken the gun."

Alice scurried from the veranda to a small two-story building that appeared to have once housed a generator. He collected a couple of loose bricks from the ground. Any weapon, however apparently feeble, was better than no weapon at all. He had no choice but to confront the cyborg, he reasoned, and he entered the building, hoping to set a trap.

The floor inside was littered with broken and rusted engineering and reeked of old engine oil. He looked at the overhead joists and saw a pulley suspended from the main crossbeam, a chain dangling to the floor. The thunderous footsteps of the approaching cyborg prompted him into action. With the two bricks tucked inside the top of his pants, he shinned up the chain and into the rafters. Then, balancing on the main joist, he positioned himself. A beam of sunlight lanced through a broken roof tile and struck his hand. If I need to, I'll get out through the roof, he thought. Settled on the beam, a brick in each hand, he waited with bated breath. The long shadow of the cyborg appeared from the entrance. This was the big moment. He'd only have one shot, and would have to hurl the brick with maximum of accuracy and power. If I can crush that metal cap on its melon, it might send it off the rails... The shadow of the cyborg grew longer, lumps of concrete and fallen brick pulverising into powder under its enormous feet. The crunching stopped, the shadow froze, and Alice took a deep breath — but silence prevailed. Moving silently, he straightened up and poked his head through the hole in the roof. Betsy was only fifty metres away. Sadly, there was another cyborg guarding her. Trapped. With his escape route shot to bits, Alice had no alternative but to entice the cyborg below into his own trap, and that would cost him a brick, leaving him only one to do the real damage. He ducked down again and got set to throw.

The shadow hadn't moved. Alice leaned down and cast the brick into the room below, hoping to draw the creature inside. It worked. The shadow moved, the crunching resumed as it walked cautiously into the room, pistol held ready to shoot. Alice swallowed. This was a huge mother of a beast, and all he had was a house brick. He felt like David up against Goliath.

He waited until it was directly below him, then stood up and heaved the brick with all his might. It impacted with enormous force, right in the centre of the skullcap, leaving a deep, deep dent. The cyborg buckled at the knees. Without waiting to see if his brick had done the trick, Alice drew the bayonet from his boot and swung down to the ground, landing behind the stunned monster.

Hearing him touch down, it turned sharply, towering over him even on its knees. Alice was too close and too quick. He darted under the outstretched arm and with one almighty shove, drove the bayonet up under its chin, through its mandible and out through its forehead. The cyborg flung its head back, and the bayonet was pulled out of Alice's grasp, catapulting him hard onto his backside on the floor. "Die, you bludger!" he screamed, scrabbling backwards. "Die!"

But the beast wasn't done yet. Grabbing the haft of the bayonet, as it got back to its feet, it dragged the blade free and cast it to the floor.

Alice wasn't impressed. "Damn!" he cursed, and dived for his brick, still lying where it had bounced to on the floor. In one quick movement, he picked it up, rolled, leapt to his feet and fired the brick with all Turk's strength, right into the cyborg's face. The missile smashed into the left eye, taking most of the nose and part of the mouth with it and leaving a gruesome cavity of smashed bone, dented metal, arcing electronics and gore.

The cyborg rocked, one immense hand pawing at its caved-in eye socket.

Seeing his chance, Alice leapt, snatching the bayonet, and clambering onto the enormous machine's back. Striking like a man possessed, with incredible ferocity, he chopped and hacked at its head, not caring where the blows landed, simply intent on doing as much damage a he could. Blow after blow he struck, until he'd sliced the impassive face beyond recognition. The monster could do nothing to defend itself against this enemy, it was like a wasp taking on a dragon. The creature's size and bulk rendered it incapable of dealing with a much smaller foe, especially while that foe remained attached to it. Automatically, it raised its arms to block the blows, and to try to grab and dislodge its tormentor. Alice simply turned his attention to them, slashing hard at the forearms until he'd hacked its left hand clean off at the wrist. It held up the stump, fusing wires sparking. Shaking its tattered head, gore from head to foot, the monster dropped to its knees. Alice braced for the killer blow. "Damn you, Robocop," he growled, quoting a favourite classic movie. "Say goodnight." With his remaining strength, he drove the bayonet into the monster's right eye. Blinded, the bayonet lodged in its main processor unit, it collapsed to the floor.

Alice left the bayonet where it was and stepped over the creature. He stopped at the doorway to look back at the body, still twitching on the floor. He spat. "Cop you later," he growled, and took off back to the warehouse as fast as his legs could carry him.

Secta turned from the window and called excitedly to the others: "Here he comes! He's all right!"

Alice almost fell through the door and collapsed, panting, to the floor. "That was one hell of a trip!" he rasped.

"Turk!" grinned Cutter. "How's it goin', mate? Did you see Betsy?"

Alice eyed Nerdo. "Morphine," she mouthed, nodding at his leg.

"Alright," he said. "Well, I've got good news and dud news." He got up, groaning. "Dud news: Turk's gone blank again."

"Yes, same here," said Secta. "I call it imposed unconsciousness."

"Sure, doc, why not?" said Alice. "Okay, good news — sort of. I had to beat one of those robot things to death."

"You had to — you beat it to death?" said Nerdo, astonished. "What are you saying? You beat a WarBot without a weapon?"

"Yeah — well, I had a couple of bricks," said Al, grinning at her. "Gave its head the bashed crab treatment then stabbed it in the eye."

Nerdo eyed him, clearly impressed. The state of his clothes bore testament to a seriously bloody battle.

"Must have been a two?" she said looking at Cutter, who just shrugged happily. "Still, I'm blown away, Alice. That's some going."

"Is that everything, Alice?" asked Secta. "Any thoughts on what we do now?"

"Well, that's where I have more good news and bad news," Al said. "Betsy's still there."

"Hooray!" said Cutter, punching the air.

"The bad news is there's one of them things guarding it ... and it's even bigger and meaner looking than the other one."

"Hooray!" said Cutter again.

Nerdo rolled her eyes. "Different how?" she asked.

"I dunno ... guess it looked more — well, more roboty than the one I necked."

"A seven or an eight," Nerdo said, with dread. "I hope it's a seven."

"Why, what's the difference?" Al asked.

"The seven has flaws they would have addressed in the eight," Nerdo said. "As far as I know they're only at concept, but if they've managed to get a prototype working, we're in the serious shit."

"Just the one prototype?" said Al.

"Frigg," she said, face pale. "What did you go and say that for?"

"Alright, look, let's not get tied down worrying about what we don't know," said Al. "Our priority is to neck that other robot bastard and get to Betsy before they blow her up or something."

"I don't think they'll blow her up for now," said Nerdo. "She's the only way to bring us into their ambush."

"I have a plan," said Secta. "But it might be risky..."

"Whatever we come up with'll be risky," said Al. "Give us the mail, Secta."

Secta started pacing, chin gripped in hand, in a style Alice remembered very well — although it looked considerably more appealing in Morri's form.

"Firstly, I need to know the working mechanism of the cyborg and the sort of weapons it possesses," he said. "What its skin is made of? How is its circuitry connected? What are its potential flaws?"

"I could tell you most of that about the lower models," said Nerdo. "But the eight? I can only guess. The basic principle on all the models was the same," she went on. "A brain-dead subject, with still-living tissue, given a holographic brain programmed using organic binary cloning from a living soldier."

"Mind cloning?" Said Secta. "I see — that's fascinating. Presumably it's only the basic drive, so to speak, cloned from a living soldier? The skill set, not the personality?"

Nerdo nodded.

"How wonderful," Secta went on. "I'd very much like to take a look at one of those brains one day."

"Yeah, well I can tell you from experience it's not that much of a thrill," said Al. "But work out how to kill it and you might get your chance."

"Sentient?" asked Secta, ignoring him.

"No," said Nerdo. "No independent thought."

"How do they merge organic with non-organic components to avoid rejection?"

"Microbial bacteria that prevent cellular decay. And they synthesized an antibody to prevent the immune system from attacking the foreign components."

"Transhumanism," breathed Secta. "They're well on the way to producing the ultimate human ... Gosh, it would be interesting to see where this goes..."

"Leave the speculation for another day, Secta," said Al. "We're running out of minutes here!"

Secta nodded sharply. He and Nerdo went into a huddle to discuss cyborg anatomy further, looking for a chink in the armour, while Al and Cutter got on with battle plans.

By noon, the relentless sun had lit up the street outside the warehouse like a concert stage. The searing heat was almost unbearable. Buildings shimmered in mirage, and the corrugated roof of the warehouse creaked and groaned as it expanded. As they kept their vigil at the warehouse window, Cutter handed his handgun to Al who nodded acknowledgement, perspiration dripping from his chin.

They had been shifting gasoline drums into rows, side-by-side and ten metres apart, all the way to the rear of the warehouse. It looked like a deadly go-cart obstacle course. Al checked the barricade closest the entrance.

"Okay, you guys get down the back and take cover," he said.

"Remember you've only got four shots, Al," said Nerdo. "Four barricades, four shots, no more bullets."

"I'll stand by in case there's a misfire," Secta said, holding four glass bottles they'd rummaged up and converted into Molotov cocktails. He took up a position near the entrance, a safe distance from the drums but close enough to keep them within throwing range.

"Are you sure you're up for this, Secta?" Cutter asked uncertainly. "Coz, I can…"

"I'll have you know I was a fast bowler in my youth," said Secta. "Don't worry about my throwing arm, young man, it is quite up to the job. And you need a head start with that leg."

"But this isn't cricket — and you're not a fella," Cutter reminded him.

Secta rotated Morri's arm like a propeller, limbering up the shoulder ligaments. "Trust me," he said. "I believe the expression is: 'She'll be right'."

Grinning, Cutter and Nerdo moved to their position at the back of the warehouse.

One last glance back at them from the barricade at the doorway, and Al slipped between the drums and dashed across the road into the prison. As he reached the generator building, he slowed to check the cyborg he'd bashed. It was still alive, still struggling to get to its feet, though it never would. "Get used to it, buddy," said Alice. "You're gonna be staring at that ceiling from now on!"

Continuing around the side of the building, hugging the wall closely to minimize detection, he came to the final corner and peered around. Betsy was on the far side of the car park. The most challenging part had arrived.

Gorrick looked at the hissing display screen formerly broadcasting from cyborg monitor two at Ursula standing beside him.

"I thought these things were supposed to be indestructible," he snapped. "Perhaps we should rename them Titanics? That is three they have now brought down. A band of ragged rebels against our top technology," he continued, sneering, "And yet they keep winning. How is this even possible?" He turned to Mennis, eyebrows raised.

"These are ragged rebels with an intimate knowledge of this technology," she said. "They are well aware of the flaws in, for example, the RF-2s. The latest casualty was a reconditioned seven. And we have learned a valuable lesson in discovering a flaw we had previously overlooked." She glared round at the team, who sank deeper into their chairs, focused to the last individual on their screens. "They will, however, find the eight a completely different proposition," she finished.

"At over three million credits a pop, I would expect so," said Gorrick, drily.

"Look!" she said, attention drawn to the pictures coming from the cyborg's POV. "There is the target!"

Turk could be seen in the distance, attempting to cross the courtyard to Betsy.

The cyborg POV provided heads-up vitals: infrared heat variance, target distancing, weapons range, weapons selection, and estimated target escape routes.

"That is Turk!" snarled Gorrick. "I thought you had knocked out his OSCI?"

"We did sir," said Mennis, desperately. "Turk and Morri, both, look!" She punched the keyboard of a separate terminal, displaying termination confirmation for both Turk and Morri.

"So how do you explain his existence?"

"There is no rational explanation, sir. It does not make any sense. Unless, of course, what he told us about a split personality is true…"

"Dammit," snarled Gorrick, irritably. "I will not have this man defeating us again, do you hear me?"

The look of bitter determination on Mennis's face said it all — she wasn't about to be outdone by Turk. She was backed by all the might of technology and science. Turk was merely flesh and blood.

"Target him!" she barked. "Lock onto his signature map!"

The operator jumped, and punched in the required commands. The feed from the cyborg's display appeared on the holographic monitor, zoomed onto Turk and locked in a clear target field around him. It blinked three times, confirming the lock.

"He is targeted," Mennis said, coldly. "The order will not be rescinded. The eight will not stop until the life force of its target has been extinguished." She turned back to the operator, and nodded. "Take him out!"

Alice was in the open, and vulnerable. It was now or never. He turned and jogged like a drunken jaywalker back towards the generator building. As soon as he was certain the cyborg was tailing him, he sped up and increased the sidestepping. The cyborg was moving surprisingly fast, judging by its heavy footsteps. It was about twenty metres behind him, closing in fast. He was banking on Nerdo's information that it wouldn't take a shot until it had locked on to him for at least three seconds. The most dangerous part would be the narrow corridor in the main building, where he would be unable to swerve. He needed to save himself some energy for a burst of speed down that corridor. He knew Turk's body was close to breaking point. Even though he wasn't feeling the pain, he knew the physical ravages of Deathball were telling on his endurance. But he had no choice. He had to drive Turk's body to the max.

Glued to the pursuit, Gorrick was losing patience. "Why does it not fire?" he snapped.

"We must be patient, sir!" Mennis replied.

"I am running out of patience for your continued failures, young lady." He looked back at the hologram. Turk disappeared inside the jail building.

"Increase speed!" Mennis ordered.

They could see Turk ahead, halfway down the corridor, about twenty-five metres away.

"Lock on and fire!" she hissed, and the heads up zoomed in, locking the running man in a blinking red frame.

Three quarters of the way along the corridor Al, responding to a gut feeling, pulled off a perfect paratrooper's forward roll. *Shing!* A bullet deflected off the wall. He grinned. Guess Morri's not the only one with a sixth sense, he thought.

When he bounced back to his feet, he was at the end of the corridor — another burst of speed and some serious zigzagging would have him safely back in the warehouse.

He raced across the road, and purposely slowed down to slip through a narrow gap between drums in the warehouse doorway. Once inside, he scurried across the floor and slid into a hide beside

Secta. Panting like he'd just run the Sydney marathon, he took aim with his pistol. Secta readied a cigarette lighter under the wick of his first Molotov cocktail. A shadow appeared in the doorway.

The heads-up hologram displayed the narrow path between lines of drums, just inside the warehouse door.

"I don't like this," Ursula said, warily.

"Take it in!" Gorrick commanded.

"But it may be a trap — those drums could be full of fuel."

"That much fuel?" said Gorrick. "Unlikely. It is a decoy. Besides, can it not withstand fire? Take it in!"

Ursula nodded reluctantly at the operator. "Take it in," she said, her face and voice expressionless.

The cyborg had to turn side-on to thread its way between the drums.

"Come on, bucket head!" Al yelled.

It turned to look at him, and he fired. Nothing ignited — gasoline simply streamed from the hole he'd made in a drum. Al looked at Secta.

"My word, isn't he amazing," Secta mumbled, awestruck by the scientific marvel before him.

"Throw it, Secta—" Alice snarled.

"Look at its features, I'd imagine it's..."

"Throw it!" Al hissed, "Or I'll shoot you!"

Secta blinked and flicked the cigarette lighter to life, ignited the wick, stood up and threw. The bottle hit, smashed and — *Whump!* An almighty explosion, accompanied by a huge fireball, catapulted both Morri and Turk base over apex and left them deafened. Shielding their faces, they scrambled to escape the roiling inferno.

Biting her knuckle, Ursula was silently willing the cyborg to survive. "Keep it moving!" she screamed.

Alice and Secta reached the next barricade, and looked back. The cyborg stepped out from the inferno, aflame but apparently unscathed.

"The skin is protected by heat-resistant crystalline polymers," yelled Secta, over the roaring flames and the ringing in their ears. "It can take over a thousand degrees Celsius! We're not trying to burn it, we're trying to fry the circuits under the skin. The next barricade should do the trick," he added, holding up crossed fingers.

Alice stood from behind the next barricade of drums, presenting himself as a target. The burning cyborg aimed its pistol and fired. The heat haze, however, impaired its aim and the bullet hit the drum in front of Alice. Its contents streamed out on the floor. Alice signalled Secta to retreat to the next barricade. Before they moved out, Secta lit the wick of a second Molotov cocktail. As he stood up to throw, the cyborg fired. The bottle shattered in Secta's hand, and the contents sprayed all over Morri's body. She lit up like a torch.

Alice leapt from behind the barricade, desperate to draw their enemy's fire. Flames from the Molotov had ignited a pool of fuel on the floor, and were shooting toward the drums ahead of them. Suddenly, Nerdo was beside them, throwing her still-wet coat over Morri, rolling her on the ground to extinguish the flames. The blazing cyborg was advancing towards them. They were trapped. Al looked at the two women, and made a call. He charged.

Gorrick and Mennis were watching in disbelief. Turk was, apparently, running directly at them, gun extended.

"What the hell is he doing?" Gorrick exclaimed, all cool English detachment gone. "Shoot him! Shoot now!"

"Well?" Ursula glared at the operator. "Fire, damn you! fire!"

"I cannot, ma'am!" said the operator, tremulously. "The circuits are overheated — they're not responding."

Gorrick began pacing, hair gripped in his fists. "I do not believe this!" he was almost screaming. "Too hot! Our three-million-dollar man is too – hot! Use another weapon in its array — surely it has one!"

He looked back at the mid-air display just in time to see Turk, sliding like a baseball player hitting home base, disappear directly under the cyborg. The POV looked down — then went static.

Alice fired a second shot up through its groin just to be sure. It was the last bullet, and it took the top of the cyborg's head clean off. Alice rolled clear just as the burning monster collapsed onto the ground and the barricade of drums ten metres away exploded into a fireball. Fortunately for Al, he was on the ground. Nerdo had already hauled Morri clear. They had survived.

CHAPTER 33
ENDANGERED SPECIES

I **T WAS DARK** when Mal swung the Commodore into the car park at the Avalon Motor Inn.

"Their car's not here. What do you think?" he said, looking around, half expecting to see Honor and Karzoff emerging from behind a tree.

"Well, what I think means zip," said Hope. "But I'm pretty sure they'll try to take you out tonight. And I don't mean for a date."

"Why me?" he said, indignantly? "Why don't they whack you?"

"My," said Hope, a slight smile playing over her lips. "Such a gentleman ... They need me as backup in case Secta doesn't return," she explained. "I can operate the equipment and duplicate the experiment. You ... well, you're expendable. Sorry," she added, as his face crumpled.

"Gee, thanks," he said. "But doesn't what you know give us leverage? Like, do I really need to be risking my life when we could just cut a deal with them?"

"No," she frowned. "They can't be trusted. So we need to book another room, right now. We can't be in the same one, they'd know it. A different room will be safer for us."

Mal's face fell even further. "Not what I had planned," he said.

"Yeah, well, the best laid plans don't always work out," she said. "Laid being the operative word."

"I ... I am not very good with guns," Karzoff stammered, from behind the wheel, as they approached the Inn.

"Ve haff a variety of veapons in ze trunk," said Honor. "Perhaps you vould prefer a knife?"

"No, I ... I do not think I have the skills to tackle him physically, do you?"

"You haff a point zere," she said, looked him over disdainfully. "Vait! I know! Tetrodotoxin!"

"You have that?" he said, astounded.

"Karzoff, I haff a variety of poisons in a dozen syringes," she said. "Some vork fast, others slow. Some are deadly, some merely subdue ze target for a time. Tetrodotoxin is quick and effective, easy to administer. Ve know vhich room is zeirs, all you haff to do is—"

"Go into their room while they are sleeping and jab him—" he interrupted.

"No, earlier," she said. Zere is no point in taking him vhen ve are tired, too. Vait for zis evening, vhen Hope is in ze shower."

"How do you know she will?"

"Karzoff, dear toad, Hope is a fastidious voman. Ve haff had a long, sveaty drive today. She vill vant to take a shower. So, ve simply get ze room next to zeirs, wait until ve hear ze wasser running, and..."

"I get the picture?"

"Roger zat."

Secta was fortunate. The gasoline from the Molotov had only splashed onto Morri's clothes, and Nerdo had smothered the flames before any serious damage was done. Sitting on the floor, still smouldering gently here and there, he looked up at Turk.

"Is she alright?" said Al, with concern.

"Just some minor burns on the backs of her hands," said Secta, markedly shaken. "Other than that, she'll be fine — thanks to Nerdo."

"Good," said Al. "I'm glad she's okay. I'm glad you both are."

"Hate to break in," said Cutter, who'd regained some equilibrium during the firefight. "But there might be another eight out there. So now what?"

"We don't have much choice," Al said. "I've gotta get to the truck. How long have we got?"

"Eight hours or so," said Secta.

"What happens if you're late?" Nerdo asked.

"Good question," Al snarled.

"Nothing, as long as I bring a note," quipped Secta. "Sorry," he added, catching Alice's expression. "Er … I'd say they'll allow a short contingency, but after that, they'll panic and then force my sister Hope to send someone after me. Worst case, they'll destroy my equipment to make it impossible for us to return. But the former scenario is more likely."

"Yeah, that'd be their form," said Al. "What's waiting for me, though? They still want me dead?"

"Quite the opposite, Alice, I assure you," said Secta. "You are now the world's most valuable commodity, and they want to own you. But on the bright side, I have the means back there to stabilize you. I just need to work out how to get us back first, and if I have to rush, I could make a mistake. That could be costly — for both of us."

Alice nodded. "Alright," he said. "Let's get this show on the road."

"Er…" said Cutter. "What's the plan? Exactly?"

Al stopped mid-stride, turned and faced the three of them.

"I'm gonna charge like a bull at a gate to the truck. You guys get to the generator building. I'll bring Betsy to you. Then we'll drive her right through those big front gates. Got it?"

Cutter nodded. "Keys are under the driver's seat," he said.

"Glad you remembered." He fired them the wave that had made metal groupies all over the world sigh with singeing desire. "Chaa!"

Alice sprinted like an Olympic champion across the street and into the main building.

Even on one leg, a crutch tucked under his armpit, Cutter kept up with the others, hot on Turk's tail. When Alice raced out of the corridor, he was travelling like the wind. He sped past the generator room, out onto the courtyard and over the car park to Betsy. Literally leaping onto the running board, he opened the driver's door, slid into the seat, found the keys and cranked her up.

With a thunderous roar and puff of black smoke, Betsy powered up. Moving slowly but gaining speed, she trundled towards the generator building. She was an awesome sight, armaments gleaming, roaring towards them before skidding broadside to a halt.

Nerdo and Secta helped Cutter into the cab, then followed. Al turned Betsy to face the gates.

Cutter hauled himself into the turret seat.

Nerdo opened a panel behind her seat and retrieved Jonno's AK-47 and a belt of ammo, handing it all over to Cutter. He was in his glory.

Al checked with them. "Sct?" he said. "Then this is it ... we either crash and burn or find freedom. Cutter, lock 'n load!" he bellowed, a savage look of determination on his face.

Rolling forward like a big A380 taxi-ing to runway, Betsy lumbered towards the gates.

"The end is about to begin!" Al yelled. He floored it and Betsy roared like a rocket, cannoning full bore towards the target. Nothing in the world was going to stop her now. The big, spiked bull-bar smacked the gates at a hundred and twenty clicks, tearing them clean off their hinges and shattering them into splinters.

Alice kept his foot flat to the floor, knowing there would be a reception committee on the other side — and he wasn't disappointed. At least a hundred-armed bikers were sitting astride their choppers, waiting for them.

Automatic lockpick in hand, Honor stood at the door to Mal and Hope's room. Karzoff stood beside her, a syringe in his shaking hand. Honor would open the door and he would rush in and jab Mal, while she covered Hope in the shower. With a nod to her comrade, she inserted the pick, and pushed open the door.

Barging into the room like a movie swat team, they found a man dressed in black suspenders and a nurse's uniform reclining on the bed. He sat bolt upright, a shocked expression on his made-up face, and let out an ear-piercing shriek. A second man came out of the bathroom in a rush; naked and wet from the shower. He collided with Honor, who threw her arms around him instinctively.

Karzoff froze, syringe poised, as realisation dawned. He whipped his hands behind his back and began to back away, stammering apologetically. "S … s … sorry!" he said. "I … it appears we have the wrong room…"

The naked man was trying to struggle out of Honor's arms. Managing to push her away, he quickly grabbed a towel to cover himself up.

The man on the bed stared as the two intruders backed quickly out of the room. Honor, with a gracious nod, closed the door behind them.

On the balcony Karzoff frowned furiously at Honor. "Well, that did not go exactly to plan, did it?" he complained. "Here!" he said, slapping the syringe into her palm. "I will not be needing this tonight!" He strode away angrily.

Honor scowled after him. "Go and check vhat room zey are in!" she bellowed, savagely.

"Go check it yourself!" he grumbled in reply.

Alice wasn't taking any prisoners. He aimed Betsy at the bikers and ploughed right through, the big truck pulverizing anyone not fast enough to get out of the way and deflecting a hail of bullets. Her spikes slashed the bikers the wheels and bull bar had missed right off their machines, and she barrelled on, leaving a trail of horribly wounded men behind.

Inside the cabin, Secta grimaced at the biker impaled on a bull-bar spike.

Cutter opened up with the AK-47, blowing more enemies off their bikes left, right and centre. It was utter chaos, slaughter: a plan Animal would live to regret hatching with Gorrick. They should have left the escapees to the cyborgs and destroyed Betsy where she was parked.

In no time flat, she'd carved a bloody swathe through the bikers and, herself unscathed, was powering away along the highway at full speed. Cutter swivelled the turret to the rear and picked off the few bikers brave enough to give chase. They did not give chase for long.

Gorrick, Mennis, Animal and two of the biker presidents watched the slaughter live on CCTV.

"Send in a drone!" Animal yelled.

Gorrick simply glared at the display. "Do you hear me?" the biker leader roared. "Send in a drone!"

Gorrick turned to him, slowly. "Unless you want to be burying the majority of your members over the next few days, I suggest you recall them immediately," he said. "We are done here." He stood and made for the door.

"I said send in a drone, Gorrick. Isn't that what the freaking things are for?" Animal growled.

Gorrick hesitated at the door, then turned and glared at Animal with piercing eyes. "One man — one man, Grand Master — has wiped the floor with everything we have thrown at him," he said, quite calmly. "You think a drone could take him out? He has beaten two RF-2's, an RF-7 and our allegedly top-of-the-line, invincible eight. He has wiped out Duke, Spike, Flaps, Drill and half your army! And you know what? You know what?" Gorrick strode across the room and stood nose-to-nose with the furious biker. "He thoroughly deserves his freedom. He won his freedom, several times over! Damn, what I would give to have him on my side. He is worth a thousand of you and your goons! Who dares wins?" He glared around the room for a moment. "He, gentlemen and lady, he dared. And he has won." He turned on his heel and stalked from the room, leaving behind a congregation of morose expressions.

When Cutter quit firing, Alice wondered whether he'd run out of ammo.

"We clear?" he yelled.

"We've done 'em, cold!" Cutter crowed.

Al let out a scream of relief, "Yeeee-haaa!"

The big truck practically rocked with the celebrations going on inside. Nerdo was jumping up and down, screaming like a schoolgirl. Secta threw his arms around Alice and planted a big kiss on his cheek then did the same to Nerdo. Cutter bounced in his gunner's chair, bellowing from the turret. "We got 'em, guys! We're home free! Waah-hooooo!"

His feet on the desk in his office at Zen HQ, Animal was in deep in doleful thought. There was a knock at the door.

"Come!" he growled, irritably.

Mennis swept into the room. "We need to talk," she barked. "Now!"

"Take a seat," he said.

Instead, she slammed the palms of her hands on his desk and eyeballed him. "We cannot allow them to get away with this!" she snarled.

Animal slid his feet off the table, leaned forward and leered back.

"I lost sixteen men today," he said. "More than forty wounded, some of 'em probably fatally. So I want his head as much as you do. No-one will be getting away with anything."

"Good," she said. "Because I have a plan."

"What've you got in mind, sister?"

She raised an eyebrow at sister, but held up her Ulink. "I can track them," she said. Their OSCIs have been shut down, but the GPS from the OSCI satellite network is operating. See?"

She leaned across the desk and showed him the Ulink display.

He took in her musky aroma and smirked.

She ignored him and continued, "They are travelling southeast on the 456. They have nowhere to hide. If we are clever, we can get ahead of them, set a trap."

"So we have all the time in the world," he said, smugly, leaning back in his chair. "And what's in this for you, Dr Mennis?"

"Redemption, Grand Master," she curtly replied.

"I see," he said. "Well yes, you have lost plenty of face, what with twelve million credits worth of hardware going up the spout. Yeah. I can dig why you'd want redemption. All right," he went on. "How do want to play it?"

"Let's take it low-key," she said. "Just the two of us. I do the tracking, you do the killing."

"You think we two can succeed where dozens of others have failed?"

"Yes," she said. "Look, years of planning went into the RF-8 project, and now it is all in jeopardy. That also affects your plans. We have seen that strength and numbers will not stop this man. So let us try stealth and cunning. I will not stand for this humiliation," she finished, drawing herself up. "So yes, we must succeed where everyone and everything else has failed, whatever the cost!"

Betsy rolled into Snake at sunset. Al parked her next to the F-200 and the J-Car at the back of Reno's Bar. They went in through rear door of the bar. Al stopped as he entered. "Let's have a drink," he said. "Drink to Jonno, Reno and Tatts. Top blokes, and didn't they go down fighting?"

Nerdo nodded and disappeared into the kitchen to rummage for beers.

"Hey Secta," called Alice. "Any thoughts on when Turk might turn up? Is there something we can do to switch him on?"

"I don't think so," Secta replied. "Seems like the OSCI has the ability to render consciousness inert. I could try stimulating your brain with the iWish if you like."

"Er ... nah," said Al. "No need. I was just wondering if Turk would need to be conscious for me to get out of him."

"That's an excellent point, Alice," the scientist replied. "I'll need to do some thinking on that."

Nerdo came in, carrying four beers.

"What's the range of a drone, Nerdo?" said Cutter, knocking the top off his beer on the edge of the table. "I'm thinking they might send one after us," he proposed sleepily.

"If they were gonna do that theyd've targeted Betsy on the highway, and they didn't," Nerdo asserted.

"Yeah, but it could still be on the cards," said Al, swigging his beer. "Look, we've got some serious decisions to make. Secta and I have got to find this Woodhedge joint, so we can bail out..."

"Woodhenge, Alice," Secta corrected.

"...But my gut tells me it's not over with Gorrick and his thugs yet," Al continued.

"You're not wrong," Nerdo added. "They've stopped trying to block my OSCI. That tells me they're using it to track us."

"I'd suggest we get to the bunker," said Secta. "It's well protected, and I can achieve a lot more there."

"Question is, do we all go? Cutter, you and Nerdo aren't obligated to continue."

Cutter and Nerdo exchanged looks. "I'd like to get Doc Dave to set my leg properly," he said. "That should take an hour or so. Then I'm sweet to go with you."

"But there's no need to go with us, man," Al said. "You'd be only putting yourself in danger."

"He just wants to make sure you leave, that's all!" Nerdo smiled.

"Nah – but I reckon Turk and Morri will need some backup once you two've done a bunk," Cutter mumbled, getting up and hobbling to the front door.

"You're making me feel guilty," Secta protested.

Nerdo joined Cutter. "I'll take you to the Doc's," she said. "Then I guess we're going to Woodhenge."

Honor was pacing the floor of the motel room, while Karzoff was lounging on the bed watching TV.

"Can you please stop chewing up the rug?" he said.

She stopped next to the front window. "I know!" she said, suddenly. "I vill haff zem arrested! Simple! Vhy did I not think of it before?"

"I wish you would make up your mind," grumbled Karzoff. "One minute you want me to kill him, next you want them both arrested. We could have arrested them ages ago and avoided this whole road trip!"

Ignoring him, and opening the curtains to look out at the night, she placed a call on her implant. "Operator!" she snapped. "Zis is — Vait! Never mind!" Abruptly, she disconnected. Karzoff! Zey are getting into zeir car. Quvick!"

Exasperated, Karzoff slipped off the bed, complaining. "Just when the movie was getting interesting..."

"Shut up, you fool," she snapped. "If zey reach Secta and Alice before us, ve vill be risking ze entire mission. Zey vill surely escape!"

"Are you sure about this?" Mal said, driving out of the motel car park. "It can get pretty cold around this neck of the woods at night."

Hope grinned. "I'm sure you'll find a way to warm me up." Changing the subject with a wry smile, she held up the ILDD. "Unfortunately, this has only a narrow field of detection — a few hundred metres at best. Secta has the more powerful model in the future. We need to be as close to the bunker as possible to detect him."

"Should've brought a blanket and pillows," said Mal cheekily, raising an eyebrow at her. "I haven't been parking since I was a teenager."

"Has anyone ever told you that you've got a one-track mind?" Hope said.

"Yes. And it's a dirt track."

He hit the music control on his steering wheel and 'Fighting for You' by Black Alice cranked up. Mal drummed his hands on the steering wheel to the beat of the song, singing along in an only slightly less powerful vocal than Alice's own.

"Verso visions disappear, a crystal crash that no-one hears, I'm breaking all those sacred rules into two, oh, I'm fighting for you!"

The Commodore sped into the night.

Honor was standing beside the car with her arms folded, impatiently tapping her foot on the pavement. Karzoff was still negotiating the stairs. He fumbled his way to the driver's side, aware of her dark mood, and fished in his pocket for the keys. He zapped open the doors, they climbed in and he started up. As he backed into the forecourt, the car made a grumbling noise.

"What is that?" he said, puzzled.

"It is nothing," snapped Honor. "Drive on!"

Karzoff shrugged his shoulders and continued backing out. But when he hit drive and moved forward, the noise increased. The car lurched to a halt. He stopped and got out.

"We have been sabotaged," he said, leaning in through the window. "Two flat tyres!"

Honor's face darkened. Karzoff could she was about to explode, and ducked back out the window to avoid the shock wave from the blast.

The electronic doors of the Zen underground parking station opened to allow a black, heavily customized, late-model TepZepi to power out of the building.

Animal looked at his driver, impressed. "This thing looks like it can go."

"Eight litre, 1,400 horsepower quad turbo," Mennis boasted.

"Yeah, well, I prefer the wind in my hair."

With a smirk, she leaned forward and hit a toggle. The roof melted open. "Like this?" she said.

"Like that," he grinned.

She gunned it. It took 14 seconds to hit 300 km/h.

"She's low flying." he grinned, getting off on the thrust. Mennis connected her Ulink to the on-board computer, and a holographic map appeared on the dashboard. A blinking red dot indicated a location.

"They are at Snake Ridge," she said, matter-of-factly.

"Guessed as much," he said. "I've already ordered reinforcements to rendezvous with us."

"Reinforcements?"

"Rebels, of course."

Her top lip curled in a sneer. "I thought we had agreed it would be only us?"

"Nothing wrong with a little insurance?"

"From now on, I would prefer you to discuss any changes to the plan with me first," she said, coldly. She was already beginning to regret their alliance. The chemistry between them could hardly be good when they both had their own separate motives. He had as little time for women as she had for men. Given the circumstances, there was bound to be acrimony between them. But for the moment, he was all she had.

Cutter hobbled into Reno's Bar on crutches, leg cast from foot to knee in a skin-tight resin that held the bone fast without restricting his movement any more than it had to. Nerdo was right behind. Turk and Morri looked up from a cubicle.

"You look almost brand new, buddy!" Al called.

"Tell you what Al, a Scotch wouldn't go astray," said Cutter, his face pale. "Can't take any more morphine just yet, and that bloody hurt." He groaned as he slid into the cubicle beside Morri.

"It's 2087 and you still haven't got anything better for pain than morphine and Johnny Walker," Alice chuckled, sliding a bottle across the table into Cutter's waiting hand. "Here. Nectar of the gods. You'll need to neck it out the bottle," he added. "Someone's nicked all the glasses."

Cutter raised the bottle in salute. "Never use 'em anyhow!" he grinned. "Cheers!"

Alice noticed an anxious look on Nerdo's face. "Something wrong?" he asked.

She looked up from her Ulink. "I'm into the Zen mainframe," she said. "There's a new firewall up around Mennis's link. That seems a bit odd to me."

Al could smell a rat. "Take a squiz at the other dude … what's-his-face?"

"Wait a sec," said Secta. "I heard Mennis say his name. Yes, that's right — Animal."

Nerdo's fingers flew. "Yep," she announced. "Another firewall."

"What does that tell us?" Al asked, taking the bottle back from Cutter.

"I'd guess they — and maybe others — are coming after us, so they've firewalled their signals to stop me tracking them," Nerdo hypothesized.

"Makes sense," shrugged Alice. "Animal's got a bone to pick with us. He's not the type to let things go."

"Can you hack in?" Secta asked.

Nerdo held up the Ulink. "This toy ain't fast enough," she said. "If we could shut down their comms network, though, that would kill their cyborg program as well."

"What do you mean?" Al asked.

Nerdo thought before replying. "Well, you two guys are going back to your time, right? But we'll still be up the proverbial creek," she said. "But if we can knock out their satellite links, that'd at least buy us some time to get our act together."

"If we did it well enough, it'd save the freaking country," said Cutter. "And who knows what else. Zen operates all over the world, and that Gorrick fella is a war going somewhere to happen!"

"I reckon he's an alien for sure," Al said. "There was talk about alien intervention in my time, but no-one could prove it. But Turk said an alien saucer even landed in Tokyo?"

"Yeah 2047," said Nerdo. "Can't forget that one. "Right after the second Korean war. Eighth of the eighth 2047: the day the world stood still. Huh! We don't know that Zen was involved, though."

"Gorrick an alien?" said Cutter. "That would explain a lot … Planted here to infiltrate and destroy the human race — yeah, I can see that!"

"Maybe they tried to do it genetically and failed," said Nerdo, "So they resorted to starting the Cyberwars."

"I don't know that your suppositions have any basis in fact," Secta interposed, "Without scientific testing there's no way to tell if Gorrick is human or alien, although it is interesting to know that a saucer finally landed to crush all the debate about the existence of life beyond Earth. That, however, is not the point. The point is that Gorrick must be stopped."

Al nodded, pinching the bridge of his nose and squeezing his eyes shut.

"Are you all right, Alice?" Secta asked, worried about signs of de-stabilisation.

"Yeah, just a bit off colour," said Al. "Too much to think about, I guess."

Secta sighed. He knew that the job wouldn't be done for Alice until he could leave this dimension a better place than he'd found it. Deep in thought, he began pacing the floor, chin habitually in hand.

"Hello," said Al. "Here comes a revelation."

Secta stopped: he had an idea.

"There's a computer at the bunker," he said. "What if..." he looked at Nerdo.

"It'd be a bit past the post, wouldn't it?" she said. "Like, circa redundant!"

"No more than I, my dear, no more than I!"

Alice jumped up. "What choice have we got?" he said. "Got to be worth a try, right?"

CHAPTER 34
ASTRAL FLASH

ALICE WALKED TO the doorway, taking a deep breath for the pre-dawn air, savouring the aroma of eucalyptus, just now at its richest.

"Alright," he said, softly. "Secta, what's your plan?"

Secta started pacing again. "In my ancient computer," he shot Nerdo a look, "There's a folder containing the top twenty most devastating computer viruses ever used. If we can get those to Nerdo, she can upload them to Zen's systems. Am I correct?"

Nerdo nodded.

"Will they still work?" asked Al.

"Well, granted, operating systems today are a lot more sophisticated than ours, but they're still essentially binary," Secta replied. "So at least one of the viruses stands a chance of getting through and causing enough mayhem to buy the time needed to take Zen all the way down."

"He's right," said Nerdo. "And something else — an eighty-year-old virus actually stands a far better chance of successfully bypassing Zen's virus protection shield, because they wouldn't be expecting it. They've probably never even heard of most of them."

"Good," said Secta. "Now. I propose that we separate. If we're in two locations, there's more chance for the plan to succeed. They're likely to come after Alice and I — after all, Turk and Morri are their two main antagonists. So all we need is time to get to the bunker and get the viruses to Nerdo. Then she'll be relatively free to put them into action."

"And what about you two?" asked Nerdo. "Will that leave you time to do what you have to do to get back?"

Secta looked at Alice, who shrugged. "We'll cross that bridge when we come to it," he said. Both men knew that they'd sacrifice their own mission if it meant saving humanity in a future timeline. Al smiled. Secta had changed.

There was a pause, while the implications of what Secta had said sunk in. Then: "How?" Nerdo asked, quietly. "If we're in separate locations, how do I get the viruses? I can't hack into your computer — the operating system won't be compatible with mine."

Secta's expression dimmed.

"Bugger!" Al swore. "Always an obstacle!"

"Wait a minute – wait!" she said, rushing over to the front desk. Digging in the waste paper basket, she hauled Reno's discarded iWish out and came back to Secta. "This has an interface designed to upload materials from any system," she said, excitedly. "It should work, even on one as old as Secta's. If we configure a link to this from my Ulink, you can use it to send the files to me — I'll show you how." Her face, which had brightened considerably, fell again. "Still one problem left — hacking Zen's satellite network. That could take ages."

"Not necessarily," said Secta, smugly. "What if you simply used the logon code?"

"That would make it possible, but how?" Nerdo looked at him, mouth open, intrigued.

"Hand me your Ulink..." Silently, she passed it over. "The code is in Morri's photographic memory," he went on. "I just need to access it." There was a tense few seconds as Secta concentrated deeply. "Got it!" he exclaimed, making them all jump. He keyed in twenty-five digits, then handed the Ulink back to Nerdo. "Over to you," he grinned.

"That's amazing," said Cutter. "How on earth—"

"Mennis made the mistake of letting Morri see the logon."

"What a memory!" laughed Nerdo. "Right, let me talk you through the upload process…"

While the two computer experts sorted out the protocols, Alice and Cutter talked logistics. "Right," said Al. "All you need to do is stay clear of Mennis and, most likely, Animal. Stick within a five-click radius of the bunker, but keep moving. That way, once the satellites are down, you're close enough to the bunker to get back for Morri and Turk."

"Roger that," said Cutter. "Are we packing?"

"You'll be sitting on your arsenal," Al quipped.

"Why Alice, you made a funny," said Secta, as he and Nerdo rejoined them. "I didn't realise you could be so witty!"

"Amazing how you get infected with wit, hanging around a genius like you."

"And he has developed taste as well. Well, well, my opinion of you has swollen, Alice."

"We'll get a doc to look into that when we get back, Secta," Alice laughed. "It could be contagious." He looked back to Cutter. "The weapons are under the passenger seat," he smiled.

Cutter handed him his pistol. "Here," he said. "Full mag."

Al took it and slipped it into his belt at the back of his pants.

"Cool. Let's go."

Sheet lightning flashed, followed by a deep, reverberating rumble of thunder that shook them all down to their boots.

Nerdo looked up at rolling purple clouds. "Going to be one hell of a storm," she said.

"Cumulonimbus thunderheads," said Secta. "No good for flying in, no good for driving under, and even worse for maintaining a satellite link."

Nerdo stopped and checked her Ulink.

"You're not wrong," she said. "Their tracking's offline."

Alice raised the J-Car door. "Good," he growled. "Gives us a head start." The four stood looking at each other.

Nerdo held out a hand. "If this goes right, this'll be the last time we talk," she said. "Shame we never got to meet face to face. Goodbye, Alice. And thanks."

He grabbed her hand, pulled her close and wrapped her in a bear hug. Startled at first, Nerdo relaxed into his embrace, smiled and kissed him on the cheek, before stepping back to show Cutter standing behind her, arms held out eagerly.

The two men laughed and grasped hands. "Can't stand goodbyes," Alice said.

"I can't stand sitting," Cutter countered. "It's been huge, man," he added. "Best of luck Al. Hope you make it back to your own time — and don't forget us, alright?" He turned to Secta. "Don't know whether to shake your hand or kiss you."

Secta took his hand then planted a playful kiss on his cheek. "Goodbye, Cutter," he said. "You really are a good old stick!" He turned to Nerdo, who grabbed his hand before he could kiss her too. "Bye, Secta," she said, grinning warmly. "You know what? I'm even going to miss you."

Secta, to his own astonishment, felt a lump in his throat. "Oh Lord, these hormones will be the death of me!" he gasped, wiping a tear from his eye. "I shall miss you too, my dear. Good luck to you."

The red dot on the holographic display froze. Ursula looked up at the sky and flicked the sunroof closed.

"The storm has killed the sat signal," she said. "We can only hope they stay in Snake long enough for us to get there."

The rain came on.

A dozen bikers, armed to the teeth, pulled their choppers into a lay-by beside the road. A big old tree would provide them some cover while they waited for their boss.

Mal parked the Commodore in the woods a couple of hundred metres from the helipad and killed the headlights.

"This do?" he asked Hope, who was busy calibrating the ILDD.

She looked up. "Yep," she confirmed. "Will the narks be able to see us here?"

"We'll see their lights long before they see us, I reckon." Mal said. "How long have we got?"

"A few more hours."

"Good," he said, and leaning across he pushed the ILDD aside, took her face in his hands and kissed her passionately. It wasn't long before they were occupying the same bucket seat and giving the shock absorbers a workout.

With the help of some reluctant motel staff, Honor and Karzoff had got their car moving again. A low mist had descended. With no street-lighting, Karzoff needed to sit forward to keep a keen eye on the road.

"Use ze high beam, you fool!" Honor snapped.

"High beam will only light up the fog and make it more dangerous," he replied, sharply. "We have plenty of time, Honor. And we know they are headed for the bunker."

"I vould haff preferred us to get there first," she said. "Still. No matter. If zey are zere vhen ve arrive, ve vill find zem. If zey are not, vc vill be zere to greet zem."

"And what will we do then?"

"You will shoot and kill Function, and we will take Hope hostage."

"I have told you already, Honor, I am an extremely poor shot. Why must we kill the man?"

"Because othervise he vill help Alice to escape!" she fired back. "It matters not, Karzoff, zat you are a bad shot. Just keep firing until you hit him!"

"But I do not want to kill—"

"Zis is not a debate, Karzoff. It is a direct order."

"I have a signal!" Mennis snapped. "They have moved!" She brought the car to a screeching halt. "They are in separate cars, a few kilometres apart," she went on. "We just passed a crossroads that would put us on Turk's tail."

"And what about the reinforcements?" Animal questioned, as she spun the car round.

"We'll have to go without them for now," she said. "We can get word to them through Gorrick to follow our signal."

The storm had passed. But not in Animal's mind. Furious, he slapped the dashboard hard.

"Such puerile behaviour," Mennis sneered. "Rather than attempting to beat up my car, perhaps you could send that message to Gorrick?"

Irritably, he grabbed the Ulink from the dash and typed an update to Gorrick.

"Turn ze lights off in case zey are already here," Honor ordered as they proceeded along the dirt road to the bunker gates.

"But I will not be able to see the track!" he complained.

"Karzoff!" she shouted. Lightning flashed and thunder resounded, punctuating her anger.

He extinguished the lights, and they crawled along the track at a snail's pace, only intermittent flashes of lightning helping Karzoff to see.

"Zere," Honor pointed. "Pull ze car into zose bushes on ze left. Ve vill vait zere in ambush."

Karzoff reluctantly obeyed, backing the car into the dense bush.

"Listen!" Honor jumped at a loud, thin squealing sound. "Vhat is zat?"

"Just branches etching huge scratches into the paintwork on the side of the car," he replied, sarcastically.

"You should haff parked front in," she said, scornfully. "You vill answer for zose scratches vhen we get back to HQ."

"Of course," he snapped, acrimoniously. "I would not expect you to take the blame! You, after all, are never the driver, you merely issue the directions and you are never wrong! So tell me, Honor, did you really want to face the bush, rather than the bunker?"

"Do not antagonize me, Karzoff," she answered, coldly. "Someone must give ze orders!"

"Yes, and someone must take the blame," he responded. "But no-one needs to be a know-it-all!"

He turned and looked huffily out of the window as a shroud of awkward silence enveloped them. He was sick of her orders. Lightning flashed again, and in the brief luminescence, from the corner of his eye, Karzoff noticed a car, relatively close by. Inside it, two figures in the incandescent light. He chose not to mention it to Honor. Instead, the consummate voyeur, he was happy to wait for the next flash of lightning. His own personal show, how delightful. He glanced at Honor. Too bad she had coolant running in her veins.

Without returning his gaze but sensing his mood, she growled, "Remove those thoughts from your filthy mind, Karzoff. I told you before, I do not fraternize with colleagues."

"Don't worry, Honor," he replied, coldly. "Your frigidity is safe with me." He went back to watching eagerly for the next flash of lightning.

"Where are they?" Honor muttered anxiously.

Karzoff smiled knowingly in the darkness.

The skies broke, and dumped their deluge on the speeding J-Car. Secta checked a rough map Nerdo had given him.

"There's a turn up ahead on the left," he said.

"Tough to see though the rain," Al answered, concentrating intensely on the road ahead. He went down through the gears, decelerating.

Knowing her OSCI signal was being tracked by Gorrick, Mennis opened a comm link so he could hear her every word.

"They are up ahead," she said. "He has turned off the highway into a side road, three kilometres on the left."

The rain started belting down ferociously.

"Woodhenge," Mennis said to herself. "Whatever can it be?"

Gorrick was seated at a Zen operations terminal, sipping a cup of tea and listening to the live audio link, static enriched by the storm.

"Woodhenge," he murmured. The operator at the terminal beside him jumped into action.

"Sir, Woodhenge is a pagan monument situated in what was formerly Federal parkland," she said. "It is a wooden replica of Stonehenge, which stands on Salisbury plain in Britain."

"I know, I know," he said, drily. "A centre for pagan ceremonies. What I do not know is why Morrigan is going there. A question for later, I feel. Send Ursula what you have on Woodhenge," he went on. "And keep her audio on speaker."

It was pouring when Alice stopped the J-Car short of the Woodhenge gate. A lightning flash lit up the Mesolithic replica.

"What the—?" said Al. "Have we tripped in time again?"

"It's a pagan quasi-dreaming worship site," Secta replied. "It's where I met Morri."

"Cool, I'm into Goths," Al chuckled.

"The bunker is underneath, better park the car out of sight," Secta suggested, rolling his eyes. "We never know who might turn up."

Alice backed the car into the bushes off the road, its British racing green colour camouflaging it amongst the trees. Had he only known it, he was parked right on top of Mal Function and Hope in their own time.

Nerdo slowed the F-200, finding it difficult to see the road ahead. The rain was so heavy even headlights couldn't cut through it.

"Never rains but it pours!" she said, jokingly. "Woodhenge is about four clicks ahead on the left … we'll keep a safe distance."

Cutter looked troubled. "I don't feel comfortable sitting on our hands like this," he said. "It doesn't make sense not to go in."

"It's a good plan, Cutter, a good mission. Just trust it. Geez, that rain is hard!"

Mennis had to hug the windscreen in order to navigate the track without headlights. She caught a flash of lightning reflecting off something in the bushes up ahead, and immediately steered off the dirt road.

"There's a car up ahead," she said, sternly.

"Where?" He checked the Ulink. "Okay, I've got them."

"Yeah, well, I can see them with my own eyes," she growled.

The longer they spent together, the stronger their antipathy grew. Mennis felt like she was on a mission with a caveman, and her sense of superiority was not lost on Animal, who played up his rough side just to aggravate her.

The rain was easing off. Suddenly Mennis noticed something else.

"Is that a light?"

"A car interior light. Someone's getting out."

Secta climbed from the J-Car carrying the iWish unit and he and Alice made for the gate. The rain was lighter now, but the deluge had left plenty of deep puddles and slippery mud to negotiate.

"Hope you know where you're going, Secta," said Al. "There's nothing here but a bunch of wooden poles."

Animal took a handgun from the glove compartment, and de-activated the electro-lock. He was about to get out of the car when Mennis held him back.

"No!" she said. "We need to see what they are doing. There might be more to this than meets the eye."

For the first time, Animal saw the logic in her suggestion. With a noncommittal grunt, he reactivated the pistol electro-lock and slumped back in his seat.

Al looked over his shoulder. "Someone's onto us, Secta," he said. "I can feel prying eyes."

"Paranoia, Alice," said Secta, confidently. "Understandable, after all you've been through." He strode through the huge wooden pillars and stopped on the grass at the other side, looking around as though he'd dropped something.

Alice stopped beside him. "What the hell are you looking for?" he snapped, impatiently. "Loose change?" But Secta had stopped, and, beaming, spread his arms wide.

"Open Sesame!" he announced.

Alice looked at him. "You've got to be kidding me," he said.

"No, that's the password," said Secta, sounding anxious. "But we have a problem."

"Yeah? What's that?"

"It's not recognising my voice. It's Morri's, you see, not mine."

"Didn't it open for you before?"

"Well yes, but over the past few days my voice has become more like hers, I suspect."

"Okay, let me try," said Al. "It might need a more masculine tone."

"Very well," said Secta. "Try to mimic me."

"Hmph. Maybe not that masculine then," said Al.

"Alice, we do not have time right now for banter," chided Secta.

Alice just grinned and took a breath, trying to recall Secta's voice.

"Open sesame!" he sang. Much to his surprise, a trapdoor opened in the turf and a light blinked on inside. "Alright!" he roared.

Animal was watching through night-vision binoculars. "There's a trapdoor in the field," he said. "They're going in."

"Arm up," Mennis said. "Time to make a move!"

"Then move," he answered, "Because if I'm right, that trapdoor will close quickly and we'll find nothing but grass."

They took off as fast as they could run.

The elevator door opened and the lights flicked on. Alice stepped into the room and looked around, amazed.

"This looks like your lab," he said.

"Yes, most of my gear is here," Secta replied. "Now, let me see … my computer is just over there." He walked over to a bench and lifted a plastic dust cover. "Ah, there she is!" He proceeded to boot up while Alice sat in the chair.

"This is where it all started — where you zapped me," he growled, bitterly.

"Yes," said Secta. "And it's where we'll both be zapped again, as soon as I've got this off to Nerdo."

"Still don't get how this is going to work," Al mumbled.

Secta established the connection with the iWish as Nerdo had instructed him, and accessed the folder containing the viruses. "Upload has started," he announced. "But there's no signal down here to send Nerdo the files."

"How will you get them to her then?"

"I'll need to send from the elevator. There'll be a signal in there."

"How long?"

"Oh, a minute or two,"

"My gut's telling me to worry," said Alice. "Not panic — yet — but worry."

Secta moved over to the cloud chamber.

"I'll fire up the other equipment to save time," he said.

"Good idea, anything I can do to help?"

"Yes — look under that chair and see how many remotes are there."

Alice got down on his hands and knees and reached under the chair. "Just one."

"Good. That means Hope's got the other one. Hang on to it, I might need it if we arrive back here."

"Hey! You just said if?"

"Oh, well … one can never be certain, Alice," Secta said with a wry smile.

"You mad professor types," grumbled Alice. "It's like mandatory for you to raise doubt when everything depends on you. Grandstanding!"

A ding sounded from the computer.

"Upload's complete!" Secta chirped.

CHAPTER 35
DEATH KNELL

SECTA STROLLED TO the computer. "Good," he said, picking up the iWish. "I'll establish the link to Nerdo." He took the iWish to the elevator, opened the door and stepped inside. "Aha! Just as I thought!" he said. "There is a signal in here. But—"

The door closed, cutting him off mid-sentence.

Thinking the door had closed automatically, Al shook his head at Secta's eccentricity. Walking to the elevator, he pressed the call button. It failed to open.

The elevator door opened and Secta found himself staring down the barrel of a gun. He quickly hit 'send' on the iWish, then hid the unit behind his back, like a naughty schoolkid.

"Hand over that device, Morri," said Mennis, "Or I will order Animal to blow your kneecap off."

Animal took aim.

"Hand what over?" asked Secta. "Oh, this? It's only an iWish. See?" He held it up. "I've been fiddling with it — interesting technology, isn't it?" He took a sly peek at the dispatch indicator. The connection was still establishing. He needed to buy more time. "Have you used one?" he asked, desperately. "I was just stepping out to get a signal for a download. I've found this marvellous little program, I'm sure you'll find it fascinating…"

Mennis snatched the iWish out of Secta's hand and peered at it. "It's sending something!" she snapped. "What? And to whom?"

"Which question should I answer first?" Secta replied.

Before anyone else could speak, Animal plucked the iWish from Mennis's hands and threw it onto the ground. It crunched under his size fifteen boot.

"Back into the lift!" he ordered, and swung the gun at Mennis. "You too."

"What are you playing at?" she growled, stepping inside.

"Getting the job done. Now press the button."

Nerdo was anxiously watching the Ulink display. "It stopped!" she shrieked. "The download is incomplete."

"What does that mean?" Cutter asked.

"We'll soon find out," she said, grimly tapping at the keys. "Fortunately Secta was smart enough to stack the files so they sent individually. I've got eight of them."

"Something must have gone wrong," said Cutter. "We should go help them."

"Need to uplink these first," she said, hacking at a speed that looked like it couldn't possibly be real. But it was.

"What on earth have they found?" Gorrick muttered, intrigued. "Check to see what that iWish was linked to."

The operator beside him commenced a digital comb for the iWish signal.

Gorrick looked up at the mid-air operations map floating overhead. A galaxy of lights, representing the live communication satellite grid linking Zen's global offices, twinkled in front of him, representing the beginning of true world domination. Satisfaction glowed on Gorrick's face.

Alice stood at the elevator door, arms folded, waiting impatiently. When they opened, they revealed a sight he was not expecting: Animal holding a gun to Secta's head.

Al slowly raised his hands.

Ursula pushed out from behind Animal and, speaking very deliberately, said: "What is this place? It is filled with scientific equipment! A weapons operations centre?"

Thinking on his feet, Al drew the remote control from his pocket and held it up. "You got that right," he sneered. "Now let hi — her go, or I'll launch a nuke at Zen."

"You're bluffing," Animal countered.

"Try me, buddy," sneered Alice. "Go on, pull the trigger. You can wave Gorrick, Zen, and all your power goodbye."

"Stand down!" Mennis screeched, not prepared to call the bluff.

"Did I hear that right?" Gorrick erupted, leaping to his feet. "Fire a nuke?"

"Sir, I found the iWish signal," the operator reported, urgently.

"And?" he barked, "Is that a priority at this moment?"

"I don't know," she said, nervously. "It used our WiFi to send a large file to a Ulink."

"What's going on?" he said, face pale. "Could they have sent missile commands? I seem to recall there being something to do with nukes in that area."

"He might be bluffing, sir," the operator suggested tentatively.

"We cannot take that chance," he said. "Do you still have Mennis's signal?"

"Yes, sir, but it's not a strong."

"It do not have to be," he said. "Use it as a locator. Launch a bunker buster missile."

"But, sir, that will—"

"I am well aware of that," he said. "How long until launch?"

"I can activate from here... around ten minutes, sir."

"Why so long?"

"There are protocols that control a launch, sir. Designed to prevent a madman from abusing the system. Not that that's what's happening here!" she added, quickly.

"What happens if it loses her signal?" Gorrick questioned.

"Once initiated it will lock onto the target. We won't need the signal anymore, sir."

"Good. Activate it, then tell Mennis to get the hell out of there," he rasped.

"Operator Two!" the woman barked. "Witness that use of IRBM, Hellfire 800 antitank missile has been authorised."

Operator Two hit a key on his computer. "Copy that," he said.

She pressed the activation key and typed a message ordering Mennis to evacuate immediately.

"Message sent, sir," she reported. "Missile launch countdown commenced."

Gorrick sat back, folded his arms and was about to let out a sigh of relief when the second operator spoke up. "Sir ... we appear to have a glitch," he said.

"With the launch?" Gorrick enquired.

"No, sir. Launch has been initiated. Ten minutes and counting. We are, in fact, losing comms."

"What?" he asked, perplexed. "What comms?"

"All comms, sir. Everything is shutting down. It appears to be a cyber-attack of some kind, possibly a virus."

"I see it, sir!" his colleague confirmed. "It has struck the satellite network, and is now in the mainframe ... whatever it is, it's shutting down our comms worldwide."

"That's impossible!" Gorrick bellowed. "How could it get through our firewalls?"

"It seems to be something new, sir. Look!"

They looked at the display in disbelief as the lights blinked out, one by one, showing that connections between Zen worlds were going down.

"Stop it!" Gorrick bellowed, "Kill it! Make it stop!"

The two main operators exchanged a look of hopelessness. "We … we can't sir," gulped the first. "It's proliferating faster than we can shut it down."

"OSCIs will go down in three … two … one. The OSCI network is down, sir."

"Holy hell!" Gorrick flopped into his chair and put his head in his hands. "Does that mean…"

"Yes, sir. No more OSCI communication. No cyborg comms. Nothing, sir. We're blind. We're done, sir."

Every monitor screen in the room suddenly went black — then a white graphic flashed on every Zen screen in the world. It read:

'CHAA! WITH LOVE, BLACK ALICE'

On his feet, mouth gaping open, Gorrick shook his head. "He has won," he said, incredulously. "He has won."

Nerdo fired Cutter a broad smile. "It's done!" she said. "Black Alice worked!" They hugged in elation. She grasped Cutter by the chin, locked eyes with him and said: "Alas, poor Gorrick!"

"Well put, my lady!" laughed Cutter, striking a theatrical pose. "Well quoted!"

Nerdo pointed at the road ahead and declaimed: "Start your engine, O Cutter! We goeth in!"

Mennis received the message to evacuate. She was about to warn Animal when she felt her OSCI connection go down.

"Drop the gun, Animal!" Al ordered, still threatening him with the remote.

Animal looked at Mennis, who nodded. Her priority now was escape from the oncoming missile. The big biker defiantly threw the gun to the floor, but as Alice bent to collect it, he grabbed Morri and heaved her at him. As they collided, Animal followed up with a vicious punch to Turk's chin. It dropped him to one knee.

"Stop!" Mennis screamed. "Stop!" It had no effect, Animal had given in to his rage and was beyond her control. She took stock. The missile was on its way, and would take care of Morri and Turk. As a bonus, it would take out Animal, whom she had come to passionately loathe, too. The attention was off her. Moving stealthily, she slipped back to the elevator. The doors closed quietly behind her.

Animal dived for the gun. Alice, still groggy from the king hit, reeled. Just then, something pinged into life in his head. Turk was back! Instantly, the soldier summed up the situation — Animal was sliding across the cement floor for the gun; he had to stop him. He leapt to his feet and was on the man in a couple of strides, delivering a powerful kick to the solar plexus. The gun skidded over to Morri's feet. She, coming back to reality, kicked it out of range, just before Animal could reach it.

"Well done!" cried Secta. "Welcome back, Morri!"

"Thanks, Secta!" she replied. "Glad to see we're still fighting!"

Animal got to his feet and shaped up to Turk.

"Um, I think while they're sorting out their differences, in the interim we'll complete the settings on my equipment," Secta said.

"Welcome back, mate," Alice thought dizzily to Turk. But Turk didn't answer. He was entirely focused on Animal. The biker let go a heavy left. Turk deflected easily. Animal, banking on a big right-hand haymaker, drew his arm back. But he'd telegraphed the move. Coolly, Turk leaned forward and Animal took the bait, lashing out with all his might. Turk dodged — the massive punch just clipped his ear — and he countered with a short but deadly flurry of blows to the head and body, his fists like a couple of pile drivers whittling away a chunk of granite. He followed up with a good hard right that smashed Animal's nose, and drew back his hand for the final blow. With all his force he drove the palm of his hand up under Animal's chin — but the man moved his head at the last second. Instead of his vertebrae being snapped by a lethal blow, he merely went over backwards. He knew he'd narrowly missed meeting his maker. Any doubt that Turk was playing for keeps was banished from his mind.

Animal shook his head, trying to clear the stars. He knew his only hope against this deadly opponent was to pull him in close and use his brute strength. But Turk was light on his feet, and though still hampered by an injured shoulder and other battle scars, he readied himself to deliver a kick that would knock the wind out of his opponent and take him entirely out of the game. Leaving himself open in a feigned lapse, Turk drew Animal into range and launched his boot at the biker's heart.

Animal had anticipated it. He intercepted Turk's foot, and lifted his leg above his head — all six feet six of him, plus the length of his arm. Turk spilled onto his back. Now it was Animal's turn to get square. Stomping and kicking, giving it everything he had, the barrage was so ferocious Turk couldn't get to his feet. Finally, he managed to swing round on the floor, knocking a kick away and throwing Animal off balance. He got as far as his knees before Animal came back at him and, with a huge kick, caught him in the chest and sent him reeling across the floor.

Seeing Animal getting the better of Turk, Morri ran over to the biker's gun and slid it across the floor to him. He snapped it up, aimed and pulled the trigger — no fire. The electro safety meant only the registered owner could use the gun. Disgusted, he flung it into the darkness.

Alice, recovering some wherewithal, suddenly remembered the pistol down the back of his pants. He overrode Turk to draw it. As Animal advanced, Alice aimed at the ceiling and pulled the trigger.

This one fired. The shot was so loud in the confines of the concrete room that it set their ears ringing.

Animal dropped to his knees, hands over his ears. Blood running down his chin, entire body battered and bruised, Turk looked at him. "I should blow you away," he said. "But I've got no quarrel with you. So get in the elevator and, like Alice would say, rack off."

"Happening!" Alice put in, quietly.

Animal got to his feet and looked at Turk suspiciously.

Turk nodded. "I'm not Zen," he said. "You'll note that your Zen buddy threw you to wolves. Maybe bear that in mind from now on." Alice growled.

The biker barked a short laugh. "I hear you," he said. "You're one tough mother, Turk, you know that?"

"Right back atcha, pal," Alice replied.

The two warriors regarded each other for a moment more, a new and mutual respect between them. Under different circumstances they might even have fought side by side — and been glad to do so.

Animal walked to the elevator and pressed the call button. As he waited for it to descend, he looked back at Turk.

"Can't say I owe you for not shooting me," he said. "But I respect you for it. You could have gone a different way." He wiped a dribble of blood from his mouth and spat more on the floor. "So let's make it square: Gorrick's ordered a missile strike. It's headed here, probably only a few minutes away. If you make a run for it — well, I won't be looking." He stepped into the elevator and the doors closed.

Turk turned to Secta who, with Morri, was buzzing about the instruments. "Did you hear that?" he said. "There's a missile on the way."

"We're in a bunker built to withstand a nuclear strike," Secta answered, without looking up. "I don't think we need have any concern."

All sorts of sounds were now emanating from Secta's apparatus. It was lit up like a carnival sideshow. "What happens from here?" asked Turk.

"Good question," said Morri.

"When I tell you to, sit in the chair and I will extract Alice and place him in that cloud chamber over there." He pointed to the large translucent sphere, which now had a faint white glow pulsating in its core.

"How can you 'extract' Alice without zapping me?"

"Alice's DNA has a marker attached, and yours doesn't. My DNA has one as well. The de-molecularizer will only extract molecules with the marker. Once extracted, the atoms will be fired from this neutron gun through a quartz prism. That will open a wormhole back to our time, and our molecules will pass through."

"Simple as that, eh?" said Turk. "And you? How will you get back?"

"Oh, you'll be able to replicate the process," Secta answered, smiling. "Once I'm in the chair all you have to do is press this button. Just think, Morri ... you'll be a free agent again!"

Turk and Morri looked at each other, and smiled.

Animal climbed from the trapdoor and looked up at the sky, seeking any sign of the missile. But there was nothing to be seen. The storm had cleared, leaving a huge full moon and a vast canopy of stars. Then he heard an engine, and saw headlights flashing across the field. A vehicle was coming towards him at speed.

Bouncing around inside the TepZepi, Mennis wrestled with the wheel, directing it over the soggy, undulating field.

Assuming she was coming to collect him, Animal waited. A servo closed the trapdoor behind him. The TepZepi skidded to a halt over it. Mennis leapt out and took off on foot.

Animal watched, bemused. "Hey!" he yelled after her. "I can't start it without the key card!"

"The car is not for you," she screamed back at him. "It is to stop them getting out!"

"That bitch!" he snarled, reaching into the car and slipping it into neutral. He quickly went to the rear and started pushing, rolling it off the trapdoor. Satisfied it was clear, he took off across the field as fast as he could run.

Nerdo was navigating the F-200 along the dirt track when she saw someone running towards them in the headlights. Mennis: and she looked like she was running for her life. Nerdo hit the brakes and watched in amazement as the woman ran straight past them without breaking stride. Then she saw why.

"Will you freaking look at that!" she yelled, pointing at a bright, comet-like trail streaking across the sky.

"Incoming, anti-tank!" Cutter yelled. "Out and under!"

Their military training kicked in. They leapt out from the car and slid underneath. Lying together they could see the full moon reflecting off the windshield of the TepZepi, sitting in the field just beyond Woodhenge.

"The bunker must be over there, somewhere near that car," Nerdo breathed.

"That's not a car," said Cutter, longingly, despite the deadly danger. "It's a TepZepi. A work of art — one of the most expensive—" the world went white. The sound was so profound that, in fact, they didn't hear it, it simply filled the world, blocking out anything other than a horrifying hissing in their ears. The TepZepi and Woodhenge both disappeared into a massive fireball as Cutter rolled to shield Nerdo with his body. The massive blast —filled with shrapnel, debris, dust, shards of wood and torn-up vegetation — hit the F-200 like a tornado, lifting the front wheels off the ground. Cutter pulled Nerdo to his chest and curled tightly around her, face buried in his arms, hoping for the best. The wheels crashed back down again, the big vehicle bouncing on its extra-strong suspension. They had to be still alive — he could feel Nerdo shaking in his arms. He gripped her tighter.

Like fireballs from a volcanic eruption, white-hot chunks of the TepZepi descended upon them. Cutter peeked out — it was raining molten metal. He'd seen it before at war and knew, provided there was only one missile and the F-200 stayed in position, it would soon be over. They had survived. Gradually, silence fell, apart from the crackling of flames from the crater, and slowly they struggled out from under the truck. They looked around in awe. Woodhenge was gone. The TepZepi had been all but vaporized, all that remained being gnarled pieces of metal and chunks of flaming tyre. A huge crater occupied the centre of the scene. Remarkably, the Wilson J car was intact, the trees that had camouflaged it had been reduced to blackened stumps.

"Goodbye, Woodhenge!" said Nerdo, glumly.

"Goodbye, TepZepi," said Cutter. "Hey, look on the bright side," he said. "That's gonna make a great reservoir for the next rain!"

CHAPTER 36
TOMORROW ON MY MIND

IN THE BUNKER it stayed pitch black, until an amber emergency light came on, making the claustrophobic darkness feel unbearably bright. Morri stirred on the ground. Turk was sitting with his back to the elevator door, scratching his head.

"Ooft!" said Alice. "That took the breath outa me!"

"That was the percussion wave from a direct hit," said Secta, groggily. "Knocked us out," he added.

Turk climbed to his feet, "Yeah, last thing I remember I was about to sit in the chair," he said. "Now I'm at the elevator. I hope everything's still—" He was interrupted by the lights flickering back on.

"Nothing to worry about," said Secta, sounding more cheerful by the second. "When the system detects an explosion it temporarily shuts the power down by ninety-five percent. Reduces the chance of a fire." He struggled upright. "It's restored now because there have been no further tremors."

"I hope the elevator isn't wrecked," said Turk. "I don't fancy being stuck down here for the rest of my days."

"Oh, I don't know," said Morri "I could think of worse company..." The two exchanged meaningful looks.

"Er... we'd better get on with getting out of here, Alice," said Secta. "It's beginning to feel like four's a crowd."

Taking a deep breath to steady himself, Turk once again took his seat in the chair. A strange whirring sound cranked up from the cloud chamber, this time it was accompanied by the sound of a servo from above Turk's head. A fishbowl-like contraption lowered into place.

"Blimey, it's like something off the set of an old sci-fi movie!" Alice said, looking up as the fishbowl lowered to the bridge of Turk's nose. "Catch you round, Turk," he added. "It's been … interesting hanging around with you!"

"In me, you mean," Turk smiled. "Yeah, guess this is goodbye, pal. It's really been an honour. I don't think I'll ever see life the same way again."

Morri leaned over and kissed Turk gently. "That one was for you, Alice," she said. "We'll never forget you."

"Just keep Turk outa trouble, alright?"

She nodded and stepped back, wiping her eyes.

"Right then, Secta," Alice said, gruffly. "Let's get this show on the road before I start whimpering. You know," he said, looking round, "I hate goodbyes. But … Chaa!"

Secta hit the button. A host of coloured lights illuminated in the apparatus over Turk's head as a low, fifty-cycle hum kicked in. The hum began to build, louder in volume and higher in pitch. Turk's face screwed up in pain. He gripped the armrests of the chair. The sound increased to an almost unbearably high pitch, Turk bucked in the chair and suddenly, everything stopped. Secta, forcing Morri to uncover her ears, walked briskly to the cloud chamber. The interface line linking the neutron gun to the de-molecularizer was blinking red.

"Oh, good," he said. "He's in there. Turk, are you with us?"

Turk tried to sit up, and bumped his head on the apparatus.

"Ouch!" he grumbled. "Yeah, I think so."

"If you can walk all right, come over here."

Turk ducked under the apparatus and slipped out of the chair. He stood wavering for a second or two, then took a deep breath and walked over to Morri.

"Feels a bit odd," he said. "Kind of … empty."

"Are you sure you're all right?" Secta asked, with genuine concern.

"Yes, Secta. Just a bit lost without my sidekick." he smiled.

"Understandable," said Secta. "It'll pass. So. Two things. First, you must return here in exactly three months time. I will leave something from the past on this chair for you. Okay? Do you remember the password?"

"Open sesame!" Morri scoffed.

"You're kidding," said Turk. "Okay, fine. Three months. And second?"

"See this gauge?" Secta pointed at a small digital meter attached to the neutron gun.

"Yes."

"See how the gauge is in red, and moving towards green?"

"Yes."

"As soon as it turns green, I will press this button here," he pointed at a button on another part of the chamber. "That will dispatch Alice back through the wormhole. You will have to do the same for me. Got that, both of you?"

"Yes," said Turk. "Um, no problem. Gauge goes green, hit the button."

"Excellent," said Secta. "It has reached green now, so here goes Alice!" he hit the button.

Turk braced himself.

There was a slight hum, a crackle of electricity arcing in the smoke-filled cloud chamber, then one tiny light flashed. It was all a bit of an anti-climax.

"Is that it?" Turk asked, expecting much more.

"Yes. Do you think it needs to be more exciting? I could add some ambient space sounds and colourful lights," Secta said.

"Nar, it was just fine, Secta," said Turk. "Just fine."

"Well, Turk," said Secta, holding out Morri's hand, "I shan't be seeing you again. Good luck old stick."

Turk took the hand and held it warmly. "You know, I didn't have you pegged as the kind of guy to save the world," he said. "But you have, all the same. Hang on to that, whatever happens next."

"Oh, it was nothing really," said Secta, uncharacteristically modest. "Alice did most of it. And you two, of course. So, goodbye, Morri," he went on. "This whole adventure would have been nothing if it weren't for you. I don't think I'll ever be the same man again after having been a young lady. You make sure you put all those remarkable abilities of yours to good use. And … I will miss you."

"Do you know, I'll actually miss you too," Morri replied. "I think you'll probably stay part of me for the rest of my life. I hope it's the same for you."

"I know it will be, Morri. And by the way, you two make an excellent team. How about keeping it that way?" He winked at Turk while Morri's face flushed.

"Secta…" she groaned, embarrassed.

"We'll do our best," said Turk, with a smile.

Secta hopped into the chair and nodded to Turk, who pressed the button to initialise the process.

"Should I be scared, Secta?"

"Not any more, Morri."

The hum began to build.

Nerdo and Cutter were standing at the edge of the smouldering crater.

"Reckon they're trapped down there?" said Cutter. "Or—"

"Don't say it," snapped Nerdo. "What is that obelisk looking thing in the middle?"

"Dunno. Looks more like a pagan worship site now than Woodhenge ever did."

The explosion had stripped soil and structure away from the elevator shaft, leaving it exposed like a tower. Suddenly, a trapdoor opened on the top. Nerdo and Cutter stepped back, nervously.

"What the…?" Cutter exclaimed.

A glow appeared from the cavity. Next second, two familiar figures appeared.

"Well, look at you," called Cutter. "Rising from the dead?"

"Guess so!" Turk called down, happily.

"Alice and Secta?" Nerdo enquired.

"Gone home," Morri answered, looking at the devastation around her. She could smell cordite, and recalled the vision she'd had in jail. The scene before her was similar — less devastating, but maybe even more frightening because of that. She glanced up at the big full moon and thought it had never looked quite so beautiful. She looked down at her hand coupled in Turk's, then glanced up at his face.

"I hope the world is a better place now," she said.

"Guess it's up to us to make sure of it," he said, gently.

The trapdoor silently closed behind them.

Cutter heard a stick snap behind him, and turned sharply to find Animal there, looking very much the worse for wear. Smoke was rising from the man's singed clothing, and his face was battered and bruised. Cutter drew a blade but a sharp call from Turk stopped him. He jumped into the crater, helped Morri down, and took Animal's offered hand as he climbed out.

"Glad to see you made it," the biker said. "Knew you was tough. Gorrick said he would give anything to have a bloke like you on his side. Now I understand. Look, he went on, stepping back. "Don't see why my people shouldn't be part of setting the world right, 'stead of stuffing it up even more. Will you accept a promise, on behalf of the biker movement, to work together against these Zen bastards?"

Turk locked eyes with the man, then turned to Morri. Still holding Turk's hand, she looked deeply into the big Rebel's mind. Animal looked her square in the eye.

She turned to Turk and nodded. "He's sincere." The look in her eyes changed to elation. She turned to face the horizon. "Together!" she yelled. "We will have a brave new world!"

Mennis stopped on the dirt track, Morri's words filling her mind. She swore bitterly to herself. "Over my dead body, girl!" She kept walking — back to Gorrick, back to Zen. Back to world supremacy.

CHAPTER 37
WINGS OF LEATHER –
WINGS OF STEEL

THE RAIN BEATING on Mal's windscreen eased. Hope was glowing in the moonlight as she reclined in the seat beside him, her gaze fixed on the ILDD. Her expression slowly changed — the device was registering a signal.

She sat up sharply. "Mal!"

He was dozing, mesmerized by the pitter-patter of rain on the windscreen. He sat bolt upright, clattering his head against the roof of the car. He turned, wide-eyed, to Hope. "What the…"

"Movement at the station!" she said, excitedly.

"Hell, you scared the livin' crap out of me," he grumbled. "Where?"

Hope aimed the ILDD at the bunker. "Over there … it's coming from the bunker," she said. "It's Secta!" she flung open the car door and headed off across the field.

"Hope, wait!" he called after her. But there was no stopping her.

Honor had noticed a light blink on and off in the bush near them.

"Did you see zat?" she exclaimed. "A car! It must be zem! Vait … did you know zey vere zere?"

"I ... I ... no ... they..." Karzoff stammered.

She had no time for him, lying or otherwise. She opened the glove box, whipped out her pistol and dropped it testily into his lap. "Zere! Now do your duty!" she snarled.

A second light blinked as Mal got out of the car.

Both Honor and Karzoff ducked down.

"That was lucky," said Karzoff. "I don't think he saw us.'

As Hope was hurrying across the field, through the light drizzle, Mal was lagging behind. "Slow down!" he complained. "What's the rush?"

"He might need help, Mal — it's still experimental," she panted back to him. "Things can go wrong, you know? This has never been done before! Besides, if we've got it right, Alice is in there too!"

The gravity of the situation registered, but just as Mal sped up, a shot rang out, causing him to instinctively hit the deck.

"Hope! Someone's shooting at us!" he bellowed.

"You reckon?" she screamed back, increasing her speed.

Karzoff was standing beside the car, one eye closed, arms extended, aiming a pistol that was waving like a flag in the wind.

"Run you fool, run!" snapped Honor. "Get after zem! You could not hit ze broadside of a barn from here!"

They took off in pursuit of their prey.

Karzoff held the pistol out in front of him, trying to line up a shot at Mal, but it was impossible with his firing arm bouncing up and down.

"Save ze bullets for ze bunker, you fool," yelled Honor. "You can shoot him zen!"

Hope got to where she expected to find the trapdoor. "Open sesame!" she called.

Mal stopped alongside her, hands on his knees, thoroughly out of breath.

Nothing happened.

They looked back — Honor and Karzoff were running across the field, Karzoff waving a pistol.

"Here come the crazies," panted Mal. "We'd better be careful, that idiot might accidentally hit something!"

Hope moved a little further away from the helipad and tried again.

"Open, sesame!" she yelled, again with no result.

"Let me try," Mal said. "Open, sesame!"

A glow appeared from a crack in the ground and the trapdoor opened right next to where he was standing. He jumped backwards, shocked.

"Far out!" he chuckled. "How's that ... it worked!"

"You know," said Hope, glaring at the hole, "I don't think this voice-recognition technology is everything it's cracked up to be."

Honor and Karzoff were bearing down on them, and were only twenty metres away.

"Move, Hope!" yelled Mal. "They're getting close!"

She hurried down the stairs, Mal at her heels.

"Come on!" Hope yelled anxiously, jabbing at the elevator call button.

"Can't we just say, close, Sesame?" Mal asked.

"No," she said, rolling her eyes. "It closes of its own accord."

"I'm pretty sure it was close sesame in Ali Baba," he mumbled to himself.

"This isn't The Arabian Nights, Mal."

"Are you sure?"

Honor reached the trapdoor first. Karzoff was out of breath and had deliberately slowed down to avoid shooting anyone.

She stopped at the trapdoor, looked down at Mal and Hope on the landing, and yelled angrily, "Karzoff! Hurry!"

The elevator door pinged and opened. Hope and Mal whipped inside.

"Close the trapdoor!" Mal yelled. "Close, sesame!"

"Will you stop that?" snapped Hope.

"Worth a shot," he grumbled.

"I told you, when the elevator reaches the bunker, the trapdoor will automatically close."

"I don't think it'll be quick enough."

The elevator door closed, just as Karzoff arrived and Honor started down the stairs.

"Imbecile!" she screamed at him, rushing to the door and repeatedly jabbing the call button, just as Hope had done only seconds before.

She snatched the gun from his hand. "Give me that!" she spat. "You haff none of vat it takes, Karzoff!" she added, spitefully. "No guts — and definitely no glory!"

Hope and Mal stepped from the elevator to find Secta standing next to his equipment, a dejected look on his face.

Hope ran over and embraced him. "Secta! You made it!"

"Yes, I did," he said, still looking forlorn.

"Where's Alice?" said Mal, coming up behind Hope.

"Who's this?" Secta asked.

"This is Mal Function," she said. "He's a friend — he's Octagon.

Mal held out a hand. "Hi, Doc," he said. "Glad you made it."

Secta took Mal's hand, much to Hope's surprise. Her brother had never held Octagon in particularly high regard.

The elevator door pinged, and Honor stepped out with Karzoff behind her. She aimed the gun at Mal and without hesitation pulled the trigger. Click. She tried again. Click, click. Realising Karzoff had emptied the magazine, she turned on him with a look that could have melted steel.

"You!" she began. She seemed to be struggling for bad enough words.

Karzoff held his hands up repentantly. "Sorry," he mumbled.

Looking like she'd just bitten into a rancid prawn, Honor threw the pistol to the floor.

"This is no way to behave, Honor!" Secta snapped. "How dare you try to shoot at anyone in my lab?"

"My my," she sneered, caustically. "A quvick trip to ze future and you've grown balls!"

Secta actually laughed. "In fact, my dear Honor, it was quite the reverse," he said.

"Enough!" she roared. "Vhere is Black Alice?"

"I have no idea," he said, glumly. "Looks like I lost him somewhere along the way."

"What?" said Hope.

"What?" said Mal.

"Vhat?" said Honor. "After all zis! You expect me to believe you haff lost him? Vhat am I supposed to tell ze President?"

"Tell him whatever you want, Honor," Secta shrugged. "It won't change the fact that I don't know where Alice is."

"I tell you what," Hope thundered, taking a step towards the SSD woman. "Why don't we all pay the President a visit. Then I can tell him how you kidnapped and tortured me and did your damnedest to undermine the experiment!"

Honor didn't move a muscle. "Is zat vhat you intend, Secta?" she rasped. "You vould double-cross me? You know ve only took Hope to prevent zat from happening!"

"I'll tell you what I intend," he said, coolly. "I intend to return to my lab. I intend to supervise the reinstallation of all my equipment, and I intend to work with my sister in a search for Alice's DNA marker. It is possible he has slipped into yet another dimension."

"How could zat be, Secta?" Honor howled.

"I warned you, Honor," he replied. "The process hasn't been perfected. Alice's condition is unstable, especially with having been exposed to it before."

"Zi same does not apply to you, it seems!"

"Just lucky, I guess," he replied, facetiously.

"Enough," said Mal. "I'm over this pair of morons. They've been tailing us for days. Let's get out of here and get on with finding my mate."

"I demand a detailed report for ze President!" Honor grated. "On my desk, first zing in ze morning!"

"You are in no position to demand anything, Honor," said Secta. "In fact, I don't think you should be in such a hurry for that report. I'm not sure how pleased the President will be to hear how you put us all at risk."

"And how pleased vill he be to discover you siding viz a dissident?" she asked, triumphantly.

Secta merely smiled. "What dissident?" he said. "Oh, you mean this dissident, who managed to overpower you not once but twice, infiltrated the very heart of your operation, rescued Hope, who was being tortured on your orders, and made it right into this top secret bunker that you commissioned as our safe house? I don't know, Honor. How do you think he'll react?"

Honor, entirely taken aback, could only step aside as Secta, followed by Hope and a grinning Mal, swept by her. A snide smirk broke out on Karzoff's face. He loved it when she was lost for a comeback.

Hope regarded her brother. He seemed somehow different. More serious, more determined. She wondered if the condition was temporary, or whether the atomic-transmutation process had given his attitude a makeover. I guess anything's possible, she thought. She suddenly realised that this wasn't merely a saying. Her brother had just travelled through time — and returned. This wasn't theoretical. This was history. Secta was living proof that they had perfected dimensional matter transfer. The evidence that the process functioned was irrefutable. The potential of their discovery was only limited by their imaginations.

Mulling over the possibilities as she walked through the cool, pre-dawn air towards Mal's car, Hope looked to speak to her brother, and realised he'd fallen behind. He was several metres behind them, and doubled up over as if in pain.

She rushed back to him. "Mal, quick!" she yelled. "There's something wrong with Secta!"

Mal was close to the Commodore. Quickly checking that Honor and Karzoff were entering their vehicle, he turned and took off back to Hope.

Secta was bent over, throwing up.

"Are you all right?" said Hope, concerned. He looked up at her, his face ghostly pale. "Just a side effect from the reconstruction process," he said, straightening up and wiping his mouth. Wincing, he felt inside his mouth with his index finger. "Damn," he said. "I'm missing a filling!"

Hope started searching the ground, "Maybe it fell out while you were throwing up?"

"No, no, it won't be there," he said. "It was made of gold. I'd say it failed to transfer because it's metal, not organic. We'll probably find it in the demolecularizer.' He chuckled.

"That's something we failed to consider, isn't it?" he said, light-heartedly. "What if someone had an implant or a metal plate in their body?"

"What's happening?" asked Mal, puffing up.

"Nothing to worry about, my friend, just a little travel sickness," said Secta. "Let's get to the car. I have a great deal to tell you."

"I can hardly wait," said Hope, enthusiastically.

"I hope it includes where to find Alice," Mal said.

In their car, on their way back to Sydney, Honor called HQ and demanded to be put through to the President. Karzoff ignored her, keeping his eyes on the road.

"You will be off zis case vhen we return," she snapped at him.

"As you please," he replied coldly.

"Mr President, sir," her voice went oily. "Vell, yes, indeed, ze mission is complete. Secta has returned safely ... No sir. Black Alice did not return." There was a long pause while she listened intently. "Yes ... of course, sir. Zank you, sir. I vill do zat, sir, you vill haff it first thing. Ve vill see you at ten, sir, after your meeting with Zen. Zank you, sir." She slumped back in her seat, then turned burning eyes on her companion. "Karzoff, my dear toad," she said, her voice strange. "I could kiss you!"

Karzoff's eyes flashed in her direction. "I beg your pardon?" he said.

"Ze President vill be presenting us both with personal commendations," she grinned.

"Wha— I ... I don't understand..." he stammered.

"Secta has successfully been to ze future and returned, yes? Do you not see? Ve do not need Black Alice. Our time traveller is Secta!"

"Does that mean what I think?"

"Indeed, dear toad," she smiled indulgently. "You vill be reinstated, and at higher rank zan before."

"That is great news! Now I can pass on that job I was offered."

"A job?" Honor asked. "You vere zinking of leaving?"

"Well ... yes," he said, looking at her again. "Many agents have received a job offer in the last few days. Did you not...?"

"I haff not had time to open my e-mail," she said dismissively. "Vhat is ze name of this company?"

"Zen Corporation," he said. "I heard you mentioned them when you were speaking with the President."

"So I did, dear toad, so I did."

Something struck a nerve with her, but she couldn't quite put her finger on what.

Secta was on the rear seat of the Commodore, looking out of the window at the dawn sky. He lowered his window and took a deep sniff of the fresh, clean air.

"Ah, petrichor," he said. "You know, nothing smells quite like Sydney at dawn after the rain. Lovely."

"What the heck is petrichor?" Mal mumbled to Hope.

"It means the smell after rain," she whispered. "Ignore him, he's just trying to show off."

Mal rolled his eyes. No change there, he thought.

"It's incredible to think you've only been away a few days," Hope said to her brother. "It sounds like you've been through a lifetime of drama! I wish we could tell what happens in the future — although by the sound of things there isn't much of one, if everyone's sterile."

"I don't know about everyone," said Secta, thinking of Morri's dream.

"I tell you what I want to know," Mal said, seriously. "And this is important, Secta."

"Yes?"

"What's it like being a chick, man?"

That caused the three of them to crack up.

"You know, I don't know if there are words to describe it," said Secta. "Coming back here after experiencing that — it's like going from black and white to colour."

Hope nodded her head, ruefully. After hearing Secta's terrifying story, she was beginning to understand some of the changes she'd seen in him.

"Maybe what you saw isn't a fixed destiny," she said. "Maybe we can start working now to change things for the better."

"It's what we've been trying to do for years," said Mal.

"And for the first time, I understand that mission," said Secta. "I have seen exactly how the future is in our hands, and that has changed everything."

The traffic was light when they reached the Sydney CBD, and they were soon on the Anzac Parade city link, passing Sydney Football Stadium.

Hope looked at the huge billboard promoting a coming international rugby test.

"I wonder if that's the same Zen Corporation you found in the future, Secta?" she said.

Secta had been resting his eyes, but they flew open at the mention of Zen. He followed her gaze. As though he'd been kick-started back into life, he lunged forward in his seat.

"Pyrmont! Drive us to Pyrmont, Mal!" he said, urgently.

"Pyrmont? Why?"

"Just do it," Hope said. "Look at his face!"

Mal turned onto the link road to Jones Bay Wharf. "That Zen Corporation on the billboard back there is an IT company," he said. "Apparently they've invented an android footballer ... prototype..." He trailed off as he realised what he was saying.

"Yes," nodded Secta, grimly. "The android footballers led to the development of the RF-2 cyborgs ... and then the Cyberwars."

Mal punched it.

"If we can stop Zen, will that ensure the safety of all your friends in the future?" said Mal, as they entered the under-city tunnel to Pyrmont. "Like, if the Cyberwars never happen, do Reno and Jonno and all them get to live?"

"Let me tell you something amazing," Secta said. "When I arrived in the future, I found two ILDD units hidden under the chair in the bunker. But when I returned with Alice, there was only one."

"Because I'd taken it," Hope said.

"Indeed," Secta confirmed.

"I don't get it," said Mal, confused.

"We took the ILDD while Secta was in the future, remember?" said Hope. "It was there when he first arrived, but gone when he went back later."

"Proving that we can alter the future," Secta said.

"I get it! Like if Alice was still there now and you removed the chair, he'd see it disappear," Mal said.

"Exactly. And if we can package a solution to solve the fertility problem, we can help mankind recover by placing it in the bunker for Morri and Turk to collect in three months' time."

"Brilliant!" said Mal. "So even if we can't avert the Cyberwars…"

"We might still be able to save the future!" Secta said.

Mal drove the Commodore into the car park at Jones Bay Wharf. It was too early for anyone to be working, only a few boats were chugging on Darling Harbour. They got out of the car and took in the view of Peacock Point, the sunrise a backdrop to the city.

"No wonder filmmakers call this the magic hour," Secta said.

"You want to tell us why we're here?" Mal rasped.

Then they heard a tune being whistled — it was no ordinary whistle for Secta. He grinned enormously.

"Took you long enough, dudes!" A raspy voice resonated off the surrounding buildings. The three of them whirled around to see Alice perched on a wharf pylon next to the peace ferry. He hopped down and ambled over. Secta was happy to see the original Black Alice — a muscular, longhaired, tattooed, heavy metaller full to the brim with attitude and a persona larger than life. But there was something missing: instead of his usual black jeans, white shirt and scarlet Cuban heeled boots, he was wrapped in filthy old rags.

"How do you expect a guy to go anywhere like this, Secta?" he growled in mock anger. "You left out the part where I arrive buck naked!"

"You're just lucky I got you back to where you left from, rather than in the middle of the city at peak hour!" Secta grinned.

"God, it's nice to be in my own body again," said Alice — and to have hair!" He combed his fingers through the long black mane that reached to the arch of his back.

Hope was so glad to see him that, despite the stench of his wrapping, she grabbed him for a big hug.

"I'm so glad you made it back, Alice," she said.

He held her at arm's length and smiled down. "Take a lot more than a bit of time travel and a war with biker gangs and cyborgs to shut old Al down," he said.

Mal grabbed Alice's arm and pulled him into an embrace. "Al," he choked, almost crying in relief.

"Function, you turd," said his friend, affectionately.

"Welcome back, mate!" Mal said, then leaned back, holding his nose. "Phew, talk about turds! You're a bit on the bugle!"

"I'd rather have him here and on the bugle than not here at all," Hope said, laughing.

"You know what, Secta, you looked better as a girl," Alice joked as they wandered along the wharf.

"Does that mean you don't fancy me anymore, old stick?"

Alice threw an affectionate arm around his shoulder. "Nah, you were never my type," he answered. Now let's get out of here. We've got work to do."

= = =

EXTRACT
SONS OF STEEL – DARK ENERGY
BOOK 3

T WAS JUST after 1 p.m. Battered and bruised, with blood seeping through his shirt from a deep cut in his shoulder, Black Alice was behind the wheel of an SUV in a desperate bid to outrun the vehicle pursuing him.

Half a kilometre away the Temple Mount could be seen in all its majesty. Alice was in Jerusalem.

Dr Secta was on the passenger seat beside him, holding an isotopic labelling detection device, or ILDD. He was shaken, unaccustomed to manic car chases.

Mal Function was on the back seat, struggling to read a map. "Take a right up ahead into Ha-Notshrim Street,' he directed.

The rear window suddenly shattered and Mal had to duck the shower of glass fragments. Someone had fired at them from behind.

Alice glanced up at the rear-vision mirror and saw a motorbike tailing them. The ancient street they were traveling was too narrow to go any faster.

With a roar the bike drew level with the passenger side door. They were unarmed – there was nothing they could do. Alice thought of ramming him — he looked across. The rider was wearing a black balaclava. As the bike accelerated and moved ahead, the biker reached behind him, dropped a small device onto the road and scooted off.

Alice immediately recognised what was bouncing on the cobblestones, but it was too late to avoid it. He yelled at the others: "A bomb!"

As the SUV passed over the small device it detonated. The power of the explosion catapulted the SUV into the air. It landed — rolled violently — skidded and stopped, propped up against the side of a building.

When the dust had settled, the mangled driver's side door in the smouldering wreckage creaked open and Alice, face bleeding from the smashed windshield, tried to climb out. He stopped dead, staring down the barrel of an automatic weapon ... soldiers had the car surrounded. A shot rang out.

Alice woke with a start, his heart pounding like a drum, mouth parched, body saturated in sweat. He reached out trembling fingers to fiddle with the light switch and flicked it on. In the weak cone of light from the single bedside lamp, he stared at his hands, pleased to find them his — he was half expecting them to be Turk's.

It had been that way for a month, ever since his return from the last time travel event. He'd wake up freaked out, confused, unsure of where or who he was. His dreams had become vivid and chillingly realistic. He had no idea whether they were a glimpse into the future or a montage of images from the past — his or Turk's. He did after all have artefacts of Turk's memory fused with his own. Whatever the case, it was confusing

Alice had been in hiding from the Oceana Government Secret Service since his return. Chief government research scientist Dr Secta, along with his sister and colleague Dr Hope, had him tucked away in their bunker just outside Avalon, not far from Canberra. The bunker had been constructed in the 1960s as sanctuary for government officials in the event of a nuclear attack. Secta had kitted it out and utilized it as a base for the last time travel mission. Hope had set up living quarters in it for Alice, while she stayed nearby at the Avalon Motor Inn. Secta remained in Sydney, in liaison with his sister to coordinate the covert regeneration program that would restore Alice to full health. So far they'd failed to stabilize his atomic structure, and he was still at risk of dematerializing at any moment.

It was critical that the Oceana Government — and, more importantly, Senior Inspector Fanny Honor of the State Security Directorate (the SSD) — were kept in the dark about Alice's existence. They still believed he was missing, presumed dead, after the last mission.

Alice checked the time: it was nine o'clock in the morning. It was easy to lose track of time down in what he affectionately referred to as the pit. It was going to be a big day for him — Secta had finally come up with something he through might stabilize Alice's condition. He'd be arriving with Hope at about noon.